The
CALUSAN

An Epic Novel Based on Florida History

by Charles LeBuff

Amber Publishing
Post Office Box 493
Sanibel, Florida 33957-0493

* * *

AmberPublishing@sanybel.com

Printed in the United States of America

Published by:
Amber Publishing
Post Office Box 493
Sanibel, Florida 33957-0493

First Edition, January 2004

Library of Congress Control Number: 2003097384

ISBN 0-9625013-2-8

Front cover drawing by Merald Clark, adapted from *Sharks and Shark Products in Prehistoric South Florida*, © 1993, IAPS Books, used by permission.

For Jean

What readers of The Calusan *have had to say—*

"Charles LeBuff has woven a stirring story about a younger, more primitive Florida. He has retrofitted two historical periods, and two different cultures, into an intriguing, adventure-filled historical novel. *The Calusan* is destined to become a Florida classic."
— *Laymond Hardy, Everglades historian*

"*The Calusan* is a shining triumph for Charles LeBuff and highlights his extensive knowledge of Southwest Florida history and its environment."
— *Betty Anholt, Historian and author of* Sanibel's Story

"Charles LeBuff writes with great empathy and humanity about both the prehistoric and historic past. Through his perceptive eyes, we envision a bygone era and rediscover an environment that still sustains us today."
— *William H. Marquardt, Curator in Archaeology, Florida Museum of Natural History*

OTHER BOOKS BY THE AUTHOR

— *THE LOGGERHEAD TURTLE in the Eastern Gulf of Mexico*, 1990. A semitechnical book on the biology and conservation of the threatened loggerhead sea turtle.

— *SANYBEL LIGHT: An Historical Autobiography*, 1998. A human and natural history of Sanibel Island, Florida, its lighthouse, and the J. N. "Ding" Darling National Wildlife Refuge.

AUTHOR'S BRIEFING

During the time it took me to write this novel, it evolved into a book of epic proportions entirely under its own steam. This is a work of fiction; however, the names of individuals associated with specific historical events, geographical places, environmental conditions, and dated events are real. Except for five individuals, the characters, whose dialogue is represented in this book, regardless of any similarity their names or occupations may have to those of real people who are now living or long dead, are fictional. The five exceptions are these historical figures: Juan Ponce de León (1460-1521), António de Alaminos (1475-15??), Jacob Summerlin (1821-1893), Edgar Watson (1853-1910), and Theodore Roosevelt (1858-1919).

In 1513, Juan Ponce, with António Alaminos at his side, discovered Florida. The beautiful land of Florida was well described in the name given it by these men nearly 500 years ago. This event and Ponce's later voyage to Florida in 1521 are included in their historical perspective to convey this novel's theme and give it context. The historical contributions made much more recently by Summerlin, Watson, and Roosevelt are part of Americana. Today, the lives and deeds of all five of these men are entwined in the historical lore of Southwest Florida.

Any racial biases and slurs reflected herein are those of the times, not mine.

Three languages are represented in this book's lines of dialogue. These are Calusa, Spanish, and English. I have made no attempt whatsoever to incorporate Calusa or Spanish conversational translations, speech patterns, dialects, or accents in this work, as I have done in a small way for my English-speaking characters. In Parts One and Three of *The Calusan* my characters convey a broad educational spectrum by virtue of their vocabularies. I have tried to interpret and capture these ranges of intellect and common sense in the dialog of these individuals. Their educational levels range from illiterate former slaves, to both poorly and well-educated Floridians, to university academics. Calusa names for people, locations, animals, and devices which are used in the text, and my depictions of their unique culture have been extrapolated from the meager literature or independently fabricated by me.

I have taken the literary liberty of applying my title's word *Calusan* to identify an individual, but at the same time I also use the word occasionally in the text as a derivative of Calusa, Caloosa, or Calosa. These are common spellings that have been used to identify this aboriginal group of people since their sad, ill-fated contact with the Europeans. The word's use in my title is also intended to identify any citizen of the kingdom of Calos. Calos is the root word from which the Spanish and English names for these people are said to have originated. Ethnologically, this extinct but relatively recent group of Native Americans is considered by modern historians and archaeologists to have been a nation unto themselves. I insist they were not simply another tribal entity connected by common origins or culture with the other primitive Florida tribes who were their neighbors when my Calusan hero was alive, when his nation was a society of viable human beings, and he and his people were secure and strong.

— *Charles R. LeBuff, Jr.*
Sanibel Island, Florida
November 6, 2003

PART ONE

THE DISCOVERIES

"Logan! Ivy! Boys, look yonder at all 'em cows. Someday there'll be more people 'n cows in this country. This lil' ol' piss aint spot on the map called Punta Rassa'll be a gateway to a whole different world, 'n' ya'll can carry that bit o' prophecy to the bank!"

— *Jacob Summerlin*
Punta Rassa, Florida, 1883

CHAPTER 1

AS THE SUN DIPPED BELOW THE RED-ORANGE-tinted western horizon and disappeared, dusk quickly descended on Fisherman Key. Flight after flight of softly grunting white ibis passed overhead, above the rusty tin roof of the weathered farmhouse. The birds were hurrying to reach their roost on a nearby key before daylight abandoned the mangrove coast.

Rhythmically rocking in his cowhide-covered chair on the porch, Ivy Clark took a sip of his coffee. As he did every evening, he was waiting—patiently watching—for the light that would soon flash from atop the tall iron tower across the rough, whitecapped green water of San Carlos Bay. Occasionally, he would anxiously glance across the mouth of the Caloosahatchee to see if less-important lights were coming on in the buildings at the tiny hamlet of Punta Rassa as its residents prepared for night. The blink of the Sanibel Island lighthouse was clearly visible across the broad bay in the twilight. Then, turning slightly to face his sleepy wife who was nodding off in her rocking chair on the other side of the table, Ivy mumbled, "Honey, the light's right on time."

Her expressive blue eyes and tone of voice revealed a slight annoyance at her husband's comment, as she responded to his words. "Dear, me! Won't you ever stop watching for that lighthouse to come on? It's been working just fine ever since we moved back to this place. Why don't you worry about something more important . . . like the lack of rain, our cistern going dry, or how our grandbabies are faring, scattered all over Florida like they are. Better yet, why don't we go inside? Aren't these bugs eating you up too? I'm going in the house."

"Oh, it'll rain soon 'nuff. The bugs ain't too bad. 'Fore yuh call it a day, will yuh pass me that lett'r from Logan's sister? I need to read it 'un more time 'fore I turn in."

"After all these years, you still have a soft spot in your heart for that ornery Cracker, don't you?"

Ivy took the envelope, then replied, in a choking voice, "Thanks, honey. I always will. I loved 'im like a broth'r. C'mere, gimme a kiss. I'll come inside directly."

After kissing his wife affectionately, the old man looked back and glanced at the distant flashing light for a few seconds more. He then reached to adjust the wick of the tall Aladdin coal oil lamp. Ivy was drawn by his emotions to once again pick up the letter and read about the final days and passing of his old friend. Although Ivy was now in his 62nd year, tears left his brown eyes and crept down the deep wrinkles of his sun-weathered face. He thought to himself, "It seems so long 'go—but my life really b'gan at Punta Rassa the day I firs' met Logan Grace 'n' went inside 'is tuff world. Where the hell've the yars gone? There'll ne'er be 'nother like 'im. Wish I coulda been wit' 'im at the end."

Ivy then straightened out his right leg, reached deep into his pants pocket, and withdrew a small polished golden disk. He slowly brought it close to his face, squinting at it through cataract-clouded lenses.

Ivy muttered, "When did I find this? *Hmm* . . . that's right! It was back in '83—35 yars 'go! I ne'er did fig're out where'n the hell this t'ing come from." As he rotated and admired the shiny flat disk held in his fingertips, a flood of silent memories welled up inside him. Then in a soft clear voice, he spoke aloud to his dead friend, "I was jus' a greenhorn kid, but yuh took me un'er yer wing 'n' pointed me in the right direction . . . well, 'most always. Yuh became my mentor 'n' best friend 'n' I've . . . I'll always miss yuh,

4

Logan. Why, if it hadn't been fer yuh takin' me ov'r to Sanib'l that firs' time, I'd ne'er found this good luck piece. It's truly brought me mighty good fortune through my lifetime. Well, truth is, it was mostly good—those damned nicknames yuh'd stick on me sometimes caused problems 'tween us. An' then there was yer moody bad temper. I'll ne'er forgit . . . I cain't git it outta my head . . . when we hooked up wit' 'em gals. I ne'er tol't my good woman 'bout 'em Cuban beauties . . . 'bout Carlita—I believe that was 'er name. To this very day, the wife don't know 'bout some o' the crap we got into together . . . some o' the dangerous scrapes 'n' situations we had to deal wit', like the killin' we had to do down there. As far as I know, yuh ne'er tol't anyone 'bout those bad escapades, 'n' I always 'preciated how well yuh kept our secrets. God bless yuh, Logan Grace. Yuh made a man outta me. Lord, where's the yars gone?"

* * *

Earlier in the day, an ominous band of low dark clouds had blown over Sanibel Island. The wind had swept across and roughened the waters of San Carlos Harbor. What little rain the clouds held had been wrung out of them, falling short of land over the Gulf of Mexico. This frontal system had been reduced to a windy and dry electrical storm by the time it reached the outer barrier islands. A cool, stiff northwest breeze, dropping humidity, and some high racing c louds w ere all t hat r emained after t he u nexpected h eavy weather had rushed past the tiny community at Port Punta Rassa.

Ivy Clark and Logan Grace, an inseparable pair of pals, were enjoying this delightful change in the weather while they watched a n a wesome fiery p anorama o n t he f ar s ide o f t he b ay. They were standing among a small crowd of people on the port's largest wharf. All eyes were switching glances between the smoke and fire to the south and the onset of a glorious sunset to the west.

The two friends stepped off the wharf and strolled along a wide pathway that meandered through a maze of wooden corrals nearly filled with noisy, skinny cattle. Spanning 30 years, the path had been pulverized into powder, crushed by hundreds of thousands of cattle hooves. Like the imminent fate of the animals wait-

5

ing in the corrals, those earlier cattle were forced from the pens and pushed along the path toward the wharf and loaded aboard a waiting vessel.

Ivy emptied his wad-filled mouth of its tobacco juice just before he started to speak. The pressurized squirt struck the powder-dry ground several feet away and raised dust. Wiping the brown drool dripping through the stubble on his chin with his shirt-sleeve, he began talking excitedly in his distinct southern drawl, "Damn, Logan! That's 'un hell o' a fire ov'r yonder! Those flames 'r' 'bout as high as any I've seen—ev'n in the piney woods back in Georgy when I was a kid. I believe that whole damned island's gonna burn, right down to the bare sand."

The unusual early spring thunderstorm, spawned by the feeble cold front, had swept over Sanibel Island. Lightning had ignited the island's tinder-dry, grass-filled central slough. The fire had started early in the day on the west end of Sanibel Island, almost at the narrow inlet that separates it from Captiva Island. Because of the steady northwest wind, the 50-foot wall of flame stretched from the Gulf of Mexico to the shore of San Carlos Harbor. The fire raced south and east toward the island's ever-tapering tip.

"Thank the good Lord no one's livin' on Sanib'l these days," Logan added. "A while back, there was 'bout 20 Cuban fishermen camped at the ol' Spanish well. Have yuh ev'r been there?"

"No, I ain't ne'er stepped foot on Sanib'l."

"It's on this side 'bout a half mile west o' the point. The Cubans rolled their smack on its side to fix the boat's bottom. I believe I heard Cap'n Wendt tell yer daddy they've all left to go off-shore 'gain, aft'r 'em groupers 'n' mackerels. It's a good t'ing, 'cause their camp was nothin' but palmetto shacks 'n' lean-tos. That fire's hot 'n' determined. Those huts'll be hist'ry once't the flames git to 'em.

"The next cowboat's not due here 'til Thursday. Let's talk to ol' man Wendt to see if he'll carry us 'cross't the bay to the island firs' t'ing in the mornin'. I'll bet if any o' Sanib'l's deer make it through that fire, they'll be easy 'nuff to find. Why, wit' no cover they'll be like sittin' ducks. I'm tired o' beef 'n' mullet. Some

6

venison would sho go down real good right now. We may ev'n find some deer that's already cooked! Ha, howdy! C'mon, let's go find the salty ol' skipper 'an' then have us a drink at Shultz's Hotel."

Ivy spit again, then turned to follow Logan who had already started to walk away, inspired by the thought of whiskey. As he got into step, Ivy took off his broad-brimmed, sun-faded hat and ran his callused fingers through his full head of wavy dark–brown hair. Although younger by a few years, he was as tall as Logan—right at six feet—but he wasn't as thinly framed, nor as bowlegged. The two young men had grown close; some people thought them to be brothers.

However, their personalities were divergent. Ivy Clark had been raised by loving parents and was reasonably educated for the times. He was likeable, well-mannered, usually jovial and wore a friendly smile on his face. He accepted his responsibilities, but on occasion Ivy could become sullen and withdrawn when pushed to certain limits. And, Logan Grace had studied him and knew every one of those limitations and how to push them.

To the contrary, Logan had received little formal schooling and was barely literate. He worked hard but had little real ambition, other than his reasonably good work ethic aimed to please cattleman Jacob Summerlin. Logan had a reputation of being a very good boss and had been Summerlin's primary foreman for over ten years. After the Civil War, his alcoholic father, a Confederate Army veteran, struggled as an itinerant turpentiner. Logan had been born into a large family that wandered the pine forests of North Florida bleeding the trees' valuable sap. He was the youngest son among nine children, By the time Logan was born, his parents had neither a trace of self-esteem nor any goals in life, for themselves or their children. Logan was raised on a long leash by his older siblings and he snapped this and broke free from all ordinary family tethers at an early age. By the time the bad-tempered, pugnacious youngster entered adolescence all who knew him considered Logan Grace to be incorrigible.

* * *

Augustus Wendt was Austrian by birth but an American by choice. Gus, as he preferred to be called, was now past middle age. He conveyed a tough and cantankerous persona, but he was respected and liked by all who knew him at Punta Rassa. He was a bachelor who drifted down the Atlantic coast to the wild Florida peninsula a few years after the War ended in 1865. Like many European immigrants in the northeastern United States, he volunteered to serve in the Army of the Potomac. Gus had seen action in a dozen major battles. He was glad it was all behind him. Almost 20 years had passed since the carnage ended and most of the pain subsided. A slight limp, the result of damaged tendons and missing muscle, still caused considerable discomfort where the Minie ball at Petersburg, Virginia, had torn away most of the flesh and some of the bone from his left calf. A compassionate and skilled Confederate surgeon had saved his mangled leg from the bone saw. Gus knew he had been lucky, but on cold and damp nights at his New Jersey home, the hurt sometimes mounted and brought tears. Sometimes it caused him to drink too much. That was his excuse anyway.

Since Augustus Wendt had been wounded, doctors had often suggested that he relocate to a drier and warmer climate. While a prisoner of war in the hellhole prison camp at Belle Island, Virginia, he considered moving somewhere else during his long recuperation. He thought long and hard about moving west. Later, after he returned home, it seemed every veteran he met or knew was packing up and heading in that direction. But Gus Wendt loved boats and the water. So his first move was to Maryland, to the waters of the Chesapeake Bay. There he bought a well-used skipjack sloop and for the next half dozen years, Gus labored as a commercial crabber.

Migrating boatpeople navigating and gunkholing in Chesapeake Bay often talked in glowing terms about Florida. It was described to Gus as the only real land of opportunity remaining east of the Mississippi. He learned the Homestead Act had opened up a fair amount of land in the state, and it was said jobs were plentiful, especially for experienced small–boat operators. The demand was increasing because coastal commerce was mush-

8

rooming between the isolated American waterfront settlements and was even expanding to international ports.

Gus Wendt had sailed into Port Punta Rassa at just the right time.

* * *

Ivy and Logan headed for the boat docks a couple of hundred yards upriver from the point of land some Spanish explorer had named Punta "Rasa" long ago. Now, with a second "s" added for Anglicized spelling, the name Punta Rassa still translates to "flat point."

"Hey, Jeff!" Logan yelled to the white-haired black man who was bent o ver furiously s craping barnacles from the fouled hull on the boatways. "Have yuh seen Cap'n Wendt anywhere?"

The once–tall African American stood, flexed and tried to straighten his back, and answered, "Yes, suh, Mauser Logan. I sho 'nough has. He be takin' Miss Alice 'n' 'er cuzzin o'er yunder to 'er daddy's place. He dun tol't me hisself he'd try'n' git back wit'n de 'our, if'n this wind hol'ts. He wuz sho it'd."

"Kindly tell 'im that Ivy 'n' me need to talk to 'im, when he gits back. We'll be at the hotel. Jus' tell 'im to give us a shout."

"Yes, suh, Mauser Logan."

* * *

Charlie C lark was a r espected h arbor pilot at the port o f Savannah when the War Between the States ended. Professional harbor pilots meet vessels at harbor entrances and direct helmsmen to the correct course headings for safe movement of large commercial water vessels in designated ports. Insurance companies, and later licensing agencies, required that specialists with long-term local knowledge of harbor entrances and channels oversee movements o f s hips t o s afeguard p assengers a nd c argo a s t he v essels enter or leave a designated shipping hub.

Reconstruction bureaucrats sent into Georgia after the end of the Civil War demanded that key positions, such as Charlie's and most of his fellow pilots in and near the major cities, be transferred to individuals who were known to have been Union sympathizers.

So, after 16 years of exceptional performance as a member of the Savannah River Pilot's Association, Charlie was forced to resign from the Association and sell his vested membership. In a state of depression, without a skilled trade to make a decent living to provide for his family in Savannah, he packed his wife, Naomi, their three children, and all their earthly possessions into a rickety old wagon. They said goodbye to relatives and old friends and headed south to find work and begin their new lives.

In late summer 1867, the Clarks arrived in the bustling port of Tampa on Florida's middle Gulf coast. Charlie promptly applied for a position with the Tampa Bay Pilot's Association. He hoped his credentials would help him start over in his chosen profession. But the buy-in costs that the Association required were well beyond the Clark's financial wherewithal. The pilot-in-charge told Charlie there was a vacant position open for a pilot boat operator and he was welcome to apply. Because his personal funds were almost exhausted, he jumped at the opportunity, anything to get back on the water and get his foot in the door. He was hired on the spot.

Over the next few years, Charlie studied the Tampa Bay shipping channel. Few mariners knew it better. When a ship was sighted offshore during his watch, he would sail out to the sea buoy which marked the channel's entrance. This navigational aid was positioned five miles west of Egmont Key. He transported a pilot who would board the inbound vessel near the buoy and provide the required expertise to safely bring the ship inside the bay to an anchorage, or if space was available, directly to its berth in Tampa. Whenever he could, he would sail out with the pilot boat and travel along with the ship to the anchoring spot or dock. By 1873, Charlie was given special dispensation to serve as a substitute pilot whenever a pilot scheduled for duty was suddenly called away or became ill.

* * *

In mid-October, the steam freighter *Liberty* puffed into Port Tampa. This vessel routinely traveled between Havana, Cuba, and Tampa. She usually made an intermediate stop at Punta Rassa to take on water for steam, coal for fuel, and to drop off and pick up freight or mail. This particular day, as a crewman steered, Charlie was on the bridge in voice control of the ship. While chatting with the skipper, occasionally he gave headings and made navigational comments to the helmsman.

Then the captain said, "Charlie, we tried to stop at Punta Rassa but Gus Wendt, the pilot boatman, came offshore in his sloop and met us all by his lonesome. He said they'd been hit by one hell of a hurricane. I guess it must've been the same one that made me late leaving Havana. It came straight out of the Gulf and its eye hit Punta Rassa direct on the 15th. They had a 14-foot tide! "'Magine that! It completely took out all the docks and wharf, the cattle pens, the warehouse, and most of the low buildings. Gus said it'll likely be several months before they'll be operational again—in fact, he said the two pilots, the Johnson brothers, left with their families and went down to Key West. Rumor is they ain't comin' back. Those old boys are the only pilots who've worked Punta Rassa since the War, and no one has any idea who'll ever replace them. There ain't nobody around Punta Rassa with the background to take on the responsibility. Gus told me he doesn't want the job. He said he's 'happy as a pig in shit' doin' what he's doin'. He prefers to just carry pilots to and from vessels.

"Charlie, you oughta slip down to Punta Rassa and ease yourself into that job. That straight channel and the deep harbor could be learned right quick with Gus's help, probably by the time they rebuild the facilities. You deserve to be a full-fledged pilot again."

That night Charlie shared this news with his wife. "I was told by the skipper o' the *Liberty*—the last boat I piloted into Tampa—that they're gonna be needin' a pilot down the coast at Punta Rassa. It's 'bout a hundred miles directly south o' here. I've heard it's a small port—not near as busy as Tampa—that ships mostly cattle. The pilots there quit after a hurricane tore up the place. I'm thinkin' 'bout catchin' a ride wit' the next mailboat goin' down 'n' look into the situation." He was testing her, trying to see if she'd agree with his impromptu plan, maybe even endorse a move for the family.

11

As she brushed her long, wavy brown hair, Naomi Clark said to her husband, "If it means yuh can become a pilot 'gain, I believe yuh should hurry down to Punta Rassa 'n' check it out."

Overhearing the conversation from his bedroom, their middle child, 16-year-old Ivy couldn't be still a second longer. He leaped into the room. "Daddy, can I go to Punta Rassa wit' yuh? *Pleeeease*? I'd sho like to see what that storm did! Maybe I could find work there too."

"Okay, son. I'd like to have yuh tag 'long."

Aboard the mailboat *Tampa Lady*, the Clarks, along with many other paying passengers, enjoyed a host of new sights while traveling south. The small sidewheel steamer stopped at settlements wherever onboard mail was bound or wherever special flags were hoisted to announce outgoing mail. By late afternoon, they reached the federally operated quarantine station on the north end of LaCosta Island, which lay on the south side of the deep-water pass called Boca Grande. They anchored for the night in a small bay between the large island and Punta Blanca.

Departing at dawn, the captain ran the inland waters to save time. To go outside at Boca Grande into the Gulf meant paralleling LaCosta and Captiva Islands and following the long curving sweep of Sanibel Island's outer beach. This would have added miles to the trip. By zigzagging through Pine Island Sound, they would reach San Carlos Harbor much sooner, but the unmarked water could be navigated safely only during daylight.

"Someday they'll have this damned channel marked," the skipper commented. "Once they turn a-loose of some money and get that lighthouse built out on Sanibel's eastern tip. They've been messin' around tryin' to justify a light for San Carlos Harbor for years now. Sort of on again off again, like a sea breeze."

"Do yuh really think Punta Rassa 'll ev'r have 'nuff commercial traffic to convince the Lighthouse Board to actually build a light station there?" Charlie questioned.

"'Til the hurricane tore things up, the port was growin' by leaps and bounds. Last year 22,000 head of cattle were loaded onto boats and shipped outta there. Once they rebuild, it'll be a busy port again and will surely continue to increase in tonnage as time goes on, at least until someone runs a rail line down this coast from Tampa."

San Carlos Harbor was an unspoiled bay in 1873. A well-defined tongue of lighter-colored Gulf water extended around the eastern tip of Sanibel Island and reached almost to the bay's center. The cleaner, denser water contrasted remarkably with the stained, less-salty water of the estuary.

Extending his arm and pointing in a variety of directions as he talked, the captain continued, holding Charlie and Ivy spell-bound. "The main ship channel's natural and a straight shot, but it's unmarked, except for a few stakes on some finger shoals. The river, known as the Caloosahatchee, flows past Punta Rassa and empties into this bay. The Caloosahatchee meanders to San Carlos Harbor from the middle of the state. Its fresh water mixes with water from the Gulf of Mexico right here at its mouth. If there's no room at the docks, vessels waitin' to come into Punta Rassa are anchored this side of Sanibel's point. The water there's about five fathoms with a good bottom for anchorin'."

The mailboat's skipper made his introductions at the dock. "Gus, this is Charlie Clark and his oldest boy, Ivy. Charlie's an old-time harbor pilot, originally out of Savannah. Like a lot of folks, his career got messed up by the goddammed Yankees after the War . . ."

Gus, quick to react and more than a little angry at the captain's remark, interrupted him and in his Austro-American voice said, "You shouldn't be using such generalities, Cap'n. Some people call me a Yankee, despite not knowing much about me because of my heavy Austrian accent. And I don't resent it because until I take my last breath, I'll believe as a Federal I was on the right side. Don't you ever call me a goddammed Yankee again! Save those kind of cheap shots for the northern politicians. It was them sons of bitches who destroyed careers and messed up reconstruction of the Union after the War. Don't take it out on the likes of me!"

"Cool down, Gus! I wasn't meanin' to upset you. I'm sorry."

Charlie liked Gus right off. He spoke his mind and wasn't shy about expressing his personal opinion. "Gus, the skipper tol't me that ya'll may be in need o' a master harbor pilot once't the port's facilities 're rebuilt."

Gus said, "That's right. The last pilots, the Johnson brothers, have called it quits. They told Jake Summerlin and a few other shippers they weren't coming back. This isn't the busiest place; I'd be lying if I told you otherwise. Whoever gets the job could make a fair to middling living. Who knows, if the port continues to grow the next pilot might get rich. Ha, ha."

"Do ya'll have a port committee here, 'r is there jus' a head man 'r agent who'll pick the new pilot?"

"No, there's a committee. Old man Summerlin is the chairman. Between you and me, he usually gets his way though, when it comes to hiring workers or making port improvements. Jake's a bit self-centered but he does have good judgment when it comes to a person's character and abilities. He may have been born and raised out in the Florida scrub in cow camps and poorly educated, but he's an intelligent and fair-minded man—despite what some of the kid cowboys around these docks may tell you.

"Jake's o ver a t h is p lace. I t's t hat b ig s tilt h ouse b y t he water. Come on, I'll introduce you," Gus said. He lamely but quickly stepped out ahead and motioned Charlie and Ivy to follow. As they walked, Charlie realized his opportunity had arrived and continued the conversation. "Gus, if I luck out 'n' do git a crack at becomin' the new pilot, what's the chance o' yuh findin' the time to run the channel wit' me a few times in yer sloop? I realize yuh don't know me, but I'd really 'preciate yer help 'n' support. I'd be at full speed 'n' ready to bring boats in once't the port is up 'n' runnin'. I'll be much obliged 'n' would be pleased to pay yuh fer yer time."

"You know . . . truth is, I expect I'll have to keep running outside the harbor to tell any inbound vessels we're not open for business—those who may be coming from Caribbean ports that aren't linked to our undersea telegraph cable and don't know we're shut down. Usually, if my schedule allows, I try like hell to go offshore after grouper at least once a week and, frankly, I do need a

14

fishing partner. You can come along with me and keep me company. We'll study all the different things I've learned about San Carlos Harbor, its entrance and channel, and Punta Rassa on our way out and in. You're welcome to copy my charts, too."

Charlie beamed. He knew that Captain Gus Wendt was a good man and they'd soon become close friends.

When the tall, thin man came to the door, Gus spoke. "Good evening, Mister Jake. I'd like you to meet Charlie Clark and his son, Ivy. They came down on the mailboat for a day or two. Charlie heard about the opening and is very interested in becoming our new harbor pilot. He worked for nearly 20 years at Savannah as a master pilot and is now a substitute pilot up in Tampa Bay."

"Don't stand out there'n the damned skeeters. Ya'll come 'nside!"

Charlie extended his hand. Jacob Summerlin firmly grasped and shook it, nodding. Then he took his enormous corn-cob pipe out of his mouth, cleared his throat, and began to speak loudly. "We sho as hell'll need a pilot right quick. Those Johnson boys . . . I was good to 'em boys! They done jus' up 'n' quit. But I cain't blame 'em—the future o' my shippin' business looks powerfully grim. That damned hurricane sho 'nuff tore this place up. They's got families to worry 'bout. We'll need a new pilot directly, once't we git the loadin' docks 'n' pens rebuilt. My best guess is that we'll be up 'n' runnin' in less'n a month, maybe this side o' three weeks. I've got all my boys workin' toward that end, that is, 'cept those I sent north to the Kissimmee Prairie country to start roundin' up the next herd o' beeves. He turned and said, to Ivy, "Say, son, have yuh ev'r hunted cows?"

"No, sir."

"If yuh're lookin' fer some steady work, yuh can hire on wit' my boys, either here at Punta Rassa 'r on the trail to bring the herd here."

Ivy swallowed nervously and replied, "Thanks, Mr. Summerlin. Frankly, I'm not the best o' horsemen. I need lots o' practice. Fact is, I ain't ne'er ridden a cow pony. I wouldn't know where to start herdin' cattle . . ."

15

Jake stopped the boy mid-sentence. "Son, the truth o' the matter is, the marsh tacky cow ponies we use have the brains when it comes to catchin' 'n' herdin' cows. The horse does all the work. A good horse'll sho 'nuff put yuh right on where yuh gotta be to work the beeves."

"I could sho learn fast, Mr. Summerlin! Fer the time bein', if it's all the same to yuh, sir, I'll take yuh up on the job helpin' to rebuild this place. I like carpenter work . . . like to make t'ings wit' my hands. It's real satisfyin' fer me."

Jake Summerlin smiled and said, "Fine, son. Yuh can start tomorrow. We have a lil' bunkhouse out yonder, the oth'r side o' the b ig c istern, n ext t o the s tump t hat usta b e t he b iggest d amn gumbo limbo tree in these parts . . . 'fore that goddammed hurricane tore it to shreds . . . the wind snapped it off. Go over there 'n' ask fer Logan . . . Logan Grace. He's a fine young man . . . looks a lot like yuh . . . well, 'cept fer the hair. He's got red hair that falls down past his shoulders 'n' his face's covered wit' big ol' freckles. Yuh cain't miss him—he stands out. Yuh'll likely hear 'im 'fore yuh see 'im. He's loud. Tell 'im I said to give yuh a place to sleep, 'n' that yuh'll be startin' to work wit' his crew in the mornin'. There's a lil' steamer comin' down the river loaded to the gunnels wit' green cypress fer the docks 'n' pens. Logan'll need all the he'p he can git!"

"Now, Charlie," he continued. "We'll have to git our lil' ol' Port Committee together to properly interview yuh fer the pilot's job—yuh know, go over yer experience, knowledge, anythin' that concerns the pilotin' business. Besides me, there's two other ol' boys. Ol' man Beatty is stayin' upriver 'round Fort Denaud, 'n' Bill Sherwin is out in the Big Cypress country roundin' up a small herd to ship. I believe he's down southwest of the big lake. Okeechobee it's called . . . it overflows into 'nother lake that's actually the headwaters of this here river, the Caloosahatchee. I'll send word to both o' 'em to come in to Punta Rassa Friday a week to meet yuh. Is that okay? I reckon yuh can come back down 'board the mailboat. Right?"

"Yes, sir! I'll look forward to meetin' the Committee. Here's my work records fer ya'll to look at in the meantime."

"Thanks. I'll show it to Sherwin. Me and Beatty . . . well, we don't read so good."

On schedule, Charlie Clark returned. He met with the full Committee, answered a few questions, and was appointed unanimously as the new harbor pilot for the port of Punta Rassa.

* * *

Gus Wendt, the pilot boat operator, had returned from the Johnson place and was busy securing his sloop to the dock when Ivy approached him and asked, "Cap'n Gus! Logan 'n' me would like to hire yuh 'n' yer boat tomorrow. Daddy told us there ain't no cowboats due 'til late in the week. We'd like fer yuh to carry us ov'r to Sanib'l in the mornin'. We wanna bag us a deer 'r two to change our menu. If yuh will, 'n' it's okay, we thought we'd ask ol' Jeff to come 'long. We plan to run the deer wit' two o' Mister Jake's cow dogs. Jeff's always done a good job o' controllin' those mean bastards in the past. They always wanna piece o' mine 'n' Logan's ass end whenever they catch us off our horses. Ol' Jeff says he likes bein' on the tail end o' the dogs. I reckon bein' a slave up in South Carolina, he was on the bitin' end a few times!"

"Boys, don't you mean *if* that fire across the harbor has burned itself out?"

Logan had seen wildfires scorch Sanibel Island before and spoke up. "I believe it will, Cap'n. The nor'wester's done picked up earlier this evenin' 'n' it's pushin' the fire toward the tip o' Sanib'l in a hurry. There's not much more grass 'r cabbage trees to burn up ov'r there. We're bettin' it'll be burned out by sunup."

"I won't touch that bet, boys. You might be right. If the fire dies and it's safe for you two and Jeff to stomp around over there, we'll go. Meet me here at the boat in the morning, about an hour before dawn. We'll decide then. Bring yourselves some food and water, enough for Jeff and those hounds too. Don't forget, bring plenty of water! Oh, if you crazy cowboys get me some venison, I'll carry you over and back for free!"

CHAPTER 2

FOR AN EARLY APRIL PREDAWN MORNING, THE COOL air was unusually comfortable. A gusty cold front had blown through during the night. But before the wind died, it had swept away thick bands of dark storm clouds. As if by a sorcerer's magic spell, the sky was now cloudless and crystal clear. The cold front had arrived, bringing with it brisk, low-humidity air. Refreshing.

Overhead, the brilliance of millions of stars was subdued by a magnificent full moon. It appeared to be suspended by a puppeteer in the western sky. A ghostly, almost daylight glow illuminated the Punta Rassa docks. Every varnished mast and spar among the small group of moored sailboats reflected the moon's crisp light, providing a flickering, delightful, holiday-like atmosphere to start the new day.

Ivy and Logan roused the black man, Thomas Jefferson "Jeff" Bowton, from a sound sleep. They told him they were running late and to hurry, get his gear together, and catch the two best hunters among Jake Summerlin's small kennel of cow dogs. Jake's favorite dogs were semiretired. Unless Jake went cow hunting himself, they stayed at Punta Rassa.

While Jeff went about his chores, Ivy and Logan picked up their equipment and walked toward the dock to meet Gus Wendt.

Since the day Ivy had started work at Punta Rassa, the two young men had become inseparable. Everyone at Punta Rassa said that Logan had adopted Ivy as his younger brother. Most of the time, Ivy admired—almost worshiped—his older buddy.

"Mornin', Cap'n," Logan muttered sleepily as he stepped to the edge of the dock. By the moonglow, he could clearly see that Gus was busy readying his sloop.

"Good morning, boys. From here it looks as though you were right! The fire over on Sanibel does seem to have petered out. Here, pass me your guns, packs, and water jugs. Where's Jeff and the dogs? We've got a falling tide and we'd best get underway just as fast as we can. The water flow will help us get there quicker."

"Here they come now." Ivy said, Then he asked in a concerned tone, "Why're yuh limpin' this mornin', Cap'n?"

"*Oh*, nothing serious. It's just this bad leg of mine acting up. Change of weather caused it. Thanks for asking. I'll be okay once the sun rises and warms things up."

Tugging against their leashes, the two huge Florida curs were pulling Jeff along. He struggled to keep from being pulled down. These dogs were a fine-tuned mix specially bred for working cattle.

Suddenly the dogs saw Ivy and Logan. In unison, they began to growl and lunge forward, all the while baring their intimidating teeth. Taken off balance, Jeff stumbled and fell flat to the ground. Before he could even try to regain his footing, the barking and snarling dogs were dragging him across the rough oyster-shell-covered ground on his stomach. In a split second, the petrified cowboys leaped from the dock into the boat's cockpit to avoid the dangerous teeth which flashed in the moonlight.

These two brutes loved to harass the horse-riders. They had not singled out either Ivy or Logan to torment, and no one had ever taken the time to find out if these dogs had bite records. Fact of the matter was, neither dog had ever bitten any of the cowboys. It was only when they sensed fear oozing through human skin that they clicked into "mean dog mode." It was a very convincing act, and it gave an otherwise mundane dog's life a little pleasure.

19

Jeff jerked on the twisted leashes and hollered, "A'ight! Dat's 'nuff o' dat shit!"

Once he clambered to his feet, Jeff began to flail both dogs' backsides with the thick leather. The tough snarling quickly changed to moanful, cowardly whimpering. The dogs realized they had overplayed the scene and reacted accordingly.

Gus, ready to shove off, barked, "C'mon, Jeff, hop in here with them noisy curs! We'll soon be burning daylight. I'd like to get as close to Sanibel as we can by sunup. You can sit to one side up top of the cabin and hold tight to the dogs. We don't want the puppies to scare these poor white boys again."

The current created by the ebb tide was powerful. Before Gus could finish hoisting the mainsail, the rushing water had already pulled the craft quickly away from the dock. What little wind remained was steady, out of the northwest. After the jib had joined the main to catch the wind, its pressure instantly filled both sails. The sloop heeled to port as Gus expertly trimmed the sails. He balanced the boat's hull and sails into a perfectly tuned water-borne missile rushing toward the dark shape of Sanibel Island.

An orange predawn glow soon began to show on the eastern horizon. The four men watched in silent awe as the sky slowly brightened. An enormous golden sun then peered above the ocean's edge to begin its daily ascent.

"Those are mighty fine weapons you boys have there," Gus commented. "Ivy, where did you ever come by such a good-looking Kentucky long rifle?"

"Cap'n, this ain't a Kentucky rifle. It's a Pennsylvania rifle. 'Cording to Daddy, his daddy—my granddaddy—had it custom made up north 'fore Granddaddy 'n' his folks left 'n' resettled in Georgy after the War o' 1812. It's a straight shootin' .50 caliber. I believe h e h ad i t c onverted f rom a f lintlock t o a p ercussion c ap 'fore Daddy was borned—to modernize it. Jus' look at this fancy patchbox 'n' the beautiful wood in the stock! Ain't it somethin'? Daddy lets me use it from time to time. It's his pride 'n' joy! I reckon Granddaddy's rifle'll be mine 'un day."

Logan chimed in. "I borrowed this breech-loadin' Springfield from Mister Jake. This cap-'n'-ball r evolver on my

hip's a Remington New Model. Pappy carried it durin' the War—
he likely kill't 'im a few Yankees wit' it. He left it to me."

Gus winced at Logan's "Yankee" remark but kept silent.

Plumes of smoke rose from scattered, still burning pockets
of fire on Sanibel Island. Isolated groups of cabbage palms, which
had been separated when the main fire rushed over the land, continued to explode in enormous fireballs. Fingers of flame reached
unburned leaf litter or grass, ignited into a flare-up, and spread
quickly to the fuel-loaded cabbage palms.

As the four men drew closer to the shore, the flare-ups
seemed more awesome. When large windblown sparks or fingers
of flame reached the palms, they would instantly flare-up with a
loud whooshing sound. These crown fires would burn out about as
fast as they flared up because not enough fuel remained nearby to
support the fire, once all the trees in that particular group had
burned. Dry ground vegetation and leaf litter had burned down to
the white shell-laden topsoil by the time the fire had burned itself
out.

"Cap'n. Let's land Jeff 'n' the dogs ov'r yonder where the
ridge followin' the shoreline ends at the big bay tucked into the
mangroves," Logan offered. "Then please carry Ivy 'n' me 'bout
three-quarters o' the way back toward the point 'n' drop us off.
We'll find a couple o' big trees to climb into fer shootin' stands.
Then we'll wait fer the dogs to chase the deer to us.

"Jeff, yuh keep a lookout fer us. Once't they start runnin',
be sho those dumb dogs're chasin' a deer, not a damn 'coon 'r a box
turtle that waltzed by last week. An' be sho they're runnin' toward
us, not the other way toward Captiva!"

"Yes, suh, Mauser Logan. We'll find yo' a mighty fine deer
'r two 'n' dese pups 'll brin' 'em right ta ya'll."

The sloop sailed away from the narrow beach. After half an
hour, they reached the second drop-off point, about two miles farther east. Holding their gear well above their heads, Ivy and Logan
slowly slid overboard on their backsides into the chilly, chest-deep
water and began to wade ashore.

"Okay, boys," Gus said with a wide grin. "Good luck and be
careful. I'll look for the three of you somewhere around here, along

the beach when I come back in, about three hours before sunset. I'm going to run offshore and see if I can catch a few grouper or tripletails. I won't be the one to go hungry tonight if you two and Jeff don't get the job done!"

Chuckling at Gus's comments, the determined young hunters assured him they would watch for his return. Both promised they would prove themselves to him and bag some game. They waved as the old man single-handedly hoisted the sails and skillfully maneuvered his craft into deeper water. Catching the wind, the sloop heeled as Gus casually trimmed the sails. He turned toward the boys, briefly returned their waves, then set to concentrating on his speed and seamanship.

"Goldurn! Ivy! This place looks 'n' smells like somebody's smoke house!"

"Sho 'nuff does. Ar' yuh positive we'll bag a deer in this barren place? Like yuh tol't me, they'll be right easy to see if there's any left alive!"

"I've hunted Sanib'l from 'un end to the other quite a few times, whenever I had time 'n' was able to git ov'r here somehow. Honest, I've ne'er gone back to Punta Rassa empty-handed. Deer thrive ov'r here. They're right smart when it comes to escapin' a fire. Hell, there's nothin' ov'r here to both'r 'em, 'cept some lucky ol' 'gator 'r crocodile I reckon. I've ne'er heard tell o' a panther 'r wolf bein' shot 'r ev'n seen on any o' these islands, 'n' they're the only real worry deer have on the mainland—other'n people like us, that is.

"There's a tall strangler fig to our left. Let's walk ov'r there so I can climb it 'n' git a look 'round to find 'nother tree fer yer stand. We need to find one wit'in a couple hundred feet o' this one. That a-way we'll be wit'in range o' any game that comes inside our firin' zone."

They continued walking toward the tree Logan had selected.

"Logan, what's that lil' white, wooden buildin' near the beach wit' the rusty corrugated tin roof?"

22

"*Oh*, that's 'un o' the cable huts. The telegraph company has two on Sanib'l. One on the bay—that 'un—'n' 'nother on the Gulf side. The cable leaves the lil' telegraph buildin' at Punta Rassa, runs un'erwater to this hut, then un'erground to the 'un on the other side o' Sanib'l. Ov'r on the Gulf the cable goes un'erwater 'gain. Then it branches off down close to the Dry Tortugas. One branch goes to Fort Jefferson in the Tortugas, 'nother to Key West. The main cable continues on down to Havana. It's a good t'ing their cable crews keep all the trees 'n' grass a good way back from the buildin's. They must've taken out all the grass fairly recently. 'Cause o' that bare sand, the fire didn't git close 'nuff to torch the hut."

As they continued toward the tree in their high-heeled boots, their footfalls caused the covering of lightweight, black, sooty ash to puff up and fall away to the side. This left a trail of well-defined white impressions in the charred landscape. Everything in view was black. The odor of smoke was almost overpowering. The lack of fresh air burned their throats. Each tied his bandanna over his mouth and nose to reduce the amount of inhaled ashy dust.

The fire had been very hot. Fighting conchs, halves of quahog clams, and other large seashells littered the land. These had been cast up from their submerged marine habitat by hurricanes many years if not centuries before. Most of the sun-bleached shells had been superheated during the fire's passage so they crumbled underfoot into white calcium dust.

The large strangler fig embraced a charred cabbage palm. The palm was once the fig's foundation, its early life support system. A layer of white latex, the rubber tree's sap, covered its trunk and stout aerial roots. The milky fluid had been extruded when the flames had scorched the bark. A few wilted leathery leaves were still attached high up in the tree's once-dense crown. The cabbage palm, a fire-tolerant species, would recover. It was not likely that the fig would be so fortunate.

After he had made a very sticky and slippery climb to a position about 20 feet up, Logan was well secured and comfortable in his tree. He sat on a large horizontal limb and rested his back against a smaller, well-positioned branch. His musket was on his lap. L ooking d own a t h is c ompanion, h e w hispered, "I c an s ee right well from up here. In case yuh're in'erested, the other cable hut done burn't up—all that's left is twisted tin from its roof. West o' here there's still a lot of smoke that's settled down ov'er t he slough. From what I can see, I'd say the grass out 'n the marsh done burn't up too. Damn! That was 'un hot fire!"

"Do yuh see any wildlife . . . any deer?"

"I can see some fresh, white-lookin' tracks that deer might've made. They're 'bout 20 yards ov'r yonder," Logan said, pointing toward the northwest. "I don't know, come to think o' it they look a lil' close together. Could be hog tracks, I reckon."

"Hogs? Yuh ne'er mentioned there was hogs here! Do yuh mean razorback hogs, 'em European boars?"

"No, these 'r' jus' wild hogs. Mister Jake says that the ol'-time Spanish explorers tried to set up a colony 'round here some-where in the 1500s. They brought livestock—hogs 'n' cows—'long wit' 'em on their sailin' ships. They turn't the hogs a-loose on the islands 'n' the beeves a-loose on the mainland, so the stock could live offa the land but be close 'nuff when they needed some. The wild cows we hunt done originated from the stock the Spaniards carried here ov'r 300 years ago. I've heard it tol't that our marsh tacky horses did too . . . our horses, Buck 'n' Cracker came from fine Spanish horses. Hogs 're still out here on this chain o' islands in pretty good numbers. If yuh git yer sights set on 'un, go 'head 'n' bring it down—so long's it's not too damn big fer the three o ' u s t o d rag b ack t o t he b each a ft'r w e gut i t! We don't wanna spend a lotta time quarterin' what we kill to haul it back out to Gus' sailboat. Too many trips!"

Ivy left Logan perched in his tree stand. He quietly walked to the other tree, slung the rifle around his neck and shoulder, and carefully climbed as high up in the slippery tree as he could to gain a vantage point. All was quiet. "The success o' this hunt," he thought, "is now 'n Jeff's hands 'n' 'em mean cow dogs. If there's any deer left in this hellhole, the dogs'll find 'em 'n' chase 'em wit'in range o' our guns."

* * *

24

"A'ight, pups," Jeff said. He crouched down to inspect what appeared to be fresh hoofprints. They were clearly visible in the sooty carpet covering the ground. As he stroked them affectionately, he spoke softly to the dogs. "Chere's wha' we's af'er. Dey's headed ina right direction, so's it's up ta yo' bad boys ta git de job dun. Ya'll git on dere tails 'n' don't let up 'til dey drops."

Intermittently howling, yelping, and sniffing the light breeze, the dogs strained against the leash. Trying to surge forward, their front legs digging into the air, each whined to be freed, imploring Jeff to begin the chase.

"Sick 'em, buyz!" Jeff yelled as he released the eager dogs from the restraining leather.

The dogs were gone in a flash . . . and a cloud of black dust!

They were in hot pursuit of something they had seen, but couldn't smell because of the charred landscape. It was close at first but was now moving away very fast. Jeff was sure the dogs were chasing whatever it was in the right direction—toward the hunters. He broke into a slow run, a gait that would not tire him, as he carefully followed the mix of prints the dogs and deer had left in the charred ground.

He quickly covered nearly a mile and found himself in what had been a long grassy clearing on the crest of a low ridge. As he jogged along, Jeff couldn't help but notice the number of gopher tortoise burrows that crowded this narrow ridge.

He spoke to himself aloud, "Lawdy, mercy! Look chere at all dese goph'rs." Because the weather was cooler than usual, most of the tortoises were safely nestled in their deep burrows when the fire swept overhead. They had survived. The few caught outside— those who failed to reach their burrow in time—had not. Many of the lucky turtles were now just outside their burrow entrance bobbing their heads and peering about, their tiny reptilian brains seemingly trying to figure out what had happened to their lush green world of yesterday.

Jeff muttered to himself, "I'd best 'mem'er dis spot. I c'n cum back lat'r 'n' catch sum o' dese goph'rs easy! I'll git me 'nuff fo' a good messa goph'r 'n' rice, 'n' I c'n sell a few. Ha! Or maybe

I c'n ev'n trade two 'r three fo' sum poontang. Dat's a heapin' 'ho'l lot bett'r'n goph'r 'n' rice! *Hmmm.* Lawdy."

He noticed that the mixed deer and dog tracks had turned slightly. "Good dogs! Dun't let 'em rest!"

It was a deer. No, two deer. The hoofprints were deep and far apart. These animals were moving at top speed and the cow dogs were baying loudly for the first time since the chase began. Their spirits were high. The dogs were fully enjoying themselves, and they were steadily closing the gap. This sure was more fun than rousing some sleepy cow out of a clump of rattlesnake-infested palmettos out on the prairies of central Florida.

* * *

Ivy could hear the dogs. Although the baying was faint, he was certain they were closing the distance between them. It began very subtly, but Ivy could feel his nervous heart start to race. Beads of cold sweat began to form on his brow and chest. As the pressure continued to build, he realized he had no clue what kind of animal the dogs were chasing pell-mell toward him. His mind raced. "Heck, I've ne'er ev'n shot at a deer 'fore. I should've come right out 'n' told Logan that to start wit'! What if I cain't git a clear shot, 'r it moves past me too quick? What if I cain't aim? Damn, what if I flatout miss? I'll only have 'un chaince . . . I may not have 'nuff time 'r the visibility may be . . .. Calm down, dammit!"

The dogs were much closer now. He could hear fire-dried branches exploding into fragments as prey and pursuers crashed through the woods. He jerked his rifle to the right in the direction of the commotion. The game was about to burst into view somewhere between him and Logan. Slowly, he sneaked the hammer back. Taking a deep breath Ivy paused, his heart pounding like tympanies in his ears.

A deafening *Boom*! broke the silence. Ivy jumped. The instant he saw the lead buck, Logan made an experienced decision and pulled the trigger on his unrifled musket. His target stumbled, then skidded, and came to rest in a cloud of soot—killed instantly. A second buck, running on the heels of the first, slowed and briefly hesitated when Logan's gunshot rang out—at the very instant Ivy's sights were aligned on its chest. *Crack*! The buck wavered briefly but refused to fall. He regained his stride and continued bounding east as the two exhausted and hoarse dogs fell in behind.

"Dammit, I missed! I missed 'im!" Ivy cried to his friend who by then had slid down the sticky fig tree and was walking over to check out his prize.

Logan shouted, "No, I don't think so. I'm sho yuh hit 'm 'n' he's hurt bad. I'll wait fer Jeff while yuh hightail it after the dogs. Yuh'd best hurry 'cause when they catch yer deer, they'll chew it to pieces. Here, take my pistol. Yuh may need it!"

"Thanks," Ivy said, as he grabbed the handgun. Then he ran into the brush in the direction the deer and dogs had gone, muttering to himself. "How'n hell'm I ev'r gonna git those dogs to back off from a wounded deer once't it's down? They damn sho won't mind me—they'll probably 'tack me fer interferin'. That's it! Logan thinks I'll need his pistol to kill those dogs from hell when they try to eat me—he didn't intend fer me to use it to put the poor deer outta *his* misery!"

Laughing at Jeff's appearance, Logan said, "Jeff, my man, I believe yuh've done gotten blacker. I reckon it's 'cause o' all the soot yuh've been runnin' through." The dog handler was wearily trudging the final few yards through the blackened brush to join Logan at the dead deer.

"Yes, suh, Mauser Logan. I's 'bout dun in, too. "Em dogs did dere job. I dun hear't two shots, di'n't I? I see yo' dun kill't 'un."

"Yup! Kill't it clean. From a stand in that rubber tree yonder. Ivy hit 'nother 'n' he's chasin' the dogs now to catch it. I don't believe it'll run too far! He hit it better"n he seems to think.

"C'mon. He'p me git a rope ov'r 'un o' these limbs 'n' we'll hoist this buck up this here tree so I can gut it. There's some rope in my pack. Then we'll carry it out to the bay so Cap'n Gus can find us when he comes lookin'."

"Yes, suh, Mauser Logan. Mauser Logan, speakin' o' bein' black, I sho' 'nuff'd like ta 'ave a mirro."

"What's that . . . a mirror? Why's that? What fer?"

27

"Yo's cuvered f'om haid ta toe wi' black soot 'n' dut. I reckon dee sap f'om dat rubber tree yo' climbed dun glue't ev'r'thin' ta yo' clothes 'n' skin. Ha! Yo's really black, Mauser Logan! Now yo' c'n pass fer bein' a black man 'n' have sum fun fo' sho' 'n' I's got de ticket back yonder!"

"What'n the hell're yuh talkin' 'bout, ol' man?"

Jeff just kept on laughing.

After gutting, they dragged the heavy buck out to the water, and doused it several times to wash away the blood and char. Logan then went back inland to retrieve his musket, Ivy's father's rifle, and the other gear.

"I'm takin' me a bath!" Logan yelled as he dove, clothes and all, into the cool water. "I brought me a change o' clothes. I had a pretty good idea this'd happen," he said as he peeled himself down to his freckled birthday suit and threw his wet clothes up on the beach.

"Will yuh please toss me that cake o' soap? It's in my bag—thanks!"

"Mauser Logan, c'n I use yo' duty trousers?"

"Why?"

"Back yunder, while I wuz trottin' af'er 'em dogs, I dun foun' a who' slew o' goph'rs. I'd like ta go back 'n' citch me sum ta cook a mess o' goph'r 'n' rice—'n' I aim ta do a lil' 'portant tradin' wi' sum. I c'n load 'em in yer britches sos I c'n tote 'em all back chere at once't."

"I swear, yuh're a crazy ol' coot, Jeff. Yeah, yuh can borrow my pants, but first grab my knife 'n' cut my hair a-loose from my neck. The sap oozin' from that fig tree done glued it together. I'll ne'er be able to wash it out. Jus' cut it off below my ears fer now. I'll ask Ivy's mama to trim it up later on."

While Logan enjoyed his bath, Jeff slowly trudged back to the ridge he had discovered earlier. In a few minutes, he caught six eating-size tortoises. He stuffed the heavy brown land turtles into the knotted legs of Logan's bluejeans. Smiling broadly, he thought briefly of his proposed menu, and then fell into a daydream. Adrift in thoughtful fantasy and grinning pleasurably, he lightly rubbed his enlarging private part and enjoyed the special glow his body was producing in anticipation of a successful sexual coup. At his age, such plateaus of erotic excitement were few and far between.

Regaining his composure, the former slave headed back to the beach with the pantload of tortoises hanging around his neck like a yoke.

"Lawdy! Yo' goph'rs're right valu'ble—worf mo'n gold. I's rich wit goph'r gold!"

Ivy w as now r unning o ver w ide-open p rairie-like t errain. Even before the sweep of the wildfire, very few trees or bushes of any kind grew here. This open expanse was now nothing but blackened stubble where healthy green, but highly flammable, cord grass once dominated. The deer had decided to continue running east, but from the length of his stride, Ivy could tell he was slowing, getting weaker. The dogs hadn't reached him yet—they were still baying. When they caught their prey, the sounds would become much more savage.

Ivy noticed he could now see both the Gulf and Bay. He knew he was quickly approaching the tip of Sanibel Island. "Where'n the hell's this deer goin'?"

He ran up a slight incline to the top of a low ridge. The soft sugar sand slowed him as he ran on the beach dune.

Only white beach and open water faced him. He had reached the very eastern projection of the island—a point of land, a mere s andspit, w here S an C arlos B ay j oins t he G ulf o f M exico. Out on the beach, lumbering back and forth along the water's edge, were the exhausted dogs. Each was baying with what little voice it had left. But no deer was in sight!

Ivy asked himself, "Where'n the world . . . ?"

Then he saw it. About 200 feet out from the dry beach swam the panic-stricken buck, instinctively trying to escape those who were intent on ending its life. But he now struggled in the turbulent riptide. Suddenly, the animal's head disappeared beneath the jumbling waves. The deer had given up and was gone.

"Damn-it-to-hell!" Ivy screamed at the top of his lungs. He stomped the ground very hard several times in total frustration.

"Now I've gotta go back to Punta Rassa empty-handed. Everyone's gonna give me grief. I'll ne'er live it down. Nobody will ev'r believe me when I tell 'em what happened to my deer, that the damn t'ing drowned on me!"

He spun around with his head lowered, humiliated and disgusted. "What'n the hell's that?" Something colorful and partly buried in the sand had caught his eye.

Ivy crouched and reached down to move away some of the powdery sand. What had he glimpsed a moment ago?

There, in a shallow depression, just inches below the surface—his angry kicking had uncovered it—was what looked like a faintly decorated clay pot. Ivy reached down and slowly lifted a large, fragile-looking container out of the sand, careful not to damage it. "What'n the world's this?" he asked out loud.

The pot was intact. Ever so carefully, he twisted off the tight-fitting lid. It resisted at first, almost as if it had been glued in place. But finally it pulled away clean. Inside were several objects.

"Hot damn, what've I found?" He fingered and closely examined each item. "This looks like a metal, maybe iron arrowhead. This other one's made outta some kinda stone," Ivy whispered. Two giant shark teeth with serrated edges and single holes drilled through each caught his eye, then several multi-faceted clear and colored glass beads.

He hesitated as his eyes came upon a small, carved, wooden statuette. It was very detailed, about six inches tall. The carving had a cat-like upper body but was anatomically human on the bottom half. "Beautiful!" He could see that it was a knife handle, and attached to it was a glossy black, glass-like stone blade.

At the very bottom of the pot was a bright metal disk. Ivy picked it out and examined it closely. Suddenly he blurted, "This looks like an ol' gold coin! It sho 'nuff's shiny."

Ivy stood up and dropped the coin into his pants pocket. He carefully replaced the lid and put the piece of pottery, which still held the other items, inside his shoulder-slung game bag. He glanced back toward the beach. He was ready to head back and join the others. But first he must convince the dogs they were to come along with him.

30

Dumbly, the dogs were still sniffing around for the deer. Ivy bravely yelled, "C'mon boys, let's go find Logan 'n' Jeff!"

He watched in stunned amazement as the dogs instantly obeyed and ran toward him wagging their tails. They were ready to quit! Now silent, they fell in behind Ivy as he backtracked to find his companions. For now, his discovery had to be kept to himself.

CHAPTER 3

OVER THE NEXT SEVERAL DAYS, IVY CLARK WAS the center of attention around Punta Rassa, courtesy of Logan Grace. Before the hunting party reached the docks on their return from Sanibel Island, Ivy had told his entire sad tale. Finding the event humorous, Logan sarcastically bestowed the title "Deer Drowner" on Ivy, along with some other unjustified degrading remarks. Ivy didn't appreciate the new moniker, nor the other insults, and let him know it.

"Logan, yuh have 'un hell o' a big mouth fer someone so puny! If yuh keep on bein' so damned ornery, I'm gonna whip yer ass! I'm not 'bout to sit still while yuh try 'n' make me the laughin'stock o' Punta Rassa!" Ivy knew he was taking a chance being so blunt. He was fully aware that Logan was quick to anger. Over the years he had seen his friend spring into many confrontational rages when challenged.

"Come 'head 'n' try, boy! What's wrong? Cain't yuh take a lil' ribbin'?"

"That's not really why I'm riled! I don't much like hearin' all that shit comin' from a so-called friend's mouth. If yuh were in my shoes, yuh wouldn't think it was so damned funny either!"

Gus interrupted, trying to defuse the argument. "Why don't you two kids cool off? Ivy, don't take everything Logan's said so damn serious. You know he's only trying to rile you. He's pulling your leg, son!"

Gus's comments seemed to help. Exhausted and irritable, the two young men simmered down and the conversation turned to friendlier topics with gentler tones. Earlier, the four voyagers had divided the venison during their short trip across the Bay. Each had stuffed their equally shared portions into canvas kit bags. Once the boat was secured, they said their goodbyes. Tired from the day's activities they plodded to their individual destinations. The dogs, still under Jeff's restraint, were also physically whipped. They made no sounds as they wearily pulled him toward their kennel.

* * *

Ivy didn't tell anyone about his discovery of the cache of artifacts. He would wait until he had a chance to closely examine the unusual objects. He dropped the gold coin back into his pocket—for the time being it would be his "good luck" piece. He put the clay pot and its contents inside a wooden cabinet at his parents' home. In his mind, he remained curious about his unusual find, but Ivy knew that no one who frequented Punta Rassa could shed any light on its origins.

Things between the friends soon normalized, and once again their lives became boring and routine. Ivy's reputation as the Deer Drowner was short-lived and the fuss between the two pals soon waned. The day after their hunting expedition, they returned to their jobs handling the small herds of cattle that arrived infrequently at the port's holding facilities.

Logan and Ivy worked for the Summerlin Cattle Company. Logan had been the cattle foreman before Ivy was hired. He decided which holding corrals the individual herds would be kept in while they awaited their passage vessels. The cowboys were responsible for feeding and watering the stock before loading the bawling bovines onto the foul-smelling boats. From Punta Rassa, the skinny Florida cattle eventually fed many red-meat-hungry peoples on the scattered Spanish and French islands, many far to the south of the Florida mainland. Some of these places had romantic-sounding names which most of the Florida cowboys had only heard of but longed to visit.

* * *

The oppressive days of summer droned on day in and day out. Life was dull and hard. High humidity, torrential rain with frightening and sometimes deadly lightning, and the black clouds of mosquitoes made living conditions miserable. These realities controlled the lives of those who lived and worked around Punta Rassa. Of all the elements that nature bestowed on the toughened residents and livestock, the mosquitoes were the worst. Most residents dreaded them more than hurricanes.

But the humans were lucky. They could escape the hungry insects by retreating to their homes at dark. Fine-meshed cotton mosquito netting surrounded their beds. Most prayed they would sleep soundly and pass the night without waking. Having to go outside in the dark to the mosquito-filled outhouse was an unwelcome fate. There was always the nearby slop jar. These primitive indoor toilets saved a trip outside—a wonderful accommodation for the very young, very old, and cowards.

The cattle weren't so fortunate. Those brought to the port in late summer or early fall didn't fare well at all. Held in open-air corrals, they couldn't escape the storm of salt marsh mosquitoes that descended on them. So Punta Rassa became almost deserted—few people or animals were able to tough it out. Occasionally, a small herd had to be driven to the port due to meat shortages on some distant island. Unbelievable numbers of mosquitoes sometimes caused these poor animals to die—literally from loss of blood from hundreds of thousands of mosquitoes piercing their skin at the same time. Cattle deaths also occurred when the insects became so thick they completely covered the nostrils of weakened, blood-drained animals and suffocated them.

Exposed outside overnight during peak mosquito season, a person could suffer the same fate. And the few horses necessary for daily operations at Punta Rassa were housed in screened and roofed structures to protect them from the bugs.

When the occasional sea breeze did not die off after night-fall, the mosquitoes became their very worst. As the wind blew across Sanibel Island, it carried millions of the bloodthirsty demons across the harbor to torture the hardened people and unprotected livestock.

* * *

At the pens early Tuesday morning, Florida's foremost cattle baron, Jacob Summerlin caught up with his two favorite cowboys. "Logan, I want yuh 'n' Ivy to bring my next herd down from upstate. Ya'll need a break from this monotonous saltwater 'n' mangrove country. I'll have Duke 'n' Mack take ov'r while yuh two're gone. They'll be here wit' their boys next week sometime. They're bringin' down a couple hundred head from the Kissimmee Prairie. Ya'll can head out next Monday mornin'. Ward's crew can take care o' 'em 'n' load 'em when the steamer 'rives to pick 'em up. I've already tol't Jeff to catch the next boat headed upriver to Fort Myers 'n' git 'un o' my wagons outta storage 'long wit' a team 'n' 'range fer some spare cow ponies from the stables. He'll be back by Friday—'r so he tells me—says he's gonna spend a night wit' some kin who live 'tween here 'n' Fort Myers. I think he's givin' me a line o' bullshit! Said he'll hurry back to start loadin' up. I want 'im to go wit' ya'll on this drive. He needs a change o' scenery, too. Jeff's a hard worker 'n' a good man. He'll be goin' 'long to take care o' yuh boys 'n' the other drover's appetites 'n' hurts. Yuh'll have to stop off at the store 'n' blacksmith shop in Fort Myers on the way north, to buy supplies 'n' git the horses."

"Yes, sir! We'll git our gear together this weekend 'n' head out early Monday. Where do we meet up wit' the beeves?"

"Yuh boys have a damn long ride 'head o' yuh. Tom Wood's hands're huntin' 'n' bunchin' 'bout 300 head up near Ocala. I've been tol't they'll meet ya'll at the cow camp on the south end o' Lake Panasoffkee. It'll take yuh 'bout a week o' long days to git there, 'n' 'bout a month to git back here I reckon."

* * *

The ex-slave Jeff Bowton had developed a strange habit since the hunting trip to Sanibel Island. Most everyone who knew him noticed it. He wore a broad grin almost constantly, and he chuckled to himself when alone, and sometimes when not alone. On this particular day he seemed happier than ever. "Ha! Ha!" he thought. "Yo' dev'lish rascal! Yo' dun pull't de wool o'er Mauser Jake's eyes 'gain fo' sho'!"

After he packed and was ready to leave, he went outside his flimsy palm-thatched shack and took his two prized gopher tortoises out of their pen. He placed each one inside a worn croker sack and threw them over his shoulder. Returning to the doorway of his house, Jeff stooped and picked up his small valise. He reached inside a partly overturned fish box that served as a table, then picked up and placed a full bottle of locally made whiskey inside his bag. Then he put his best straw hat on his white-haired head and started walking toward the dock. After a short wait, he climbed aboard the wood-burning steamboat that would take him and a few other passengers up the Caloosahatchee to Fort Myers.

As the boat moved away from the dock, Jeff said to himself, talking aloud to his silent cargo in the sacks, "Yup, yo' goph'rs'll be worf mo'n gold'n Fort Myers t'night. When I gits ta de quarters, I's gonna fin' me de bes' ho' 'n town! Ya'll're a-footin' de bill! Godamighty! I cain't wait; it's be'n sicha long time!" Once again he fell willing victim to that special glowing pulse in his crotch. His smile broadened.

* * *

"Mornin', Alice! Where're yuh 'n' yer folks headin' this beautiful day?" Alice Johnson was the oldest daughter of Bob and Ruth Johnson who had homesteaded Fisherman Key, which lay offshore from Punta Rassa. His younger brothers, Alice's uncles, had been the harbor pilots at Punta Rassa until the Hurricane of '73.

Ivy had talked to Alice occasionally when she happened to visit Punta Rassa—whenever Logan wasn't around to cramp his style. He guessed she was one, maybe two years at the most, younger than he was. Since he had first met her, Ivy thought Alice was the prettiest woman he had ever seen. Blonde and petite, Alice was very attractive and this demanded attention. She was the belle of Punta Rassa! Anyone with reasonably good eyes could see he was right. She boarded with an aunt in Fort Myers during the school year and was well-spoken. With her education completed Alice was once again living on Fisherman Key with her parents.

"*Oh*, hello there! Good morning, Ivy. How are you? I haven't seen you in quite a spell."

"I'm doin' right well, Alice. I've been 'round, but I'm fixin' to leave out next week to he'p bring a big herd in fer Mister Jake."

"Before I completely forget, thanks for that venison you and Logan sent over to us with Cap'n Wendt. My folks, my little sister, and I sure enjoyed it! Today we're all heading down to Johnson's Mound for a family reunion."

"Where's that?"

"It's a key, an island, down there." She was pointing south toward the island to the left of Sanibel Island, on the opposite side of the wide entrance to San Carlos Harbor. "It's in a long bay behind that outer beach. One of Daddy's older brothers homesteaded it about the time Daddy applied to the Government for our land.

"When everyone in the family who lives close enough shows up at one of our reunions, it's a lot of fun. I love to meet all the new babies that have been born into our family!"

"Tell me, how'd the place git the name Johnson's Mound?"

"Because we're the Johnsons, silly!"

"No, I mean Johnson's *Mound*—why do ya'll call it a mound?"

"*Oh?* Their place sits on top of a big Indian mound. Haven't you ever seen one? Some are really huge! I believe it may be the highest land along this coast—all man-made too. Our place over yonder sets on one of them, although Daddy has leveled a lot of it to cultivate crops. The shell and dirt mix grows some right nice vegetables."

"Yeah, I've eaten lots o' 'maters yer daddy's growed. What kinda Indians?"

"The old-time Indians. I believe they were the Calosas— those who lived along this coast a long time before the Seminoles came this far south. The Calosas built the mounds from shellfish remains. From what I've been told, they didn't farm—just lived off the sea the best they could. Daddy says the mounds are nothing more than old garbage dumps. I reckon those Indians just ate the creatures living inside the shells and fish, or anything else they could catch or kill. Things must have been real hard for them back in the olden days."

"They must've been. I'd sho git mighty tired o' chewin' tuff ol' clams all the time. I git tired 'nuff o' chewin' on Mister Jake's stringy beef. I believe I found 'un o' those Indian mounds, a small 'un, ov'r on Sanib'l not too long 'go."

"Really? You'll have to tell me about it sometime. Right now, I've got to run. It was sure nice to talk with you again, Ivy. I'd best get back to the dock and get in the boat. They're waving at me to hurry. Why don't you come over and have supper with us some Sunday?"

"I'd love to when I git back wit' the cows. Yuh jus' let me know when!"

"I will . . . I certainly will. I'll send word when I know you're back. It'll be real soon after that. I promise!"

Ivy smiled as he walked away to go back to work. He was very fond of Alice and proud she had presented him with a warm thought. He had something to look forward to and at the same time take with him on his trip.

* * *

Jeff made it back to Punta Rassa on Friday with the wagon—minus two gopher tortoises, his bone-handled pocketknife, his new hat, and his only pair of shoes. He was flat broke, utterly exhausted, and seriously hung over. He longed for his bed. His once-happy grin soon became a defensive smirk after several people asked, "Jeff, how was your trip upriver to Fort Myers?"

Jeff had accomplished what he had anticipated for months. A pleasure-talented young black lady had fulfilled both his sexual and emotional needs in the segregated colored quarters of Fort Myers. He was satisfied. The experience had been worth everything he had given to it—or paid for it! What limited parts of the romp he could clearly recall, despite the whiskey, that is! He was-n't the least bit interested in sharing the events of his recent sexual encounter with noisy, big-mouthed, cow-smelly white folks.

From Jeff's appearance, Ivy and Logan knew he had some kind of interesting adventure upriver. They were unrelenting and determined to pry the details from him. But Jeff was used to their shenanigans. The old man stood his ground and remained tight-lipped. He knew his sex life had again entered another familiar uncomfortable dimension—a long dry spell. So he resolved to ignore his interrogators and enjoy what good thoughts he could remember. Jeff refused to share them with anyone.

*   *   *

The layover to buy supplies took longer than expected. Jeff charged everything to Jake Summerlin's account. This included sacks of corn meal, rice and beans, and cloth-wrapped sides of cured bacon. Jeff was careful when he bought the bacon, remem-bering Logan's words, "When yuh buy that bacon, yuh best be sho yuh git slabs that don't have no damn buttons!"

Several wooden crates containing salt mullet started from Punta Rassa with them. Fresh-killed birds and game and freshwa-ter fish augmented these supplies for the duration of the round trip. Drinking water was essential and several wooden barrels had to be rinsed clean and filled with drinking water from the deep flowing sulfur water well at the store. While Jeff shopped for groceries, Logan and Ivy moved the team and other horses to the town's blacksmith shop. They inspected the horses' shoes and had some reshod.

They spent the first night away from home in the pineland east of Fort Myers and south of the Caloosahatchee on the eastern bank of a smaller river called Twelve-Mile Creek. The next day, because the creek was so deep, they had to ride southeasterly almost to the stream's headwaters before they could cross it. Once across this water barrier, the group of men and animals turned northeastward. They now traveled east again, paralleling the main river.

Late on the third day from Punta Rassa they forded the zigzagging, narrow Caloosahatchee. The three men did not see any other people until they had nearly reached their destination. This was wild, unspoiled land. Only cows and pigs and a few horses had sullied the natural systems.

The river crossing was relatively easy for the horsemen, Mildred the veteran herd-leading cow, spare cow ponies, and unburdened extra harness horses. But it was treacherous for the heavy, fully loaded supply wagon and its straining four-horse team. The tumbling water in the Caloosahatchee raced downhill after leaving Lake Flirt. Its dark, tannic-acid-stained water was heading for the Gulf of Mexico near Punta Rassa.

There were not many safe crossings along the unbridged wild Caloosahatchee. The traditional fording place had a firm bottom and was shallow enough for safe passage—except when the river was at flood stage. The three men, the cowboys who would join them, and the cattle they would drive south would pass this way again in a few weeks.

The trio from Punta Rassa, Jeff, Logan, and Ivy, crossed just before dark, then stopped for the night. They were bone tired. Out in the middle of nowhere they quickly made camp, spreading their ground cloths and bedrolls in a Spanish-moss-draped live oak hammock. Indeed, this was a welcome change from looking at mangrove trees all day.

And the night sounds were very different.

"What'n the hell's makin' that God-awful noise out in the woods?" Ivy yelled suddenly as he threw off his blanket and leaped to his feet. He was not quite fully awake and nearly fell into the roaring fire which Jeff was busy banking for the night.

Logan turned over and asked sleepily, "What's wrong lil' feller? Ain't yuh ne'er heard a painter 'fore?"

"What's a damn painter? I've ne'er heard no noise like that! Someone out there must be dyin'. It sounds to me like a woman screamin'!"

"A painter's 'nother name fer a panther—painter's what Pappy always called 'em. Some folks call 'em a cougar. It's a big ornery calf-killin', long-tailed cat." Winking at Jeff, Logan continued. "We'd best all be on our guard tonight. That devil might try to sneak in here 'n' drag 'un o' us off in the palmettos. I reckon we should've brought 'un o' Mister Jake's dogs 'long to protect us!"

"Yuh ne'er tol't me 'bout no man-eatin' cats! Is he tellin' me straight, Jeff? Jeff?"

"Reckon he is, Mauser Ivy. I dun hear't sum bad stories o' wha' panthers c'n do ta peoples, 'specially ta white folks!"

Almost pleading, Ivy asked, "Ar' we gonna take turns stayin' 'wake tonight—to keep the fire burnin' 'n' guard the stock 'n' each other from that damned scary cat? If it ain't safe fer us out in the open like this, I'll ne'er be able to git any sleep! I wish I was back 'n my own bed!"

Nearly asleep and fully enjoying his prank, Logan yawned and answered, "Oh, we'll be safe sho 'nuff. That cat done likely kill't some poor woman—didn't yuh hear that sad screamin' sound? That meal 'll last the cat through this night. But tomorrow night's 'nother story!"

"*Good God*! How do ya'll 'spect me to sleep?"

Soon, all were soundly asleep. The sounds of human snoring drifted through the dark woodlands and mixed with the night sounds.

Jeff was the first to rise and begin the new day. He dutifully stoked the fire, then built a grill over it made from a metal grate supported by logs on each side of the fire. A blue porcelain pot, in which he would brew strong coffee, came next. Beside the coffee pot, Jeff set down a huge cast iron frying pan. He began to fry strips of thick, hand-cut, buttonless bacon. When this was done to his liking, he scrambled a dozen eggs mixed with lots of diced hot peppers. They would be eating these hearty, man-sized breakfasts for the next few days—until the supply of hen's eggs Jeff brought ran out! For weeks after that, breakfast would be much simpler, shared by everyone who was part of or visited the nomadic cow camp. Black coffee, bacon, and johnnycakes would fuel their bodies and get them started each day in the saddle.

Jeff, Logan, and Ivy followed a wide, well-worn, and meandering cattle trail through open, roadless, unfenced range. Naturalized cattle and hogs shared their habitats with native deer, black bears, panthers, bobcats, wolves, turkeys, caracaras, sandhill cranes, and countless coveys of bobwhite quail. Mildred, the experienced trail cow, was tethered to Jeff's wagon. Once again she would lead a wild herd of cattle back to Punta Rassa.

Long day rolled into long day, and the next, and not much happened between them. The terrain soon changed once they left the immediate floodplain of the Caloosahatchee. Now into their fourth day they were traveling almost due north over rolling sandhills in the ridge country of central Florida and dodging around beautiful cypress-bordered lakes dotting the countryside. The sand ridges were covered with short-needled sand pine, rosemary, turkey oak, and sometimes dense stands of impenetrable saw palmetto. Speedy scrub lizards and their faster striped relatives, six-lined racerunners, dashed for cover. Startled wild cows and white-tailed deer evaded the men and domestic animals, disappearing into the vastness of the green wilds. Once in a while, large defensively poised eastern diamondback rattlesnakes blocked their path.

"Shoot dat damned ol' rattler, Mauser Logan. He'll bite 'un o' us 'r a cow on de way back if'n yo' dun't."

"Nope. I don't kill't nothin' I cain't eat—ne'er have, ne'er will! That noisy diamondback has more title to this scrub country 'n any o' us does. He's sho 'nuff lettin' us know that too, ain't he? Jus' listen to that big buzztail son-o'-a-bitch! If we sidestep 'round 'im, we'll git by jus' fine!"

On their eighth morning out, Logan spotted a distant spiral of smoke rising from the flatlands on their side of a vast prairie bordering a large lake. He remembered seeing this beautiful panorama a few years before, when he first ventured this far north as a greenhorn kid on an earlier cattle drive. Logan thought, soon they would reach the smoke—a cook fire marking their destination. He would meet the other drive foreman, transfer responsibility for the stock, and assume supervision of the dozen or so wranglers that would help him move the cows south. He'd become the trail boss, but he secretly hoped the herd wouldn't be ready to move when he arrived. If they were lucky, Ivy, Jeff, and he could rest a day or two before starting back. He didn't look forward to the grueling, slow, and exhausting trip back to their home base on the distant seashore.

The animals now sensed others of their kind nearby. The horses perked up as they reached the crest of the final ridge which overlooked the broad flatland between them and the lake. Controlling their excited mounts and looking down at the cattle-covered green prairie before them, Ivy, Logan, and Jeff each sensed an independent feeling of relief.

Turning in his saddle, Ivy said, "Logan, here come a couple o' riders. They're haulin' ass! Look's like they've seen us. Yeah, they're wavin'!"

The riders continued to approach at a gallop. Now within shouting distance, the lead rider, a big black-bearded man, hollered, "Is that yuh, Logan? I'll be a son-o'-a-bitch! Logan Grace, 'tis yuh, yuh damned ol' cow-lovin' 'Cracker!' It's me . . . Jehu!"

Excitedly, Logan took the man's outstretched hand and yelled, "I'll be goddammed! Jehu . . . Jay Rivers, yuh mean ugly bastard! I don't believe I've laid eyes on yer sorry hide fer better 'n two yars. I didn't reco'nize yuh 'cause o' 'em bushy whiskers. I heard a while back that yuh'd been kill't by the ol' man o' some lady yuh were beddin', yuh crazy coot! It sho's hell good to see yuh!"

"Nope. The ol' geezer jus' winged me! I heard he damn near beat that good-lookin' wife o' his to death though—ov'r me! Do yuh believe that? She was somethin' else, nice to look at, 'n' man, she were the finest kind in bed! Damnation! It's sho 'nuff good to see yuh after all this time! How's yer hammer hangin'?"

CHAPTER 4

JEHU RIVERS AND HIS PARTNER WEBB McCOY HAD been hunting cows in the dense scrub when he saw Logan and the others approaching. The cow hunters were working as a team: two horsemen and a dog. They slowly made their way among the dry rolling hills, carefully searching thickets of sand pine, oak, and palmetto for wild cows in hiding. Jehu and Webb were traditional and tough Florida cow hunters. They stood a breed apart from ordinary men. Like Logan Grace, they were "Florida Crackers."

Six mounted men stayed close and worked the main herd, constantly circling the grazing and bawling cattle to keep them in a loose but contained bundle. A separate team of three men slowly rode through the herd and inspected the hide of each cow. They cut out unbranded cattle that were accidentally mixed in with the marked animals. Individuals scarred with a brand other than Jacob Summerlin's "cSc" were roped and pulled from the main herd. These were moved about a half-mile away to a smaller herd being held together more tightly than the animals in the main herd by one mounted man and five well-trained dogs

The men and dogs who found any unbranded cows drove them to the main herd. They were roped, thrown to the ground, and their legs tethered. Immobilized, they were quickly branded with a red-hot piece of forged iron, burning the "cSc" into their hides, then they were tallied as property of the Summerlin Cattle Company. When 300 head were rounded up, the herd would be driven to Punta Rassa and loaded aboard a cramped boat bound for Havana, Cuba.

Before sundown, everyone knew their new trail boss was in camp, along with a skinny white kid and a cranky, bent-over old black man. As soon as he arrived, Logan asked foreman Tom Wood to spread the word to all the cowhands that everyone on the payroll should assemble at the cook fire, once the cattle settled down for the night.

Logan waved the men in and announced, "Boys! I'm only gonna need 'bout ten o' ya'll wit' the wagon 'n driver that're already part o' the roundup crew to make the trip to Punta Rassa wit' these cows. I believe ya'll knowed that up front! Tom's given me a list o' those who wanna make the drive. Looks like 'bout 12 o' yuh, all tol't! Mr. Summerlin's a fair man. He said I could keep that many o' yuh on the payroll.

"Tom tells me ya'll've done a great job 'n gathered 'bout 290 head. He said ya'll' 're some o' the best cowhands he's ev'r had! Tomorrow we'll hunt these ridges 'n the prairie fer 'un last day. In 'bout 30 hours, we'll start movin' 'em south. We'll pick up a few more head 'long the way to git the herd up to the 300 the boss man's expectin'. Fer those o' yuh who won't be comin' 'long, I un'erstand that the Kirkland outfit needs hands down at their Kissimmee camp. Ya'll that'll be leavin' us, see Tom 'n' me tomorrer evenin' 'bout yer pay. We'll settle up then."

At sunrise, the drive started on Logan's schedule. After sleeping on the proposition, Jehu Rivers decided to stay with Logan and the herd. He had never traveled to Punta Rassa before and was looking forward to spending a few days on the ocean with his old friend. Jehu tasted seawater only once, years ago when he was a boy. Around the fire the night before, Logan had told him stories about the giant fish that frequent the waters near Punta Rassa. Jehu Rivers loved to fish.

45

Jehu had a ready sense of humor and an infectious smile. His short black hair and generous beard made him look much more mature than he was in actual years. Because of his good looks, mature appearance, and personality, Jehu Rivers also learned about the ladies much earlier than his teenage cohorts did. In some towns he was popular because of his wit and good looks. Yet in others, these qualities got him into trouble over women.

Like most young men raised in the wild Florida interior, Jehu had limited career choices. He would have to work timber, chase cattle, or follow a farm mule. In his late teens, Jehu decided chasing cows on horseback was the best career for him. He left the family farm in central Florida's lake country and drifted down to Wauchula. He found work on the open, unfenced cattle range of 19th Century Florida and met Logan Grace. Both grew up to become skilled horsemen.

The two cowboys were about the same age, so it was natural that they quickly bonded and formed an enduring friendship. Like Logan Grace, Jehu Rivers was slim and rangy, and like Logan Jehu could be mean-tempered, but he was not as short-fused.

The 305-head herd was short less than a half-dozen when the tail of the last cow left the Lake Panasoffkee cow camp. They started out slow and tight, head to tail. But by the end of the first day, Mildred, the veteran lead cow, had led the herd less than ten miles. The rest were stretched out half a mile behind her.

Along the way, the cowboy's lives became pure simplicity. Many wondered, "Why'n the hell did I choose this livelihood? Sho as hell not fer the food . . . nor the money!" Ivy Clark still had that special youthful exuberance about being a cowboy, but before this trip was over, he'd find himself thinking more and more about Alice Johnson and his future. Sometimes he'd fantasize and dwell on *their* future.

Twenty-six days later, the entourage reached the north bank of the Caloosahatchee. Logan decided to camp for the night so the stragglers could catch up. They would cross the river the next morning.

* * *

The battle-scarred behemoth was king of his watery domain. He also ruled the land several yards out from the river-bank. With slow side-to-side thrusts of his powerful tail, his four limbs held tight against his body, he cruised where he pleased. He feared nothing. This giant bull alligator was truly lord of his world.

Forty-seven years ago, his mother built a nest from rotting grass on the marshy shore of Lake Okeechobee. His life began with a series of high-pitched grunts, from the inside of a dark egg. His was one of two dozen she had carefully buried.

Despite a life full of threats, he proved himself to be a survivor. An otter once held him firmly, intent on biting off the hatchling's head. But with a series of grunts, a weak pinching bite, and a squirming lunge, he freed himself. Such experiences made him tough and smart.

This river-wise bull had reached adult length many years ago. But like other reptiles, he continued to grow in length and girth over time. He would grow until he died.

Forty years before, as a wandering six-foot-long youngster, he ventured from his birthplace. He followed a trickle of water leading him into the dark water of Lake Flirt. Later, his travels brought him to the Caloosahatchee. He arrived there quite by accident, carried by the outflow draining westward from the series of shallow lakes.

With enormity of size came a change of diet. Eating small animals no longer satisfied his appetite. The occasional swimming or drinking deer, cow, hog, or raccoon was his usual prey, and large soft-shelled turtles flattened further between his powerful jaws. Not many flightless creatures trying to cross his river, within his view, lived to make the swim back.

* * *

Each cowboy's saddle was laden with personal gear, essentials for a horseback rider who worked cattle. Each carried a bedroll for sleeping and a poncho for protection from the elements. But the two most important tools of the cowboy trade were the two items coiled on the front of the saddle near the horn: the lariat and the bullwhip. Lariats were used to catch, help restrain, and move cows. The long bullwhips were also used to move cattle, but more importantly, they helped steer a herd in the intended direction.

Astride his buckskin gelding, Buck, and pointing upriver, Logan started things moving, "Ivy! Head east to that bend in the river. Signal me if there's a boat comin' this a-way. Bob, yuh do the same t'ing where the western oxbow begins to turn. If either o' yuh see a boat headin' this a-way, stop the damn t'ing so we can cross't these cows! I don't want some boat pilot blowin' a damn whistle 'r a horn 'n' spookin' 'em. That'd spread these cows to hell 'n gone! Jehu, yuh 'n' Webb he'p Jeff 'n' Willie git their wagons 'cross't 'fore I start the beeves!"

With nearly worn-out spurs, Ivy nudged his mare, Cracker, in the ribs. The palamino-colored swamp tacky instantly side-stepped away from the herd, and horse and rider soon disappeared into the thick palms and oaks lining the river.

The tassel on the end of Logan's tightly braided leather bullwhip hovered for a split second over Mildred's head. Then, with a well-trained, artistic flick of his wrist, the 18-foot-long whip made an explosive sound. *Crack!* The noise made a racket like a rifle firing. Above the heads of the now wide-awake, bawling, and milling cattle, other whips cracked around the bunched-up live-stock. *Crack! Crack! Crack!* The frightened herd began to move toward the sloped bank of the Caloosahatchee, away from the noisy horse-mounted crackers. Years earlier, as they too tried to escape the frightening sound, other cattle had passed this way and beaten down the once-steep embankment of the fording place.

Ivy and his fine horse, Cracker, meandered through the woods at a trot, trying to keep the river in view. After breaking through some dense leather ferns, they crossed a shallow creek. Stopping at the confluence of the two streams, Ivy scanned the Caloosahatchee from a swampy point of land jutting out into the river. Although a thin mist hung veil-like a few feet above the water, it was clear to Ivy there were no boats in the area. A few anhingas, known to Ivy as snakebirds, were busy fishing. When their heads and long snake-like necks broke the surface, they tossed their small fishes into the air, caught them head first, and then swal-lowed them whole.

48

Ivy's eyes again panned the upstream section of the river. Squinting in the poor light of dawn, he thought he saw something drifting downstream toward him. He focused on the dark object and said to himself, "What the hell's that out in the middle o' the river? It's no rock. *Huh*, looks like a big log, but damn! It's movin' downstream faster'n the current!"

It finally dawned on him what he was looking at. Ivy yelled out loud, "God-a-mighty! It's a 'gator! It's the biggest damn 'gator I've ev'r seen! C'mon, Cracker, let's git back to the herd 'n' warn Logan!"

As the spurs dug into her hide, Cracker spun around and ran crashing through the tall ferns. Ivy continued pumping her. Ivy knew that by now the herd had already started across the river. He'd have to get there quick and warn Logan and the others . . . if the huge alligator didn't get there first!

Submerged just inches below the river's surface, the alligator moved toward the cattle crossing at top speed. There were no ripples on the surface, nor sounds of any kind to give a clue to his presence. There was no alert. He had selected his target and was moving in on it. It was a moment of climactic and primeval savagery and nothing could stop his momentum.

When he was close enough to be heard over the commotion of lowing cattle, cracking whips, and shouting men, Ivy screamed at the top of his lungs. "Logan! Logan! There's a big 'gator headin' this a-way! He's the biggest 'gator I've ev'r laid my eyes on!"

Logan screamed back, "Where the hell is he?"

Reaching Logan's side, Ivy yelled breathlessly, "I lost track . . . when I lit out . . . to git back here . . . to warn ya'll! When I las' saw 'im, he was highballin' it this a-way!"

The river was choked with cattle. The large animals and horses could walk all the way across, but the smaller ones lost their footing and had to swim. A struggling heifer on the herd's east flank was the doomed target.

49

Suddenly the dark water erupted like a frothy geyser, and the unfortunate cow bawled painfully as the monster alligator lunged out of the depths. He caught her by the neck with his huge jaws. Immediately the reptile turned, trying to drag the resisting animal away from the shallows into deeper water. Despite the young cow's frantic attempts to impale her attacker with her left horn, the alligator was much too powerful. Once in deep water, he took her with him to the bottom.

Logan screamed at the top of his lungs, "Ivy! Cross't ov'r 'n' git yer rifle outta Jeff's wagon! When that son-o'-a-bitch comes up fer air, blow 'is goddammed head off! Stay here 'til yuh kill't the bastard! We'll put 'n end to that wise ol' 'gator's bullshit today! Once't 'n' fer all!"

It didn't take long. Feeling the prey finally go limp in his vise-like jaws, the alligator decided it was time to surface. A partially buoyant dead cow was easier to drag away through the water than across the bottom. Then he'd retire to a secluded spot and begin his feast in private. He had avoided human contact for most of his life, although a time or two bullets had whizzed very close to his leathery hide.

As the alligator came up with the cow, the surface of the water hardly broke. Slowly, he began to swim toward the oxbow slough where his cave was located. All that showed of his water-borne presence was the top of his head, with its large protruding eyes, and the nostril mound at the end of his snout. Occasionally, lifeless and floating cow parts sank and others rose to break the mirror flatness of the water.

Ivy crossed the river again. It seemed to him that the northern bank of the Caloosahatchee was clearer. There was less tall vegetation growing close to the bank, and the light was better. He would have a better view and, when he saw the alligator, he would have a clearer shot. Less likely to miss!

Calmly whispering to his horse, Ivy said soothingly, "Steady, Cracker, I believe I can see Mr. 'Gator. Damn, he's big! He's gotta move 'head jus' a lil' bit more 'n' I'll have a fair shot at 'im."

He placed a cap on the nipple of the already-loaded rifle, slowly cocked it, and raised it to his shoulder.

"Steady now, Cracker." Ivy said as he patted his horse on the neck after he lowered the heavy rifle and rested it across the front of Cracker's saddle. Ivy was waiting for a clear shot when the enormous reptilian head reached an opening in the tree line separating them. Ivy Clark stood in the stirrups and reached into the pocket of his jeans, feeling for the familiarity of his good luck piece. Subconsciously, as he rubbed the gold disk between his thumb and forefinger, his shooting confidence increased. He raised the rifle and brought the butt plate firmly against his shoulder a second time.

Sitting motionless, Ivy thought, "Logan tol't me once't that a 'gator's got a brain 'bout the size o' a sewin' thimble. If I'm gonna do this son-o'-a-bitch in, I've gotta take my time. I've gotta shoot true. I cain't miss this one. My eye's gotta be right on the money. I gotta hit that puny brain." Then aloud he whispered, "Easy, Cracker."

Bam! The shot echoed along the river bottom and bounced back and forth off the banks and tall trees. The alligator simply stopped; the dead cow slowly floated free. Then the huge reptile rolled over—dead!

Rising high in the stirrups and waving the rifle, Ivy yelled, "Deer Drowner! My ass, Logan Grace! Now, yuh gopher-necked cow hunter, yuh can call me 'Ivy, the giant killer!' C'mon, Cracker, let's git back to the crossin'. We'll haul that rascal to the bank 'n' measure 'im."

Several minutes later, he skillfully threw his looped lariat and caught hold of one of the alligator's legs. Ivy dragged the dead monster into the shallows. Then with Cracker's help, he hauled the heavy carcass partly out of the water and straightened it out the best he could. Ivy's bullwhip was a standard 15-footer, three feet shorter than Logan's. He uncoiled it along the alligator's back, aligning the end of the handle even with the tip of the snout.

"This's a mighty big 'gator! He's two feet longer'n my whip. He's 17 feet long if he's a foot! I declare! An' Logan's nowhere in sight! He'll ne'er believe me! I wish I had one o' 'em new-fangled picture makin' machines!" Ivy severed a front foot to carry back to the herd and show Logan. He would show Logan the evidence to prove he had indeed made the kill. Otherwise, Logan and the boys would never believe him.

Cracker burst out of the water and lunged up the bank of the south shore of the Caloosahatchee. Ivy spurred his Florida cow pony, nudging her into a canter as they maneuvered through the trees. Like others of her unique marsh tacky breed, the small horse was extremely fast and comfortable in this gait. The mare charged toward Logan. The foreman was riding along the front left flank of the herd and working his loud bullwhip to get the cattle moving again after their river crossing. *Crack*! *Crack*! Ivy stood and stretched stiffly upright in the stirrups. Both of his arms were raised high in the air over his head as Cracker surged forward, unreined. In his left hand Ivy held his grandfather's rifle, in the other hand he gripped the dripping, bloody foot of the huge alligator he had slain. Ivy pumped his hands up and down, as he shrieked, "Logan! Hey, Logan! Look here! Here's the livin' proof I kill't the son-o'-a-bitch!"

* * *

Punta Rassa looked the same as it always did to Ivy. After all, the place never changed. It smelled just the same too. The cattle pens were empty, awaiting the herd. Charlie and Naomi Clark were happy their oldest son, Ivy, now a strong, strapping cowboy, had returned safe and sound.

Stumbling over his own words in delighted excitement, Ivy reported, "Daddy, that ol' rifle o' yers did a mighty fine job fer me this time. I used it to kill the biggest bull 'gator that's likely ev'r lived in the Caloosahatchee, 'n' I did it wit' 'un good, carefully placed shot! Jus' like yuh always tol't me to." He then proudly went on to tell his parents in detail about the alligator and the other adventures he had on his first cattle drive.

"Mama, have ya'll seen Alice Johnson lately? I wonder if she's come ov'r from 'er folks' place to pick up their mail this week?"

His mother knew of Ivy's growing interest in Alice. It was becoming obvious. Winking at her husband, she answered, "I don't rightly know, son. Yuh might check wit' Cap'n Gus tomorrow. He may've seen Alice 'r 'un o' the other Johnsons 'round the docks."

Fully enjoying his soft bed, Ivy slept late his first morning back at the port. A real bed for a change, not the hard sandy ground. But by mid-morning he was at the docks talking to Gus Wendt, getting caught up on all the news and local gossip.

"I'm glad you're back in one piece, Ivy. Your father told me this morning about the big alligator you shot."

"Yes, sir, he was somethin' else to see, Cap'n. He was longer'n my bullwhip!

"*Oh*, tell me, any o' the Johnsons come 'cross't this week?"

"I don't think so. I haven't seen their skiff on this side."

"Cap'n Gus, can I borrow a rowboat? I wanna go ov'r 'n' visit Alice 'n' carry their mail to 'em . . . if there's any."

"Sure! You're fond of Alice, aren't you?"

Ivy was stunned. He realized for the first time himself how much he cared for Alice. No one had ever bluntly asked him that question before. Not even Logan had dared. He drooped his head when he felt his face begin to flush. He glanced away fidgeting and shifting his feet. For the first time in his life Ivy Clark was nearly speechless and the gap of silence widened. Then, looking Gus directly in the eye, he blurted, "Yes sir, Cap'n! I sho 'nuff like 'er. I like Alice Johnson a whole bunch!"

Ivy rowed the half-mile across the river to the Johnson place and tied up to their dock. He walked briskly up the steep, shell-covered pathway to the big weathered, tin-roofed farmhouse. It was set on concrete piers atop an Indian mound. Outside of Johnson's Mound it was the highest place in these parts. When he knocked, Alice herself came and quickly opened the screen door.

Completely surprised to see Ivy at her door, Alice leaned against him. She intended to give him a gentle hug of greeting, but uncontrollable emotions took hold and she squeezed him tight and kissed his mouth. Alice blushed and said, "Ivy, you're back! *Oh*, I'm so happy, Ivory Clark! I've missed you so much!" She threw her tanned arms around his neck and kissed him again. Again, squarely on the mouth!

Astonished, Ivy felt Alice's firm, full breasts against his chest, and the blood rushed to his face and other limbs. His mind raced and to himself, he said, "Golly . . . Ha, howdy! I ain't ne'er been kissed that a-way 'fore. *Oh*, Alice, I liked that. I hope yuh do it 'gain!" He regained his composure and took her by her soft warm hand as the beet-red blush changed his complexion. Then Ivy said aloud, "Same here, Alice. I thought 'bout yuh a whole lot while I was out'n the wilderness wit' 'em cows, 'n' each night I'd dream o' yer sweet voice 'n' pretty face! I've a lot to tell yuh. I'll start wit' the most important—'bout a giant 'gator that 'tack't the herd . . .."

"Thanks for bringing over the mail," Alice shouted as Ivy took the oars and began to pull away from the dock. "We'll see you back over here this Sunday. Mama said, 'around noon.' Don't you dare be late!"

* * *

"Yuh boys made right good time," Jake Summerlin said as Logan and the drovers were punching the last few cows into the crowded holding pens.

"Yes, sir. We brought in 304 head, includin' the ol' leader cow, Mildred. I only lost 'un cow, Mister Jake. I'm sho Ivy'll fill yuh in on all the details o' that lil' problem. Which he solved."

"I'm sho he will. I'd like to see yuh'n Ivy ov'r at my place this evenin'. After yuh've settled up 'n' paid off all the hands."

Jacob Summerlin poured three glasses of his favorite sipping whiskey and passed one each to Logan and Ivy. Then he started, "Boys, I cain't make this trip to Cuba wit' the beeves. I need to find someone else to go down wit' the cattle, handle all the business wit' my agent, 'n' collect my money. Do either o' yuh have any idea o' who I could send?"

Logan answered, "No, sir."

Jake Summerlin pounded his fist on the table as he laughed in his own unusually loud, cackling style of laughter, "Hee Ha! Hee Ha!" Then, in a more serious tone but still smiling, he replied, "Hell's bells, boys! Why, I'm gonna send yuh two down there! What do ya'll think o' that?"

Logan had been to Cuba before with a cattle shipment. He thought that trip was his last. Most who knew about his shenanigans doubted Jake Summerlin would ever send him there again. A memory flashed through his mind about how his last trip to Cuba turned out. "Mister Jake knows what happened when I went to Cuba wit' 'im. Now he wants me to go down to Havana 'n' handle his affairs? He must be pullin' our legs!" Then he spoke aloud, "Are yuh joshin', Mister Jake, 'r 'r' yuh truly serious?"

"I'm as serious as a goddammed stampede, boys! I cain't pull it off myself this time. Too much happenin' 'round here. The boat'll be here Wednesday mornin' fer loadin'. It'll be a combination shipment: my cows 'n' a load o' cypress. In Havana, after the beeves 'n' timber 're unloaded, they'll wash the boat 'n' load a cargo o' 'bacca leaf, processed sugar, 'n' syrup, all bound fer Tampa. That'll give ya'll two 'r three days to explore Havana. Do yuh git my drift? Hee Ha! Hee Ha! *Oh*, Lordy! I'd give anythin' to be a young squirt 'n' full o' piss 'n' vinegar 'gain in Cuba!"

Then Jake Summerlin composed himself and his tone became more serious. "Now, boys, bear'n mind this trip won't be all fun 'n' games! Yuh'll meet up wit' Raul Martinez in Havana. Remember 'im, Logan? He's my broker in Cuba. He'll pay yuh 'n' yuh're to bring back my money. All in gold!"

Jake nearly stopped talking as his words slowed and he began to speak in an apprehensive loud whisper through clenched teeth. "I'd prefer to send three men. I do believe it'd be safer that way. Yuh boys know there's been a hell o' a lotta trouble goin' on in Cuba, don't yuh? The goddammed Spanish have been steppin' on 'n' squashin' the Cuban people fer longer 'n I can 'member. Somethin's fixin' to happen down there politically. I believe it'll happen fairly soon 'n' I want my money protected! Logan, who else is there 'mong yer drovers yuh can trust if yuh asked 'im to go 'long wit' ya'll?"

Acting as if he were giving the question considerable thought, Logan hesitated. Then he responded, "My ol' buddy Jehu . . . Jay Rivers is good in tight situations, Mister Jake. He's already plannin' to hang 'round Punta Rassa fer a week 'r two. Jay don't know it yet, but I'm fixin' to put 'im on yer payroll. Like Ivy, he's ne'er been to Cuba. I'm sho I won't have to twist 'is arm 'r drag 'im 'long wit' us!"

"Okay. I've knowed Rivers' daddy, Ray, fer yars 'n' yars. He's good people. Done 'n' ov'r wit' . . . hire 'im . . . it's the three o' yuh to go!"

"Logan, yuh tote a fine-lookin' sidearm . . . believe yuh tol't me once't it was yer daddy's. What 'bout yuh, Ivy—'n' Rivers? Yuh both have pistols?"

Nervously, Ivy answered, "No, sir, Mister Jake. I've ne'er owned a holster gun, 'n' I believe all that Jehu carries is a shotgun in a saddle scabbard."

Jake walked over to a large wall cabinet, opened it, and removed t wo n early new C olt r evolvers. E ach w as h olstered i n matching, fancy-tooled leather belts. He turned and said, "Here, Ivy. I'm loanin' these to yuh 'n' Rivers. Here's a few boxes o' cartridges too fer ya'll to practice wit'. I mean serious practice—fer both clearin' the pistol from the holster 'n' quick 'n' dead-accurate firin'. 'Em goddammed Cubans can draw like greased lightin' 'n' hit a gnat's ass from half a mile away!"

Squinting, almost glaring, Jake Summerlin finished in a serious, fatherly tone. "Now, I want yuh three boys to be careful. Yuh'd best practice some too, Logan. I don't want none o' yuh boys to shoot yerselves in the goddammed foot if yuh git into a scrape in Havana!"

CHAPTER 5

GOOD MORNING, MY GOOD MAN! I UNDERSTAND you're the dockmaster here at Port Punta Rassa?"

"Yes, sir! You're looking at Cap'n Augustus Wendt. I'm the dockmaster and the pilot boat operator. What can I do for you?" Gus replied as he extended his hand.

Taking his hand, the thin, dandy-dressed, dark mustached stranger spoke. "I'm Dr. Francis Corning from the Philadelphia Archeological Society. I'm looking for a gentleman by the name of Johnson—Robert Johnson to be exact. I've been corresponding with him and he told me he lives near the port. Would you be kind enough to direct me to his residence? He's been expecting me and I'm late!"

"That's Bob Johnson's place over there," Gus said pointing northward to Fisherman Key. "You can see their place on top of that high mound on the eastern end of the island. Their boat dock is on this side and Bob has both sides of the channel marked with poles."

"Thank you very much, sir!" Dr. Corning turned and briskly walked back to his boat. He told the boat's captain what he had learned, and the skipper began to bark orders to the crew as soon as Francis Corning stepped on board.

* * *

Alice Johnson was sitting on the dock watching the tall, white wading birds fish the nearby tidally flooded grass flats. Darker and smaller reddish egrets, with their wings spread wide, ran erratically through the shallows in pursuit of minnows. They were comical and caused Alice to smile. Her long blonde hair was down and waving in the gentle breeze. Anxiously waiting for Ivy, Alice could see him struggling against the river's ebb tide as the Caloosahatchee made its routine trip between Punta Rassa and her island home on Fisherman Key. As the distance separating them narrowed, Ivy waved and Alice's heart began to race. It had only been a few days since she had briefly held him in her arms for the first time. Since then, she found she missed Ivy worse than she did during the long weeks he was away on the cattle drive. She was confused and her mind wandered. "I've known Ivy since he first moved to Punta Rassa and his folks brought him to prayer meetings. I've always thought he was so polite and handsome. Why have I suddenly developed these strong feelings for him? I wonder. Does he care for me? *Oh*, I do hope so! Mama told me she can tell I've been smitten by the love bug because of the way I've been acting lately."

Ivy couldn't wait to get there. Each oar stroke moved him closer to Alice. He too fantasized and his thoughts drifted around inside his head. "I'm gonna sweep 'er up in my arms 'n' kiss 'er right off. I'll be straightfo'ward 'n' frank 'n' tell 'er flatout how much I think o' 'er. That is, if 'er folks ain't watchin'."

He continued in thought. "*Hmm*? Whose boat is that tied up to the dock? I've ne'er seen that 'un 'round Punta Rassa 'fore!"

Several men were sitting lazily along the edge of the pier, their feet dangling inches above the water. Some were sleeping, others were nodding off, and one or two were quietly fishing. Ivy assumed they were associated with the steamer berthed alongside the Johnson's dock.

He rowed the last few yards at a furious pace. Although now out of the main tidal current, erratic swirling eddies worked against his efforts, forcing the tiny rowboat south and toward the bay. Finally, an exhausted Ivy reached out, caught hold of the dock with one hand, and sprang out of the boat. In the other hand, he tightly held the coarse hemp rope, which was tied to the bow. Ivy quickly tied a bowline and dropped the loop around a piling.

A smiling Alice stood in front of him. Ivy took her hand and pulled her to him. She didn't resist but both were uncomfortable, hesitating before the small audience of sleepy fishermen. The couples' bodies and lips did not connect. Any preconceived plans either of them had for a more intimate greeting were foiled.

Hand in hand, Ivy and Alice walked along the angled pathway toward her house. Ivy asked, "Whose boat is that tied up at yer dock?"

"A friend of Daddy's. A professor from some museum up north is visiting. They never met face-to-face until today, though they've been writing to each other for quite some time. He's a famous archeologist, or maybe an anthropologist, named Dr. Corning." She paused and smiled, then added, "Sorry, but I haven't really paid much attention. I've other important people and things on my mind, I reckon. He's here doing some kind of Indian survey. I believe he told Daddy he hired the steamer and crew up in Tampa."

"Good mornin', Mrs. Johnson. Thanks fer lettin' Alice invite me ov'r fer supper," Ivy cheerfully said as he and Alice entered the large living room. With its metal roof above the trees, the large house received lots of fresh air. Ivy found it to be more comfortable than his folks' place at Punta Rassa. And it was much cooler than Jake Summerlin's bunkhouse where he lived with Logan Grace.

Hearing Ivy's voice in the living room, Bob Johnson shouted, "C'mon back, Ivy! My friend 'n' I're out here on the back porch havin' a smoke."

After his daughter and Ivy stepped onto the screened porch, Bob Johnson continued. "Doctor, this is Alice's friend Ivy Clark. He stays ov'r at Punta Rassa. He works fer the Summerlin Cattle Company. Ivy, this is Dr. Corning from Philadelphia."

Ivy shook the well-dressed man's hand firmly. The slim gentleman then said, "I saw you battling that ebb tide and Alice told me you were crossing the river to join us for dinner. If Alice had mentioned sooner she was expecting you, I would have sent my boat across to pick you up."

Ivy smiled. "Much obliged, but I was makin' the most o' that current. Ridin' atop a horse has put 'nuff muscle in my butt, but not 'nuff in my biceps. Rowin' helps build the arm muscles."

Amused at the young man's wit, Francis Corning smiled as Ivy continued. "Alice tells me yuh're here to do some kinda survey. Hope yuh don't find me too nosy, but can I ask what yuh're actually surveyin'?"

"Care for a smoke, son?" Dr. Corning offered Ivy a long, thin cigar. "These are the finest made in Tampa, from the very best Cuban leaf!"

"No, thank yuh, sir. I've been known to dip a lil' snuff 'r chew, but I ain't ne'er smoked none. I ran outta 'bacca on my last cattle drive so I give it up. I don't miss it much these days!"

"Good for you, son. Wish I could quit!"

"I'm leading a team of scientists to map Indian sites along this coast from Charlotte Harbor to Cape Romano. We'll locate, map, and do a surface survey for artifacts at the sites we catalog. A few years ago, I learned of the Johnson family's reputation for knowing about the ancient Indian midden mounds and their exact locations. I've been corresponding with Bob and his brother, who lives at Johnson Mound, for nearly a year while I was putting plans for this trip together."

Ivy frowned, glanced uncomfortably at Alice, and listened closer to this man's strange way of talking. He had never heard anyone so highly educated speak before, and at first he had trouble following the doctor's fast-paced speech and Yankee accent.

The archaeologist continued. "We know very little of the Calusa culture. Some Spanish documents provide insights but not a complete understanding. What other evidence that remains available has been mostly forgotten and is nestled—hidden, if you will—within the vast network of their old shell middens. None of these have ever been systematically investigated by a professional."

Ivy interrupted, and asked, "Ar' we talkin' 'bout the Calosas, the olden time Indians that I've heard once't lived in these parts?"

"That's correct, Ivy. We archaeologists have dubbed them with the name Calusa, C-a-l-u-s-a. I've been fortunate enough to have been appointed as principal investigator by the research committee at my institution. Following this trip for basic inspections, I hope to secure funding and return here to launch a major study in the near future."

Alice and her mother, Ruth, joined the three men on the breezy porch. Alice carried an oversized tray with tall glasses and a large pitcher. She asked, "How would ya'll like a refreshing glass of fresh-squeezed limeade? I just picked the key limes from our citrus grove and Mama squeezed them. She and I don't believe they were really ripe enough, but we probably won't be able to tell the difference because they're so tart anyway. I've sweetened it with some cane syrup we made."

Ivy was parched from rowing across the river. He was delighted when everyone seated at the table asked for a glass, too.

Ivy's curiosity was piqued and he wanted to hear more. "Dr. Corning, what 're yuh studyin' those mound-buildin' Indians fer? I done heard they'd gone extinct, 'r so Mr. Summerlin says. He tol't me they left these parts nearly 200 yars 'go. Mister Jake said they flat disappeared from the face o' the earth!"

Francis Corning chuckled at the young man's comments. "What you've been told is correct. The Calusa no longer exist as a people, although their bloodline likely still exists in Cuba. I believe that following their contact with Europeans in the early 1500s, they were destined to vanish."

"Why did they disappear, doctor?" Alice interjected.

"The Spanish and other European explorers brought diseases and disease-bearing vermin to this hemisphere. Later, enslaved African blacks introduced devastating tropical diseases. The Calusa and many other Native Americans had no immunity and could not cope with the new deadly, contagious infections. These infectious diseases, warfare with other tribes, and battles with the Spaniards contributed to their demise. The Calusa were a proud, warring, and fierce people. They completely dominated their aboriginal neighbors, but it was the virulent diseases brought here by us Old World Caucasians and subsequently the maladies of the Negroes that decimated the Calusa population. Some students of their civilization have claimed in the scientific literature that those rare surviving tribal members who did not pair up or inter-marry with the early Spanish colonists, or later the immigrant Seminole Indians, migrated—no, escaped—to Cuba."

Alice spoke up again. "Ivy found some very interesting Indian stuff over on Sanib'l Island a few months ago! Didn't you, Ivy?"

Days after finding the artifacts, Ivy had secretly shared his discovery with Alice. He had since just about forgotten the deco-rated clay pot that held the trinkets. Reacting to Alice's question, he reached into his pocket to touch his good-luck piece, part of the small cache he had found.

"Yes, I did."

"Tell Dr. Corning about them. Show him and Daddy the beautiful gold coin you found!"

Ivy nervously fumbled for words. "I was huntin' on Sanib'l 'n' found what seemed to me at the time to be a low man-made mound o' sand. It was too perfect in shape wit' its flattened top to be a natural ridge, so I guessed someone'd built it. It was made from gray sugar sand, not ordinary white beach sand. I fig'red the sand'd been carried there 'n' dumped to make the mound. I don't 'member seein' many seashells on the surface, so I'm sho it wasn't original Sanib'l dirt someone'd heaped up. Sanib'l's natural soil's mostly shell. I sort o' accidentally found a colorful clay pot buried a few inches below the mound's surface. The pot had a few t'ings inside, includin' glass beads 'n' this gold coin in my pocket. I've adopted the coin as my good-luck piece. Would ya'll like to see it?"

"By all means!" Francis Corning responded excitedly.

Ivy withdrew the lucky amulet from his trouser pocket and held the rim firmly between his thumb and index finger for every-one there to see. The soft fabric of his pants' pockets had polished the disk's surface to a bright golden luster, but the deep indentations of the casting had retained a patina, which helped define the small disk's features.

Ivy continued his tale. "My good buddy, who's also my boss, Logan Grace, says it's a Spanish gold doubloon that was likely brought to Sanib'l a few hundred yars 'go by some olden-time explorer."

An electrified and intense Francis Corning asked, "May I examine it more closely?"

"Yes, sir!" Ivy passed the bright disk to the archeologist.

Francis Corning placed a pair of reading glasses on the bridge of his nose and carefully and silently began to inspect Ivy's pocket charm. Then he took a small hand lens from his jacket pocket. It was similar to a loupe a jeweler uses to evaluate the quality of gemstones. He scrutinized both sides of the disk. Everyone could hear some nearly inaudible *"ohs"* and *"ahs"* as the scientist took his time examining the piece.

He looked up at Ivy almost gasping for breath. *"Egad*! Young man, this isn't some everyday antique gold coin dropped by some Spanish seaman. It's a well-cast medal, probably one worn by someone important. With my magnifying glass, I can see where a ribbon eye had been soldered to the back. But this has somehow been detached and lost—broken away—from the surface of the side without any detailed relief. This is certainly a significant and exquisite piece. Discovering . . . finding this is a major discovery!

"I know you don't want to part with it, but may my photographer and artist photograph and draw it for my expedition portfolio? They can do this right away, while you're visiting with Alice. They're down at the boat relaxing and fishing. I'll have them set up their equipment and get started straight away! Will you take me to the site where you discovered it? Also, when can I examine the container which held this and the other artifacts?"

Ivy hesitated, thought it over, then answered. "It's okay by me. Jus' so long as yer men can do the picture takin' 'n' drawin' today, while I'm here. I'm not turnin' a-loose o' this piece fer very long. I've growed right fond o' it!"

"That's fine. The medal will be in the best of care. The photography won't take long and the artist can finish in an hour or two. I assure you, both men are trustworthy and very skilled at handling artifacts."

Satisfied he had protected his ownership of the good-luck piece and conveyed his concerned consent, Ivy continued. "I'd be happy to show yuh the place where I found it, if we can schedule a trip to Sanib'l. But there's 'un condition."

"What's that, Ivy?"

"I'll take yuh to the spot where I found it, but if my mound turns out to be someone's grave, I won't stand fer it bein' robbed 'n' left uncovered like Alice's uncle does at Johnson's Mound. I was raised to have more respect fer the dead . . . any dead person . . . than to let that happen. So, I need to be sho yuh'll take only man-made t'ings 'n' leave any bones in the grave. Otherwise I won't show yuh!"

"I'll agree to those terms."

"Yuh can take a look at the other t'ings I found as soon as yuh come ov'r to Punta Rassa. Best make it fairly soon though. I'm leavin' fer Cuba wit' a shipment o' cattle this Wednesday mornin' early!"

"How long will you be in Cuba?"

"*Too long*!" Alice exclaimed aloud with slightly more emotion and volume than she intended. Embarrassed, she lowered her head and blushed. Then she quickly excused herself and left the porch to help her mother in the kitchen.

"I should be back at Punta Rassa wit'in a week 'r so, I reckon!"

"I may have to postpone looking at your collection, Ivy, until mid-month. We're supposed to meet a group of Seminole Indian leaders upriver on Tuesday to look at some inland sand mounds. I'll be sure to stop at Punta Rassa on my way back to Tampa from Key Marco."

Francis Corning then thanked Ivy for sharing his remarkable discovery. He added, "While you're down in Havana, and if you have enough time, look up an old colleague of mine at the University of Havana. His name is Dr. Jorge Gomez. He's very knowledgeable about such artifacts. Show him your splendid golden disk to see if he has any ideas about what it may be. Here, I'll write his name down for you."

Ivy and Alice left the house. "Dr. Corning sure got excited over your gold piece, didn't he?"

"He sho did! Yuh know, this coin 'r medal, 'r whatever it is, has brought me a streak o' good luck since't I found it!"

They walked along a wagon trail, which passed through the middle of a patchwork of long narrow fields of half-grown vegetables. The trail was a triple set of ruts gouged into the sand and shell soil. Over time, many wagon wheels had made the outer ruts and the hooves of the mules and horses had made the middle one. It was a few hours before they were expected back for supper and the couple wanted to be alone. They wanted to be as far away from other people as possible on this small, curved, 60–acre island.

Ivy was carrying his borrowed Colt revolver. He and Alice would u se the unpopulated end o f F isherman Key a s a shooting range. Ivy practiced, honing his skills at drawing and firing Jake Summerlin's fancy six-shooter.

Ivy rambled, "I went on a cattle drive, saw new country 'n' critters, 'n' kill't the biggest bull 'gator anybody can 'member in these parts. In a few days, I'll have the chance to visit a foreign country. I don't think that's too shabby fer a saltwater cowboy! Do yuh? The most serious lucky t'ing in my life nowadays, though, is yuh, Alice. I'm the luckiest person in these parts, walkin' here wit' yuh beside me, holdin' yer soft hand 'n' listenin' to yer sweet voice."

Alice smiled, lowered her head and blushed, and ever so softly squeezed his hand in acknowledgment. Ivy felt it.

Suddenly he stopped dead. Alice continued walking but was able to take only a few more steps. Their arms fully extended, Ivy forcefully spun her back to him. As their bodies slammed together, Ivy's open arms snatched her petite figure in his embrace. Aggressively but gently, he kissed her anticipating lips. This was a special kiss, long and affectionate—a spontaneous but serious kiss—much more intense a nd i ntimate t han t heir first. Looking into her happy, sparkling blue eyes, Ivy muttered, "Alice, my sweet Alice. I love yuh!"

Alice was completely taken off guard. Surprised and dumfounded to say the least! Not by Ivy's romantic actions and words, but because she was overjoyed. Alice was emotionally over-whelmed by his words.

"Ivy, I've been totally in love with you for months. It seems like I've cared about you forever!"

Nestled securely and safely in his strong arms, and without any inhibitions, she hugged him. Then, with urgency, her separated moist lips kissed him in return.

As they resumed strolling, slowly, arm in arm and mind in mind, Ivy never saw Alice so completely happy. Each was fully engulfed in their shared new feelings. The young lovers were now soulmates. From this moment on, they would be inextricably connected. Whatever the future held for their relationship, the passage of time would lack the power to subdue the memories created by their now openly professed love for each other.

CHAPTER 6

DAWN WAS STILL SEVERAL HOURS AWAY BUT THE port of Punta Rassa was already wide-awake. Under the expert guidance of harbor pilot Charlie Clark, the *Kissimmee Cloud*, the flagship coal-burning steamer of the Summerlin Cattle Company, was brought into the harbor earlier during the night. He turned her so that she was snugly berthed along the cattle-loading wharf, her bow facing out toward the channel entrance.

After the crew enjoyed a short nap, the deck mate rousted all hands to ready the companionways and ramps in the dim light of kerosene lanterns. They were preparing to take aboard the second part of the *Kissimmee Cloud*'s cargo. The lower holds already contained 20,000 board feet of milled cypress lumber. The small, roofed-over, open-air compartments that formed the upper three decks were to become the cramped temporary quarters for 400 head of gaunt scrub cattle as they made their first and last sea voyage.

Pilot boatman Gus Wendt was preparing to leave the dock in his sloop, the *Punta Rassa Pilot*. He needed a head start to keep port operations on schedule. He'd be underway just as soon as there was enough light. In a few hours, Gus would rendezvous with the sea-ready *Kissimmee Cloud* in deep water well offshore and south of Sanibel Island's eastern point. On station, Gus would move his sailboat in near the cattleboat, which would be moving just slowly enough to still maintain steerage. With both vessels making minimal headway, Gus would cautiously move his sloop to the leeward side of the *Kissimmee Cloud*'s hull, just close enough for pilot Charlie Clark to grab hold of the sloop's high railing and step onto the deck for the trip back into port.

Jake Summerlin bought control of the shipping facilities from the telegraph company after the disastrous '73 hurricane, and the Summerlin Cattle Company rebuilt the port. Punta Rassa was now a very busy shipping point. About 25,000 head of beef cattle departed for Cuba each year. On average, one commercial vessel a day sailed from Punta Rassa.

Jacob Summerlin charged his cow-shipping competitors modest pen, feed, and loading fees. If another cowman's cattle were transported on any one of the three Summerlin steamers, like every other shipper who owned a vessel, Jake added a standard but stiff transportation surcharge. No one in the Florida cattle business who dealt with Jacob Summerlin wondered how he became so wealthy. However, most other people around Punta Rassa considered his charges fair.

Logan, Ivy, and Jehu arrived in the predawn glow ready to go to work. Dockworkers had already prepared the loading ramps to transfer the sleepy but noisy cattle from the pens to the ship. Temporary portable fencing forced the cows to travel to certain ramps. The three mounted cowboys cut out ten head, moved them toward the ship, and then stopped the oncoming herd to create a gap. Then they started ten more forward. Deck hands prodded and shoved ten cows into each compartment.

When the stalls on the lower deck were full, the loading procedure slowed. Booms were swung out from the ship, block-and-tackles were connected to these, and each oncoming cow was fitted with a body sling made from tough canvas. These were connected to a dangling hook, and each cow was individually hoisted to other deck levels.

After more prodding and loud cussing, 408 head were finally secure aboard the cow-crammed *Kissimmee Cloud*. During the loading of the animals as well as their feed and water, the engine-room crew was busy firing the boiler, and building a head of steam.

"Well done, boys!" Jake Summerlin hollered over the noise.

"Logan, I wanna word wit' yuh 'fore yuh git 'board!"

"Yes, sir, Mister Jake."

The two stepped away from the ship as the others boarded. They walked into the quiet dawn shadow of a huge gumbo limbo tree.

"Here's the shippin' manifest fer the cows. Cap'n Boutchia has the papers on the lumber. He'll handle clearin' the wood 'n' the cows through customs at Key West. This envelope has the paper-work fer Martinez 'n' 'is office address in case he ain't at the dock in Havana to meet yuh. After yuh boys leave, I'll send 'im a wire that yuh're on yer way. If yuh have any kinda problems, work 'em out through Raul. That's what I pay 'im fer!"

Then Jake's tone of voice changed. His words became more serious and he spoke slower. "I want yuh to know here at the very beginnin' that I'm holdin' yuh personally responsible fer what 'mounts to the success . . . 'r failure . . . o' this trip ya'll're 'bout to take. I don't wanna hear nothin', no rumors 'r otherwise, 'bout anythin' like the bullshit yuh pulled on yer last trip down to Havana! If I do—boy, yuh'll ne'er work 'nother Florida cowherd! Yuh hear? I'm as serious as a goddammed stampede!"

"Mister Jake, I promise, sir! I've done a lotta growin' up since my last trip to Cuba. Yuh've given me a hell o' a lot o'respon-sibilities on this trip, handlin' yer gold 'n' all. I won't let yuh down. Promise!"

"I'm expectin' yuh to do yer extreme best. 'Un more t'ing, watch out fer Ivy! I like that boy! If ya'll git to drinkin' that rotgut Cuban rum 'n' runnin' 'em whores, be damn careful. Drink a good brand 'n' stay clear o' the loose gals on the streets 'n' those hangin' 'round the docks! If ya'll're inclined to whore-hop . . . I know 'bout these t'ings. I was young once't too. I'll send a wire 'n' tell Raul Martinez myself I want yuh boys to have some first-class women!"

"Yes, sir, Mister Jake. Okay!"

69

"Here's some spendin' money. Consider it an up-front bonus 'n' share it equal . . . that's a three-way split!"

"Yes, sir! I know—I will!"

Metal clinked against metal as the cash fell into Logan's open hand.

He quickly chanced a peek into his palm, then thought to himself, "*Holy shit*! Six 20-dollar gold pieces!"

The cattleboat's whistle sounded and someone aboard was yelling at the top of his lungs. "C'mon, Logan! The Cap'n says fer yuh to hurry! We're shovin' off!"

"Thank yuh, Mister Jake. We'll see yuh in a week 'r so," Logan yelled over his shoulder. He sprinted toward the ship and vaulted onto the deck as the last line was cast free.

All lines were loose, the cargo was secured, and everything was aboard that was supposed to be. The boiler was stoked and a full head of steam was ready to start them on their adventure. The helmsman gave the ship's horn a long and loud blast, signaling that they were underway. The *Cloud* slowly drew away from Punta Rassa and picked up speed, bound for the blue waters of the Gulf of Mexico and the Florida Straits.

Logan and Jehu stood side by side at the bow. Logan was pointing out coastal features and landmarks to his friend. Ivy had already joined his father, Charlie, who was piloting the vessel. They were standing topside with the ship's captain and the helmsman in the pilothouse.

"Daddy, I've always been amazed how yuh're able to keep in the middle o' the channel, day 'r night, 'n' pass safely 'tween Sanibel's tip 'n' Bowditch Point yonder."

"I use a combination o' techniques, son. Mostly compass headin's 'n' bearin' triangulations offa fixed positions. I ev'n use the dim lights from the port if I'm inbound at night. Ha! I've heard that people claim I've been at this job so long I can run the channel blindfold durin' a hurricane! Ya'll know that's not entirely true! Don't yuh? Ha! Truth is though, no vessel I've piloted has ev'r touched bottom comin' into 'r leavin' this harbor!

"Eventually, the Lighthouse Board'll wake up 'n' heed the petitions that've gone up to their headquarters through the yars.

Folks that work the sea or depend on waterborne transportation have been askin' fer a landfall light here off'n on fer 'bout 50 yars! Letters from people wantin' a lighthouse at Port Punta Rassa have also been sent to the Congress. Both're up 'n Washington 'an' that town moves at a damn snail's pace. That is, unless someone slicks the course wit' lotsa money. I believe when the political climate's right, which'll come to pass someday, they'll build a lighthouse nearby, maybe at the entrance to San Carlos Harbor. The way we've seen shippin' traffic increase ov'r the ten years we've been in these parts tells me it'll happen! When they build a lighthouse, they'll install a system o' buoys, daymarks, 'n' range lights. 'Un usually follers the other if Congress sets 'side 'nuff money!"

The captain spoke up. "Charlie, I was told by one of the Tampa Bay Pilots—Tom Zajicek—you remember him, don't you? Well, he brought us out of Tampa this trip. Tom says he's been told by one of the lighthouse keepers at Egmont Key the Government was tryin' to set aside land on Sanibel Island to build a light station. So it's finally in the works!"

"That's right good news, Cap'n. Sho hope it's true 'n' not 'nother damned rumor!"

"Bring 'er to slow 'head 'n' dead true on the helm at a bearin' o' 240 degrees," Charlie Clark barked. "The pilot boat's tackin' to come 'longside to pick me up. Hol't that speed 'n' compass headin' 'til I'm 'board the oth'r boat!"

"Yes, sir, Mister Clark!"

"Cap'n Boutchia, have yer man at the helm bring'er back 'round to 190 degrees 'n' hol't 'er on that course after I git off. At that headin', yuh'll pick up Loggerhead Key Light offa yer starboard this evenin'. Good luck, sir, 'n' be safe." Then Charlie turned and climbed down to the main deck to reach the pilot's perch. In a few moments, he would step aboard Gus Wendt's fast closing sailboat.

Ivy joined his father to say goodbye. Charlie spoke to his son, "While Cap'n Boutchia is clearin' his cargo through customs at Key West, why don't yuh check into the facts 'bout a new lighthouse on Sanib'l fer me? The Lighthouse Service's District Office

71

is located in the same buildin' as Customs. Son, yuh might wanna check on jobs wit' 'em if the stories're true. Yuh know, yuh cain't work cattle fo' the rest o' yer life!"

"That's a good idea, Daddy. I'll be sho 'n' do that!"

"Yuh boys be careful'n Cuba. It's a lot different down there 'n what ya'll're used to. I'll see yuh when yuh git back. Have fun, but behave yerself!" Charlie Clark said then stepped onto the deck of Gus Wendt's heeling pilot boat.

Ivy and Jehu couldn't believe how clear and blue the water became once the ship moved offshore and beyond the zone where the water from the Caloosahatchee and the Gulf of Mexico mixed. Always trying to be the center of attention to impress his coworkers and any onlookers, Logan played the part of a well-seasoned ocean traveler. He didn't let on to any of them that when he had made his previous Cuban voyage, he was completely overcome by the ocean's motion. So far this time, the low swells caused the vessel to rock only a little. It was not uncomfortable and all the novice sailors, both human and bovine, were faring well. So far!

As the day wore on and the atmosphere heated, the smell of cattle waste grew. For those working below decks, the stench filled each breath, but the experienced cowboys and cowhaulers took these foul odors in stride. However, the half-dozen people who had booked passage from Tampa to Havana aboard the *Kissimmee Cloud* did not fare as well as the crew. The constant nauseating stink of the voluminous bovine excretions caused upset stomachs for their unfamiliar and weaker constitutions. For the time being, all of them stayed topside to take advantage of the plentiful supply of fresh ocean air. Later, the three cowboys joined the other landlubbers in bouts of miserable seasickness. All somberly assumed bent-over positions along the lee rail, all choking and gagging as they hurled epithets at and sent vomit to the denizens of Davey Jones's locker.

CHAPTER 7

LOGAN! THERE'S THE KEY WEST LIGHT DEAD ahead! You hear me? You awake? Logan!" Captain Bob Boutchia yelled. Then with firmer words, he repeated himself loudly to wake the napping cowboy.

"*Huh*? . . . sho . . . I heard yuh, Cap'n . . . I weren't asleep."

"*Bullshit*! Do you always snore while you're awake?"

"I told yuh, I weren't asleep!"

"You sure can't convince me, boy! But then, who gives a flyin' shit anyway! I'm bringin' the ship to the wait anchorage near the sea buoy and we'll set and ride the hook for the rest of the night. I'll bet it'll be dawn or better before the pilot gets out here to take us in."

Still half asleep and refusing to ever admit it, Logan replied, "Okay, Cap'n. Oh, 'fore I forgit. Ivy says he needs to go ashore to do somethin' fer his daddy while we're at the rev'nue dock. If yuh think there's time 'nuff. How long can I tell 'im he'll have?"

"If he gets off the boat as soon as we dock, I expect he'll have about an hour. Yeah, at least that! It really depends on how much crap Customs gives me—how long I have to argue about their high-priced duty? Seems they've raised the damned tariffs each time I've cleared Key West this year. Them Spaniards are about as bad as our American boys when it comes to gettin' their hands into old man Summerlin's pockets when we leave Cuba with freight comin' back!

"We might be held up if there's no pilot to take us back out to sea! I hope we can be underway again by early afternoon at the latest. It might take us longer to cross the straits than it did to get here from Punta Rassa. The sea conditions are always worse and slow us down. Ha! You remember your last round trip across the Florida Straits with me, don't you, Logan?"

Slightly irritated at the captain's stabbing question, Logan interrupted him. "Yes, sir, I 'member! I've been eatin' crow 'n' tryin' to forgit ever't'in' 'bout that trip ev'r since!"

The captain thought he detected an air of disrespect in Logan's voice. So he countered, "I'd sure like to see the Cuban coast on the horizon in the mornin' without smellin' you boys and the others' puke. These goddammed cows I haul around for a livin' stink bad enough!"

Logan was really irritated now. He suddenly grabbed his lantern and angrily stomped off the bridge and climbed below to the top cattle deck. He'd check them before retiring. Later, visibly upset and cantankerous, he joined his coworkers in the open-air bedroom. Far too familiar with his sometimes dark and violent moods, Ivy and Jehu knew when to give him a wide berth. This was one of those times. Each knew he'd be in a better mood in the morning.

The three exhausted and sunburned cowboys slept soundly through the night. Their canvas hammocks hung from posts in an open compartment behind the pilothouse. The night was warm and humid, but the fresh sea air made sleeping comfortable.

The red dawn slowly rose out of the eastern Atlantic Ocean. As the sun climbed higher above the lower Florida Keys, illusions created by atmospheric magic slowly altered its fiery brilliance and size. When the brightening new day provided enough light for all to see, a whistle sounded. The boys rose with the others to start their shipboard chores feeding and watering the cattle. Working as a well-tuned and experienced team, they soon finished their work.

Sleep had improved Logan's attitude. He decided it was best to stay clear of the mouthy captain.

The young men enjoyed their breakfast of coffee, bacon and eggs, and hot fresh-baked biscuits. In the still air of dawn, while the cattleboat rode at anchor, the aroma of the cook's frying bacon masked the constant stench of cow dung. The hungry passengers soon joined the cattlemen in the galley for the first meal of the day.

The *Kissimmee Cloud* had barely stopped and the first mooring line secured when Ivy jumped over the rail onto the wooden wharf. He headed for the nearby Government building where the captain had told him the district office of the Lighthouse Service was headquartered. He had important questions to ask. One was for his father, the other a vital inquiry for himself.

Ivy entered a large office and walked over to a huge oak desk where a busy paper-shuffling young man, not much older than he, was seated. Ivy cleared his throat and spoke. "Good mornin', sir. My name's Ivy Clark."

The clerk politely returned Ivy's greeting and offered his assistance.

Ivy continued. "My father's the harbor pilot up at Port Punta Rassa 'n' he asked me to stop here while I'm 'n Key West. I'm travelin' 'board a cattleboat that's waitin' to clear Customs. We're headin' down to Havana 'n' I don't have very much time. Is there someone I can talk to 'bout what ya'll's plans 'r' fer a new lighthouse near Punta Rassa? On Sanib'l Island, so we've heard."

"Mr. Curtis, our District Engineer, can likely answer any questions you have. Let me see if he's free at the moment. Excuse me. I'll be right back."

Ivy glanced around the room. He had never been inside such an official-looking building. He was impressed. Photographs and construction drawings of lighthouses along with maps and charts of the Florida coastline covered the walls. He walked to the nearest wall and began to inspect the pictures and other illustrations of the important light-supporting structures that safely guided seafarers. He was astonished to find they were so varied in design. No two looked alike. Then an official-looking document caught his eye. He walked to it and started reading to himself: "'Roster o' Personnel, Seventh District, U. S. Lighthouse Board'. *Hmm?* Damn, what we've heard's true. There 'tis, plain as day, 'Sanib'l Island Light Station'. There's no people assigned there so far. That's why the Primary 'n' First Assistant columns 're marked 'Vacant'! Damnation! That's good news! Sho hope I'm not too late!"

"Mr. Clark, Mr. Curtis will see you in just a few minutes. Would you like a cup of coffee?"

Already full of coffee and about to wet his pants, Ivy replied, "Yes, sir. I certainly would. Thank yuh."

Ivy barely had time to fix his coffee, quickly snatching a half-teaspoon of sugar and a few drops of canned milk. He didn't get these luxuries on cattle drives. Hearing his name called, he looked up and saw a tall full-bearded man poke his head past his half-opened office door. "Mr. Clark, come in."

"Good morning, lad. I'm Laban Curtis, District Engineer. What brings you to our office so early?"

Ivy quickly gave the man a rundown on his father's pilot position and his special interest in a possible lighthouse at the entrance to San Carlos Harbor. This gave Ivy's visit somewhat of a quasi-official purpose. He hoped beginning the conversation this way would open the door for his later, more personal questions.

Engineer Curtis proved to be very interesting and full of information. "It's true. We're finalizing plans to construct our newest Gulf Coast light stations in this district. One will be on Sanibel Island; the other will be a replacement further north at Cape San Blas. Congress has appropriated the money, but we recently hit a snag because of land-ownership problems on Sanibel Island. The Board hopes to resolve the land-title question with the State of Florida shortly.

"All bids have been received for construction of the new light station, and I expect to award contracts for the various elements this next month. Barring any unforeseen circumstances, a lighthouse will be operational on Sanibel Island the first quarter of the next fiscal year."

"*Wow*! My father's gonna be mighty happy to learn that! Mr. Curtis, will there be any jobs at the new lighthouse? Either durin' construction 'r after it's done? My father says I should git outta the cow business. I'd like to find work o' a more permanent kind."

"Why, I imagine there will be! We encourage contracting firms to whom we award contracts to use local tradesmen and labor sources wherever possible. I'm sure we'll hire someone new to help staff the light station, a Lighthouse Establishment Assistant Keeper. The Primary Keeper is usually someone who is promoted from within the ranks, but the Assistant Keeper is usually recruited from a list of applicants. If you're interested, our clerk Jim, outside at the desk, has the applicant's list and application forms. I imagine it'll be five or six months before the district's Chief Inspector of Lights will interview anyone. But the sooner you get an application in, the better!"

Ivy was ecstatic, offered his hand, and excitedly blurted, "*Oh*, thank yuh so much. Yuh answered all my questions! Good day 'n' thanks to yuh 'gain, sir!"

After stopping at the clerk's desk, Ivy ran, even gleefully skipped a few times, back to the *Kissimmee Cloud*. The application was hidden in his shirt pocket. He intended to keep it secret from his companions.

With the Customs hassles now behind them and once again underway, the boys' routine duties aboard returned to monotony. The three cowboys took it easy. Each lazily leaned on the railing watching their progress toward the endless horizon. They were engaged in man-serious, meaningful conversation. Fascinated, they watched leaping dolphins alongside the prow as they raced to keep up with the ship. The young men were bonding, friends sharing tales of cow drives, weather, family, and ladies. Logan had to tell Jehu about the infamous Sanibel Island deer hunt and the saga of the Deer Drowner . . . again.

Ivy thought, "If Logan tells that damned story 'nuff times to 'nuff people, it'll become part o' American folklore. It'll either make me famous 'r embarrass me no end!"

His first impulse was to immediately challenge the mention of that embarrassing escapade. But Logan must have read his mind, or had a premonition of some kind, because he suddenly shifted his storyline and started talking about Ivy killing the great Caloosahatchee alligator. Ivy decided he'd avoid confronting the storyteller, so he let the irritating issue slide.

Jehu Rivers had been curious for some time and now decided the time was right. He bit the bullet and asked Logan, "Why the hell does ol' man Summerlin come down so hard on yuh whenev'r he brings up yer last trip down to Cuba?"

"Boys, I really don't wanna talk 'bout that miserable trip. I've been tryin' to forget it ev'r happened!"

Jehu could always read Logan like a book. He knew how far he dared go with this, so he continued. "Hell's bells, son, it'll probably do yuh some good to talk 'bout it. If yuh cain't talk 'bout it wit' us, who the hell're yuh gonna talk to? Yer mama? Some damn preacher?"

"I reckon if 'un o' yuh boys had gone through what I did down in Havana, yuh'd try 'n' forget it, too!"

"*Jesus Christ*! What the hell'd yuh do? Kill't somebody?"

"Yes! Goddammit! I sho 'nuff did! Now're yuh two royal pains-in-the-ass happy?"

"Lord've mercy! Damnation! If I'd known, I sho 'nuff would ne'er 've pressed yuh. I'm sorry!"

"Yuh've no need to be sorry, Jay. It was my own doin'! An' I'll tell yuh straight out, if it weren't fo' Mister Jake, I'd still be rottin' 'way in some dungeon cell in that goddammed Morro Castle in Havana!"

Ivy was bewildered. "What the hell happened? How'd yuh kill't somebody? Ar' yuh bullshitin' us? If yuh 'r', it's not very funny!"

Logan cleared his throat, and said, "No, boys, it's true! I got myself in 'un hell o' a situation when Mister Jake took me to Cuba. I swear, I ne'er thought he'd ev'r ask me to go back!

"I fell in wit' some bad company, got drunk, 'n' ended up in a whorehouse. The whore's boyfriend . . . 'r pimp . . . 'r some oth'r piece o' shit . . . broke into the room wit' a knife. It was a setup. The son-o'-a-bitch was gonna rob me!"

Logan stopped talking and stared out at the horizon. He spit at the water below as he collected his thoughts. "I come to my senses 'n' jus' managed to roll offa the woman when I saw his knife. I jumped up 'n' grabbed his arm wit' the dagger. We fought ov'r it . . . more like wrestled. I somehow got the knife a-loose from 'is grip 'n' it fell free. The instant it hit the floor, I grabbed it. I reckon 'tween bein' half drunk 'n' scared to death, I stuck the knife in the bastard's guts . . . clear up to the hilt. The whore was screamin' out the window. Before I knowed it, a pair o' Cuban constables busted into the room wit' drawn pistols. I still had my hand on the knife. The Cuban's blood had gushed ov'r both o' us, 'n' when the police got there, the thievin' bastard screamed fer his last time. He let out a final blood-spewing breath 'n' collapsed dead on the floor."

Logan paused again. Grimacing, he hung his head, then a second later he threw his arms up in despair, and went on with his story. "Lord knows, boys. I didn't wanna lose my money 'n' only tried to defend myself. I ne'er meant to kill't the poor bastard, but he had messed wit' the wrong man! I think the cop on my blind side knocked me in the head. When I came to, I was bound 'n' chains, hands 'n' feet, in that Cuban jail . . . 'n' wit'out my god-dammed britches!

"No one from Mister Jake's outfit knew where I was at. They didn't have a clue 'bout what happened to me 'r where I disappeared. They went back to Punta Rassa wit'out me. Fo' all anyone knew, I could've been dead I guess! Boys, I sat in that hellhole fo' weeks 'til 'un o' Raul Martinez's men discovered me. Mister Jake pull't out all the stops, I reckon. He was determined to find me if I was alive! Thank the good Lord he didn't give up!"

Jehu glanced at Ivy and rolled his eyes.

"I never did have any kinda hearin' 'r nothin'. But not long after, Ed Filip—Eduard, that's Martinez's right-hand man—found me, the charges was dropped, 'n' I was turned a-loose. Mister Jake must've paid someone off bigtime to git me out. Hot damn! An' not prosecuted! I still cain't believe it! He won't ev'r tell me the full story, but he sho as hell hol'ts the whole t'ing ov'r my head. As yuh boys've seen, he loves to rub it in ev'ry chaince he gits!"

Awed, Ivy commented. "That's the damnedest story I've ev'r heard. Yuh're sho 'nuff 're 'un lucky son-o'-a-bitch!"

Further into the windy Florida Straits, the ship began to toss. "Man alive, the water's gettin' mighty rough!" Jehu said.

"It damned sho 'nuff is!" Ivy added.

"Ha!" Logan laughed. "Boys, believe me, the worst is yet to come!"

Those words had barely left Logan's lips when Jehu whispered, "Lordy mercy, boys! I'm gettin' sick! I'm gonna puke!" He tried not to let anyone else overhear but gave himself away when he ran for the deck railing with one hand over his mouth. Ivy and Logan had noticed earlier that Jehu began to look pale but didn't relate it to the rising sea swells.

Jehu's sudden illness seemed to start a chain reaction. The telltale heavy salivation, yawning, dizziness, and nausea caught them all by surprise. It wasn't long before Jehu's coworkers and all the passengers had made their own dashes to the rail. Each stood beside another in their own private hell, with guts wrenching as their full stomachs involuntarily heaved up their fine breakfasts to the fishes.

* * *

"C'mon you good-for-nothin' shiftless cowboys! I can already see the Havana Light. We're about 20 miles off the entrance. It's time to come to, children. Wash your pretty faces and pull your weight! That's what Jacob Summerlin pays you for!" Captain Bob Boutchia of the cattleboat *Kissimmee Cloud* shouted through the predawn darkness.

Logan had been catnapping between the dry-heaves most of the night. His equilibrium was shot and he couldn't walk well. It was also hard for him to stay awake after the captain had roused them. He knew what must be done, and he had to be finished while they were still far enough off the Cuban coast.

With a voice hoarse from vomiting, he urged his coworkers on. "C'mon, boys, let's git to it! Ya'll cain't feel no worse'n I do.

"Ivy, yuh go fo'ward to the bridge 'n' ask the cap'n to have his boys start the pumps. Jehu! Git yer ass outta that hammock! Git below 'n' check ev'ry scupper to be sho they's not blocked. Then uncoil the hoses so we can move 'em 'round. I'll be there directly!"

The auxiliary deck pumps were soon sucking hundreds of gallons of seawater each minute from the ocean. The three men aimed their high-pressure hoses at the filthy decks around the cows' hooves. This was the only chance they had to clean the cattle decks before the ship docked. The cleanup had to be done at sea, as a cargo of filthy cattle might result in a fine from the Spanish authorities. The Cuban officials didn't want Havana Harbor to become more of a cesspool than it already was.

The cleanup went well and by the time they were done, they had reached calmer waters. Seeing land, the jubilant crew began to anticipate their short liberty. Havana was their kind of town! The cowboys and passengers were beginning to feel better as the *Kissimmee Cloud* entered Havana's protected harbor and smoother waters.

Ivy and Jehu joined Logan to watch the ship being berthed. Logan whispered just loud enough for them to hear. "There he is, boys! That man in the white Panama hat on the wharf, that's Raul Martinez. The short fella next to 'im wit' the white beard is Ed Filip. Martinez is Mister Jake's broker here in Cuba. He's an honest man who'll treat us right. Filip's a lil' strange actin'. His mind wanders 'n' he seems to live in the past when he's drinkin' rum . . . worse, he's mean when he's on tequila. The ol' bastard is set in 'is ways. I do believe he'd be right dangerous if yuh were his enemy. But he's trustworthy 'n' yuh can count on 'im. While we're here, try to keep both these men on yer side.

"Here's a lil' somethin' Mister Jake tol't me to give yuh boys." Logan dutifully passed each of the men their two 20-dollar gold pieces. "That's all the money yuh'll git from me, so yuh'd best hol't onto it as long as yuh can. Spend it wisely!"

Ivy was dumfounded. "This is more'n a month's pay! Why'd he give us so much?"

81

"Mister Jake says we all did a great job gettin' the herd to Punta Rassa. He tol't me it was a bonus fer us 'n' we're to have fun! Now let me tell yuh 'bout the fun yuh can 'spect . . .!'"

When the cattleboat was secured to the wharf, the cowmen walked down the gangway with their luggage. Minutes before, a smiling Captain Boutchia had told Logan they'd be departing early on Monday morning.

The three cowboys were feeling much better now that their boots were firmly on solid ground again. None of them had stopped to consider they would have to reboard the *Kissimmee Cloud* and cross the miserable Florida Straits again to get back.

Logan didn't say anything aloud. "Great balls o' fire! he thought. We've got three full nights 'head o' us 'n this place!"

Havana was a wide-open city and she never slept.

CHAPTER 8

A FTER FORMAL INTRODUCTIONS, RAUL MARTINEZ spoke first. "I've reserved a room for each of you at the Park View Hotel for the next three nights. It's a nice place in the heart of the city. It's on the Prado. Eduard is going to stay close to you most of the time. That's one of my many instructions from Mr. Summerlin. You know how the man operates; he insists I follow his orders to the letter. I assure you, Eduard's not going to interfere in your . . . *ah* . . . lustful ways. But he'll be there to keep you out of trouble or danger. Do you understand?"

In unison, the three eager cowboys agreed, "Yes, sir!"

"The captain said he'll have the *Kissimmee Cloud* loaded and ready to leave early Monday morning. Eduard will pick you up at the hotel and take you to the bank to meet me when it opens Monday morning. I'll receive payment for the cattle and lumber later today and transfer it to you Monday morning. We'll withdraw Mr. Summerlin's money in gold. Just as he wants."

"Yes, sir!"

"That two-horse carriage at the end of the wharf is mine, gentlemen. Come, pick up your luggage and let's be on our way," Eduard Filip said in his strange non-Spanish accent. "We have about a half-hour trip to your hotel."

As they left the vicinity of the busy port, with its boats and ships, cranes, dry docks, warehouses, and busy workers, the road turned into a wide, tree-lined double avenue with a broad, center, park-like raised sidewalk. Couples strolled along this baluster-railed walkway or relaxed on the many stone benches under the massive tropical shade trees. The avenue had a private, refreshing, and cooling atmosphere about it.

"This is the Prado," Eduard informed them. "There are several of these broad, well-planned avenues criss-crossing Havana. I suggest that during your visit to the city, you stay within sight of the Prado. It's usually well patrolled by the local police. I'm telling you this for your personal safety, especially if you find yourself alone. Havana has all kinds of people. Some of the bastards would slit your throat just for a fresh-lit cigar!"

Logan spoke up. "'Member my story, boys? Pay 'tention to Ed's wise words o' caution! What happened to me happened 'cause I was stupid. I didn't heed 'is warnin'!"

"Boys, you can all call me Ed."

They left the waterfront and were traveling between rows of quaint, European-style buildings. Sounds of female voices began to drift down through the early morning air. Some women waved at the passing carriage. Some yelled words of greeting, others outright invitations. "Hey, boys! Hello, Yankees! Come here, Mister. Let me show you what I have for you. I have something tucked away just for you!"

Ed shouted back a few obscene comments. "You ladies are sure starting work early today!"

Still curious, Ivy asked, "What're those girls yellin' at us fer? I'm havin' a hard time un'erstandin' what 'tis they're sayin'. Why're they callin' to us, Ed?"

"Let me check your ears, son," Ed said as he winked at Logan. He reached up and mock-examined Ivy's ears one at a time. "For Christ's sake, boys! His ears are soaking wet! Your friend Ivy isn't dry behind the ears yet! Ha!"

Logan taunted, "Ivy, they's whores advertisin' their wares. We're not gonna mess 'round wit' 'em. Ed's gonna take us to a genuine first-class whorehouse, 'r so Mister Jake promised me! Yuh 'r', ain't yuh, Ed?"

"Yes. This time a round, y ou're t o m eet t he b est w omen your money can buy in Cuba! Trust me!"

"We're gonna go to the hotel first, ain't we, boys? *Huh*, Ed? 'Fore I git laid I wanna shave, a bath, a drink, 'n' a cigar! In that order! How 'bout ya'll?" Jehu chimed in.

Their enthusiasm was cut short when Ed Filip announced, "The first thing any of you will do is unpack your pistols and hand them over to me. Mr. Summerlin wants them locked in the hotel safe until Monday when it's time to go to the bank. He told Raul he doesn't want to deal with any more dead Cubans."

The Punta Rassa cowboys and their strange-talking chaperon were enjoying their lunch on the veranda of the Park View Hotel when Ivy spoke up. "Ed, how far's it from here, 'n' how long'll it take to git there from here, to the University o' Havana?"

"Are you walking or riding?" Ed Filip queried with a smile.

"Howev'r I can git there, I reckon."

Logan tried to antagonize his friend. "What the hell do yuh wanna go to the university fer? Yuh gonna become a student? Son, yuh'll git all the education yuh'll need o'er the next three nights! Ha! Right, Ed? Jehu?"

"There yuh go 'gain, cut'n the fool when I ask a serious question! Stop 'n' think 'n' yuh'll 'member I tol't yuh I met Dr. Corning at Alice's place a while back. Well, he suggested I look up someone by the name o' Dr. Gomez at the University o' Havana while we're down here."

"Dammit, don't git so feisty! Yer sense o' humor's done gone to hell, son!"

"Tell you what, boys," Ed offered. "I planned to take you sightseeing around Havana this afternoon. So happens the university campus is along the route I was going to take. What do you say we stop there long enough for Ivy to look up this Dr. Gomez?"

"Suits me," Logan conceded.

Slowly sipping his tall Pina Colada—his fourth—Jehu raised his drooping head. His words were somewhat slurred. "I don't give a shit! Long's it don't cut into my social life . . . if ya'll know what I mean?"

"Good! We'll leave just as soon as we finish lunch. I'll let the driver know," Ed said as he stood up and walked toward the carriage.

*   *   *

Havana was once the major hub of financial and commercial activity for the New World territorial possessions of Spain. All trade, to and from the Atlantic colonies and some from the Philippines bound for Spain passed through Havana. As a result, the city was very diversified. Spain's once-splendid and powerful colonialism lasted more than 300 years, but now its majesty was in decline. Throughout the Caribbean basin, known as the Spanish Main, new nations were rising from the ashes of Spain's once-powerful globewide empire. In 1883, Cuba was still writhing beneath Spain's heels. Revolt was in the air, whispered about in the shadows, and planned in the minds of the downtrodden Cuban people. Rallying patriots of freedom appeared in Cuba. For Spain time was running out.

The drive through Havana took them into beautifully landscaped residential neighborhoods and along avenues lined with ornate government buildings, banks, and museums. When they arrived at the university, Ed spoke to the gatekeeper in fluent Spanish. "Good afternoon. We're looking for someone by the name of Gomez, Dr. Jorge Gomez. Can you direct us to his office?"

"Yes, sir, he's the head of our antiquities department. He's Cuba's chief archeologist. You'll find his office on the lower floor of the third building on the left."

"Thank you, lad."

The curved driveway passed through colorful manicured grounds. Well endowed with a variety of beautiful flowering plants, both sides of the white shell-surfaced road conveyed a unique tropical lushness.

Ivy entered the high windowed, airy building and walked down a long hallway in the middle of the structure. He examined every d oor-mounted s ign s earching for the office o f Dr. G omez. Finally he found it and knocked.

From within, a deep Spanish voice resonated. *"Entre."* Understanding the word "enter," Ivy opened the louvered door and went into the room. "Hello . . . Hello . . . Anyone here?"

The basal voice spoke again, this time in perfectly clear English. "Yes, I'm in here, in the collection room. I'll be with you in one moment."

Before actually seeing the man he was talking to, Ivy impatiently asked, "Ar' yuh Dr. Gomez?" His words echoed in the hollowness of the high-ceilinged room.

"That is correct, sir! You're speaking to the Dr. Jorge Gomez . . . the *only* Cuban-born Gomez who to my knowledge ever received an education!" As his words trailed off, reverberating around the room, a tall white-haired man wearing a white frock and wire-framed spectacles walked through the open door.

"What can I do for you, young man?" he asked with perfect diction and pronunciation. "I don't have the opportunity to speak to many Americans. I'm happy that you're here to visit me, giving me a chance to speak your language again."

"Doctor, my name's Ivy Clark. Yuh sho 'nuff speak perfect English, sir. How . . . where'd yuh learn to speak it so well?"

"I received my doctoral degree in archeology from your great college at Harvard. I lived in the Boston area for five years in my youth while a student. I learned your language and customs quite well. Now, what brings you to my office?"

"I'll git right to the point. I've friends waitin' outside fer me so I don't have much time. I met Dr. Francis Corning a few days 'go near my home in Florida. I showed 'im a very unusual . . . *ah*, artifact, he called it . . . I found on Sanib'l Island. It's on the Gulf Coast not far from where I live . . . ."

". . . *Aha*, yes. I know of the key known in my language as *Puerto Sur Nivel* . . . your Sanibel Island!"

What does Por . . . Puerto Sur Nivel mean?"

"*Aha*! That was the original name given to Sanibel Island by the Spanish mariners who first visited and charted it many hundreds of years ago! It means a 'South Level Port'."

"*Hmm*? When I tol't Dr. Corning I was comin' to Cuba to help deliver a herd o' cattle, he suggested . . . no, insisted . . . I take the time to look yuh up 'n' show yuh what I found." Ivy then gave the archeologist a quick description of his discovery.

"Do you have the artifact with you?"

"Yes, sir. I do."

"Come into the library—I'll have a look at it!"

Ivy followed Dr. Gomez into the library. Hundreds of books were systematically arranged on wall-mounted shelves suspended above glass-enclosed display cases. These glass cases were crammed with archeological artifacts that Jorge Gomez had collected over a lifetime of field research in Cuba.

"All right, Mr. Clark, have a seat. Let's have a look at your mysterious artifact."

Ivy reached deep into his trouser pocket and by feel selected his good-luck piece from among the two gold pieces and some smaller coins. He dropped it into Dr. Gomez's open palm and sat down on the stool next to him.

Looking down casually at the polished, nearly flat disk Jorge Gomez brought it closer to his eyes. After a few quiet moments, he muttered, "*Aha*, it's beautiful! You are indeed fortunate to have found such a remarkable artifact. Now, if I understand you correctly, Mr. Clark . . . may I call you Ivy?"

"Sho."

"You found this with a few other objects in a clay pot buried in the ground?"

"Yes, sir. I actually found it when I kicked the sand 'n' uncovered it." For a split second, a thought raced through Ivy's mind: "Maybe chasin' that damned deer weren't so stupid after all! Otherwise I wouldn't've discovered the pot."

"Please describe the area to me. What was the lay of the land? What did the land look like?"

Ivy gathered his thoughts. Then he started slowly, "I was on the very eastern tip o' Sanib'l. The place where I found the pot was a lil' bit higher'n the surroundin' open beach, 'n' the sand was definitely different 'n the reg'lar beach sand."

"What do you mean, different?"

"The sand was real fine. There weren't no seashells in it like reg'lar Sanib'l sand. We usually call this sugar sand, but this was real dark, a gray color, not pure white like real sugar sand."

"Can you remember anything about the land other than it was elevated? If so, what was the mound's general shape?"

"I reckon it's sort o' diamond-shaped, maybe 50 feet 'tween its longest points 'n' 'bout three 'r fo' feet higher'n the beach. I noticed it was flat on top."

Jorge Gomez continued his careful examination of the medallion, his experienced eyes scrutinizing each design character on the disk. His eyebrows gave away his intense interest in the object, and Ivy picked up on it right away.

"In my professional opinion, Dr. Corning is correct. This is a medal. But it's no ordinary medal! First, it is made from the highest quality casting gold. It's almost pure gold! Therefore, it's not the kind of medal awarded to some ordinary person. Whoever received this was certainly a very important individual. If not royalty, then someone of major political importance."

Dr. Gomez paused, stroked his beard and frowned before continuing. "Since you discovered it buried with more primitive artifacts—you said an arrowhead, a projectile point of some kind—and a few glass beads, I'm sure this piece originates from a very early period. I wouldn't be surprised if your find has been buried on Sanibel Island for 300 years or more. I'd judge it's been there since just after the time of contact!"

Ivy scratched his head and asked, "Beg yer pardon. What do yuh mean by 'time o' contact'?"

"'Contact' is a term we use to identify an event in time when we Europeans first met . . . first contacted the aboriginal peoples of this hemisphere . . . the Indian natives."

"I un'erstand."

"Secondly, based on your description of the discovery site and the fact that this medal was buried in a primitive ceramic container tells me its original owner was completely unaware of its whereabouts. I'd judge the Calusas constructed the diamond-shaped mound you described. I'm sure you know about the role they played in your region's history."

"Well, all I know 'bout 'em is they's all dead. I believe extinct's the word. They built huge, high mounds from the shells o' the different kinds o' seafood they ate. I reckon they lived in small towns on those mounds, too. I've a friend who lives on 'un 'o those ol' shell mounds on a lil' island near Punta Rassa."

"The sand mound you described to me is unlike the shell mounds. The sand mounds were often used as burial places, but they also had religious importance. The mound that held your discovery is what I like to call a spiritual mound. The pot was certainly buried there along with the mortal remains of the person who last owned it and its contents. That individual was most likely interred at the same time, and his or her bones are probably resting just inches from where you kicked up the pot.

"When do you leave Cuba to go back home?"

"Monday mornin'."

"If I can make the arrangements, and you have no objections, I'd like to go back to Florida with you and see this site first-hand."

"I've already told Dr. Corning I'd take 'im there as soon as I git back."

"I don't believe that will be a problem. Francis Corning and I know each other. In fact, we're old friends and I think he'll welcome my participation. He's already invited me by asking you to show me this medallion. The old boy knew full well that when he asked you to show it to me, he'd be drawing me into this investigation!"

"It's okay by me. But frankly, I reckon yuh'd best clear passage wit' the cap'n o' our cattleboat, the *Kissimmee Cloud*, to be sho it's okay wit' 'im 'n' he has room fer yuh."

"I'll do that straightaway this afternoon. Before you leave, may I make a wax impression of your medal? Later today, my students and I will make a casting of it. I'll do some further research between now and Monday. By then, I hope to share some preliminary findings with you."

"Yes, sir."

*   *   *

90

"*Goddammit*! I t's 'bout time!" Logan griped. "I thought someone had captured yuh 'r some good lookin' Cuban girl'd grabbed yuh by yer crotch!"

With a sidewise glance at Logan, Ivy climbed into the buggy. "No such luck. I hurried best I could!"

Jehu suddenly came to. "Speakin' o' women, I'm ready fer 'nother drink, boys 'n' hungry fer un' o' those dark-skinned petunias!"

"Boys!" Ed Filip said. "We're going to visit a rum distillery today and a cigar factory tomorrow. Sunday you may have free— for shopping or you can even join me at church if you wish."

"*Church!*" Jehu moaned. "Yer're not gettin' me inside no church. Yuh wanna cause the roof to cave in?"

"Me neither!" Logan added.

An hour later, the group was comfortably seated in the sampling room of Havana's major rum distillery. The subjects of conversation had been mixed and each man had tasted a variety of the spirits made there. All were feeling the effects.

Logan asked, "Ed, where the hell're yuh from? Yuh sho 'nuff have a weird accent. Yuh're not American, 'r Spanish, from best I can tell."

Ed put down his half-full glass of tequila, then shot back in a hostile tone, "Why do you fret about where I'm from?"

"I'm not frettin'. I'm jus' tryin' to figure it out fer my own satisfaction. I'm curious. Ha!"

"Me too!" Jehu added siding with his buddy.

Ivy decided not to get involved. He'd just sit back and see where the conversation would go.

After glaring at Logan for a few seconds, and tugging his neatly-trimmed beard a few times, Ed decided to answer. "You're right. But I can speak both languages and several others! I don't talk about myself much, especially to kids young enough to be my children. But it's going to be a long night of drinking and playing wet nurse to you boys. So, if you want to hear a sad tale, I'll tell you one!" An intoxicated Ed Filip then raised his glass and belted down the remaining tequila.

"You see seated before you a man who should be long ago dead. One who is a disappointment to himself and should be in some grave far from this place. Please pour me another glass!"

"Hell, we've all had our share o' scrapes, Ed, 'n' survived. Why the hell're yuh so down on yerself 'cause yuh're still kickin'?" Bottle in hand, Logan then reached to refill Ed's empty glass.

"I was born in Poland. I grew up in a time of hardship and financial despair. Like many eastern Europeans, I left my homeland and traveled west. Survival was my goal. But my dream for a new life in one of the richer countries of western Europe failed too. Broke and unemployed, I like many others sought security in the armed forces of an adopted country. I joined the French Foreign Legion in 1851, and it was there that I found my niche—a purpose for my life. I rose quickly through the ranks and was selected for officer . . . training. I attended the French military college at Saint-Cyr. Eleven years following my enlistment, I reached the rank of captain while marching across the deserts of North Africa. Not bad for a poorly educated Polish farm boy, *huh*?"

"If yuh were in the French army, how'n the hell'd yuh git to Cuba?" Logan, now all ears, raised his chin from his elbow-propped palm and asked.

"The French government, headed by Napoleon III, sent troops to Mexico to help support Maximillian, the Archduke of Austria. You see, Napoleon had offered him the crown of the newly organized Mexican Empire. I arrived with two Foreign Legion battalions and landed at Vera Cruz, in Mexico, on March 28, 1863. Over 20 years ago now. I was the commanding officer of the 3rd Company.

"My men were toughened veterans of desert campaigns in Algeria and Morocco and other distant places, but the diseases of Mexico were much worse. They quickly decimated our troops. My orders were to move inland to reach the city of Puebla which was under siege by the Juarista Mexicans. But not long after we landed, a sickness—I learned later it was Yellow Fever—laid many legionnaires and officers low, including me. Scores died!"

Ivy's jaw dropped in disbelief. "Yuh survived a case o' Yellow Fever, Ed?"

"That's right. As I lay near death in a crude hospital, my colonel appointed someone to replace me! He assigned someone else to lead my company! Captain Jean Danjou volunteered to lead 62 legionnaires and two other officers to Puebla in my place! On April 30th, at a tiny spot on the map known as Camerone—which will long live in Legion history and tradition—he and my brave 3rd Company faced 2,000 Mexican calvary and infantry. Danjou was mortally wounded soon after the battle started. But before he died, he h ad t he m en a nd o fficers o f t he 3 rd C ompany v ow that t hey would not surrender. Three of my legionnaires survived. Had I not been too ill to march, I too would have died a glorious death with my brave men. To this day, I resent that providence did not permit me to die as well that day, leading my fearless legionnaires."

The three cowboys gawked at one another, awed into silence by Eduard Filip's revelation of his past.

Ed continued. "After the Mexican campaign ended, I elected not to reenlist for another five years. I mustered out of the Legion in Mexico. I drifted over here to Cuba about 18 years ago and found work with Raul Martinez. And sometimes I have to babysit snot-nosed American kids!"

"Goddammit! I ain't in no mood to be talked to like that!" Jehu yelled, jumping to his feet and raising clenched fists in Ed's direction.

Standing up to face Jehu, Logan pleaded. "C'mon, yuh don't wanna do that. The ol' man'll take yuh down real quick, I'll bet. If not outright kil't yer sorry ass!" Logan prepared to grab his drunken friend quickly if necessary. If either man threw a punch, he'd try to stop him. "Cool down, boys, 'r somebody's gonna git hurt!" Logan shouted in frustration.

Surprisingly, both men nervously obeyed him without comment and sat down. Ivy could clearly see the anger in Ed's glaring eyes and thought, "If Logan hadn't stopped 'em, there would've been un' helluva brawl in this place. I believe ol' Jehu would've gotten the short end o' the stick."

"C'mon! Let's git back to the hotel 'n' git some grub. I could eat the north end outta a southbound skunk! I'm flat starvin'!" Logan announced to the other three men. He stood up, swayed dizzily, and clinked a 20-cent tip down on the table. He let everyone in the place know he was ready to leave.

"Good idea!" Ivy agreed immediately. Giving Logan's idea to leave his full support, Ivy stood up, also put a tip on the table, and then started toward the door. He suddenly discovered he had serious difficulty standing and walking straight. He had never consumed so much alcohol at one sitting before, so he was totally unfamiliar with its effect on his balance. He thought he heard two other coins loudly slap the table behind him as he wobbled out the door behind Logan toward the waiting carriage.

It was nearly dark when the three noisy, alcohol-saturated men staggered into the lobby of the Park View Hotel. Ed Filip stayed with the buggy; the driver took him to some prearranged place. The loud group of Punta Rassans now bubbled over with camaraderie. They laughed, joked, and sang together.

Each man staggered directly for his own room. The plan they had agreed on was that after freshening up, they would regroup a little later in the hotel dining room. But instead, each stupored man collapsed across his soft bed and snored the night away.

* * *

"Good morning! I'd like to send a wire to the Punta Rassa telegraph terminal. That's in Florida. In the United States." Jorge Gomez instructed the telegraph clerk at the Havana terminal early Saturday morning.

"Yes, sir. Do you have the message ready?"

"Yes, but it's in English. Any problem with that?"

"Not at all, sir. I'll send it immediately. Will there be a reply?"

"No, there won't."

As the clerk held the handwritten paper in one hand, he tapped out the message with the index finger of his other hand on the telegraph key. The apparatus soon clicked rapidly, making a rhythmic sound unintelligible to an untrained listener—the dots and dashes of International Morse Code:

"TO DR. F. CORNING . . . PUNTA RASSA . . . FLORI-
DA . . . USA . . . IN REPLY TO YOUR WIRE . . .
INSPECTED AND AM COMPLETELY INTRIGUED
BY SANIBEL ISLAND MEDALLION AND SEEING
ITS DISCOVERY SITE . . . WILL ARRIVE THERE
WEDNESDAY WITH IVY CLARK AS YOU SUGGEST-
ED . . . JORGE . . ."

"Your message has been received at Punta Rassa, sir. Do you have any other communications to send this morning?"

"No, that's it for now. How much do I owe you?"

"Three pesos, sir."

"Here you are, and this is for your timely transmission," Jorge Gomez added. After he passed the three pesos to the clerk, he tossed an extra coin into the man's expectant hand.

The message was transcribed at the tiny Punta Rassa telegraph station and was ready for delivery to Francis Corning. He and his team had recently returned from the upper reaches of the Caloosahatchee.

The telegrapher yelled to a black man who was working nearby. "Jeff! Hey, Jeff!" Jeff Bowton, the former slave and Jacob Summerlin's favorite colored man, was busy swinging a scythe back and forth. Its curved saber-like blade was cutting the thick grass and weeds around the hamlet.

"Yes, suh, Mauser George, suh. I's comin'," Jeff Bowton hollered back. He'd been answering to white folks since he was born a slave in South Carolina, and despite 20 years of freedom, his voice still conveyed the tone of the required—no, demanded—air of respect a black man had to yield to a white man in the deep south.

"Yes, suh! Whats c'n I do fo' yo'?"

"That little steamer that came down from upriver this morning—that's it at the dock, isn't it?"

"Yes, suh. I do b'lieve dat's de very boat!"

"Take this telegram over there and if a Dr. Corning is on board, deliver it to him. Now, Jeff! Don't you dare read that telegram! You hear me?"

Ha! Ha! Lordy, 'ave mercy, Mauser George! Yo' sho 'nuff's joshin' wit' ol' Jeff, Mauser George. Yo' 'noz I cain't read nary a lick!"

Still laughing out loud at the agent's silly humor, Jeff plodded along the dusty cattle trail leading to the boat docks. He welcomed any kind of break from swinging that confounded scythe, or from any kind of hard work nowadays. He had tolerated a lifetime of physical labor and the effects were catching up with him.

"'Lo! Yuh'n de boat! Suh! Is dere a Dr. Corning on bo'd wit' ya'll?" Jeff shouted.

"Yeah, he's on board. He's down below. Hold yer horses a couple o' minutes. I'll fetch 'im topside!"

In a few minutes, Francis Corning, his sunburned face half covered with shaving cream, came up from below decks. He cracked a half-smile and said, "Yes, my good man. I'm Dr. Corning. What can I do for you this fine morning?"

"I's a tel'gram fo' ya, suh. Mauser George de tel'graph 'gent o'er yunder dun writ it out'n axed me ta brin' it ta ya. Chere 'tis."

"Thank you. Here, this is for your trouble," Francis Corning said, and flipped a shiny nickel into Jeff's open hand.

CHAPTER 9

FOLLOWING A NIGHT OF FITFUL SLEEP SPRINKLED with bouts of nausea and a few intense nightmares, Ivy awoke to the strange early-morning sounds of the big city . . . and someone pounding on his door. He rose, dressed, and dragged himself out of the room. He found his companions downstairs huddled at a table in the hotel dining room. The bellhop had just been dispatched to Ivy's room to make another effort to rouse their young friend.

"Well, son, it's 'bout time yuh crawled out!" Logan exclaimed as Ivy approached the table.

"Boy, yuh look like yuh been to hell'n back! What's the matter? Yuh don't look so good! Yuh got the miseries?" Jehu just had to toss in his two cents worth.

His voice strong with a hint of aggravation, Ivy barked, "I feel awful! My head hurts like a bull stepped on it! Why'd yuh boys let me drink so damn much?"

Ed Filip joined in. "These two, and myself for that matter, don't feel much better than you. The fact is, we don't show it because we've had more practice at hiding a hangover than you."

"So this's what a hangov'r feels like? I feel like I'm seasick all ov'r 'gain. No more fer me! Damn, my head's throbbin'!"

"Here, boy! Grab hol't o' the horns o' the bull that gored yuh!" Jehu then offered Ivy his nearly full glass of the killer Cuban rum.

"Yuh mean yuh're drinkin' that shit already? This early?"

"Boy, I'm on vacation! It'll be a long dry spell once't this 'un ends! Here, take a swallow 'n' yuh'll feel better directly."

Ivy did. Gagging he got it down, then thought, "Well maybe I do feel a lil' better. Hell, all o' 'em's drinkin' already." Then he called out, "Waiter, I'll have a rum 'n' an American coffee when yuh've time, please. The Cuban coffee I had last night like to kill't me!" Then, again in silence, he evaluated his condition. "Maybe that's why my guts're on fire 'n' I feel so damn poorly. It's probably 'cause o' that strong Cuban coffee."

The day was a repeat of the previous afternoon. More sight-seeing, strange-tasting foods, and alcohol. Late afternoon found the three cowboys and Eduard Filip sitting in an outdoor restaurant along the busy Prado. The topic of conversation was the many attractive women parading the shaded avenue. As they passed, most all the ladies smiled at the gawking men. And some of the girls flirted openly.

Ed snapped them back to reality. "I promised I'd get you boys some female companionship. I have orders to keep you out of trouble—including jail—and seeing to it you get to sow some wild oats . . ."

". . . Yuh got that right. 'Specially the part 'bout my wild oats!" Jehu interrupted. "I'm sho 'nuff glad I didn't whip yer ass yesterday ev'nin'! Ha!"

"Yuh'd likely be in a Cuban hospital 'r an un'ertaker's par-lor, Logan countered. Yuh're crazy as hell if yuh think fer 'un minute yuh'd've won if yuh'd tangled wit' this French Foreign Legionnaire. I've heard 'bout those bad boys!"

"Shit! I'd've cleaned the place wit' this dude," Jehu said breaking into laughter. He patted Ed on the back so he'd know he was genuinely joking.

"You boys will be boys, won't you?" Ed responded and then challenged them. "We'll see tonight just what kind of men you are once you get up under a skirt!

"As I said earlier, I was told to arrange female companionship for you. I made those plans before you arrived in Havana. Now, are you American gentlemen ready to perform?"

"Hot damn!" Logan blurted. "Lead on, ol' timer!"

Ivy, inexperienced at the prospect of an intimate encounter with a woman and apprehensive about his ability to fulfill the role, tried to convey his enthusiasm too. But Ed could read the boy's uncertainty as to what was going to happen next and how he would measure up.

Ed hurried them. "Eat up, you horny squirts, then we'll settle up here and get back in the buggy."

The building looked like any other upper class Cuban residence. It was ornate by American standards, especially Punta Rassa standards. The house had an elegant European flair. Its architectural theme was present on all the houses that lined the quiet streets of this well-to-do neighborhood. Ornate columns, red- and orange-colored Spanish-tile roofs, and scroll-cut gingerbread adornments gave the building a graceful, even traditional, Cuban appearance. To an uninformed passer-by, this could have been the home of a prominent Havana professional, perhaps a physician, lawyer, or religious leader. But it wasn't. It was Havana's infamously best and most expensive house of ill repute. This was the house such professionals discretely visited from time to time, usually *after* dark.

"Henri!" Ed called to the black carriage driver. "I hired another buggy and expect it any minute to help take us back to the hotel. Our group will soon be bigger. We shouldn't be here too long. I'll be back in a few minutes."

"Yes, sir, Mr. Filip. I'll be standing by. Take your time."

The anteroom of the house was nicely arranged and decorated in good taste. Colorful paintings hung on its walls and those of the adjoining larger parlor. Several statues lined both well-lit rooms. The paintings and sculptures were explicitly sexually oriented, purposefully placed to arouse clients passing through the front door seeking age-old human bonding and pleasure.

"Have a seat, boys. How about a drink?" Ed tempted them. He walked over to an elaborate, hand-carved mahogany bar on the far side of the parlor.

As Ivy and Jehu sank down in plush chairs, Logan answered, "Why the hell not?" He joined Ed to check out the types and brands of liquor available. "Hot damn! I'm gonna try some o' this Canadian whiskey. I heard it was right good. C'mon Jay! Ivy! I reckon it goes wit' the package. Right, Ed?"

Ed laughed, nodded, and said, "Right! Enjoy, because you boys are footing the bill!" Logan flopped down with his whiskey in another plush chair near Jehu and Ivy.

"Mr. Filip, how very nice to see you!" a thin, well-dressed black woman said in a low, smooth Spanish voice. She had quietly entered the room from behind a half-drawn curtain near the bar. Instantly, the three polite Punta Rassans stood.

"*Aha*, Madame Perez. It's indeed a pleasure to be in your presence. Before such beauty, I'm struck speechless!"

"*Oh*, Mr. Filip, you're so gracious. Have you always been such a charmer?"

"Yes, my dear, and I speak from the heart! These are the young Americans about whom I spoke."

In perfect English with a scarcely perceptible accent, Madame Perez began to talk to the three fidgety cowboys. She knew they were nervous and tried to make them comfortable, calm any fears, and eliminate any apprehensions. "Welcome to Havana, gentlemen. I trust your visit to our fine city has been enjoyable?"

Speaking for the group, Logan replied, "Yes, ma'am. We're havin' a good time. What do sailors call it? *Oh*, yeah, a liberty. Ed's takin' good care o' us. Right, boys?"

Jehu and Ivy nodded their heads in agreement but kept their eyes scanning the erotic artwork. They were still too spellbound by their surroundings to speak.

"My girls are here to serve your special needs. They will fulfill your most intimate fantasies. But be assured they are not common streetwalkers and do not come cheap. Our fee is 12 pesos.

This is payable directly to me after you have made your personal choice. This charge covers the services of the young lady of your choosing, but you are obligated to pay for her food and drink during your time together. You must also treat her like the lady she is. For this small cost she will thrill your manly sensations tonight. All night! Are you each ready to continue?"

Logan spoke right up. "Yes, ma'am! I believe I can speak fer Jehu 'n' Ivy too. Right, boys? Yes, ma'am, the three o' us're ready. I cain't speak fer Ed. Ed, 'r' yuh joinin' in this party? Sorry, I ne'er thought to ask 'n' yuh ne'er did say."

"I don't believe so. I have a lady friend I share my life with. It is tempting, but I don't need any on the side. I have all I can handle at home. They're ready, Madame Perez. Boys, I'll be waiting for you outside."

After Ed made his exit, intentionally timed so as not to embarrass the nervous cowboys, he joined Henri who was grooming the resting horses.

Clap! *Clap*! The madam signaled the ladies who were quietly waiting and listening in the next room. It was their cue to enter the parlor. One by one they strutted into the room. In an almost surreal environment, with the air saturated by a variety of fragrant perfumes, ten gorgeous girls lined up in front of the astonished cowboys. The objective of this beauty parade was for each man to select a woman with whom he would share his evening.

"Does any o' 'em speak English?" Logan asked.

"Yes, they do. Some very well. Others speak what you Americans call pidgin English. Each will understand what you'll expect of them to have your needs—your urges—fulfilled."

Jehu did his best to interpret what he thought was happening. "So, we're here so's each o' us can pick 'un o' these beauties? Have I got it right?"

"Yes, sir!"

Without any hesitation, Jehu shot back, "I'll take that beauty in the light yeller dress, wit' the yeller flow'r in 'er hair. The third girl from the right, wit' the coal-black hair 'n' dark skin." He couldn't keep from staring at her, and thinking, "Goddamn! She's beautiful. What a body! She's the finest kind! Am I dreamin'?"

Jehu's thoughts were interrupted as the tall, full-figured mulatto named Juanita smiled, stepped forward, and demurely walked toward him. She took his hand, sat on his lap, wrapped her arms around him, and gave him a friendly hug.

Logan chose next. "The blonde does it fer me, boys! My pappy done tol't me once't they're more fun 'cause they git dirty faster. I'm fixin' to find out if ol' Pa was right? 'Gain!" Then Carmen, a petite but chesty blonde joined him in his overstuffed chair.

"C'mon, Ivy, pick one!" Jehu said urgently.

"I'm fixin' to! Hold yer damned tater!"

Ivy was scared, and he knew that Logan and Jehu knew it. His mind raced searching for something to say. "I don't know why the hell I let those two talk me into comin' into this place! Reckon if I didn't I'd ne'er hear the end o' it though. Hope Alice ne'er hears 'bout this! These women're all so damned pretty. I don't know which 'un to pick! Maybe the 'un wit' the big smile 'n' skin-tight white dress." He announced his decision, "Believe I'll choose the 'un at the end. I'll have the girl wearin' the white skirt."

Ivy selected Carlita Fernandez. Although she appeared to be in her late teens, Carlita was not a novice prostitute. She was a veteran whore who had been working in the brothel for over a year. Like many economically deprived, attractive, young Cuban women, money drew her into the ancient trade. Prostitution offered a means by which she could elevate herself out of Cuban deep-rooted poverty. Once she made the decision to sell her body, her looks had taken her straight to the top of the whore heap, to the first-class brothel of Madame Perez. She attended finishing school at her madam's expense, wore the best clothes, and was regularly showered with expensive gifts from her highly satisfied clients.

Carlita did not begin work this night with glowing exuberance. If she performed well, she could usually anticipate a generous tip. But tonight she had to entertain another inexperienced, penny-pinching, crude young American. She knew what was coming and silently considered the night ahead. "Just my luck! This kid's another beginner! They always have to be helped along the way. He'll try and prove himself to himself and his crude companions." But she was a professional so continued smiling, held out her gloved hand, and approached Ivy squirming in his seat.

"Hello, I'm Carlita. You are?"

"I'm Ivy." He gingerly took her hand in his and continued. "Yuh sho 'nuff're 'un fine lookin' lady, Carlita. Yuh're as purty as a picture 'n' perfect in ev'ry way!"

"Thank you, sir!" She said and smiled softly. Then looking directly into his eyes, she continued, "You think I look good now? Wait until later, when I take my clothes off and you get to touch me!" Then, lowering her voice, Carlita continued in a whisper. "Maybe you'd even like to see my female parts up close?" After enticing him with her candid but calculated message, she twisted, nestling her well-shaped buttocks into his lumpy lap.

Ivy blushed, then glanced around to see if Logan and Jehu were listening, or watching, or had noticed the color of his face. They weren't. They hadn't. Each was too busy talking and fondling their new live toys to notice him.

Later, after the carriages had dropped them at the hotel and Eduard Filip had said his goodnights, Logan decided he and Carmen would take a walk along the Prado. Before dinner, he wanted to enjoy one of the cigars he had bought and get to know Carmen better. Logan called to his companions, "C'mon, boys! Let's walk 'long the parkway 'n' enjoy the cool ev'nin' 'n' a smoke 'fore we eat some chow 'n' bed these gals."

Jehu shook his rum-soaked head and blurted out, "*Eat!* Yuh got eatin' on yer mind? Yuh're as daffy as a dumb duck! Damned if I'm gonna think 'bout food at a time like this! Not fer a while anyhow! We're headed fer the sack! I'll catch up wit' ya'll later. We'll be at the hotel!"

After the refreshing and nerve-settling walk, the two couples headed for the hotel. Logan was hoping to find Jehu waiting for them. He wanted to protect his old friend from himself. When he was drunk, there was no telling what kind of trouble he could get into. Jehu was not in the bar, so the foursome went into the dining room for dinner.

Following their delicious, traditional Cuban meal of roast pork and black beans and rice, Logan and Ivy tossed back a few shots of Canadian whiskey. Their female companions enjoyed imported wine in tall-stemmed crystal glasses. Suddenly they heard a commotion in the lobby.

A familiar voice boomed above the ruckus. "Goddammit, Juanita! I can make it on my own. I don't need no damned he'p from some runt nigger in a monkey suit!" Jehu screamed as he pushed the black-skinned bell captain aside. He continued to rant, "I'm lookin' fer my buddies! They're 'round here somewheres! Logan! Ivy! Boys, where'n the hell 'r' ya'll?" Jehu screeched at the top of his lungs.

Logan pounded his fist on the table making the silverware jump. He glared at Ivy and said, "Go out there 'n' git that damn drunk, will yuh? Tell 'im I said to shut the hell up 'n' come in here! If I go, I'll likely knock the shit out o' 'im!"

"Yer ol' buddy's a reg'lar pain in the ass sometimes!"

"I know that, but he's good-hearted. Usually, ev'n when he's drinkin'. Yuh know, don't yuh, that he'd give us the shirt off his back? He'd prob'ly die fer me!"

"So this is where yuh dandies 'r'! Boys, I'm havin' 'un hell o' a night! Juanita 'n' I come up fer air. Didn't we honey? Waiter! Bring my lady 'un o' these fancy glasses o' wine 'n' a glass fer me. I'll share some o' this liquor my friends have."

The whiskey reinforced Ivy's courage. His admiration of Carlita was increasing in proportion to his alcohol intake. He was tiring of this six-sided conversation and Jehu's nasty mouth. He wanted to withdraw, to be alone with Carlita. "So, 'r' ya'll gonna sit here drinkin' 'n' bullshit all night long?"

"Hell, boy, we got these ladies fer all night! What's yer damn rush?"

"Damn it, Jehu, yuh've got 'n answer fer ev'rt'in'! Yuh 'n' Logan know as well as I do we didn't hire these girls to sit here 'n' listen to our life stories all night. Fact is, I'm ready to take Carlita up to my room 'n' git some o' what I done paid fer!"

Roaring with laughter, Jehu countered, "Go 'head, but don't let 'er eat yer cherry! Juanita's 'n eater. Ain't yuh, honey? Ha! Ha!"

"C'mon, Carlita. Let's dump these smart-ass drunks 'n' go upstairs!"

Ivy never saw a naked woman before. Not even a picture of one. He hadn't touched a woman's exposed breast since his mother weaned him years ago. And Carlita knew how to take her clothes off just right. She stood where she knew the dim gaslight on the wall would provide the proper amount of glow. She controlled the shadows playing on her smooth olive skin. Carlita slowly and erotically exposed herself to Ivy. She knew how to excite a man, how to arouse him completely while disrobing. Ivy was gloriously excited and she watched his progress through his pants. She moved her silk-soft fingertips across his lower abdomen and began to undo his belt. A few moments later he too was nude, standing before her in fully erect splendor.

Without a word, Carlita moved closer to him and took hold of his fully aroused organ. Ivy never flinched as she stroked him, then began to back him up toward the bed, steering him with her hand. When Ivy's legs contacted the edge of the bed, she turned him loose. Carlita giggled and gently shoved him backward. He lost his balance and fell flat on his back onto the mattress.

Ivy could see her smile as she slid onto the bed, her body just inches above his. Impulsively, he reached up and clutched her perfectly formed, youthfully firm, and voluptuous breasts. Ivy gently squeezed her nipples between his thumbs and forefingers, and he felt the firming of erectile tissue responding involuntarily to his touch. But Carlita was interacting with Ivy as woman to man, not as a reciprocally loving person. Remaining vocally silent, Carlita concentrated on her skills as she crouched above him. She took his blood-engorged organ in her hand and began to settle on her knees. As she lowered herself, Carlita aligned him and both felt the penetration begin.

In silence, Ivy concentrated on his senses. *"Oh, my God! What's she doin' to me? I cain't believe this is happenin'! It's* better'n I ev'r heard. Better'n Logan 'r Jehu said it'd be . . . this is truly unbelievable!"

Slowly, Carlita began to gently rise and fall, and Ivy's body stiffly rose from the bed as he tried to push himself deeper inside her each time their bodies came together. She began the joint pelvic and muscular rhythm practiced by all good female lovemakers. Her professionalism was showing and Ivy was the beneficiary. Words were bouncing around in his head. "*Oh*, I ne'er 'magined it'd be like this—*sooo goood*!" Primitive sounds left his mouth as he swooned, "Don't stop, Carlita! *Oh* . . . Please . . . No . . . Don't . . . *Don't stop*!"

CHAPTER 10

ACCORDING TO MANKIND'S LONG-ESTABLISHED religious mores, Ed Filip was already awash in a sea of sin. Right or wrong, Ed firmly believed that living life to its fullest demanded that humans frolic sexually. Based on that belief, he had spent a lifetime loving women and fornicating with whores whenever the opportunity arose. He also knew that such intense bodily activities required physical recuperation but not spiritual redemption. Sleep was the most important of these elements.

So, in Ed's opinion, the behavior of the three Punta Rassans were normal manifestations of primitive human drives which had been put on mankind's shoulders by The Creator. And Ed was kind. He allowed the three young men to sleep until nearly noon, but now it was time for them to rise and shine. One by one, he knocked on their doors to roust the sleep-deprived, sexually drained, and hung over young men. He thought, "Thank God it's Sunday! Their last full day and night in Havana! I have only 24 hours more to keep my eyes on their every move. Tomorrow my life will be back to normal."

Eduard Filip's orders from Raul Martinez were simple and perfectly clear. Under no circumstances were the Punta Rassans to get into confrontational situations with Cuban nationals. Ed's overall plan was to keep them in a group so he could control their actions. S o f ar, t hey b ehaved w ell f or u ntamed k ids. B ut J ehu Rivers was the worst. He had been on the brink of a drunken tirade and close to assaulting Cuban citizens a time or two.

Eduard wouldn't be happy until he ushered his three temporary wards safely aboard the *Kissimmee Cloud* and waved goodbye as they steamed toward the northern horizon, homebound for Florida.

After he woke them, Ed instructed each to inspect their personal belongings. He wanted to make sure their money and other property, which he insisted they conceal when they checked in, hadn't walked out the hotel's front door with the whores. None of Madame Perez's girls were known to steal from their clients, but Ed preferred to be on the safe side.

Once they arrived in the dining room for brunch, Ed didn't ask any specific questions about their sexual adventures. Instead he barked, "You b oys l ook l ike hell! Are you g oing t o live, J ehu? Logan, your eyes look like you hardly slept a wink!" After the four were seated at the dining room table, he continued to nudge them awake. "Ivy, you don't look as bad as these two! Did you boys get your money's worth? Are you all petered out? Ha!"

Logan was the first to sluggishly respond. "I cain't speak fer Ivy 'n' Jehu, but I'm caught up fer a while. Caught up on both my whorin' 'n' drinkin'. I'm takin' it easy today. No women fer me tonight! No, thank yuh! I wore it down to a nub last night!"

"Same here! Ha!" Ivy interjected.

"I cain't believe yuh two!" Jehu mumbled. "I done tol't Juanita when she left this mornin' to come back to the hotel tonight. I'll tell yuh both straight out here 'n' now! I ain't sharin' 'er if yuh boys decide to git horny later on this ev'nin'!"

* * *

Logan, Ivy, and Jehu spent the rest of the day exploring the shops near their hotel. They leisurely looked for souvenirs for relatives or some kind of special, personal memento to remind them of this trip years later. At dusk, Ed found the three lounging on the

Prado gazing at passing women. Ed and the Punta Rassans reassembled in the Park View's dining room. In a more serious tone Eduard Filip addressed his charges. "Boys, you continue to keep quiet about tomorrow. We don't want any Cubanos to learn what we're up to. I'll be here at the hotel tomorrow morning around 7:30 to have breakfast with you and pick you up. We're supposed to meet Mr. Martinez at the bank when it opens at nine. It's just a few blocks from here. I'll tell the clerk at the front desk to wake you up early enough so you'll have time to settle your accounts and check out. Don't forget to claim your pistols from the hotel safe. Be sure you load and wear them! You never know what might happen when so much money—especially in gold—moves through the streets of this city. Get a good night's rest so you'll be alert. It's imperative you have all your faculties about you first thing tomorrow morning! I'll see you then. Stay put, too! The hotel staff's watching your behavior. I'm sure if word reaches Jake Summerlin that you didn't obey my instructions, your services with his company will no longer be needed, and a job in your line of work will become difficult to find!"

Through with his sermon, Ed rose from his chair and left the dining room and the hotel. Upon reaching the sidewalk, he started toward the waiting carriage. Out of the corner of his eye, he saw a familiar overdressed woman approaching the hotel entrance. "Juanita? Is that you?"

"Yes, sir, it is." the woman answered and walked closer.

"You're here to meet with Jehu, I understand?"

"Yes, sir. He asked me to return and share his bed again tonight."

"Are you moonlighting? Does Madame Perez know you arranged to come back to the Park View tonight?"

"I beg your pardon, sir?"

"Does the madam know you're here to spend the night with last night's client?"

"No, sir . . . I'm . . . I'm here on my own . . . because I like Jehu."

"Honey, you and I both know that's bullshit! My dear girl, I suggest you stay the hell away from this hotel tonight! If you don't, Madame Perez will hear about it! Understand me?"

"Yes, sir. I understand."

Juanita spun around on her tall spindly heels and disappeared into the Havana darkness. Ed's charges would all sleep soundly this night—much sounder than Jehu had hoped.

"That bitch ne'er showed up last night!" Jehu roared and pounded his fist repeatedly on the breakfast table. "I stayed up all damn night waitin' fer 'er! Well, part o' the night. Guess I fell 'sleep 'round midnight. See, like I done told't yuh two, yuh damn sho cain't trust no woman, 'specially a whore!"

"I slept like a baby," Logan said.

"Me too," Ivy added to help Logan aggravate Jehu.

"I'll bet ya'll . . . hell, two to 'un . . . outta what's left o' my bonus money that she don't come to the docks to see me off like she promised either! She said she'd . . ."

Visibly upset at Jehu, Logan stopped him in mid-sentence. "Wait a damn minute! Jus' what'n the hell did yuh go 'n' tell that goddammed whore? When we're leavin'? 'Bout the gold?"

"Goddammit! Don't holler at me like that wit'out any reason! I'll kick yer sorry ass! Fer yer information, I ain't told't nobody nothin' 'bout nothin'—'cept maybe Juanita! I was drunk 'n' not thinkin' straight when she started askin' me all those damn questions! Who the hell's she gonna tell, anyhow?"

"Yuh 'n' that damn rum! I hope it don't prove to be yer downfall. Yuh'd best not let Ed find out 'bout this!" Logan griped as he jumped to his feet and started pacing around the crowded dining room. He had to give this new crisis some serious thought. Then he cracked a smile. Ed had arrived and was busy talking to someone out in the lobby. When he finished, Ed joined the two somber-faced boys who were still seated and picking at their meals.

"Why so blue, boys? Are you unhappy about leaving Cuba? And what's wrong with you, Logan? You upset about something?"

"No, I got a cramp'n my foot 'n' I'm walkin' it out. Those two 're okay."

"Have you boys checked out?" Ed inquired.

"Yeah, we're all set to go," Logan said and pointed to their meager luggage stacked against the wall.

The Punta Rassans were mulling over their experiences in Havana. Each would leave Cuba with his own individual both good and bad memories. The fond memories would be shared later with others. The shady parts would be recalled only in dark bars, around the fire at cow camps, and whenever the three reconnected later in life. However, some things would be forever kept to themselves and never, ever shared.

Ed had a carriage waiting. Tethered to the rear of the wagon were two handsome but nervous saddle horses. When the three men joined him, Ed spoke firmly. "Okay, boys, gather around. This is the plan. I'll ride up front with Carlos. He'll drive the rig. Ivy, you'll ride with us . . . just sit there on the tailgate. Logan, you and Jehu are to ride these horses. I've ridden both and they're fast and spirited. I know, you finicky characters will probably think they're not as good as your half-wild horses back home."

Eyeing the strange-looking English saddles, Jehu interrupted him. "What'n the hell kinda saddles 're these ponies wearin'?"

A little irritated, Ed said, "Those aren't your ordinary roping saddles, but they'll do. They'll have to, that's all we've got! When we get to the bank, we'll load the special freight in the wagon. Logan! Jehu! You two will ride lead . . . point! Stay 20 or 30 yards out in front of the wagon. I'll let you know when to turn and what direction to take. We're going through the old part of the city because that neighborhood has the fewest side roads where someone could ambush us or cut us off. Ivy, you stay put and watch our ass-end! Any questions?"

Although anxious glances passed among them no questions were asked.

Twenty minutes later, the five men arrived at the ornately constructed bank building. Ed went inside. Soon he, Raul Martinez, and two bank guards came out the front door. The two guards were carrying a small but heavy strongbox.

The locked box was placed on the bed of the wagon and the guards returned to the steps of the bank, remaining close by. Raul

Martinez walked over to Logan. The Cuban reached up, shook his hand in greeting, and passed Logan a fountain pen and slip of paper. In a hushed but clear voice, he said, "This is Mr. Summerlin's gold. As he instructed, I'm turning it over to you for safekeeping and delivery to him. Please sign this receipt to acknowledge this transfer and your responsibility for its protection."

"Yes, sir," Logan said as he took the paper. Without reading it, he signed on the line where Raul Martinez was pointing.

"Ed will accompany you to the *Kissimmee Cloud* and provide any help he can to protect this shipment. Ivy and Jehu, I enjoyed meeting you both. I hope you can come back to my country sometime. Logan, I'll be pleased to tell Mr. Summerlin how well you performed . . . excuse me, ha . . . behaved on this trip. Goodbye to the three of you, and good luck!"

"Wait a minute, Mr. Martinez. Jus' how much gold's there inside that lil' box?" Logan couldn't resist asking.

"Plenty! There's $10,800 in gold bullion and coins—American—in that heavy little chest. There's $6,000 from the lumber and the rest is from the sale of the cattle."

"*God Almighty!*" Logan whistled through pursed lips. "Some people I know'd kill fer a helluva lot less'n that!"

Ed reminded them. "That's why you're all wearing firearms! There are many people in Cuba who would too, for much, much less. Be on your toes!"

Again Ed cautioned them, this time deliberately soft-toned and dead serious. "We've got about two miles to go, people. Some of the city that we'll pass through this morning isn't safe at any time, even for a small army like ours! Ha! Today you'll travel through one of the unsafest places on earth. You're about to step over the edge and teeter on the brink of hell!"

"That mis'rable son-o'-a-bitch! Ol' man Summerlin sho is a pip! He ne'er told me we'd be gettin' into any kind o' a chaincy situation!" Jehu said, but in a much more hushed voice than usual. Even as they huddled together and quietly talked among themselves, curious riders and pedestrians glanced in their direction. Some people stopped and openly stared. It didn't take anyone brighter than a cow chaser, or a banker, or a former military man to know some major financial transaction was going on for all to see out in the open street.

"Okay, boys! Same positions and straight ahead." Ed barked as Carlos snapped his buggy whip. The wagon began to roll. "We'll move very slow, slower than normal for a moving wagon or a walking horse. Also, keep an eye on me, because we'll stop occasionally to see how other wagons or riders react. If there's any bad men around, we want to get them to pass us and end up out in front!"

Not long after they left the bank, Ivy noticed a horseman acting erratically as he followed behind them. The rider would drift from side to side of the avenue, even loop around when the wagon slowed or stopped briefly.

"Ed! Can yuh hear me?" Ivy whispered.

"Yes, I can! Go ahead!"

"There's a rider on a roan back here. He's maybe a lil' more'n 100 yards away. I believe he's follerin' us! He don't seem to be goin' any place in particular 'n' he's keepin' his distance."

"Okay! Watch him real close. If he starts to close up on us all of a sudden let me know right away!" Then Ed reached down and released the strap securing the double-barreled, 10-gauge Greener shotgun to its rack behind his knees on the seat support.

Ed then raised his voice so all could hear. "Keep your eyes wide open, Carlos! Logan! Jehu! You both check out every intersection before we enter it! Scan the buildings on both sides, too. Double-check anywhere a sniper may be hidden. Watch for people or riders who don't act natural! If you think anyone is approaching us too fast, holler at him, draw your pistol, and wave him off! In Spanish, it's '*Alto*.' If he don't stop, shoot him! And, goddammit, I mean shoot to kill! Then we'll stop and fight the rest of the bastards!"

"Okay, Ed!" Logan and Jehu each nervously shouted still looking straight ahead.

The procession slowly meandered through the narrow streets of waterfront Havana. Grim poverty was everywhere. Old, dilapidated, unpainted shacks prevailed. A combination of swill and human waste slowly flowed through a grid of open ditch-gutters. The place looked almost deserted. Ivy thought, "Ev'n the poorest o' the niggers 'n' Indians don't live in such squalor at home."

Logan was riding front left and was a few yards farther out than Jehu. He was approaching a junction where two side streets intersected the roadway. Suddenly, Logan pulled his horse up and dropped the reins. He raised his left arm with palm forward and with his right hand snatched the long pistol from its holster. "Stop! Stop right where yuh 'r', Mister! *Alto!* Ed!" Logan hollered at the top of his lungs. "There's a guy here . . . he's movin' toward me mighty fast. I tol't 'im to stop, both in English 'n' Spanish, but he ain't slowed down yet!"

Ed saw the man trotting toward Logan. He faced him and shouted in Spanish, "*Pare, ahí donde está, hombre!*"

"I've got two riders comin' up fast ov'r here, too! Stop yuh two!" Jehu yelled in a combination of languages as he raised his hand high.

The three riders slowed their horses to a walk but kept coming toward the main road from both sides. After Jehu drew his pistol, he waved at the two riders on his side to stop. He shouted for them to stop again, both in English and in a crude attempt to duplicate Ed's Spanish. But the men continued to approach.

The rider on Logan's side moved into the intersection and stopped directly facing Logan. Then in pidgin English, he yelled, "Good morning, Mister gringos! I have been told that you have come to Havana so you may die! We are here to take your money and help you into hell where all American pigs belong!" As these last few words left his mouth, he quickly drew a pistol from a shoulder holster, held it at full arm's length, and pointed it at the Summerlin Cattle Company's box of gold.

This show of bravado from the man who apparently was the leader signaled the two riders near Jehu to draw their handguns. One of them howled, "Poor little gringo bastard boys! You'll never see your whore mothers again!"

A second—an instant—later, Logan quickly aimed and fired. His shot was accurate. The slug tore into the first horseman's chest. Without a sound, the already dead man tumbled from his horse onto the filthy street. Before his body hit the earth and crumpled in a distorted and grotesque pile, Ed stood up, aimed, and fired one barrel of his shotgun at the trotting horse and rider coming straight at him and the wagon. The rider was bent low in the saddle trying to reduce his target profile. As the horse closed faster the rider's and horse's heads blended as one and were hit by the load of buckshot as the pattern barely started to open. Both died in an instant and skidded to the ground together in a heap.

The rider behind the wagon, pistol drawn and cocked, then charged the wagon. Terror-stricken but still able to think, Ivy raised his pistol, cocked it, and took slow aim on the figure galloping toward him. *"God, please he'p me!"* Ivy pleaded silently as he fired. A split second later, a bullet from the attacker's pistol crashed into the buggy just inches from Ivy's shoulder. But it was not soon enough or close enough to have affected Ivy's deadly accuracy. Blood and bone erupted from the back of the chaser's head, and without a sound, the lifeless body toppled from the charging horse. Momentum catapulted the corpse over and over several times after it struck the ground. The body didn't stop tumbling until it almost reached the wagon, close to Ivy's dangling feet. Taking a deep breath, Ivy hesitated and then looked down at the still corpse. He couldn't believe what he saw. *"Jesus Christ Almighty!"*

But Jehu was still in trouble. The one remaining robber had turned his horse to run, trying to escape the gringos' deadly fire. But in a last ditch desperate effort, he spun around in his saddle and fired at Jehu. Although he was at point-blank range, the moving horse threw off his aim. The bullet struck Jehu in his left shoulder. Realizing he missed, the shooter tried to recock the single-action revolver for another shot. But the second barrel of Ed Filip's powerful shotgun rang out first, hurling a load of 00 buckshot at the horseman with a force that nearly cut the man in two. The impact of the lead knocked him sideways off the uninjured horse. As he fell, his right leg snapped, leaving his bare foot hung up in the stirrup.

"Owww! The son-o'-a-bitch hit me! Gimme a hand, boys!" Jehu shouted in pain, his voice full of disbelief.

"Are there any more of the thieving bastards?" Ed shouted. He tossed the empty shotgun to Carlos and barked, "Reload this, quick!" He spun away, drew his pistol, and raced to help Jehu.

Ed and Logan reached the wounded man at about the same time. Jehu was slumped forward in the unfamiliar saddle, almost resting on the horse's neck. He moaned and groaned whenever the nervous horse shifted and jiggled him.

Despite the pain, Jehu muttered, "Boys, look at this critter twist 'round. I believe he's causin' me to hurt more'n this damn slug is all by its lonesome. Jus' like some ordinary horse'd do—'un who ain't ne'er catched a cow! But maybe he's gettin' ev'n wit' me fer not likin' his sissy saddle. *Owww!* Did yuh git 'em all?"

Logan replied excitedly, "Yuh bet yer sweet ass we did, ol' buddy! Ev'ry last one! Least ev'ry 'un we laid eyes on. How bad're yuh hurt, Jay?"

"The son-o'-a-bitch got me in the shoulder! Thanks, Ed, fer nailin' his ass. I saw yuh blow 'im to smith'reens right after he shot me. I declare! Yuh kill't 'm right on time . . . 'fore he could cock, aim, 'n' git 'nother shot off 'n' finish me!"

Ed replied, "Glad I was able to. Say, where's Ivy?" He looked toward the wagon and yelled, "Ivy! Are you okay?"

"Yeah, I'm okay! I'm not hurt—jus' sick!" Ivy shot back, anguish in his voice.

Ed Filip barked, "C'mon, men, help me carry Jehu off his horse and into the wagon. Ivy! Ivy, we need your help over here. Come on! Help us get Jehu into the buggy!"

Jehu was bleeding severely. The four men carefully slid him off the nervous horse and into the wagon next to the gold-filled chest. Ed cut away the blood-soaked shirt, examined the wound, and fixed a temporary pressure bandage around Jehu's shoulder. This would slow the flow of blood, but it was obvious he would require a physician as soon as possible.

"Carlos! You take Jehu's horse and ride to the Port Authority's office. There's a military surgeon attached to the company of Spanish regulars bivouacked there. Tell the doctor to meet us at the *Kissimmee Cloud*. I think he'll find it at the Customs wharf. Be sure you mention my name and explain what happened here! After you do that, go to the boat and tell the captain what happened. Tell him we'll be there soon as we can. *Fast!*"

"Ed!" Ivy said, his face ghostly white and shiny with tears streaming down his cheeks. "Take a walk wit' me ov'r to the person I shot. Yuh too, Logan! It won't take but a minute. I want yuh both to see this. Ya'll're gonna have to see this to believe it!"

Although rushed to reach medical attention for Jehu, the three men took the time to gather around the body. It was merely a heap on the dirt road, its face tilted downward. Only one side was visible from above. The long jet-black hair at the rear of the skull was already matted with hardening blood. Some blood still flowed across the head behind the right ear, forming tiny rivulets. These randomly dripped across the dark skin. Open yet lifeless, dark eyes stared vacuously at the dirt.

Ivy started to cry again and said between sobs, "Does she look familiar to eith'r o' ya'll?"

"*She?*" Ed retorted in amazement.

"Yuh mean to tell me it's a woman?" Logan asked in shocked disbelief.

"That's right! I kill't a woman! That's not all. Take a good look . . . a closer look at 'er!"

Ed Filip dropped down on one knee, reached over, and took the corpse by its hair above the forehead. He pulled the head up and away from the road to look at her face. Slow recognition spread across his countenance. After all, he had been the last of the group to see her alive. "*God Almighty*! It's the whore! It's that damned Juanita. The bitch was in cahoots with the three other dead bastards!"

"I cain't believe I kill't a woman!" Ivy sobbed.

"Snap out of it! You did what you had to do. She'd have killed you to get the gold. Don't you ever doubt that for the rest of your life!" Ed blurted out. Then he paused, thinking and mentally reviewing the chain of events which had resulted in four dead people. Killed only moments ago by his, Logan's, and Ivy's hands. Then, he continued, "I don't think it would be smart to let Jehu know about this. Not just yet anyway. He has enough to endure, okay?"

117

Ivy wasn't completely numb. He knew Juanita tried to kill him . . . and she wouldn't be standing above his dead body crying! Had she and her friends been successful, she probably would have spit on his corpse and kept on going. These thoughts brought him back to full reason. "Okay! It's done 'n' ov'r wit'! Let's git Jehu to the boat so the doctor can work on 'im. He's got a bullet that has to come out 'n' the faster the better!"

Jehu complained and yowled in pain at every wagon bump as the team of horses galloped through the streets toward help. Ed was no longer concerned about potential robbers hiding in the shadows ready to pounce on them. Any that tried would be dealt a similar fate as had befallen the four who lay dead in the road behind them.

* * *

The Spanish doctor was on the scene. He saw the wagon and lone rider coming fast, then instructed two uniformed soldiers to ready the stretcher against which one of them was leaning.

Ed stopped the team so the wagon's tailgate was just beyond the *Kissimmee Cloud*'s gangway. "Dr. Alvarez! Ricardo! Thanks for coming. I'm delighted to see you. This man in the wagon has been shot by bandits—their final mistake!" Ed yelled excitedly in Spanish as he leaped from the carriage with the agility of a much younger man.

The uniformed doctor replied, "It's good to see you, too, Captain! It's been a very long time. We must hurry! The *Cloud*'s captain has prepared a well-lit cabin for me to work in. Follow me."

Ed Filip continued, "Yes, it's been a long time, old friend, much too long. Logan! Ivy! Help the soldiers get Jehu onto the stretcher."

Ivy moved in to help. As he did, he glimpsed a familiar figure standing at the railing and watching the drama unfold on the wharf below. "Why I declare! That's Dr. Gomez the archaeologist on board. I reckon he's comin' to Punta Rassa wit' us." Ivy thought as he helped lift Jehu onto the stretcher.

* * *

An hour later, the surgeon was finished and Jehu was coming around. As the effects of the ether wore off Dr. Alvarez spoke to his patient, "Mr. Rivers, are you awake?"

Jehu hesitated, tried to clear his groggy head, and then mumbled, "*Huh*? Oh, yeah, I'm okay. How bad am I hurt? Am I gonna make it?"

"You're a very lucky man. I was able to remove the ball in one piece. It didn't break into fragments and ricochet against nearby bones. That would have torn up more flesh and require more extensive surgery. Your collarbone is fractured where the round struck it. You should be hospitalized in case of any possible complications. However, I understand the situation completely. I urge, and I'll tell the ship's captain and Mr. Grace, that while the cargo is processed at your American customs in Key West, you're to see a doctor. You must have your wound examined and redressed. You're a lucky young man!"

Jehu muttered, "Yes, sir. Thank yuh very much. How much do I owe yuh?"

"You owe me nothing. My old commander and friend from the adventuresome Mexican days of our youth, now so long ago, shall buy me a drink or two in payment!" He glanced over at Ed Filip and winked.

Captain Boutchia had already settled with Spanish Customs officers and paid the export duty for his return cargo. They were now transporting cigar-grade tobacco leaf, processed sugar, and syrup. The shipment was bound for the Port of Tampa, with intermediate stops in Key West and Punta Rassa. He had been held up too long and was anxious to be underway.

Ed said his goodbyes. "Ricardo, I'll stop in and see you later this afternoon at your headquarters.

"Logan, Ivy, and Jehu, you're good and brave men. I'll never again think of you as boys! I was proud to be with you in that tight spot this morning. You're each as brave in a skirmish as any of my legionnaires ever were. Jehu, you take care of that shoulder. I may see all of you again one day if you ever return to Cuba.

119

"Now, I m ust h urry b ecause b y n ow t he a uthorities h ave arrived on the scene of our shootout and have launched an investigation. I'll handle the situation on your behalf—attempted robbery and self-defense—but the sooner you three are out of Cuba, the better. Goodbye!"

Ed turned and walked to the horse Logan had ridden, mounted up, and began to trot away. Before the roadway curved, Ed Filip stood high in the stirrups, turned around, raised his arm, and waved farewell.

CHAPTER 11

RECROSSING THE DREADED FLORIDA STRAITS wasn't too bad after all. No one aboard the Kissimmee Cloud was seriously seasick, and without any work responsibilities, Logan and Ivy acted like tourists on an ocean cruise. Jake Summerlin's gold was locked in the ship's safe, and Jehu Rivers was resting comfortably in bed.

When they left Havana, the captain told them he expected to be at the U. S. Customs dock in Key West by dawn. The Key West lighthouse beacon was now in view. They decided to sleep until the ship docked.

Logan, Ivy, Jorge Gomez, and a handful of other passengers stood along the rail watching the seamen tie the spring lines to bring the vessel snuggly alongside the pier. A small group of men stood on the dock waiting for the ship to be secured. Logan suggested to Ivy, "Let's git offa the boat while they're takin' care o' this duty bullshit 'n' stretch our legs."

As they started down the gangway, someone in the group on the dock called out, loudly, "Hello, aboard! I'm looking for some one by the name of Logan. Logan Grace! I understand he's aboard?"

Logan laughed and said, "Well, he's halfway! I'm Logan Grace. What can I do fer yuh?"

"I'm Dr. Mick . . . Laurence Mick! A Mr. Martinez in Havana wired me to meet your boat to examine a gunshot victim . . . a Mr. Rivers?"

"Yes, Doctor. He's tucked away topside in a cabin—better quarters'n the rest of us had. He was awake when I checked a few minutes 'go. He said he hurts like hell but seems okay."

"Let me get my medical bag and I'll have a look."

Jehu's bandage hadn't leaked during the night. That was a good sign. The physician carefully cut away the wrapping and inspected the sutured bullet wound. Other than severe bruising, the condition of the injury appeared to be within medical standards.

"Mr. Martinez told me that Mr. Summerlin owns a cottage here in Key West, and he's made it available for your recuperation. No, he strongly insisted . . . demanded . . . that you use it! I'm to assign a nurse to care for you until, in my opinion any danger of infection in your shoulder has passed. Only when you've fully recovered will I release you from my care."

Fearing he was going to be abandoned, Jehu winced, propped himself up on one elbow, and said, "Hell, Doc. That's mighty nice o' Mister Jake 'n' yuh, but I've gotta git back up to Punta Rassa to work. I cain't 'ford to stay here!"

"There's no physician at Punta Rassa to see to your care. You're not able to work. You know that, don't you? You'll remain on the Summerlin Cattle Company payroll while you're convalescing. Correct, Mr. Grace?"

Logan hesitated, then said, "I reckon . . . yeah, that's right, Jay. Mr. Summerlin'll take care o' yuh."

"Then it's okay wit' me, I reckon. So long's the nurse is a looker 'n''ll crawl in the sack wit' me! Ha!" The doctor winced, but Logan and Ivy knew their friend was completely serious.

"You realize, don't you, that there's always a threat of serious infection in a gunshot wound? Your friend in Havana was very smart indeed to have a military surgeon take care of you early. They're certainly the most experienced when it comes to treating wounds of this kind."

* * *

About five miles from Punta Rassa, the familiar shape of Captain Gus Wendt's perfectly trimmed sails approaching the *Kissimmee Cloud* was a welcome sight for Ivy and Logan. The fast-closing sloop was about to deliver Charlie Clark to pilot the steamer to its berth. Soon, the gold-filled strongbox would rest secure in Jake Summerlin's small vault. With that, their trip and its responsibilities would be over . . . except for those good and bad memories that time would dim but could never obliterate.

Ivy whispered, "Logan, I've been meanin' to talk to yuh 'bout somethin'."

"Yeah, what's on yer mind?"

"I'd like to keep our whorin' down'n Havana 'tween the three o' us . . . keep it a secret! Okay?"

"What's the matter, son? Yuh don't want yer mama 'n' daddy to know yuh done been a bad lil' boy?"

"Damn! Cain't yuh git serious fer jus' a damn minute? I don't give a shit if my folks find out! I'm grown 'n' on my own . . . holy Christ, I'm 26 yars ol'!.. I don't have to answer to 'em no more! It's that I don't want Alice Johnson to hear 'bout it. If she does, at least right now, I believe she'd think a whole lot less o' me. Yuh know, don't yuh? I'm fixin' to seriously court that girl!"

Logan knew the two had grown close but reacted with surprise. "Yuh 'r'? I swear I didn't know. She sho's a cutie. She ne'er paid any attention to me. Bet she's been savin' 'erself fer yuh! No, yuh can count on me. I won't ev'r tell Alice 'r anyone else 'bout yer whorin' ways! Ha!"

"Thanks. I do appreciate that. Much obliged."

Ivy saw Alice clearly now. She was standing alone out on the edge of the dock, fidgeting and shifting from side to side. Every second or so, she rose up on her toes and waved wildly at the approaching steamer. Jake Summerlin stood a little farther back. He was talking with the workers waiting to take lines to be thrown from his ship.

In a few moments, the vessel stopped and was brought up tight against the wharf. As soon as he was sure he could span the distance, Ivy leaped for the dock. Alice stood resolutely in his landing zone. When his feet hit the weathered cypress planks, she caught him in her arms, steadied him momentarily, and hugged him affectionately.

"*Oh*, Ivy! I missed you so much! I'm really happy you're home, safe and sound."

Ivy hugged her firmly and kissed her lightly on the lips. Blushing, he then introduced her to Dr. Jorge Gomez, the Cuban archaeologist. He had disembarked and joined the couple and the others on the dock.

"Dr. Gomez," Alice said, "Dr. Corning is aboard his boat. It's tied up at my folks' place over on Fisherman Key. That's that little island over yonder," she said pointing. "I rode over here early this morning with Cap'n Gus in his tender. Dr. Corning said he'd come over in a small boat to get us both when he saw the *Kissimmee Cloud* coming into port. I'll keep a watch for the boat, but if he arrives sooner than later, you two can visit with Mr. Summerlin. That's him . . . the tall, older man now boarding the boat. I believe Dr. Corning knows Mister Jake. Don't ya'll forget and head off for Fisherman Key without me! Don't ya'll dare leave me marooned over here with Ivy! Ha!

"Ivy, come, I'll walk you to the bunkhouse so you can put your things away. And before I forget . . . Dr. Corning arrived back from upriver only yesterday. He wanted me to ask you if tomorrow would be good for you to take the day and go over to Sanib'l? Where did you get that nice looking pleated shirt?"

"Why, thank yuh, Alice. I bought it in Havana. I wore it today so yuh'd be sho 'n' see it. I knew yuh'd like it.

"As far's I'm concerned tomorrow's a good day. How'd he know Dr. Gomez was wit' me, *huh*? I'll have to check wit' Logan first, to find out what's goin' on work-wise. Reckon I won't know 'til he gits here'n' talks wit' Mister Jake. He's comin' in wit' Cap'n Gus."

"Well, let's see if we can find out what's going on tomorrow before the doctor arrives to take me back home. He said if ya'll are going over to Sanib'l, he'll be here at Punta Rassa at dawn to pick you up. Dr. Gomez will be staying with him on his boat. Ivy, if you do go to Sanib'l in the morning, can I go along with ya'll? I want to be with you . . . to do things with you . . . every chance I get!"

"Why, sho yuh can. I'll be right proud to have yuh."

Before the day ended, Ivy had Logan's permission to take off work on Thursday, and plans were made for the next day's expedition to Sanibel Island.

Ivy described the Cuban trip to his parents, younger brother Donald, and Alice before Francis Corning convinced her it was time to go home. It was nearly dark. Before Alice left, Ivy distributed his few souvenirs to his family and her. Talking about his ordeal made him feel better inside, although he didn't tell the whole story. He intentionally left bits and pieces out—fragments he wasn't ready to reveal or discuss.

* * *

As the steamer inched toward the eastern tip of Sanibel Island, Ivy and Alice huddled in the bow, his right arm tightly around her thin waist and his other hand resting on her well-defined hips. They made small talk and watched a pod of bottle-nosed dolphins. Some of them leaped completely clear of the water as they played.

As the steamer neared the beach, Ivy climbed to the bridge and spoke to the helmsman. "'Cordin' to Cap'n Gus Wendt—he knows these waters better'n anyone—there's plenty o' water right up to the beach here on the bay side."

The boat slowly eased ahead until its bow touched bottom a few yards from the shore. A crewman suspended a ladder over the side, and one by one those going ashore climbed down and waded to the beach.

Once ashore, Alice commented, "I just love to come over here, 'specially right after a strong storm, like a winter nor'wester. The shell collecting is fabulous then. You can find so many different kinds of beautiful shells that the waves wash up on the beach."

125

Ivy, Alice, Drs. Corning and Gomez, and four other men whom Ivy didn't know gathered on the beach. But one of the others seemed familiar to Ivy. After a moment, he recognized him as the artist who drew the picture of his good luck piece for Dr. Corning. All, except Ivy and Alice, carried backpacks and a variety of tools and other equipment including shovels, sifting screens, and a tripod with a surveyor's transit attached.

Ivy and Alice carried shoulder bags containing food and water they had brought along. Ivy wore his regular everyday attire: Denim jeans and shirt, riding boots, and a worn broad-brimmed felt hat dirtied by fingerprints. Alice wore brogans, and a long, lightweight cotton dress she had made herself from flower-patterned flour sacks. She had her long blonde hair tucked inside a white sunbonnet.

Dr. Corning stepped forward and addressed the group: "We're here to investigate a possible aboriginal mound which Ivy Clark discovered several months ago. In that mound he found some very, very interesting artifacts. Some of you already know Ivy recently brought this discovery to my attention . . . very generously I should add. Based on my examination of the materials Ivy found, I asked Dr. Gomez, who's an authority on such Spanish artifacts and antiquities, to come up from Cuba and join us as we look at the discovery site. Ivy, I don't think you knew for certain that Jorge was coming along until you saw him as a fellow passenger aboard Mr. Summerlin's freighter. I knew he would! Yours is a very exciting and mysterious find. If you're ready, please lead the way."

One of the men stepped forward and cautiously passed Ivy a machete. Then Ivy began to hack an opening through the burned but still standing vegetation. This soon became a narrow trail over which he would lead the group inland. Before he had gone too far, Ivy turned around and called out, "Okay, ya'll follow me. Watch where yuh step through the brush 'n' grass. An' carefully check the sides o' this trail I'm makin', too. Sanib'l's famous fer its big diamondback rattlers."

Questioning expressions, fearful glances, and rumbling noises of apprehension rippled throughout the group. Alice stepped in line behind Ivy, far enough to avoid his razor-sharp, swinging knife. The others fell in one by one behind her.

Ivy carefully selected the easiest way forward through the thicket. He sliced away at fire-killed sea grape and buttonwood branches so the party could penetrate the barrier close to the water's edge. Going was slow for the first few yards. They moved obliquely from the water, heading toward the very tip of Sanibel Island.

Once the group was clear of the burned and recovering trees, bushes, and strong vines near the beach, the terrain became more open. Then it became almost barren, with dry desert-like soils and a hardy incompletely burned plant community. Thick sedges and grasses were mixed with clumps of sharp-spined prickly pear cactus and Spanish bayonets. Not more than ten yards from the very tip of the island, they stumbled through a thick barrier of sea oats and climbed a low knoll. Most recognized the abrupt rise in terrain as the mound they came to examine.

"It's pretty much as I remember 'n' described to yuh, Dr. Corning," Ivy began. "See, it's level 'cross't the top, 'n' if yuh walk 'round 'n' look at the outer edges, yuh'll see it's diamond-shaped like I tol't yuh."

"Definitely man-made! Do you concur, Jorge?" Francis Corning asked his scientific colleague.

Jorge Gomez was excited. He had removed his Panama hat and was busy wiping his face when he answered in a muffled voice through his handkerchief. "Without question!" After moving his hanky away, he said, "Will you please ask your men to start clearing some of the plants away so we can make proper measurements and survey the site accurately?"

"Yes, by all means! Frankly, I've never seen such a mound as this before."

"Nor have I!" an eager Dr. Gomez interjected, nearly shouting.

Dr. Gomez continued. "I'm sure we'll find it to be quite special. If it is of Calusa origin—and I believe it is, because of the artifacts you discovered, Ivy—it must have been very important to their social order and culture? I'm certain this pile of sand played a major role in their ceremonial and religious lives."

While the men trimmed away the plants to better decipher the shape of the mound, Francis Corning asked Ivy, "Just where did you find the ceramic vessel—the pot? Can you remember?"

"Yes, sir! I stuck a small conch shell into the sand directly on the spot where I kicked up the pot. Let me see if I can find it."

Ivy walked to the inland end of the mound, kneeled down, and scanned across its surface looking toward the east. He stood, took half a dozen steps forward, kicked at the sand, and dislodged the nearly concealed sun-bleached horse conch. He yelled excitedly, "Here 'tis Dr. Corning! This is exactly where I found the pot!"

Francis Corning then addressed the group. "We're going to examine this site somewhat differently than others we've surveyed or removed artifacts from in the past. Dr. Gomez has studied and evaluated the new wave of field archaeology recently developed in Europe. We'll apply that technology here today."

Jorge Gomez outlined the new procedure, and the archeological dig started in earnest. First, a nine-yard square grid, with the discovery site at its very center, was measured, staked, and cordoned off with twine. As Drs. Corning and Gomez began to survey the mound, the four other men started to open the site with shovels. The uppermost topsoil was methodically cleared away a shovelfull at a time, dropped into a metal bucket, and carried away from the site. This sand was then carefully dumped onto a portable, table-like, swinging sifting screen. Each piece of material that failed to pass through the mesh was meticulously inspected before it was discarded. A few inches of soil at a time were removed in this way over the entire site, one square yard at a time. The excavation proceeded slowly, although the soil's characteristics made digging easy.

While the others worked, Ivy and Alice walked out to the beach. They kicked off their footwear, left them on the beach, and strolled along the edge of the surf admiring the wilderness and natural beauty of Sanibel Island. Long before, prehistoric humans walked this same white, shell-strewn beach. No one lived here permanently, although legends persisted that about 50 years ago, people tried to start a settlement on the island. It failed, partly because the mosquito ruled here most of the year. From time to time, commercial fishermen camped on the beach, but Sanibel Island, like most of southwest Florida, was considered too harsh a place to live. But Ivy knew this was about to change: Two lighthouse keepers and their families were soon to become the island's first permanent residents.

Reaching the hard, damp sand along the water's edge, the couple slowed their pace but continued to walk in unison. Nearly a foot taller than Alice, Ivy tilted his head to look down at her as she talked. "Ivy, look how the two different colors of water meet and make a pie-shaped pattern."

"Yeah, Cap'n Gus tol't me that's called a rip tide. It happens when water carried by a strong ebb tide rushes outta the Bay 'n' Pine Island Sound real fast 'n' meets water from the Gulf o' Mexico. He tol't me it's really dang'rous fer a swimmer 'r small boat, 'specially if there's a strong onshore wind blowin' from the opposite direction 'gainst the tide. The combination makes the water treach'rous. 'Specially fer a swimmer!" Silently, to himself, he added, "Ev'n fer a wounded deer!"

As they strolled, Ivy and Alice were sometimes ankle deep in water whenever a strong wave bounced up the beach and surrounded them. Alice was talkative, almost a chatterbox. She reminisced about her childhood and talked of family, her love of reading, and concern for her future. Not once did she say she thought herself outside the mainstream—stuck as she was, by her own choice, in the sleepy hamlet across the Bay. She had no expectations other than to be happy and productive. She would leave her parents and Punta Rassa behind when she was ready, and would do so on her own terms. Ivy listened intently, occasionally interjecting his hopes and plans for his life and future. They glowed. They were happy.

"Ivy, did I just hear someone? Listen!" They paused, ears pricked. "Yes, I did! Someone's calling you. We'd better hurry back and see what's going on!"

Hand in hand, they jogged to rejoin the main party. Ivy could see Dr. Corning standing on the edge of the mound. He was

129

waving, signaling them to hurry. He seemed excited about something.

"Ivy, the diggers found something. I thought you'd want to be in on this."

"Yes, sir!"

Jorge Gomez was on his hands and knees staring into the shallow hole. The artist was also crouched down but lower, inside the excavation. With a small brush, he was busy whisking away sand partially covering three stained objects laying crosswise in the sand. Ivy judged that the three crossed objects were only inches below and in the exact same location where he kicked the pot out of the sand.

Francis Corning then gave some instructions. "Ira, when Ralph uncovers those, I want a few photographs taken for our archives, before Dr. Gomez removes them for examination. Warren, before we forget, let's plot their specific location. What do they look like to you, Jorge?"

The Cuban replied, "Whatever they are . . . I do have an idea what they are . . . I've never seen such artifacts in a Calusa mound before!"

After Ira took several photographs, Jorge bent farther over and pulled the three long, slightly flattened, curved objects out of the sand.

Dr. Gomez then stood up and took them to a portable table that served as an examination station. With a small soft-bristled paintbrush, he swept away the remaining particles of sand which still adhered tightly to the articles. Then with a large magnifying glass, he began to carefully scrutinize the pieces.

"Why, they look like ol' sea cow ribs to me!" Ivy exclaimed.

"Ivy, you never cease to amaze me!" Jorge Gomez said. "But you're correct. They're manatee ribs. That's what you people in southern Florida call sea cows. However, these are not ordinary manatee ribs. Take a look, Francis." He passed Dr. Corning the hand glass and one of the bones.

"Egad! I'll say! Utterly splendid!"

Ivy had seen many sea cow ribs before. Occasionally, someone harpooned one of the giant marine mammals and towed it to Punta Rassa. Such a kill instantly created a party atmosphere, a feast in which the highly prized and delicious flesh was shared with everyone in the community. Ivy and Logan owned matching scabbard knives with ornate, handcrafted handles made from the heavy, dense rib bones of manatees. They were highly polished and resembled ivory. The knives had once been Christmas gifts from Jacob Summerlin.

Francis Corning continued to examine the bones carefully. As they lay buried for centuries, they had become considerably stained by tannic acid and other chemicals leaching down through the fine sand. They were now nearly brown. Then he suddenly realized what his colleague was referring to when he noticed the faint markings. The ribs were engraved on both of their wide, flattened surfaces with small pictures.

"Why, this is . . . is . . . fine scrimshaw. Whoever rendered this piece of work was a true artist. Egad! You're right, Jorge! Who would ever imagine finding something of this caliber in a Calusa mound? I was surprised at the quality of work that had gone into both the ceramic vessel and the wooden carving, but these pictographs are fantastic! Men, continue digging, but dig carefully. There's no telling what else you might find!"

The two archaeologists hovered like doting mothers over the bones. Scientific terms spoken in whispers passed between them about what they were looking at. Of particular concern was the orientation of the tips of the ribs before they had been exhumed. They were crossed but not at right angles. The largest was buried the lowest and its tips pointed east and west. The narrow third of each of the other two crossed over the eastern end of the bottom rib. Their free, uncrossed ends pointed directly at the north and south extremities of the corresponding "points" of the mound.

"I've absolutely no idea what this apparent specific directional orientation means. Do you, Jorge?"

"No, but it must have some significance. It'll take thoughtful study and perhaps some additional expertise. Let's examine and evaluate the pictographs. Perhaps if we can comprehend their meaning first, we may come to understand the totality of this site and its mysterious contents."

"Dr. Corning, come here, please!"

Along with Ivy and Alice, the scientists returned to the dig site and looked down into the depression.

"Doctor, I've uncovered a human skull!" Ralph Brogdan exclaimed when he looked up and saw them standing above him.

Looking down at the skull, Francis Corning commented on his assistant's discovery. "From its orientation, and the fact you've found an individual cranium at that elevation, suggests to me that this is an extended burial. I'll venture that the skull and other remains you'll soon uncover are those of the artist. I've thought from the very beginning, whoever was the artist would also rest here. He was someone important. That's very, very obvious."

Curious as to what was going on, Alice asked, "Dr. Corning, may I ask you a question?"

"Yes, you may, dear."

"What's an 'extended burial'?"

"Well, the Calusans usually placed their dead in charnel houses, which were closed shelters in which the flesh was allowed to decompose. Then periodically, the various bones of the deceased were gathered, bundled together, and placed in baskets with identical body parts from other village residents. All were laid to their final rest in a religious ceremony at a scheduled mass burial. However, in an extended burial, a complete skeleton was buried following a grandiose ceremony, much sooner after the person's demise than a common person. A typical grave was dug and the decedent's bones were placed in their normal positions: face up, as is customary for a body in our modern culture. In the Calusa world, primary and secondary chiefs, principal priests, and political nobles were interred horizontally—their bodies extended. Based on the other artifacts that Ivy found, I'd say this man . . . I'm assuming we're looking at the bones of a man . . .?"

The excavator interrupted. "Dr. Corning, from the heavy brow on this skull, and the dimensions of the limb bones, I'd say this individual was male. Indeed, a tall man . . .."

"Thank you, Ralph . . . a Calusa man who more than likely didn't fit into any one of the exalted social positions I just mentioned. He was probably a non-religious, non-political person. Likely someone who, because of his artistic achievements or some other noble deed, attained a very special status. Perhaps he was an important Calusa hero."

"Dr. Corning! There are also some poorly preserved wooden figurines buried here. They're about six inches tall, I'd say. But no matter how careful I am, when the brush hits them they break up and disintegrate," the man kneeling in the excavation added.

"Let me have a look," Francis Corning replied and stepped into the hole to see what his assistant had found. "*Hmm*. From what I can see, they are very unusual in both appearance and craftsmanship. They look like kneeling human figures, but the upper torsos have odd feline, almost cat-like, features. Why, they're perfect duplicates of the knife handle in Ivy's pot. Very, very interesting. I don't know of any way to preserve them perfectly, but I'll melt some paraffin while you dig around a couple of them. We'll encapsulate them with wax. That'll hold them together until we get them back to the university laboratory. We'll figure out then how to stabilize the wood."

"Dr. Corning! I'm sorry to interrupt you again, but can you come here please and take a look at this bone!"

Standing on the edge of the excavation, Francis Corning asked, "What in the world is it, Ralph? Be careful uncovering it!"

With his small brush, the cautious excavator slowly swept sand from the large, brown-stained bone. The outline and mass of the object was patiently uncovered while the group of men and Alice, drawn by the tone of Ralph's voice, stared into the grave in awed disbelief.

"*Dear God in heaven!*" Dr. Corning exclaimed. "It's the skull of a *horse*! What in the name of God are the remains of a horse doing in a Calusa burial site?" The whole group stood wide-eyed and dumfounded as they nodded slowly in agreement that it was indeed a horse's head. The scientific team could scarcely believe what they were looking at.

Jorge Gomez broke the silence. "This further supports the overwhelming evidence this is a post-contact burial . . . but where . . . how did a horse come to be buried with this Calusan?"

A subdued, concentrating, and awestruck Francis Corning replied, "We'll never know! Photograph and map it! We'll leave it as we found it!"

Laymond Daughtry, the expedition's biologist, had been busy digging at the opposite end of the excavation from where Ralph had uncovered the skulls. He had just exposed the long human leg bones when he noticed the top of something embedded in the sand and positioned between them. Carefully, he continued uncovering this dark-colored object. With the sand around it removed, he thought it time to bring it to someone's attention. "Dr. Corning . . . sir, come take a look at this!"

"What in the world is that, Laymond?"

"Doctor, to me it looks like a leather case of some kind. It's been encapsulated in a thick covering of black mastic-like material, almost like tar."

"When you have it free, bring it to the examining table, please."

The leather material had rotted away in one corner, and over time, fine sand had seeped inside. After Laymond carefully extracted the item from the tight-packed sand and climbed out of the hole, he carried it to the table. Francis Corning began to gently brush away the clinging sand and commented, "This is some kind of waterproofing overcoat that was applied during the case's manufacture. The outer layer helped preserve this remarkable artifact. *Hmm*, I don't see any other way in. Please pass me a knife. Let's have a look inside."

He carefully made a lengthwise incision through the tough material. "This indeed looks as though it's leather."

Intently watching the procedure, Ivy added, "It looks like sea cow hide to me."

"I agree," Laymond said. "I can't think of any other hide, at least here in Florida, that's this thick except manatee. That's an excellent deduction."

Pleased with receiving the compliment in the presence of Alice, Ivy continued, "Well, what's inside it, Dr. Corning?"

"This day has been full of surprises, so let's see," Francis Corning said. He wanted to open the container without removing any of the leather, so he made some lateral slices leading from his first cut. He peered into the dark interior and continued his description of what he saw. "It's not entirely filled with sand. I can see at least two large objects inside." He reached inside and withdrew a wooden item nearly two feet long.

As he held it up for all to see, Jorge exclaimed, "Why, it's an atlatl!"

"A what?" Ivy asked.

"It's an atlatl! A dart caster . . . a spear-throwing stick once used by some Indian cultures. Look at the craftsmanship in the carvings. Why, it's absolutely beautiful! Most of these I've seen have been much more fundamental, simple in design. Francis, don't you think it strange that we've found this weapon here in Florida? The atlatl is an archaic device. It is virtually unknown in most non-Arctic North American Indian cultures—the bow and arrow replaced it ages ago. Some archaeologists, myself among them, have concluded that there was some genealogical connection between the Calusa and the Aztecs of Mexico. This atlatl provides supporting evidence of such a historical connection. If both peoples were simultaneously using the same weapon during the same time period, up until soon after contact, the connection was likely historically recent. We know the Aztecs were using atlatls as recently as 1519, because they used them against Hernan Cortés and his forces when he invaded Mexico. If the Calusa used the spear-thrower here, it could well account for the fear Spanish records tell us that the surrounding tribes held for the warriors of the Calusa nation. This is just mind-boggling!"

"What else's in that t'ing?" Ivy asked.

Reaching into the case again, Francis Corning withdrew another carved piece of wood. "Look at this, Jorge! It's an Indian saber. Just look at the detailed work . . . how the teeth are set into it. What are they, Laymond?"

"Dr. Corning, may I examine it?" the biologist asked. After carefully looking it over, he continued, "The teeth are tiger shark teeth. Their size matches the two drilled teeth in Mr. Clark's pot. They're much larger than any recent or even fossil teeth from this species I've ever studied in any collection. There are a few references in the ichthyological literature of tiger sharks that supposedly reached very close to 30 feet long. I'd say these teeth came from a 30-footer. Who's to say such a giant fish never swam in these waters 350 years ago?"

Further examination of the case's contents revealed several well-oiled hardwood atlatl dart and arrow foreshafts, each still holding a variety of projectile points. These included bifaced stone dart points and arrowheads. One shaft was tipped with a large tooth from the lower jaw of a bull shark.

As the morning progressed, several other artifacts were removed from the grid. Most seemed to be associated with the person in the grave, including several large whelk shells that had been drilled to secure handles for use as hoes or hammers, two additional unbroken pots, and two beautifully-carved wooden ceremonial masks. The masks were rotted and started to fall apart when touched. Like the figurines, they were generously covered with paraffin and packed in wooden cases with the other items. As time permitted, the cases were carried overland and stowed aboard the steamer that rode at anchor just off the Bay beach.

At the excavation site, the two archaeologists were huddled together in serious conversation. "Francis, the more I think about the position of those manatee ribs, the more this site intrigues me. I've seen similar bone and stone arrangements at both surface and burial sites in Cuba and on a few Caribbean islands. It's always been my opinion that such an arrangement was well planned, executed in an accurate solstice position in relationship to the compass bearing indicated by the pointers . . . in this case an arrangement of bones. In my opinion, the pointer rib buried here is definitely aligned with the sun's position at the summer solstice. I'm sure when you review the data with a reputable astronomer, you'll find

136

my idea has credibility. The man whose bones we uncovered today was probably laid to rest during a summer solstice ceremony.

"From the time of his burial, contemporary and future tribal storytellers had the responsibility of maintaining the historical record of this person's life. This is the foundation on which primitive legends were based. Stories of his deeds and those of other important people were passed down through the generations to commemorate the talents and deeds of the individuals. These tales of legendary warriors and heroes comforted the Calusa until they were too few in number and too dispersed within their own territory. I'm sure the storytellers had little impact when the surviving small group of the once-powerful Calusa entered their final days as a true bloodline-independent people. Finally, they were forced to abandon their homeland forever."

"I follow and agree with what you say, Jorge. Had their storytellers survived the ages, the Calusa would not be the enigma we strive to comprehend today." Francis then looked skyward and paused.

"Here we are, ignorantly standing in the very center of their former universe! Perhaps the pictographs on the manatee ribs will shed some light on this person.

"Tell me . . . I'd forgotten to ask . . . what, if anything, have you learned about the gold medal Ivy found here?"

"*Ah ha*! There's been so much excitement since I arrived at Punta Rassa, I completely forgot about that. While Ivy was in Havana, I made two castings of the medallion. Incidentally, they turned out very nicely . . . each face casted perfectly. I kept one in my collection and sent the other to Spain, to the General Archives of the Indies in Seville. Actually, I sent it to an old colleague of mine whom you may have met, or at least you may be familiar with his work—Dr. Fabio Herrara. His specialty is early Spanish medalists and the recipients of such commemorative awards. But as you know, overseas mail is slower than a snail. The reply will take considerable time, perhaps many months. In the meantime, we may learn how Ivy's medal got into an ancient Calusa ceramic vessel, and inside a special burial mound, when we sit down long enough to examine the pictographs carved into the manatee ribs and on that pot."

Now back at the edge of the excavation, Francis Corning addressed his team. "Ralph, Warren, Laymond, Ira—you've all done an outstanding job today. Earlier, I agreed to conditions on which Ivy insisted before he would lead us here. Those terms will be honored! All skeletal remains are to remain in this burial. Go ahead and start back-filling the site. We'll let this Calusa gentlemen remain undisturbed; his eternal rest shall not be violated any further by our hands!" Then his thoughts began to sift through the day's events. "*A horse*! How in the hell did a horse get into this Calusa man's grave?"

CHAPTER 12

WITH ALL ABOARD IN A SUBDUED MOOD, THE deck hands tugged the anchor loose from the sandy bottom, and the steamer puffed away from Sanibel Island. As the beach slipped farther a stern, everyone took a silent mental note of the growing void between them and land. The island had enraptured each of them and there was little joy in leaving. They were not eager to return to their real-time lives.

As the boat moved across the slick surface of San Carlos Harbor on gently surging currents, Ivy and Alice stood together in the bow enjoying the fresh, cool, moving air of dusk, as it whispered past. Bound in each other's arms, they talked, and watched the beginning of another spectacular sunset.

"Alice, I'm goin' back down to Key West fer a few days next week. I plan to catch a ride on the next boat leavin' Punta Rassa that's headin' south. When we stopped there on our way to Cuba, I picked up'n application fer a job wit' the Lighthouse Board . . . fer a job at the lighthouse they're gonna start to build soon ov'r on Sanibel. I'll deliver it'n person, 'n' check on Jehu's condition, too. Maybe if he's better, I'll fetch 'im back to Punta Rassa wit' me."

"I didn't know you were seriously thinking about getting out of the cattle business! Why?"

"Don't yuh think I should make more money 'n' settle down after I marry yuh?"

"*Huh*? . . . Marry me? Why, I declare, Ivory Clark! You've never asked me no such thing!"

"Well, I'm askin' yuh now! If I git the job I'm fixin' to apply fer . . . will yuh marry me?"

Alice paused, then suddenly turned away. She wished she had time to think . . . of what to say . . . hoping for some quick privacy. If only she had a moment to compose herself, to fashion an appropriate response. But there really wasn't time. She knew she had to be spontaneous.

Alice turned back to face Ivy with a broad smile and moist sparkling eyes—glistening t ears r evealing h er i nnermost j oy and sincerity. Ivy soon realized she was overwhelmed by his words. He waited.

"Ivy, I love you! I'll marry you whether you get that job or not! As far as I'm concerned, the sooner the better!"

Ivy hadn't thought this far ahead, so he wasn't prepared for her quick positive response. He stuttered, "Wha . . . What'd yuh . . . What'd yuh say?"

"I said, of course I'll marry you! I've loved you so very much, for so very long! As a matter of fact, my mother and father often asked me—for the best part of the past year—when you were going to 'pop the question'? Ha! Do you reckon they were pushing me? Maybe they're afraid I'll end up an old maid! I usually joke by saying I was planning to ask you myself. When I think the time is right! Am I too outspoken? I was raised to be proper, but I really don't know how to react. No one ever asked me to marry him before! I'm right proud I'll be able to tell my folks you actually asked me first! Ha! They may not believe me!"

On sudden impulse, Ivy grabbed Alice low around her waist, just above the full sweep of her hips, and pulled her closer to him. As their moist, partly separated lips met, he shivered with excitement, squeezing her tighter against himself. Before the next kisses, which were improving with experience and passion, he caught his breath and whispered in her ear, "*Oh*, Alice. I've told yuh how much I love yuh . . . since the day I 'rived at Punta Rassa ten yars ago . . . when I first saw yuh prancin' 'round on the cattle docks!"

"I know." She moved her face back a few inches from his but remained firmly in contact with his grasp. She continued, "Please don't think it forward of me, but you know, don't you . . . seriously . . . we can go ahead and get married right away. That is, as soon as we do some planning and whatever else has to be done."

"We wouldn't have no place to live. Later on, if I didn't git the lighthouse job, I'd have to keep workin' fer Mr. Summerlin to support us. That means I'd be off cow huntin' sometimes 'n' I don't believe I want my wife movin' into Mister Jake's bunkhouse! That's fer damn sho!"

"Wait! You're forgetting the empty cottage on Fisherman Key. The one my uncles used to live in when they were piloting out of Punta Rassa. Daddy's kept it up fairly well since they left. With a little work, it would make a cozy home for us to start out in. I'll ask Daddy if we can use it, if you want me to."

"Okay, but I'll ask 'im . . . at the same time I ask 'im fer yer hand'n marriage!"

"I didn't know you were so old-fashioned!"

The next day, right after work, Ivy rowed over to the Johnson place. It was to see Alice, of course, but the real reason was matrimony.

That afternoon, Bob and Ruth Johnson gave Alice and Ivy formal approval to marry. They were pleased their daughter selected Ivy to become her husband. Use of the one-bedroom cottage, the one next door to the house Captain Augustus Wendt rented, was also granted. That is, on one condition. Alice would have to continue helping her parents work the small farm whenever Ivy was at work or away on a cattle drive. The small talk between the four then drifted to wedding plans.

"Ivy's going down to Key West this week," Alice said. She then took a deep breath, paused, swallowed hard, and went on. "I believe I'll go along with him. As far as we're concerned, we can get married down there . . . instead of having to wait weeks for the circuit preacher to show up over at Punta Rassa. I don't want to go upriver to Fort Myers to get married by that old preacher in that little church."

Showing signs of being a little upset, Alice's usually reserved mother spoke up. "Honey, yer father 'n' I prefer yuh have a real weddin' 'n' reception hereabouts than go off way down yonder in that wild town o' Key West!"

"Mama, truth is, I don't want a big grandstand of a wedding! Later on, we can have a reception over here at the cottage, once we make it homey. Or, we can do it at Punta Rassa in Mr. and Mrs. Shultz's place.

"Mr. Summerlin's already told Ivy we can stay at his place on Key West for a few days after we get married. Our honeymoon will be a wedding gift from him. So he told Ivy!"

"Well," Bob Johnson said, "if that's what yuh kids want, it's fine wit' us. Right, Mama?"

"I reckon it'll have to be; their minds 'r' done made up!" Ruth curtly commented. Then she picked up the shuttle and tatting resting on her lap and changed the subject to her plans for dinner.

* * *

The *Everglades Egret* was a shallow-draft coastal steamer that made regularly scheduled trips between Punta Gorda and Key West. It carried mail, freight, crates of fruit and vegetables, and passengers between the small settlements that were popping up along the mangrove coast. The roundabout trip to Key West would take at least five days—or it could take a week, giving the engaged couple more time to plan their future.

At the very last minute, Jake Summerlin decided to send Logan Grace along with them, not to cramp their style, as Alice thought at first, but to secretly carry $10,000 in Cuban gold to deposit in his bank on Key West. Only Logan and Ivy knew about the gold. Alice wasn't too happy when she learned Logan was coming along. She was concerned and asked questions when he and Ivy showed up to board the boat wearing sidearms.

Late on the first night out, before retiring to their separate sleeping quarters, Ivy confided to Alice the real reason why Logan was aboard. After kissing her goodnight, he went topside and looked around for Logan. Ivy thought, "I don't wanna keep any secrets from Alice . . . well, maybe jus' a few, fer the time bein'. What she don't know won't hurt 'er."

Bravely piloted, the *Everglades Egret* didn't stray from the poorly defined channel in the dark. She arrived safely at Chokoloskee Island a few hours before dawn. Chokoloskee is an important gateway into the wild Florida interior. Small rivers in the region meander from the Big Cypress Swamp, at the western fringe of the Everglades, and drain into several large bays. One of these shallow bodies of water surrounds Chokoloskee. The half-dozen families living permanently on Chokoloskee were mostly vegetable and lime farmers. They traded with scattered bands of Miccosukee Indians, who roam this wild country hunting and fishing, and white settlers with homesteads on nearby islands.

At sunup, two rough-looking male passengers prepared to leave the steamboat. They looked preoccupied. They were busy loading supplies, camping gear, and several shotguns into a canvas-covered canoe which had been towed behind the steamer from Punta Gorda.

Logan Grace was wide awake and feeling friendly with the world as a whole. Loudly talkative this morning, he was also curious. He walked to the stern rail, leaned over, and casually greeted the two strangers. "Good mornin'! Say, where're yuh boys headin' wit' all 'em armaments? Ya'll've 'nuff firepower wit' yuh to start a war. I ain't heard nothin' lately 'bout no Indian uprisin'."

"It's none o' yer goddammed business, sonny!" the older of the two men answered bluntly.

Logan hadn't expected so hostile a reply. After all, he hadn't spoken to the man before, nor were his innocent queries out of line. The man's harsh rebuttal had tilted Logan's mood.

"*Son-of-a-bitch*! I'll make it my business now . . . when a couple o' strangers come into my backyard packin' firepower like that. Ya'll done come down here to shoot somethin'! It's likely not

143

deer by the looks o' 'em big shotguns. S'pose yuh could kill't deer nuff wherev'r the hell 'tis ya'll call home! Where's home, boys? Ya'll talk like goddammed Yankees! Yuh boys Yankees?"

The stranger answered again, this time much louder. "Mister, I think yuh'd best mind yer own goddammed business! I've already done told't yuh that! Don't yuh un'erstand plain English?" As these hostile words left his mouth, he noticed the revolver on Logan's hip.

"Why, yuh no 'count son-o'-a-bitch! Yuh've no reason to talk to me that a-way. I only asked yuh a simple damn question!"

Ivy heard the commotion and knew what was coming. Logan was getting aggressive and might fly off the handle any minute. Someone was about to get hurt. So, in an attempt to restore civility, he positioned himself so he could step between them should the need arise. Intentionally interfering, Ivy said, "Yeah, Logan, seems to me these fellas 're sho 'nuff Yankees. That don't give yuh any call to pick on 'em . . . 'r hurt 'em! I 'member what happened to those three bad Yankee boys from Ohio when they pissed yuh off!"

Bewildered, Logan looked at Ivy. "*Huh?*"

The younger of the two men was squatting down in the canoe stowing gear. He finally spoke up. "Mister, we ain't Yankees 'n' we ain't here to cause problems fer yuh people. Actually, Mr. Watson 'n' I 're down here from Lake City to visit wit' an ol' Army buddy o' his. His friend has a place up Turner River, which we un'erstand is a few miles inland from this here Chokoloskee Island. Later, w e plan to do some plume-bird huntin' ' long the coast at some o' the big bird roosts we've heard tell 'bout. To make a lil' extry cash to help pay fer this trip."

"Ya'll're aigrette hunters?" Logan asked, his voice conveying his anger and disgust. "Yuh done come down here to kill 'n' maim birds fer their damn feathers . . . to let their babies starve to death on their nests? I believe ya'll 're either too late 'r a lil' early! Them birds ain't nestin'—they ain't wearin' plumes now. Yuh'd waste 'em poor birds jus' to decorate some high-falutin' city woman's bonnet? I declare! Ya'll must be the original brave great white hunters I've done heard tell 'bout! I ain't ne'er shot anyt'in'

144

I weren't gonna eat! 'Cept a poor 'scuse fer a man once't! Yuh two 'r' totally sorry! Killin' 'em beautiful birds jus' to jerk a few feathers outta 'em. Tonight when I say my prayers, I ain't wishin' nothin' but bad luck on the likes o' yuh two piss aints!"

Sure he was now in control of the confrontation, Logan was unrelenting and continued raving. "I'll add a lil' hex o' my own to strengthen up 'em prayers, too. I hope each o' yuh meets up wit' a giant cottonmouth back 'n' 'em fresh-water creeks 'n' he bites each o' yuh on the cheek o' yer sorry asses! Yuh're sho as hell lucky my ol' buddy ain't here wit' us this mornin'. He wouldn't be as tolerant as me. Jehu Rivers wouldn't stand fer yer foul-mouthed shit . . . would he, Ivy? He'd pull outta few o' yer chicken-shit feathers! Yuh sorry bastards!"

Ed Watson was livid and, like Logan, almost out of control. He approached Logan and stood eye-to-eye and toe-to-toe with him. He shouted in Logan's face at the top of his lungs, "Sonny, my name's Edgar J. Watson . . . *Mister* Watson to the likes o' yuh, yuh skinny, long-haired squirt! Don't ev'r forget my name! After I visit my ol' friend up Turner River 'n' shoot all the goddammed plume birds I wanna, I'm headed down south o' here to a place called Chatham Bend. I 'spect to take title to that place this trip 'r next 'n' move down there to homestead 'fore too much longer. Next time yuh git nosy, 'r wanna shoot off yer mouth, 'r show off fer yer friends, 'r feel a lil' suicidal—c'mon down yonder 'n' visit me on the Chatham River. I'll put a genuine hexin' on yer sorry hide 'n' nobody'll ev'r find a trace o' yer goddammed bones!"

Logan was about to cross the line. His fists were tightly clenched and he was on the verge of belting Ed Watson in the mouth. Instead he snarled, pivoted on his heels, and stomped away toward the other end of the boat. The confrontation was over and done with, but one of the adversaries was a grudge-keeper and would never forget the incident. He hoped that one day Logan would wander into his domain. No one in the island country knew it, but Logan Grace was indeed lucky—again! He had turned his back on a dangerous man and walked away unscathed. Others had tried to escape Watson's hellish wrath, but rumors would then spread of how they quickly died when an unexpected bullet or blade penetrated their backs.

* * *

The remainder of the trip was uneventful. Logan stayed by himself, sulking and in a bad mood most of the time. His rage seemed endless because of the way the trip had started. The steamer stopped at two more settlements in the green mangrove myriad of the Ten Thousand Islands, and at three more in the chain-like string of islands known as the Florida Keys before it finally reached the Monroe County seat at Key West.

On board the *Everglades Egret*, Ivy and Alice sat and talked for hours or worked as a team on Ivy's application for employment with the Lighthouse Board's seventh district headquartered in Key West. The stops gave them the opportunity to leave the boat for short walks. Whenever they found themselves out of sight from the other passengers and intimately secluded, they practiced improving their new-found romantic skills.

Although he had no personal knowledge about lighthouse operations, Ivy definitely had a few pluses on his side to help him qualify for the job. He was young enough to learn the responsibilities as well as the peculiarities of the position. Lighthouse keeping was a poorly compensated but greatly admired profession, and lighthouse keepers took their work very seriously. Ivy also had local knowledge of the Sanibel Island area, an advantage the selecting official would certainly consider when reviewing his application.

Ivy was applying for the assistant lightkeeper's job. Duties would include maintenance of the structures to be built at the new station, including the light tower. He was experienced in maintaining buildings and small boats. Alice was quick to pick up on these kinds of work experiences and encouraged Ivy to write concise narrative statements that described similar duties he had been assigned during his years with the Summerlin Cattle Company.

* * *

At Key West, after the gold was safely stored inside the bank's giant vault, Logan went on alone to the Summerlin place. Still in a disgruntled mood, he was anxious to check on Jehu.

Now on their own, Ivy and Alice stopped at the Lighthouse Board's district office. Ivy handed the completed application to the same friendly clerk he had met on his last visit. He learned the closing date for applications wouldn't be until the first day of December, which was still several weeks away. The clerk let on that there weren't many applicants, and no applicant was already a keeper who wanted to transfer. Once again, the bad reputation of remote Sanibel Island and its mosquitoes had reached the ranks of the U. S. Lighthouse S ervice. The final s election w as e xpected next year, by March 1, 1884, when construction of the light station was supposed to start. All Ivy could do now was wait.

Getting directions from the office clerk, Ivy and Alice carried their luggage to Jake Summerlin's cottage. This was quite a "cottage." Built on tall pilings, the large, white-clapboard, metal-roofed house was surrounded by a wide veranda. After they climbed the broad stairs, Ivy knocked on the door.

Before long, a heavy-set, late middle-aged, coal-black-skinned woman came to the door and exclaimed, "Howdy, young-uns! Ya'll mus' be Mars'er Ivy 'n' Miss Alice! I's Ruby. Mars'er Jake dun sent me a letter . . . I c'n sho 'nuff read 'n' cipher sum! He tol't me ya'll'd be chere this week. I's dun got 'is be'room ready fo' ya'll ta use. Once't ya'll git married dat is! Ya'll cain't sleep t'gether 'til yo's hitched! I's dun got de word! Dere ain't gonna be no foolishness 'round chere! No, suh! Mars'er Jake'd ship Ruby back ta Georgy!"

Both were embarrassed by the maid's remarks. Ivy blushed, squeezed Alice's hand, and said, "Yes, ma'am!" After composing himself h e asked, "Scuse me, m a'am, ' re my friends here?"

"Why, dey's out on de po'ch havin' a pi'cher o' my fresh-squeezed key lime juice I dun mixed up 'n' took 'em a while 'go. Dey's 'spectin' ya'll ta join 'em soon's ya'll git chere!"

Ruby turned to lead them to their friends, but she hesitated and spun completely around, looked at Ivy, and asked, "Tell me,

147

suh, how's Mars'er Jake's color't man, Jeff Bowton, doin' dese days? He dun stopp't comin' down chere ta see me sum time 'go. He wuz sho 'nuff a cutt'r yars 'go! Tell 'im fo' me dat 'is Georgy peach axed 'bout 'im 'n' I miss jukin' wit' 'im like we usta when we wuz boff young . . . 'n' he wuz sum kinda stud! Ha! Give 'im a big hug fo' ol' Ruby!"

"Why, Jeff's doin' jus' fine, Miss Ruby, though age'is catchin' up wit' 'im. He's yet on Mister Jake's payroll. I'll sho 'nuff tell 'im that yuh was askin' 'bout 'im, but I don't know 'bout givin' 'im that *hug*!"

As he sipped his glass of limeade, Jehu told the group he seemed to be recovering from his gunshot wound "slow but sho." The doctor or nurse still visited once a day to clean and redress the wound. "It don't look like I'll be goin' back to Punta Rassa with ya'll this trip," he told his concerned friends, who were all seated with him around the oval porch table.

"Why?" Alice asked.

"*Ah* . . . complications." Jehu said, but offered no further explanation.

"What kinda complications?" Logan asked in a concerned tone. "Yer shoulder's not infected . . . is it?"

"*Ah* . . . nope. *Ah* . . . I'll tell yuh boys the details lat'r."

Alice detected from the drift that her presence was no longer wanted at the table. From here out would be pure man talk anyway. She was used to leaving the room whenever men began to stammer and act strange. She did so many times while growing up on Fisherman Key, whenever her father's friends visited and their conversation became focused and serious.

Earlier, Ruby had invited Alice to tour the large house. She would take Ruby up on the offer now. Sometimes, such things as withdrawing when you aren't wanted just naturally fits into place.

"What'n the hell's wrong wit' yuh?" Ivy followed up in a loud whisper once Alice had made her excuse and left the porch.

Very quietly, haltingly Jehu answered, "Boys, I don't want what I'm 'bout to tell ya'll goin' any farther 'n the three o' us! Yuh both hear? An', if ya'll don't 'cept what I'm sayin' 'n' promise not to tell anyone, I'm clammin' up!"

Logan replied first, "Sho 'nuff, Jay. Okay, Ivy?" Ivy nodded in agreement and Logan anxiously continued, "Now, what the hell's the matter wit' yuh?"

"I don't rightly know how to tell ya'll this? I've worried myself sick 'bout havin' to do this, 'n' had to eat some humble pie! Well, it seems . . . 'cordin' to Dr. Rand . . . I've got a really bad dose o' the goddammed clap!"

"*The clap!*" Logan blurted, much louder than he intended. Then more quietly, "How the hell'd yuh git the clap . . . shot up like that 'n' all? Yuh done been sneakin' out 'n' whorin' here in Key West wit' that bum shoulder? Hot damn! Yuh're a hell o' a lot tuffer 'n I thought yuh was, ol' buddy!"

"Tuff, hell! Yuh 'r any oth'r fool should know I caught it in Cuba! It was that goddammed dirty whore Juanita that give it to me! I'd like to git my hands on 'er! I'd flat kill 'er! The sorry no 'count bitch!"

Logan and Ivy were stunned. They looked at each other in total disbelief, speechless. After a few minutes, each thinking of how he should respond to the news, Ivy asked, "How do yuh know when yuh've got the clap? I don't really know too much 'bout these kind o' t'ings?"

"It started out wit' the inside o' my peter burnin' like fire! Felt like a hundred piss aints bit me inside it whenev'r I took a leak. Then it got so bad . . . I'm swelled up inside, I reckon . . . I flat couldn't pass water. That's when I panicked 'n' sent Miss Ruby fer my doctor. He put a long tube up my hossywhop so I could piss! Right now it hurts worse 'n the damn bullet hole.

"The doctor said he can cure me, but it's gonna take a while yet. From what lil' bits 'n' pieces he's done tol't me, it damn sho won't be much fun neither! So, I reckon I'm stuck here 'n Key West 'til he gits me cured.

"*Pleeease* . . . please don't tell Mister Jake! The doctor says he won't tell 'im. I'd kill that clappy bitch if I could git my hands on 'er! Right here! Right now! Like Mister Jake always says, 'I'm as goddammed serious as a stampede!'"

Ivy swallowed, looked over at Logan, who nodded to him affirmatively, then said, "Yuh've been through hell, that's fer damn sho! An', there's somethin' yuh should know 'bout right now! It cain't wait no longer! Logan 'n' I've been waitin' 'til it was the right time to tell yuh. We didn't tell yuh earlier, 'cause at the time yuh were shot up pretty damn bad 'n' we didn't wanna upset yuh. We both thought it best if we'd save all the details 'til yuh got better. Yuh know don't yuh, neither o' us were sho yuh were gonna pull through this 'r not . . .?"

"What the hell're yuh tryin' to tell me? Spit it out! I ain't in no mood fer yer damn games!"

"Jehu! Shut up! Yuh don't ev'r have to upset yerself 'r worry 'bout gettin' revenge on Juanita 'gain! Now, hush up 'n' listen like I asked yuh!" Logan said in a low but clearly angry tone. He spoke slowly because he wanted Jehu to understand each word. Logan didn't want to repeat himself.

Jehu responded in rage, his eyes squinting and exuding malevolence. "What the hell're yuh talkin' 'bout? I'm tellin' ya'll, when I'm healed I'll catch a cowboat that's headed down to Havana 'n' find 'er! I 'll cut 'er goddammed dirty whore o' a throat fer puttin' me through this misery!"

"Jehu! Listen close! I'm fixin' to tell yuh this only once't, 'n' Ivy ain't ev'r gonna talk much 'bout it no more!"

"Go 'head. I'm listenin'."

"Ivy's already done kill't Juanita!"

"What the hell'd yuh jus' say?"

"Goddammit, I said fer yuh to listen close. Be quiet 'til I finish! Juanita was in wit' that pack o' bastards that tried to rob us in Cuba. She was the rider that came up from behind the wagon. Ivy blew 'er head off! He kill't 'er dead 'n' sent 'er to hell wit' one shot!"

"*God-a-mighty*! *Lord Jesus*! I've thought a lotta 'bout that run-in lately. It was prob'ly my big rummy mouth that give it all 'way 'n' led 'em sorry bastards to us. Boys, I'm truly sorry, but I got shit-faced drunk when I was wit' 'er 'n' must've talked too much. I'm sho glad neither o' yuh boys, 'r Ed Filip, was hurt . . . 'r wors't, died on my 'count. I reckon me gittin' hit, now this dose

150

o' clap, was all my own doin'. Damn! Yuh both must know how sorry I am. I hope there's room in ya'll's hearts to forgive me."

"Yeah, we know, Jay. We already have. I reckon what's done's done 'n' we'll all have to live wit' what happened. Fer me . . . I'm gonna try my best 'n' forgit it ev'r happened. Now, tell me somethin'?" Ivy asked.

"What's that?"

Logan broke in, "Where do yuh hide the rum 'n' whiskey 'round here? I'm parched, 'n' we've got a weddin' comin' up we have to he'p celebrate!"

CHAPTER 13

WITH LOGAN GRACE AS BEST MAN, IVY AND ALICE were married in a simple civil ceremony at the Monroe County Courthouse. Following the nuptials, Logan said his good-byes and booked passage aboard the next Punta Rassa-bound steamer.

Following a three-day honeymoon at the Summerlin cottage, Mr. and Mrs. Ivory Clark returned home to begin their lives together on Fisherman Key. Ivy was soon back in his routine: working six days a week for the Summerlin Cattle Company. Long workdays at Punta Rassa, occasional lengthy horseback rides with Logan into the interior of Florida, and slow cattle drives back to the port kept him busy. Alice wasn't fond of the times her husband was away from her and their bed. But she knew from the beginning that when their relationship became serious, this would be their lifestyle until a better career opportunity for Ivy came along.

In late February 1884, the residents and workers around Punta Rassa sensed progress in the air. The port's telegraph office received advance notification, in the form of a cable from Key West, that the contractor selected to build the new Sanibel Island Light Station was gearing up to begin work. The Lighthouse

Board's district engineer and the contractor's representative would arrive late in the month to begin layout and construction. Soon, several carpenters and laborers from Punta Rassa and Fort Myers were hired. The contractor explained to the construction crew that the project would last about five months.

At first, Ivy considered applying for a job on the building project. In the end, he decided that when near his home, he'd rather sleep in his own bed. Otherwise he would have to stay on board the cramped worker's barge resting at anchor on the Bay side of Sanibel Island. He'd be stuck three miles away from his house and Alice for nearly a week at a time. Ivy appreciated all the benefits of his marriage.

When the castings and other foundry work were completed, the wrought-iron components of the light tower were shipped from New Jersey to Key West. The prefabricated collection of parts would remain there aboard ship until the contractor was ready for their delivery to Sanibel Island. When assembled, they would become a pyramidal skeletal structure rising some 112 feet above sea level. After the concrete foundation was poured and sufficiently aged to support the heavy structure, the wrought-iron parts were scheduled for shipment to Sanibel Island for assembly. A team of ironworkers, specialists in such dangerous elevated work, would erect the tower.

By late April, the complete inventory of lighthouse parts left Key West aboard a schooner. Halfway between Key West and Sanibel Island, the boat was struck by a violent early tropical storm plowing northward out of the Caribbean. Very quickly, the surface of the Gulf of Mexico turned savage and perilous. By the hour, the storm's ferocity mounted. Unknown to the seamen, its unrelenting fury would rage around them for days as it moved slowly northward through the Gulf. The captain of the heavily laden vessel was determined to remain on schedule and reach protection inside San Carlos Harbor in the lee of Sanibel Island. So the sailboat continued toward its destination.

As usual the Punta Rassa pilot boat operator, Captain Gus Wendt, rose before dawn and was standing at his telescope on the porch of his Fisherman Key cottage. His cup of fresh-brewed coffee helped him fight off the cool, gusty wind that had arrived during the night. Gus dutifully scanned the dark watery horizon between Point Ybel and the barrier islands across the broad opening into the Bay. Through the wind-driven salt mist, he made out the shape of a large sailing vessel far offshore. After observing the boat for a few minutes, he assumed the vessel was tacking toward the port's entrance channel.

Gus and Ivy made it across the Caloosahatchee to Punta Rassa in record time, thanks to the powerful wind generated by the rising storm. Charlie Clark was waiting for them at the berth of the sailing sloop named *Punta Rassa Pilot*.

"She's still too far at sea! I can't see any lights or daymarks to tell me she's requesting a pilot," Gus reported to Charlie, who was watching the schooner's progress though his hand-held telescope. "I don't believe they've reached the sea buoy anchorage. They're still underway, so they're not displaying any signals yet."

Charlie then offered, "I reckon if yuh're up to it, we can head out 'n' meet up wit' 'em. That'll save a lil' time! That must be the freight schooner that's carryin' the parts fer the lighthouse. Logan gotta cable that was sent to Mister Jake a few days 'go notifyin' the port that they'd be arrivin' in the harbor. What do yuh think? Is it too ruff out there fer yer boat?"

"Nope!" Gus replied. "With this wind, I think we have a clear shot and can get there and back quick enough. I'm ready if you are!"

Once they cleared the lee of Sanibel Island, the two men were at the full mercy of the wind and ocean swells. The waves were mountainous by Gulf of Mexico standards, but the experienced seamen continued undaunted. They met the wind-whipped swells diagonally. Gusts of wind vaporized the breaking crests, further reducing visibility as the dawn broke.

"I believe she's tackin' back to the nor'east," Charlie yelled above the fury of the 40-knot wind. He was unable to hold his telescope steady enough for a good look. As each cresting, mountainous swell passed beneath the sloop's hurtling hull, the stem dug deeply into the wall of water presented by the next and the next. Wave after wave of foaming water flowed over the bow and cabin and cascaded into the cockpit, swamping it and drenching both men before draining out through the scuppers.

Charlie yelled again, "Let's try to intercept 'er when she comes 'bout to tack. It's gonna take a while to bring 'er inside in this weather. I don't know why'n the hell the skipper didn't turn back to Key West 'r the Tortugas when he hit this stuff? He must be 'n experienced blue-water cap'n 'r don't know how to read a barometer!"

"Or he's crazy as hell!" Gus added. "This wind's too strong! I have to drop the jib and reef the main. Take the tiller and bring her into the wind for me, will you, Charlie?"

With wet, cold-numbed fingers, Gus buckled a strong leather harness around his chest and wrapped the free end of its connected heavy lifeline to a stout cleat on the sailboat's gunwale. Then he crouched down to the deck. On hands and knees, he slowly crawled forward to grab and retrieve the jib. The loosened sail blew over the port side with the sheets still attached. Hand over hand, Gus hauled the soaking wet triangular sail aboard. After securing it, the elderly mariner stood, braced himself against the wind, and reefed the mainsail to reduce the amount of sail exposed to the wind. This slowed the boat by slipping more of the heavy air, improving the boat's control. Still, the distance between the two sailing vessels closed fast.

Back at the tiller, Gus Wendt was about to call on all the foul-weather skills he had. He shouted over the wind, "I'll come along side her first—my port to her starboard—so you can talk to them . . . if anyone can hear us above this damn wind!"

"Okay!" Charlie shouted. He reached for the bullhorn mounted on the cabin bulkhead.

"Ahoy, the schooner!" his voice boomed. "I'm the harbor pilot! Permission to come 'board on yer lee side?"

Soon, a tall, stooped-over man fought his way across the schooner's deck, leaning into the wind and sea spray. Finally he grabbed the railing and put his horn to his mouth. "Hello, pilot boat!" His high-pitched voice was barely audible over the din of waves crashing against the wooden hull and the wind screaming through the rigging of both boats. Catching his breath, he continued, "I'm the skipper of this vessel . . . the *Martha M. Heath*. Be advised, sir, that I haven't requested the assistance of a pilot. Since my destination is not Port Punta Rassa, I decline your services to bring her into San Carlos Harbor!"

Astonished at this response, Charlie paused, then shouted back, "Aye, sir! Have yuh someone 'board wit' local knowledge o' the channel yuh're 'bout to enter?"

With a heavy New York City accent the schooner's skipper yelled back through the horn, "No, sir. I have charts. I'm transporting property of the United States Government—bound for Sanibel Island. The Federal Government is self-insured. My company's lawyers insist because of that, and other provisions of the shipping contract, we're not required to obtain your services. I'll bring her to the anchorage in the harbor myself!"

Charlie glanced at Gus and shrugged his shoulders. Again, turning to the schooner, he yelled through his bullhorn, "Very well, Cap'n. We'll record in our logs that yuh declined the services o' the Punta Rassa harbor pilot. I wish yuh 'n' yer crew well in this weath'r, sir!"

He nodded to Gus and instantly ducked to avoid the swinging boom of the mainsail as Gus came about, ready for the rough return to the safety of less violent waters.

As the vessels parted, the schooner continued her tack to the west. It was the captain's intention to come about far enough offshore that he could tack to a position off Bowditch Point, then make one final tack to reach the protected waters behind Sanibel Island's Point Ybel.

Charlie and Gus watched in awe as the schooner continued offshore on a westerly course. "I believe the schooner's in peril ov'r that bottom," Charlie observed. "'Cause o' 'er draft, she'll ground once't she comes 'bout 'n' begins 'er tack. What do yuh think?"

"I believe you're absolutely right," Gus replied and pointed his sloop more to windward. He wanted to slow their progress to watch possible events unfold.

With her reefed sails violently luffing, the schooner came about well south of Sanibel Island. The helmsman began a broad reach toward the northern tip of B owditch P oint. Had visibility been c lear a nd t he s ea h eight n ormal, t he b oat's lookouts or the helmsman would have seen the extensive shoal. It was only a few feet beneath her keel as they turned and committed to a northeasterly heading. As the schooner raced along, the water was getting shallower fast.

Suddenly, the *Martha M. Heath* struck the shoal with a thunderous, splintering *thud*! Her keel bounced along the bottom as successive broadside swells pushed the 207-ton schooner higher onto the submerged sandbar. In minutes, the schooner foundered and broached. She was very close to capsizing.

The several impacts dislodged the cargo stored on deck. Broken l oose f rom t heir f asteners, i ron l ighthouse p arts t umbled across the listing deck and fell overboard. Still erratically pitching and twisting, the grounded schooner then struck the metal parts heaped beneath it on the bottom. With great, aching groans, the wooden planking cracked, the vessel took on water, and the hull started to fall apart. Still more of the cargo spilled from the swamped holds into the turbulent water.

Gus had turned the pilot boat and was making good speed toward the foundering schooner. He and Charlie offered assistance to the seamen scurrying on the deck frantically trying to release and lower their two lifeboats. The *Martha M. Heath* was breaking up right before their eyes.

Gus grabbed the bullhorn. "Cap'n! Rig a buoy just in case your vessel breaks up completely . . . so your cargo can be found and salvaged! We'll take a few of you back with us and send out a larger boat for those we can't."

The schooner captain yelled back through his bullhorn, "Thank you! Come alongside. Please take as many of my men with you as you can. Once we launch and board our lifeboats, the rest of us will wait for the boat you'll send out to us. Thank you, sir! I believe you're right! I'm afraid my boat's going to break up completely!"

Gus answered as loud as he could, "If there's not a boat and crew at Punta Rassa brave enough to come out after you, I'll come back after you myself!" He knew he would have to keep his word.

As Gus brought his pilot boat within inches of the vessel's hull, five crewmembers and finally the first mate of the foundering schooner leaped from the foaming water-covered deck and onto the gunwale and bow of the pilot boat. The first mate barely landed upright on the rain-slick deck. He grabbed the tall rail to keep from falling over the side.

"Jack!" The captain yelled. "As soon as you're able, send a telegram to the chief engineer in Key West! So he can send a salvage team up here. Better tell him to send a tender and a crane barge . . . and a diver too! I'll notify our office after I get ashore."

"Aye, sir!" the first mate yelled back. The gap between the two men widened as the sloop began to tack away.

On the way to Punta Rassa, safely in the lee of Sanibel Island, Charlie Clark silently reflected on what just happened. "Cap'n, I wouldn't wanna walk in yer shoes!" He felt a sudden twinge of sadness for the stubborn skipper and his lost boat. Unfortunately, the maritime gossip grapevine—his reputation of losing a boat after refusing the legitimate service of a harbor pilot—would haunt the man for the rest of his career.

Two lighthouse tenders, one towing an enormous barge with a hard-hat diver aboard, arrived on the scene four days after the accident to begin salvage operations. Despite the continuing rough weather, the tenders anchored as close as they could to the wreck. The more powerful of the two steamships pushed the barge over the sandbar as close as possible to the sunken cargo to get the crane in operating range.

By the time the heavy weather subsided, most parts of the light tower had been lifted off the sandy bottom and formed a pile of disarrayed metal on the barge. At the end of the salvage operation, most parts were accounted for, except for two or three of the smallest fittings for the lower gallery rail. The salvaged parts arrived at their destination a little late, saltwater-soaked, but close enough to schedule that the delay didn't hinder the project.

As the light station construction proceeded, the people of Punta Rassa carefully followed its progress with interest. The two white, clapboard-sided keeper's quarters and the partially completed light tower were clearly visible across the harbor. The excitement over the unfortunate demise of the *Martha M. Heath* was soon forgotten and life on both sides of San Carlos Harbor returned to normal.

In mid-May, Jacob Summerlin returned to Punta Rassa by boat from Tampa following a lengthy trip north. Now back at work, he and his foreman, Logan Grace, were watching as Ivy Clark and two other cowboys loaded a small herd of Cuba-bound cows onto a steamer. As they watched, all Jake Summerlin could do was complain this morning. He raved about the declining price of beef, the oppressive heat and humidity, the absence of rain, and the comfortable cool weather he had been forced to leave behind in the northeast.

Suddenly changing the subject, Jake said, "I've been meanin' to ask yuh . . . the skipper o' the lil' freighter that carried yuh 'n' Ivy down to Key West tol't me that yuh'd some kinda run-in wit' 'noth'r passenger. What was that all 'bout?"

Nervously, carefully picking his words, Logan replied, "I was tryin' to make friendly small talk wit' a man who turned out to be 'un surly son-o'-a-bitch. From the very start, he got on 'is high horse wit' me! It weren't my fault at all! I swear, Mister Jake!"

"Whoa, son! I ain't fixin' to chew yuh out! Did yuh ev'r find out who he was?"

"Yes, sir. I believe he called hisself Edgar . . . Edgar Watson."

"*Ed Watson*! From north Florida . . . 'round Lake City?"

"Yes, sir! I believe that's where 'is sidekick said they hailed from. Yuh knowed the man?"

"Yeah, I sho 'nuff do. Last I heard he was out west, in Arkansas 'r the Indian Territory. I met 'im once't 'r twice't through the years. He's a small-time cow hunt'r who usta gath'r 'n' drive lil' herds to the commercial docks at Tampa fer shippin'. He don't like me! I ain't ev'r taken his bullshit seriously, so he ain't ne'er brought no herd down to Punta Rassa. Yuh were right, Logan, he's sho 'nuff no 'count . . . mean as a damn croc-a-gator! Yuh're lucky he didn't shoot yuh to start off wit', 'r slip up behind yuh later 'n' stick a knife in yer back! What the Sam Hill was Ed Watson doin' down in Chokoloskee country?"

"He tol't me he's fixin' to buy a place down south o' Chokoloskee on the Chatham River."

"He's a land baron now, *huh*? 'Em folks down yonder'll regret the day Watson becomes their neighbor! I'm as serious as a goddammed stampede!"

In a perplexed tone, Logan shyly asked his mentor, "Mister Jake, what's a croc-a-gator?"

"Yuh're Florida borned 'n' raised 'n' yuh ain't ne'er heard o' a croc-a-gator 'fore now, boy? I declare!"

"No, sir . . . I ain't."

"Why, son, it's a alligator at 'un end 'n' a crocodile on the oth'r! They's mean as hell! Yuh knowed what makes 'em so damn mean don't yuh?"

Now completely puzzled, Logan thought for a minute or two, hesitated, then replied, "No, sir."

"Hee ha! Hee ha! A croc-a-gator's so mean 'cause he ain't got no bunghole . . . he cain't shit! Hee ha!"

The conversation probably would have degraded further had Jake not noticed Jeff Bowton, Punta Rassa's only black man, headed for the cattle loading gates, hobbling faster than usual. Barely within range for his crackling voice to reach, Jeff yelled, "Mauser Ivy! Mauser Ivy! I's gat a tel'gram chere fo' yo'. It dun 'rived jus'a minit 'go!"

Trotting over to meet him, Ivy reached down from his horse, Cracker, and took the yellow paper with its hand-written telegraph message from the weathered old black hand of the messenger, whom Ivy respected. "Thanks, Jeff. Come 'round lat'r to the back door o' Shultz's place. Let 'em know yuh're there 'n' I'll buy yuh a drink this ev'nin' after work!"

Jeff's eyes gleamed with anticipation. "Yes, suh, Mauser Ivy!" He'd happily be there, even though he always had to go to the back door.

Jake and Logan walked over to Ivy and Jake asked, "Anyt'in' wrong, son?"

"No, sir. It's from Dr. Corning. He's that Yankee archeologist . . . the Indian expert who was here a few months back. He says that 'im 'n' his friend, Dr. Gomez, from Cuba'll be comin' to Punta Rassa 'round the first o' next month. They wanna meet wit' me 'gain. Says here they've some interestin' news on that buried Indian stuff I found ov'r on Sanib'l."

* * *

The two archaeologists arrived at Punta Rassa from two different directions and two days apart. By the time Drs. Francis Corning and Jorge Gomez landed at the port, Ivy was away working elsewhere. Since he didn't know the exact day the scientists were arriving, life in the cattle business went on as usual. Logan had sent I vy to w ork a small h erd o f Summerlin cattle awaiting shipment. They were grazing in the natural pastures a few miles away near the Caloosahatchee settlement known as Iona. He and two other cowboys worked a three-day rotating shift with the herd, and then another trio of drovers replaced them. However, if there was room for the cattle in the Punta Rassa pens, the cows were herded toward the port.

This worked out to the liking of the two old academic friends. It gave them time to compare their notes, share individual findings, and argue preliminary theories about Ivy's Calusa-related discoveries before sharing the information with him, as each had independently promised. Perhaps more importantly, they would have at least a day of free time to do some sport fishing with Gus Wendt in the little-fished rich waters of San Carlos Harbor and Pine Island Sound.

Ivy rode into Punta Rassa at dusk. He was exhausted but happy to learn both scientists had arrived. He had worked overtime, so Logan agreed he could have a few days off to spend with the two archaeologists.

Ivy made his excuses soon after he found the professors at the Shultz Hotel. After brief cordial greetings, he explained, "I'm tired 'n' dirty, ya'll. I haven't been home fer a few days 'n' I believe I'd best spend a night wit' my wife if I'm to be free to spend some time wit' ya'll. Okay? Ya'll un'erstand?"

Francis Corning grinned and nodded in agreement. "That's fine. We can begin tomorrow morning. Is that all right with you, Jorge?"

"Yes, that's fine with me."

Ivy rose from the table to leave. "Okay then, I'll see ya'll 'round firs' light tomorrow, here at the hotel."

As Ivy turned to walk away, Francis Corning added, "Ivy, please bring along the pot tomorrow . . . with all the artifacts you found inside it. I have the photographs and drawings of them, but it will be advantageous if we can closely examine the actual objects you discovered . . . to help Jorge and I validate our interpretations."

"*Huh? Oh,* yeah! I sho will, Doctor. I'll see ya'll in the mornin'. Good night!"

It was well after sundown and Ivy had missed his usual ride home to Fisherman Key with Gus Wendt. Despite his weariness, he rowed one of the port's skiffs across as fast as he could. As he drew closer, the boat sliding quietly over the surface of the Caloosahatchee, he saw Alice sitting on the dock next to a bright kerosene lantern. She was waiting for her husband with anticipation. She didn't like to be separated from him at all.

* * *

Ivy and the two scientists met early the next morning over a steaming pot of fresh-brewed coffee in the cozy dining room of the Shultz Hotel. They began with casual topics, such as fishing and cow stories and the progress of the Sanibel Island Lighthouse. The latter brought the purpose of their get-together to the fore, the subject's commonality connecting these three men.

Because of the construction activity a few miles across the harbor, Francis Corning voiced his concern about the future integrity of Ivy's discovery site. "Have you been over to the island to see if the work crews have damaged the site where you discovered the artifacts? Is it gone . . . leveled?"

"No, sir. They've built some good-sized wharves on each side o' the point 'n' cleared some land fer the buildin's 'n' lighthouse, but ev'r't'in' else's been left pretty much alone. I think it'll be okay. I don't believe anyone ov'r there knows anyt'in' 'bout it!"

"That's a very good point," Jorge Gomez added.

"Well, I've been waitin' to learn what all these t'ings 'ar', what they mean," Ivy began. "I reckon ya'll have some answers, 'cause yuh wouldn't've traveled all this way if yuh didn't? I'm much o bliged that yuh've come so far jus' to tell me 'bout this stuff." Ivy then reached into his pocket, withdrew his good luck piece, and snapped it down loudly on the table next to his other prized discoveries he had already taken out of the pot. "Let's not forgit this piece! It's sho 'nuff brought me good luck . . . some of which I don't wanna talk 'bout."

Jorge Gomez, the visiting Cuban archaeologist, picked up the medal and began to finger it. Just barely audible, he muttered, "*Aha*! This is an intriguing piece of history. Let's discuss the other items first . . . I like to save the best for last! Ha!"

"Okay. First, the pot itself," Francis Corning began. "After I got home to Philadelpia I sent copies of the drawing and photographs to experts, including leading archaeologists in England and even as far away as Egypt. All who reviewed them agreed that not only is the pot exquisitely made, it is far superior to any known Calusa ceramic vessel. The pictographs around its outer circumference were rendered by . . . well, a super-talented individual. It's unlike any known Native American work of art. It's extremely detailed, much superior to the art of the Central American Mayans."

The archaeologist peered over the top of his reading glasses as he continued speaking in a serious tone. "Furthermore, we believe the art is autobiographical and identifies important events in the life of the artist. In the known Calusa culture, we are sure that pottery was created customarily by the women, and was very primitive, to say the least. However, the intricate detail and the color pigments used in your piece are unknown in Calusa pottery-making. Its origin is also baffling because some kind of polishing or glazing process was incorporated in its manufacture. The opinion expressed by researchers who've examined the paintings and photographs give overwhelming credence to the notion that this pot was made by a man, not a woman . . . very likely the same man who rests for eternity in the burial site which harbored your discoveries safely through the centuries. Ivy, this container is in itself a priceless example of primitive Native American art!"

"I totally agree with Francis, Ivy," Jorge Gomez excitedly added, as he butted in. "I'll remain forever awed by the beautiful form, relief renditions, and glazing of this piece."

Ivy leaned back in his chair, raised his arm to signal an interruption, and said, "Excuse me, Dr. Gomez," Ivy interrupted. "Ya'll're tellin' me the pot yuh're holdin' is one o' a kind?"

"That's correct. Nothing like this has ever been found in a prehistoric site in this hemisphere! It's priceless!"

Francis Corning resumed leading the discussion. "Before we talk about the details of the pot, let's finish discussing the things Ivy found inside it."

"Fine, go on."

"These beads are trade beads brought to this part of the world by the Spanish. Before the introduction of glass beads, the Calusa adorned themselves with necklaces, bracelets, and even earrings made from bone and seashells. The two tiger shark teeth are very similar in size to those that were set into the saber we found in the grave. The two teeth were very special, probably worn as jewelry by this Calusan.

"The two projectile points are very interesting. The larger, the stone point, is made from chert. Chert occurs in limestone deposits as far south as the northern parts of Florida. I'd say the man who originally owned these artifacts made this point. It's an example of the finest of the arrowhead maker's craft. The metal arrow-like point was also handmade, but with a forge and anvil by a more modern craftsman—a European blacksmith. This point is known as a quarrel; it tipped the business end of a bolt. A bolt is a small, stout arrow propelled by a crossbow. Crossbows were Spanish military weapons in wide use at the time of contact. They were standard issue before reliable firearms were perfected and universally distributed. I'd guess our Calusa artist acquired this point after the material from which it's made intrigued him."

Dr. Corning stopped talking and cleared his throat before he picked up and scrutinized the next item. After a moment of silent but obvious admiration for what he was holding, he continued. "This knife blade is made from volcanic glass-like stone called obsidian. This particular type is known as lace obsidian. If I hold it up to the light you can see lace-like lines in it. . . . look!" As Francis held the dagger toward them he twisted his wrist to move the blade around to backlight it. Ivy and Jorge moved closer to see the unique translucency and internal pattern of the black stone. "Until now, obsidian was unknown from other aboriginal sites in Florida. The nearest source of lace obsidian is across the Gulf of Mexico in the Yucatan. Your discovery—this, and the atlatl we uncovered—suggests some connection between here and there."

Francis Corning took a minute to again admire the black blade, then continued. "*Ah*, next is the knife's handle, the figurine that resembles . . . both feline . . . cat . . . and human features. Remember? We found an almost duplicate carving at the burial site on Sanibel Island, although it was not as well preserved as this one. In years past, both Jorge and I have examined what we believe were exact copies of this carving from several Calusa sites in Florida. Again, they weren't as well preserved or detailed as yours. Unfortunately, all were in a state of advanced decay and couldn't be preserved. Yours is most remarkable! We assume that all were carved by the masterful hand of the same man."

Ivy admired the kneeling hardwood figure with its catlike face. He wanted to know more and asked, "What's this carvin' made from, 'n' what was it? Do ya'll have any ideas?"

Jorge Gomez answered. "In the past it was difficult to determine the type of wood used in the similar carvings because the wood fibers were too spongy. Through the centuries, and because of direct burial, exposure to dampness, and insects, they quickly disintegrated. This particular carving was well-preserved, according to the experts I consulted with, because the wood from which it was made had absorbed a volume of sodium chloride: salt from seawater. I've talked to several tropical botanists and showed them photographs of this carving. Most are of the opinion that the wood is buttonwood . . . genus *Conocarpus*. This is a hardwood tree growing here in the coastal wetlands. In today's world, I'm told, it's harvested and rendered into commercial charcoal."

Ivy responded, "*Oh*, yeah! I know a few people who cut buttonwood fer a livin'. They pile it up tight in cone-shaped stacks, cover it wit' sand, 'n' burn it down into a lil' bit o' charcoal. It's a helluva lotta work! The tree's purty common on the islands in these parts. It grows outta the salt wat'r, high'r up on the land'n the real mangrove trees do. I've ev'n whittled on buttonwood myself. It's hard as hell but polishes up right nice. Ol' Jeff, Mister Jake's nigger . . . the color't man here at Punta Rassa . . . uses it to smoke fish 'n' meat."

Jorge Gomez winked at Francis Corning, then continued. "We can't really answer the second part of your question with accuracy. Its use was certainly of a religious nature; perhaps it represented the spiritual unification of the animal world with that of the Calusa people. The statuettes aren't mentioned in the few existing written accounts of Spanish priests regarding their contact with Native Americans in Florida. We may never know its true purpose or role in their extinct culture!"

Jorge Gomez again took the pot in his hand. He admired it as he slowly turned it on his open, flattened palm. "If we look carefully at the pictographs, we may reach back in time and gain insight into the man who created this piece and the statuette. In my opinion, and that of several notable students of North American aboriginal archeology, these drawings indicate major events and accomplishments in the life of our artist, the maker of this beautiful pot and the collector of the artifacts it held.

"The first drawing is a baby figure. Two people, whom I assume are its parents, are holding the youngster. They're standing on a land mass that remarkably resembles a map: an astonishingly accurate rendition of the outline of Sanibel Island. My interpretation of this scene is that our ancient artist was born there, and he is the child. The next few pictures depict his growth to manhood. He was a good gatherer, a fisherman, and a warrior. If you look closely at the fourth picture, you'll notice he's seated, and on the ground around him are arrowheads, ceremonial masks, and one of the cat-like figurines. All are products of his ingenious creativity. In this next one, he's m anufacturing a c anoe. The next is a p anoramic composite a nd i llustrates a Spanish s ailing v essel s urrounded b y Calusa war canoes. Arrows are falling out of the sky onto the Spaniard's ship. This illustration depicts a major battle. Next, our man is depicted as an adult, standing with his arm around his wife, and two children.

"Ivy, here." Jorge passed the pot to its finder, then held out his hand and pointed. He touched the pot and continued. "Take this eyeglass and look carefully at this final pictograph. Take your time. Tell us what you see?"

Ivy squinted and scrutinized the side of the pot. He concentrated for a few seconds, then blurted out in excited amazement, "Godamighty! I ne'er noticed . . . I cain't believe it! It's my good-luck piece!"

"Yes, it is! In every absolute detail!"

"Can ya'll believe this? I swear!"

"That brings us to the final item: the gold medallion on the table. Its possession was important to this early American artisan. Remember when you visited me in Havana, I made a casting of your medal? I mailed it to a colleague in Spain. After months of research, my friend advised me of the progress he was making. We know when the medal was made, but details about its original recipient haven't been determined. Francis and I are confident we'll ultimately know, but examining sloppily-kept Government archives in Spain takes time."

Francis Corning was excited and blurted out *the* question, *the* reason the two scientists had returned to Punta Rassa: "Would you consider donating or loaning any of these artifacts to my university for our museum collection? Jorge and I came all this way to tell you what we've learned about your remarkable discoveries. In our opinion, they should be safeguarded in an institution for posterity, perhaps eventually in the Smithsonian Institution in Washington. Calusa artifacts of this quality will never be found again!"

"Doctor, to be perfectly truthful, I cain't rightly answer that question. Alice has sho 'nuff growed 'tached to this pot 'n' the wood statue, 'n' ya'll knowed what I think 'bout this gold piece.

I'll talk wit' 'er this ev'nin' 'n' I'll let yuh know how we decide in the mornin'. Okay?

"*Oh*! If we do let yuh use 'em, would yuh put a sign up that says they was donated by Ivory 'n' Alice Clark o' Punta Rassa?"

"Yes, I'd certainly agree to that!" Francis smiled. "Tell Alice I'll even put it in writing."

"Fine, I'll tell 'er that. Alice is a good Christian person but likes to be recognized fer 'er good deeds . . . 'n' thanked."

The day was ending and the fiery sun would soon seem to fall into Pine Island Sound. Ivy sat on the edge of the boat dock admiring the brilliant sunset, waiting until Gus Wendt was ready to call it a day and head home. On the short trip to Fisherman Key, Ivy was pensive. He was mentally cataloging all the information he had learned about the clay pot full of artifacts nestled in his pack. He was looking forward to sharing all he had learned with Alice.

"Ivy, there's a letter here for you. Hurry! Come open it! Daddy brought it over this afternoon," Alice shouted when she saw Ivy's boat slip silently up to the dock in the twilight.

"Who's it from?" Ivy yelled as he hurried up the path from the dock to his home.

"It's postmarked Key West. It's from the Lighthouse Board. Hurry, honey! Open it!"

Habitually, as he had done since discovering the gold disk in the cache of Calusa artifacts on Sanibel Island—and before he did *anything* important nowadays—Ivy dug deep into his pocket and felt for his good luck piece. Touching it, he rubbed the golden disk, seeking its fortuitous comfort. With his confidence fully bolstered Ivy reached out and took the envelope from Alice.

PART TWO

THE ORIGINS

"Just look, Antón! It's exactly as I remember! The Florida *is* a land of lush greenery and flowering beauty. On the other hand, I recall, too, that its natives are bellicose and savage. We may have to fight, but we'll take this land from them and colonize it."

—Don Juan Ponce de León
At sea, off the coast of Southwest Florida, 1521

CHAPTER 14

T HE NIGHT WAS ABLAZE WITH WHITE FIRE-LIKE LIGHT
as the broad-beamed wooden canoe sliced through the salty, eye-
burning chop. Paddling furiously, four young men propelled themselves
selves over the glowing, churning water, as they entered the Gulf of
Mexico. They had left the smooth water of the "Bay of Calos" and
were rounding the eastern tip of the "Great Seashell Island." The
water-borne light was caused by the abundance of bioluminescent,
microscopic, marine organisms in the water. These were at their greatest profusion because of the warm seawater. The glowing water presented an eerie and brilliant aura to the paddler's surroundings, but the
white spontaneous light would be temporary this particular night. Its
intensity would soon be nearly overwhelmed by the competing bright
silver glow of the full moon. The moon was rising steadily above the
dark eastern horizon.

They boat was made by combining the use of fire and primitive
tools to shape the trunk of a giant slash pine. Its makers had turned the
log into a graceful watercraft. Propelled by broad-bladed cypress paddles, the canoe pitched and rolled as the powerful riptide produced
counteracting top and bottom currents. These eddies taxed the young
men, as they tried to safely negotiate their passage.

The paddler in the stern bellowed, "Okay! Now! Together! Stroke deep!" As the words left his lips, he stabbed his pointed paddle into the water as deep as he could reach. His paddle was longer than those used by his companions because it also served as a rudder. Twisting the paddle steered the vessel toward the calm surface closer inshore, beyond the control of the agitated riptide. His crew, three nearly naked and completely soaked paddlers, responded and dug their paddles deep into the water. Each took powerful strokes, pulling the glowing water toward them. The hull surged forward, toward the more placid surface they hoped to soon reach—the sooner, the better.

The steerer yelled, "Mando! Keep paddling as hard as you can on the right side—until I tell you to stop. That'll help me make the turn better. And then paddle on the left after we've turned and are moving parallel to the beach. We have to keep the boat clear of the breaking waves!"

Breathing hard, frowning and noticeably peeved, Mando responded, tersely, "Panti! I don't know why you made me sit in front? You know that I've had little experience with these kinds of things! Remember, I'm not an experienced rough-water boating person like you three." Mando took a deep breath, exhaled, and continued, "My boating has been limited to the shallow lagoons and calm creeks around home! Each time I make the mistake of visiting you, you get me into some kind of scary situation! I'm going to stop coming to visit you and your family, if I ever have to come along on one of your crazy expeditions again! I warn you, for all the danger you're putting us through tonight, we'd better not return empty handed!"

"Don't worry, cousin, we won't. Now, again! Dig in deep! Again!"

The dugout canoe was cruising along parallel to the moonlit beach. They were just outside the zone where the moderate-sized waves broke on the land and spilled their cold light when the water rushed up the beach. The moon had risen and was washing the sea and white beach with its glow. The luminescent waves had become more subdued because of the brighter competing moonlight.

"You can ease up now! As long as we stay out here just beyond the breakers we can paddle slower. Barto, that was the roughest ride I ever made around the point. It had me scared!"

"*Huh*? What did you say, Panti? I can't hear what you're saying! My ears are getting worse, especially with the added noise of this surf and wind. What did you say?"

Panti yelled again, louder, "I wouldn't want to slide around and get beat up like that every time I come out here. Now that the moon's rising the tide's changed. It's beginning to flow back inside. Maybe we can finish soon and head home with the help of the incoming tide."

Barto was Panti's friend since infancy. He had become a specialized diver who collected large seashells—weapon and implement grade conchs and whelks—from deep water. Although he was young, the rigorous year-round demands of breath-hold diving had already permanently affected his hearing. Barto excitedly agreed with his pal's comments, and replied, "I wouldn't want to try this in one of the regular canoes. This one that you designed using your outrigger idea handles really well in rough water. I've no doubt there aren't any Calosa boats anywhere that are made better, or are more seaworthy, than the one we're in. We should rig a sail and take a trip down to the "Big Southern Island"—the mountain island—sometime!"

"You three can make that trip without me!" Mando added. "You two are really special—no, just plain crazy is more like it! I've always thought you both were mixed up in your heads. Do you believe the storytellers when they spin those tales about a big mountainous island that's supposed to exist somewhere to the south of our people's land?"

"Yes, I do!" Panti replied, and continued talking, "Before he died, my grandfather—my mother's father—told me stories about the war parties he sometimes went on to that place when he was young. Our bravest warriors sought reprisals for raids those people made on our villages in Calosa territory south of here. I know it exists!"

"Well, like I said, count me out!" Mando replied sarcastically.

The fourth member of the party had remained silent throughout their ordeal. After all, he was the youngest of the quartet and this was his first nighttime canoe trip into the Gulf of Mexico. Kardah was frightened and at a loss for words, but he listened.

The canoe rocked slightly as it glided along on the water, above the wash channel created by the tumbling surf. The alert Calosa Indian adolescents were now paddling slower, in a less exhaustive cadence of paddle strokes. They made good speed over the shimmering surface of the Gulf. By now, the brilliant moon dominated the sky on this rare cloudless summer night. Usually, late June nights in Southwest Florida are densely overcast and the thick clouds periodically drop voluminous amounts of torrential rain. Then, too, there are the violent thunderstorms, which dispense powerful winds, add frightening booming thunderclaps, and deadly lightning. The moonlight flooded the sea, the wide white beach, and the dense vegetation covered the low dunes of the curved island they were skirting. The glow cast a considerable amount of light over the landscape and provided long-range visibility for the Calosans.

"This is certainly easier paddling, isn't it? I'm worn out from all that work!" Panti announced after he had finally caught his breath. "Are you three watching the beach?"

"Yeah!" His alert companions replied in unison.

The young men in the canoe were on a sea turtle egg collecting expedition. In late spring and summer the eggs of these marine reptiles were a vital part of their people's sustenance. Several different kinds of sea turtles visit the barrier islands and nest on the beaches of the Calosa nation.

After making the turn, they had covered less that a quarter mile. Mando suddenly turned around, faced the stern, and screeched, "Cousin! I see a one-way turtle track across the beach ahead! A turtle's up in the grass!"

"Good job! See, you're an important person to have along on the hunt." Panti shoved his paddle straight down, deep into the water on his right side, and expertly trimmed its angle for steerage. The heavy canoe started its deliberate turn toward the beach.

Panti shouted another series of orders. "Keep paddling! Hard! A few yards out from the beach I'll signal and we'll all leap overboard. Mando, you pick up the bow line and take it with you. We'll lighten up so we can get the canoe as high on the beach as the waves will push it. Don't forget we may need to load a turtle and the closer we are to it, the better!

"Okay? Get ready . . . *Jump!*"

A few moments later, the drenched quartet huddled together on the beach. They closely examined the track the turtle had left when she struggled to move across the soft sand. As Mando had perceived from offshore, there was indeed only a single crawl across the beach. This indicated the animal crawled up the beach, but not yet back down.

Panti broke the silence, and said, "Take a look at those front flipper marks! They're really wide apart and the grooves they made in the sand are opposite one another. I think we have a big green turtle in the grass on the higher part of the beach. Barto! Slip up there and see if she's laying eggs. If she is, we'll let her finish before we turn her! In fact, we'll let her get back close to the water before we do that—so she'll be closer to the canoe. That'll make it easier for us to move her into the boat."

After a few moments, Barto was back. He dropped down to sit on the sand, and reported, "She's covering her eggs. She'll be headed this way in a minute or two. I'm going to lay right here on the beach and rest until she does."

It wasn't long before they all heard a commotion coming from the dry grass. After completing the laborious task of concealing her eggs, the huge green turtle had turned around in the clump of sea oats and was heading back to the water. Her bulk and weight tore up dry grass, and broke pieces of driftwood as she pushed through the wall of vegetation. Her mission was accomplished, the open beach was in her view, and she started to leave the grass. The turtle could see her goal beyond the breaking surf as it struck the edge of the land a few yards away. At that instant, eight human eyes were busy scanning the upper beach when her dark, sand-covered shape suddenly appeared at the edge of the waving sea oats. The turtle paused, raised her small head, and with a foul breath exhaled in an explosive *hiss*. As the sound trailed off, both of her front flippers were extended forward. With powerful force, they were dug deeply into the sand ahead of her. Then, with a series of shell-raising lunges, she pulled herself forward, again and again, toward the safety of the sea.

"Kardah! Turn her upside down before she gets into the water!" Panti said with a broad grin on his face that Kardah failed to notice. The smile was visible to the others because the moonlight flashed across Panti's teeth. They also saw the mischievous twinkle in his eyes.

"I've never turned one of these over before . . . alone . . . are you kidding me?"

"No, I'm not kidding! Grab her under the side of her shell, lift up, and flip her over. Hurry!"

The youngest and most inexperienced of the turtle hunters did as he was told. After all, Panti was the leader. Of course, by now the lunging green turtle had seen the boys and was picking up speed in an effort to elude contact with the unrecognized figures coming toward it. Kardah ran up to the animal and placed two hands under the edge of its shell. With the shell firmly in his grip, he raised the side of the turtle a few inches off the sand, but was unable to muster enough strength to lift it high enough to upset it. He lost his hold. With a loud *thud* the heavy turtle fell back against the sand and struggled toward the water.

Barto stepped up, laughed aloud, and said, "Let me show you how it's done." It was obvious someone would have to do something quick, because the heaving turtle was inches from the rolling surf and freedom.

Barto grabbed the edge of the shell and lifted, but then quickly brought his right knee against the shell to help keep it in an elevated position. At the same time, he repositioned his hands and arms, preparing his grip to push, instead of lift. The turtle was up on the edge of its shell. One flipper was flailing in the air and the other was throwing great amounts of sand into the sky. Barto gave the green turtle a little push and it fell to the beach upside down. Despite its disorientation it continued throwing voluminous amounts of sand, now with both front flippers.

"Wow! I don't think I've ever turned one over that was quite so big! You gave it a good try Kardah, but Panti didn't give you the best of instructions. We knew he was toying with you. All of us, except you, saw that grin on his face. The secret is using your knee."

Panti laughed, proud of his practical joke, then said, "Mando, take Kardah to the nest and show him how to find the eggs. Barto and I will truss the turtle and get it ready to load."

The boys backtracked on the wide set of tracks the green turtle had left in the beach surface. Well inside the sea oats, a large disturbed area of loose sand and uprooted plants gave away the location of the nest to Mando's experienced eye. The turtle's movements during covering had camouflaged the exact location of the eggs, but he quickly eyed a spot where he thought the eggs were buried. By close examination, Mando had mentally judged the position of the turtle's final sand-sweeping front flipper marks in relation to the turtle's size. These gave him an approximation of where he thought the eggs were located.

Mando stood above the nest and stretched and flexed his muscular body a few times before kneeling on the sand. He was ready to proceed, and said, "Green turtles dig much deeper nests than the moss-backed loggerheads do. Based on the size of the turtle and the position of the flipper marks in the sand, I'd say her eggs are right about here." Mando marked an "x" in the sand with his finger then continued his lecture with an air of authority. "There are several ways to find the eggs. We could probe into the sand with a pointed arrow shaft until we pull it up with egg yolk on it. Panti doesn't want us to do that though, because eggs will be broken and wasted. We'll scoop the sand away, then make a hole about half way to our knees in depth." He had risen to his feet again and dragged his foot across the beach around the x, creating a limiting circle inside which he instructed his inexperienced apprentice to begin digging. Mando then kneeled down again to help.

Soon, the sand was removed by hand to a diameter and depth that met Mando's approval. He stopped digging, stood up, stretched, and gave instructions. "You stand in the pit and push one of your feet firmly against the bottom. Keep moving your foot around and do that until the sand gives way and you feel an unusual soft spot. That's where you'll find the eggs!"

Kardah did as as he was told. He began to systematically apply foot pressure on every square inch of the bottom of the hole they had just dug. After a few moments, the sand under his foot gave way with a strange spongy sensation. Kardah knew he had found the nest.

The egg collectors hurried back to the beach after they filled the basket with more than 100 round, soft-shelled eggs. Panti and Mando were reclining on the beach waiting. They were already finished with the grisly task of securing the turtle for loading.

The turtle's four flippers had been punctured near their outer ends. Panti had double-laced and secured braided cord through the bleeding holes. Each flipper was pulled to its full extension, drawn across the turtle's bottom shell and tied to another angled flipper opposite it. After being trussed in this manner, the turtle strained to move its muscular appendages, but found movement impossible.

The canoe was pulled off the beach slightly, so it wouldn't bottom-out and be hard to move after the heavy marine reptile was loaded. The foursome dragged the turtle into the water and positioned it about mid-ship. It was lifted into the boat after a long pole, usually used to push the canoe through shallows, was shoved between its bottom shell and flippers. All took hold—two at each end—and with great effort the turtle was lifted by the straining young men. It was raised high enough to clear the canoe's gunwale, then lowered onto the boat's bottom, positioned between the outrigger spars.

"Let's rest and eat before we head back." Panti suggested, then added, "I'm beat! Barto, pass me my water gourd out of the canoe, please . . . and about a half dozen of those eggs."

Mando spoke up, and asked, "Bring some for me and Kardah too will you, I'm starving!"

Panti took three of his eggs and walked into the water. He bent down and washed them off. Some of the eggs were still damp, covered with a clear fluid produced by the turtle's reproductive system. On others, sand tightly adhered to their paper-thin, soft shells because of the sticky liquid. After swishing the eggs to remove the unwanted materials, he rejoined his companions and sat cross-legged on the beach facing the water.

Taking an egg with the thumbs and forefingers of both hands, Panti pinched the shell and pulled his hands apart to tear it. Once the opening was enlarged sufficiently, he brought the egg to his open mouth and dumped its contents inside. The large yellow yolk was then crushed between his tongue and hard palate and he slowly swallowed the thick mixture of yolk and albumen. Panti reached for another of the nourishing protein-rich eggs and repeated the process.

As the young men ate and relaxed, they stared toward the spectacular star-studded heavens, or looked in awe at the changing brilliance of the sea as the low surf raced toward them but fell short of reaching them. As young adults almost universally do, each contemplated their selected sights, they exchanged serious commentary about their observations, and even ventured to talk about the unknown origins and mystery of their lives in relation to the natural world.

When their appetites were satisfied, and their paddling arms sufficiently rested, the boys readied to return to the calmer bay and home. They would stay as close to the beach as possible. Another turtle may have landed and left a fresh nest since they last passed.

CHAPTER 15

NOW IN HIS LATE TEENS, PANTI WAS TALLER THAN average and very muscular. It was evident to his peers he had unique intellectual and leadership skills. His verbal expressions and extroverted personality conveyed an aura that demanded respect from those he interacted with. He also possessed an uncanny and exuberant sense of humor, showed remarkable love for his family, and special kindness to his closest friends. Just over six feet tall, Panti was known as one of the most aggressive and bravest warriors among the Calosa. Most who knew him were convinced Panti was destined to become famous among his people.

Panti's attire and appearance were traditional. He was usually barefooted, the soles of his feet toughened from a life-long absence of footwear. He could walk on razor-sharp oyster beds without cutting his feet. His body was naked except for a soft buckskin breechcloth. Only during the coldest winter months would he don other garments. His breechcloth was held in place by a braided, knotted belt that he had crafted from soft, buckskin. The flaps of Panti's loincloth were decorated with delicate pigmented designs. A twisted leather band usually held his clean, glossy-black, shoulder-length hair on top of his head, out of his eyes, and off his neck while he worked. At other times, his hair was usually gathered into a ponytail. Like his Calosa contempo-

raries, Panti's thighs, arms, and the upper cheeks of his face were decorated with painted markings. Like all males he spent considerable
time maintaining his personalized body art. Other than one permanent
tattoo inside his left forearm—tattoos were rare among the Calosa—
Panti's body adornments were temporary and regularly altered to meet
his personal tastes and moods. His jewelry, which Calosa warriors
wore to display their social rank, consisted of wrist and ankle bracelets
made from nickerbeans and seashells. He regularly wore a necklace
made from a combination of the sea beans, seashells, and bird bones.
The tubular lightweight bones were etched with complicated designs.
On important social occasions Panti tied long turkey gobbler beards to
his armbands and wore a necklace he had fashioned from the claws of
black bears he had killed for their hide and as food.

Panti was considered by those who knew him to be a serious
person, one who studied the natural world and was comfortable in the
complex hierarchical culture in which he lived. Panti was a devoted
student of his environment: to a much higher degree than his peers. His
visual interpretations manifested his specialized talent and superior
intellect. Panti had a reputation of being honest, friendly, gregarious
and amenable. On the other hand, he was also known to be deliberate
and fearless.

A powerful unified people, 10,000 strong, the Calosa were at
their political and social pinnacle. They had dominated neighboring
peoples of the South Florida peninsula for nearly a millennium.

Five tassels of human hair were attached to his wicked looking,
shark tooth-studded, war saber. Panti had cut these from the heads of
the five lesser enemy warriors he had personally killed in hand-to-hand
combat. He slew several others from afar—with arrow and atlatl dart.

Panti was born in the small village where he still lived, worked,
and contributed. The community his family inhabited had been in use
for a few hundred years. But it was small in acreage and population
when compared with much older and larger Calosa towns. His village
was originally crowded onto a low, sparsely vegetated, spit of land. It
was no more than a sandbar, a small peninsula. It sometimes appeared
to be connected to the Great Seashell Island, at least at low tide. A large
oval-shaped bay, known to the Calosa as "Grassy Bottom," separated

the village from the the main island. The broad Bay of Calos isolated the site from other islands situated to the east and closer to the mainland.

Like most Calosa settlements, Panti's home village rested on a growing waste heap—a midden—a mounded mixture of dead seashells and sand. Originally, this location was selected because it was suitably exposed to weather elements, close to deep water, near a bountiful year-round food supply, and its foundation was stable. Stability of the land was important. Tidal- and weather-caused water currents quickly eroded many sites which otherwise appeared suitable. Here, with these forces at a minimum, the village prospered. Over time it grew in both geometrical dimensions and population.

The tightly packed soil of the mound system was slowly developed by strategically dumping food byproducts. The height was not as great as that of other neighboring Calosa middens. The maximum elevation was a little over eight feet above sea level and the mound was constantly being expanded laterally to increase livable space. This height was sufficient to cope with high tides caused by minor storms, but would not provide protection from complete inundation because of major hurricane surges.

Their well-made, palm frond thatched dwellings were raised on stout posts above the ground an additional few feet. These were open-sided unless inclement weather required hide or woven palm panels to be inserted along the sidewalls to prevent rain or cold wind from chilling their sleep. Additional structures included an open-air communal cookhouse and a small communal lodge. The lodge was used by villagers for assemblies or when temporary refuge from the sun or bad weather might be needed.

Panti was sparked at an early age to be a skilled craftsman. His paternal grandfather, Ronna, was a local weapons maker of high reputation. Panti sat for hours, watching the processes with which his father's father tediously created beautifully formed arrowheads and dart points. By the time he was ten years old the boy could make hunting and fishing points from stone, shell, and bone.

Panti occasionally accompanied his grandfather and small groups of warriors, and weapon makers from nearby communities, on lengthy boat trips. They traveled to regions far beyond the limits of the

Calosa domain. They went to the distant areas to obtain chert and other commodities. Chert is a hard stone from which the various types of points are painstakingly created. They also bartered with friendly people they encountered, or accepted weapon points as tribute payments from others who their nation's king-like leader sometimes dominated. Point makers, allied to the Calosa or not, were held in high esteem because their stone and bone products were essential commodities. Arrowheads yielded game and fish and provided a means of protection. Because they were usually not retrievable, their acquisition or manufacture had to be constant. Their production was linked to the success of the Calosa's overall economy and strong-arm treaties with neighbors.

"Grandfather! Where did you get that beautiful black-bladed knife you always wear in your deerskin sheath? Did you make it?" Panti asked.

Smiling, looking down at the knife, the gray-haired old man withdrew it from its soft leather scabbard. It flashed in the sunlight, as he held it up, and answered, "No, Panti. You asked me that question once before, when you were a very young tot. Don't you remember? This blade is very old. It's been handed down through our family. My father gave it to me and someday, I'm sure, it will be yours. My grandfather once told me this is a very special . . . no, a spiritual blade. He told me it was brought here when our ancestors came to this place to find freedom. When they escaped from the land of the stone pyramids—from far away across the Great Water. From a place even more distant than the Big Southern Island which has mountains. The black stone it's made from is unlike any I've ever seen."

The perfectly flaked edge was extremely sharp, made from shiny-black, glass-like stone, and dagger-like in design. The knife had a thin, tapered, well-proportioned blade about six inches long. The deer antler handle the blade was attached to was plain but functional.

Ronna continued talking. "This blade needs to be hafted to a new handle. I made this one when I was about your age . . . no, I was a little older. Why don't you start looking for a piece of suitable wood for a new handle. When you find the perfect piece, you can carve one for it. I'm sure with your wonderful talent the new handle will turn out much better than this old one."

Panti took his grandfather's challenge to heart. Days later, he discovered a perfect piece of wood from which he would produce a replacement handle. He found it while hunting deer with a group of his friends. It was hidden among an old forest of salt-killed trees, on the desolate, glaring white sand flats beyond the western edge of Grassy Bottom. The partially buried piece of wood that caught his eye was an old, well-weathered, salt-saturated piece of heartwood from the common hardwood with which the women of his village smoke fish, and use in their cook fires. "This beautifully grained piece of buttonwood has hope," Panti thought, as he imagined the final carving. He would work the wood with care and strive to make it unlike any knife handle he ever saw before. When mated with the magnificent black blade, the pairing would be one of a kind—unlike any other. It would become the finest knife in the land of the Calosa.

* * *

During the boat trip north along the wild Florida coast, Panti spent every free moment working on the new knife handle. After all, his grandfather had presented the challenge, and was watching his progress. Panti's tools were simple. For the detail carving he used shark's teeth. These were mounted on wooden handles, were extremely sharp and cut and scraped away the hard wood remarkably well. Those with the saw-like serrated teeth worked especially well. Scrapers made from chert were used when it was necessary to smooth or otherwise work the piece of extremely dense and heavy wood. Final smoothing was done with shagreen—pieces of rough, sandpaper-like, sharkskin.

From the beginning, Panti envisioned a knife handle unlike any made by contemporary Calosa craftsmen. Foremost, he wanted it to be strong and possess a spiritual identity. It would have to mount securely to the mystic blade. After all, it must last his lifetime because his grandfather told him he would become heir to the ancient blade. He was convinced the carving must be graceful in dimension, practical in actual use, and rendered in a manner that properly paid homage to his personal spiritual totem. The embodiment of the carving's beauty must unite this totem with his spirit and be a unique creation. It would be forever recognizable as the fine art of Panti. Like any artist, of any era, he found himself reaching for immortality, even as a teenager.

Once carving began, his level of creativity quickly heightened and Panti skillfully started roughing-out the black blade's three-dimensional handle. The wood would be fashioned to become similar in appearance to the totem figure he had self-tattooed inside his left forearm. This was a strange kneeling figure, composed of two almost surreal elements—one half was human-like, the other half was animal-like. His carving must gracefully meld the human figure, which he perceived as himself, to that of the panther. Immediately after Panti's birth, the village priest had dedicated the cat as the newborn's spiritual totem.

The secretive panthers of the inland forests rarely visited the offshore barrier islands near Panti's home. The Calosa held these large, powerful cats in high spiritual esteem. Panthers were never killed. To do so would be contrary to ancient Calosa laws. The storytellers told it was a mighty panther that protected the Calosa's forefathers from the indigenous peoples when they first arrived on the shores of what was now their kingdom. Although the panther was commonly claimed as a totem by Calosa males, no artists had perfected the style—much less the ability—to duplicate the extraordinary tattoo Panti had etched and inked into his arm.

The dozen men in the two canoes had been sailing north for more than a week, pushed along by small deer hide sails. On the second day out they had left behind the deep inlet which led into the "Great Bay of Dolphins." A week later, they sailed past the broad water entrance of the enormous "Bay of Danger." The latter was the northern boundary of the domain of the Calosa. The multi-tribal peoples who lived along the lengthy circumference of this bay regularly paid tribute to the Calosa. The leaders of the Calosa demanded this primitive taxation and the weaker tribes avoided armed conflicts with the Calosa kingdom by paying tribute. As the days passed, Panti and the others grew apprehensive. To a man they knew once they left the safety of open water their trip would become hazardous.

At night they camped on the beaches of small, uninhabited islands. These narrow barrier islands stretched one after the other along the coast. Occasionally, islands they passed contained well-established villages. Carta, the leader of the expedition, knew from experience on which segments of the island chain it was safe for his party to land, and which to give wide berth. Although all the coastal tribes adjacent to the kingdom of Calos feared their warriors, a small group of Calosa travelers could be overwhelmed by a larger war party as they passed through foreign territories.

A few days after they had passed the Bay of Danger, the continuity of the chain of islands began to break. The islands became smaller, fewer in number, and were spread farther apart. In the absence of barrier islands, the land of the mainland reached to the water's edge. Those of the men aboard the canoes, who had made this trip before, knew by the change in the landscape and character of the shoreline that they were nearly halfway to their destination. More than another week would pass before they reached the mouth of the "River of the Stone." Here they lowered their primitive sails and masts, picked up paddles, and began the long trip inland on this broad, flowing river of dark, fresh water. Their ability to outwit any surprise attackers would be lessened, and their escape or defensive movements constrained, because of the River of the Stone's narrowing width as they moved upstream.

For many in the canoes the trip took on a depressing monotony. Those not directly involved in sailing found too much time on their hands. These passed the long hours with a variety of ordinary endeavors. A few fished continuously, trolling behind the boat in hopes of an exciting catch. Fishing required time and skill, plus it supplied food for the travelers. Some talked constantly—about home, family, battle experiences, men they had killed, and victories they had counted. Others complained of the weather, the length of the trip, and feared what unknowns lay ahead for them. Panti listened, occasionally looked up, and leisurely assessed the changes in the land. He continued working on the piece of buttonwood.

"Grandfather! I've finished my . . . your . . . knife handle. Shall I mount it to your blade?" Panti said with satisfaction and passed the carving to his grandfather. Ronna was napping, leaning comfortably against an outrigger strut.

In astonishment, he awoke and took the carving from his grandson's hand. He spoke intentionally loud enough for all aboard to hear, when he said, "Panti, you never cease to amaze me with your great talent. I've never before seen such skills among our people."

"Nor have I!" Carta added.

Someone else aboard muttered, "You'll become the greatest of us all, Panti!"

Panti's grandfather continued to brag on his grandson. "There has never been such a great artist among our people before you, Panti! No one was ever given your gifts, your ability to carve wood and bone, or decorate pottery, tattoo, and create the best weapon points. We're all makers of points and simple tools, but none of us has any real creative abilities beyond that trade. The storytellers of the future will praise you and your good works! The women and children shall sing songs about your great talent!"

"Oh, Grandfather. Stop! You're embarrassing me."

CHAPTER 16

P ANTI HAD NEVER SEEN A RIVER LIKE THIS ONE. IT WAS quite unlike the mangrove-bordered Great River which emptied into the Bay of Calos across from his home. The mouth of this waterway was dominated by dark-colored marsh grass, not red mangrove trees. In fact, the coast was noticeably treeless. As the hours passed, the paddlers labored against the out-flowing current. They strained to move the cumbersome canoes upstream. As they proceeded inland, the ground slowly rose in elevation, fractions of an inch per mile. On the second day a mix of freshwater and upland woody vegetation appeared on the barely emergent banks of the river's wide floodplain.

On their fifth day since leaving the Gulf of Mexico, the banks of the river had risen and turned into steep, eroded bluffs of strange-looking, stratified soils. These had varying colors, contrasts, and thicknesses. This landscape was totally unfamiliar to Panti, who asked, "Grandfather, what makes the land along this river's bank so strange?"

"We're getting close to our destination. The different layers of dirt and rock you see on the banks give the River of the Stone its name. I've been told that the water flow washed away the dirt and stone to create the river's channel. Through the passage of the ages, rushing water has exposed the special stone we've traveled so far to find."

"I've never before seen the natural stone of the earth Grandfather, the stone from which we make some of our weapons and tools. I've only worked with small pieces that reached us through trading. Please show me some when you see it." Panti asked.

Soon, Ronna stopped paddling, turned around, and spoke to his grandson. "Do you see that little beach ahead and to our left?"

"Yes, I do."

"See that light-colored thick layer of rock, about halfway down the face of the bluff? That's what we're looking for! If you look carefully as we get closer you'll see places where the bank has been dug out and the pieces of the lightcolored rock have been broken away. We'll find the hard stone in that rock layer."

The party's leader, Carta, interrupted their conversation. Speaking in a low tone, just loud enough for all to hear, he said, "Finally, we're here, men. Ronna, after we beach the canoes, take Karmp and Turpa with you, climb the bank, and scout the area. We must be extremely quiet. We don't want to frighten any people or antagonize warriors who may be living or hunting nearby. We're few and couldn't defend ourselves very long against a larger and stronger force. Everyone—except Panti—is to loosen the stone we have come here to collect. Panti, you'll stay with the canoes. Keep their bows pointed downstream, and the hulls floating free of the bottom. In case we need to quickly abandon this place!"

It wasn't long before Ronna returned. He peered over the edge of the densely vegetated bank and smiled. Loud enough for everyone digging or near the boat to hear, he said, "We haven't seen or heard anyone. I posted Karmp and Turpa—one in a tree, the other on a ridge—to serve as lookouts. I'll stay hidden here to protect them should they need to withdraw." He reached over his back and withdrew a long-shafted dart from his deerskin quiver. The feathered end of the dart's shaft, opposite that tipped with the chert point, was deeply concave. Ronna fitted this depression over a prominent raised spur he had carved as part of his atlatl. Two fingers, one of which passed through a large hole in the throwing stick, tightly held the cane shaft in position against the spur. Ronna raised the light but deadly weapon to a resting position on his shoulder, turned away, and silently disappeared into the dense palmettos.

189

The chert-mining operation went smoothly. The quality stone they sought was in good supply near the narrow sandy beach where they had stopped. Large chunks of the heavy rock were carried to the beach and piled near the canoes. Carta carefully watched the mining operation and when he was satisfied they had collected enough, he exclaimed, "That's enough! Now, get your axes and let's move into the woods to cut a supply of bow wood. Panti, I want you to stay here with the boats. Keep alert! Watch the river in both directions, and the opposite bank, too. We may not be the only ones about on this river on such a beautiful day! Follow me, men. Let's be quick! We'll soon be on our way home."

The eight men spread out into the forest and were joined by the two warriors whom Ronna had earlier assigned as lookouts. They would search the hardwood-dominated woods for high caliber hickory trees. Straight-grained small trees, which were mostly limbless at their lower levels, would be selected and felled. Next, six foot-long sections of trunk were chopped from the downed trees. Wedges and hammers would then be used to split and quarter the pieces lengthwise into staves. Later, when the wood was seasoned and dried it would be worked with hand tools to produce powerful bows. It wasn't long before all the men were out of sight. Panti stood nervously alone beside the bobbing canoes.

Lost in thought, Panti's mind wandered. "Why did Carta make me stay behind and guard these boats and a pile of rocks? *Huh*! What's that noise?" He slowly turned around, listening intently, trying to determine where the faint, pulsating, dull sounds he had just heard were coming from. Straining to hear, his mind raced, "It's coming from somewhere upriver." The sound again echoed along the river bottom, *Dum-da-dum Da-dum*. "It's a drum!"

Anxiously, Panti crouched in the cool water between the canoe hulls and continued to look around. He was still unable to pinpoint the exact direction from which the drumbeats were coming.

"Who's that?" He asked himself—suddenly startled when he saw a half-crouched human figure moving through the brush along the shore about 100 yards upstream. The man was moving at a fast pace and coming in his direction. Whoever it was, Panti knew the person was not from his party. First, because none of the men from his group had gone off in that direction, and second, this person had short hair and wore feathers in it, and he was covered with tattoos! Panti leaned over, reached into the canoe, and grabbed his bow and quiver. He would prepare to fight. Or, at least he would be ready to defend himself, should the person approaching send threatening signals, or attack him outright. As an afterthought, he again stretched and reached inside the canoe. He withdrew a large seashell he had made into a horn. This was a simple but very effective Calosa signaling device. The horn's mouthpiece was a small hole drilled at the end of the huge horse conch's spiraling tip.

Panti fitted a bull shark tooth-tipped arrow to his bowstring, held four other arrows in reserve in his hand that held the bow, and waited. He didn't have to wait long. Another man had silently moved, unobserved, to within 100 feet of him and suddenly stood up. Seeing another possible adversary, a compounded feeling of fright and excitement knotted his stomach. Panti had felt overcome this way before in similar threatening situations. He liked the rare sensation. The first person he had sighted continued to walk along the riverbank, picking his trail through the brush, and continued to close the distance between them. Panti saw the man was carrying a bow with a fitted arrow at the ready for launching. He was getting near lethal range with his weapon. Like Panti, the man was gripping additional arrows in his bow hand, and similarly was ready for rapid, successive firing. Instinctively, Panti rose and stood straight. He brought the conch shell's tip and its orifice to his mouth, inhaled deeply, and blowing with the full force of that breath he offered the horn's full volume in the direction his companions had gone. *Toot-ta-toooot!* He dropped down onto one knee, partly protected by the hull of a canoe, and took a firm grip on the arrow and bowstring. Slowly he drew back the arrow, sighting along the straight cane shaft with its black feathers, ready to send it speeding on its deadly course. But, at the sound of the blaring horn the strangers were noticeably alarmed. Both stopped their advance.

Ronna was the first to respond to Panti's alarm signal. He remembered that when Carta passed him he had said Panti was left alone to protect the boat. It was Panti who had sounded the horn! Ronna had to be sure his grandson was safe. Rushing and breaking through the sharp-stemmed saw palmettos on the river bluff, he surveyed the riverbed, and immediately focused on the problem. *"Panti! I'm here!"* He shouted and raised his arm with open palm to signal a warning to the two men threatening his grandson.

The man nearest Panti looked up at Ronna, made eye contact, and raised his arm in reply, recognizing his presence. Ronna continued talking to Panti. "I can tell from their headdress they're local people. They're usually friendly. They've never caused a problem for those of us who make the trip here to collect the stone. In fact, when I was young I spent happy times among these people."

The strange man standing in front of Panti started to speak. His language was different, unlike that of the Calosa, but as he spoke slowly and haltingly he occasionally uttered a known common word Panti could understand. Above them, Ronna understood each word as the man said, "I'm Okeena, a warrior leader among the mighty Yustegas. Who are you people? What brings you to this river?"

Ronna cupped his hand to his mouth and yelled, "Okeena, you've grown old and wrinkled since we last talked and hunted together!"

Surprised to hear such words, the Yustegan looked at Ronna and shouted, "Who are you who claims to know me and foolishly talks to me that way?"

Ronna started to climb down, then descended by sliding upright down the steep embankment. Stumbling but regaining his footing when he reached level ground, he walked closer and continued speaking. "Old man . . . old friend, you're now a chief of the great Yustegas! Do your eyes fail you? Don't you recognize me?"

Confused, the old Yustega warrior narrowed his eyes and spoke. "Few live men dare talk to me in such a tone and use those words. Your use of my language tells me you're not of the Yustegas. You talk of *my* age and *my* skin?" Okeena had lowered his hand and stepped closer to Ronna. Squinting, he examined the stranger walking toward him and continued talking. *"Hmmm.* You too are an ancient o ne. You have wrinkled skin, too. And your back is bent and your head droops! You call me friend! Do I know you? Have I seen you before?"

"Old man of the Yustegas, it's me Ronna . . . Ronna of the Calosa!" Ronna stepped forward, reached out, and took the extended hand of the astonished man who now stood in front of him smiling.

"*Yult*! Come over here!" Okeena yelled to his surprised fellow tribesman who was watching the friendly meeting of the two old men. Yult placed two fingers on his lower lip and gave a series of shrill whistles. One by one, a dozen Yustega warriors stood up and came out from their hiding places in the nearby vegetation. They walked forward and gathered with the others next to the canoes, as Okeena addressed them. "Men, this old man is my friend Ronna of the shell eating people—the Calosa. They live many days south of here. From time to time . . . probably more than once . . . I've told most of you stories about him!" Okeena turned and motioned one of his companions closer. "Ronna, this is Yult. He's my oldest son. I'm happy that once again our paths cross and he has the chance to meet you. I've told him and our young people much about you.

"We're camped not far upriver. Some of our women were frightened when they saw your band arrive. Come to our camp, rest, and feast with us. We have much food to eat and you can tell me the news from your land and events in your life since we last talked, so long ago."

Ronna put his arm on Panti's shoulder and said loudly, for Okeena and all the others to hear, "This young man, who was guarding our canoes, is my grandson, Panti. He is a brave warrior and the finest craftsman among my people. This is his first trip to this river. There are ten others in our party who traveled to this place to collect raw materials. Our leader is inland with the others. They're cutting bow wood from your strong nut trees. When he returns I'm sure I can persuade him that we should visit with you for a few days. We can work and begin to break down the stone, and a have a good long rest before we begin the tiring journey home."

Okeena smiled and said, "Good, old friend. My men and I will return to our camp and I'll have sleeping arrangements made for your party. I'll let the women know they're to prepare food for guests. Tonight we'll brew the black drink, dance, and celebrate our reunion!"

The Yustega camp was a large seasonal assembly of people. Nothing about the settlement was really permanent. Small grass- and bark-covered shelters were arranged in a semicircle a few yards away from the edge of the river. A larger open-air lodge was centrally located in this half circle. Men, women, and children milled about on the riverbank as the heavy canoes slid to rest on the white sand beach fronting the camp. They watched as 12 strange-looking men disembarked and joined the residents.

The Yustegas rarely hosted groups of visitors. They were not known for aggressiveness, or high levels of warfare, but they were a proud and independent people. The Yustegas supported a long-established truce with their neighbors. In no one's memory, including elders like Okeena, had there been war among the neighboring tribes of central Florida. Peace would not have prevailed if any of these people were unfortunate enough to have parts of their domain share a common boundary with that of the Calosa.

Ronna and Okeena first met at a time when each was ending his teens. They were grown men, each close to the present age of Panti. Forty years before, the canoe in which Ronna had traveled to the River of the Stone was severely damaged when a violent windstorm broke off a giant live oak limb. The tree limb fell onto the boat and smashed it in half. The seaworthy canoe had to be replaced before the Calosa expedition could begin their trip back home. Construction of another canoe took several weeks. During this time, Ronna and Okeena met by chance. People from both groups were collecting chunks of chert along the sides of the river. The young men quickly became close friends and spent every moment they could together. They hunted, fished, and explored the countryside. Each learned the other's language. By the time Ronna had to leave, the two were blood brothers. When they parted, each believed they would one day meet again. Through the years, each thought of the other from time to time. Now, near the sunset of their lives, the destiny of true friendship had come to pass. Their paths had indeed crossed again and, ironically, at the same place.

Panti noticed right away that the Yustegas dressed differently than the Calosa. Another of his first impressions was that he and his people were taller than they were, too. Unlike the Calosa body painting, the Yustegas adorned their skin with permanent tattoos. They also decorated their leather garments with a variety of unusual colored beads. Their headdress included broad, completely beaded headbands, and apparently the number of eagle feathers, turkey gobbler beards, and black bear claws included in this decorative covering indicated an individual's rank in the culture's hierarchy. Okeena wore the most elaborate headdress among the clamoring excited people running to greet the mysterious visitors when they stepped onto the beach fronting the village. Panti also noticed their hair. It was much shorter than the traditional long hairstyle of the Calosa. Yustega males and females of all ages had straight black hair that extended slightly below their ears. The women wore no headdress but some had wooden combs, colorful bird feathers, or magnolia blossoms in their hair.

"Come to our main hut. There you'll find food and drink! My father invites you all to enjoy our hospitality!" Yult announced loudly and by glance and smile invited Ronna to repeat what he was saying.

His words were translated into the Calosa tongue by Ronna who found he still understood the long unheard words uttered earlier by Okeena, and now by his son. After a lifetime, he translated the unfamiliar Yustega words with little difficulty. The skill returned to him quickly.

Panti was excited. He hoped he would have an opportunity to meet the artistic members of this tribe. He wanted to learn how they made their weapons, tools, and pottery? How they created the intricate bead designs on their clothing mystified him? With uncontrollable curiosity he mingled with the crowd, to investigate, despite the snarling, menacing dogs. Feigning complete aggressiveness, but not brave enough to make contact, or at least so Panti thought, their bared teeth warned him he was not welcome by all residents of this village. He would have to earn their trust.

He wandered through the camp looking for work areas, places where things were made and repaired. The dogs and children followed him. Crowding around, the daring children touched his strangely decorated body and ran their fingers over his colorful body art, reached up to feel, and even pulled his long, shoulder-length hair. Some dared to tug at his breechcloth. The dogs continued their loud barking. In between b arking e pisodes t hey w ould s it, t hrow u p a r ear l eg, r aise small clouds of dust, and whine as they sought to do serious damage to an irritating flea or two. The games of the children and dogs continued as Panti roamed at will through the village of his hosts.

Edible nuts were a rarity in the climate and environment of Panti's homeland. Occasionally, he stooped down and picked up mockernut hickory fruits that had fallen from the canopy of the tall mature trees overhead—those fruits that gray, flying, and fox squirrels hadn't whisked away to eat or hide somewhere. Ronna had told his grandson stories about these seeds and how good the dry ones were to eat—once they were cracked open and the tasty kernel was accessible. His grandfather had pointed them out to him shortly after they had arrived in Okeena's camp. The mostly empty dried husks of several species of hickory littered the ground. The mockernut kernels had a unique sweet flavor that Panti's taste buds were totally unfamiliar with.

Panti reached a place on the downstream edge of the camp. Here a group of women were busy removing the skin from a recently killed deer. They could not take time to join in the festivities until this task and the cooking which would follow was done. The animal had already been beheaded and its hind legs strung up tightly to the top of a strong tripod made from three cypress poles. Skillfully, with razor-sharp stone knives they expertly removed the deer's skin. This was placed in a basket and carried away for later processing.

A bent-over, middle-aged woman stepped up to the deer. She made a long incision down the middle of the animal's belly. This cut penetrated the flesh but was not deep enough to completely sever inner membranes to expose the intestines and organs. Finished, she stepped back and stretched, then leaned forward again, and expertly cut through the remaining tissue, from the head end up. The deer's innards dumped from the body cavity in a heap at her feet. Another woman stepped up, then another, and as one of them held the various sections, the animal was soon quartered by the other. The venison was to be cooked and eaten tonight.

Panti turned around to walk away, but he bumped into someone. The collision knocked the smaller person to the ground. Unnoticed, a Yustega woman had sneaked up behind him and was closely examining his body art and strange hairdo. The young lady was caught off balance by the impact with Panti and she had fallen over backwards. Unhurt, but completely startled, she screamed in surprise. The younger children began to laugh and taunt her because of her rather comical predicament.

She looked up and screeched at them in words unintelligible to Panti. "This isn't funny! You brats leave me alone!" He could see a twinkle of impish delight in her coal-black eyes as she scolded the children.

Embarrassed, Panti scowled at the noisy youngsters, then reached down and offered the girl his hand to help her rise off the ground. She hesitated, then smiled, and took the offered hand with both of hers. Panti gently pulled her upright onto her feet. As the young woman brushed the dirt from her skin and deer hide clothing, Panti dared to discreetly look her over. He judged she was about a foot shorter than him and seemed to be close to his age—maybe just a little younger. Her straight black hair was longer than that of the other women he had seen in the village. It glistened, was neatly combed, and nearly reached her shoulders. She wore several strands of beaded bone necklaces and had similar bracelets on both wrists. Once she cracked the first smile, she never stopped smiling. This expression of pleasure and her delicate facial features set her apart from the other Yustegan woman who were somber-faced. Her teeth were white and perfect. They were not stained and ground down like his were becoming—dental features common to all adult Calosa men and women. Calosa teeth were worn flat because of a lifelong diet of tough, sand-gritty shellfish.

Panti had started to notice the attractive sexuality of women a couple of years ago. Recently, he developed feelings for a few young Calosa ladies. None of those relationships became serious.

His mind asked questions. "Why does this girl look so special? None of the other women that I've seen here are as pretty. Nor do any of them have such a well-proportioned figure or such a perfect complexion. Her legs are beautiful!" Panti shyly smiled, offered his open palm, then spoke in a gentle convincing tone with words she couldn't understand. "I don't speak your language but if you'll come with me we'll find my grandfather. He can talk to you for me."

The woman seemed unafraid and took his outreached hand. He was so different than the young men among her people. She trusted him from the start. Despite his strange hair and painted body this tall Calosa man was handsome—and a gentleman. Hand in hand they went in search of Ronna.

CHAPTER 17

RONNA AND OKEENA TALKED NONSTOP INSIDE THE palm-thatched, open-air lodge. After all, they had 40 years of life's experiences to catch-up on. As soon as Okeena, the Yustega chief, finished a round of tales, he listened intently as Ronna told of his life in the faraway Calosa nation.

"We've been at peace for years. There are still minor skirmishes with the Tequestas who live across the great land of lazy water and grass to our east. I don't think they'll ever stop trying to move into our southern frontier. Calos, our supreme leader, won't allow large raiding parties, like those of my youth. They used to keep the neighboring people under control. Our leaders seem to be content with receiving token tribute payments of commodities instead of full-scale war to settle border conflicts. Panti's father, Pundon . . . well, Panti too . . . both have been in deadly combat a few times. Both proved themselves b rave warriors and defenders of our way of life. I'm pleased that neither my son, Pundon, nor my grandson, Panti, have been seriously injured in battle. Or, worse!"

Okeena suddenly interrupted his friend, saying, "Speaking of your grandson, Panti, here he comes now."

Ronna looked up as two smiling young people walked to where he and his old friend were seated.

In his usual exuberant tone, with wildly gesturing histrionics, Panti started talking. "Grandfather! Look who I've found! Isn't she beautiful? She can't understand a word I'm saying . . .!"

"I can, don't forget that!" Okeena interjected as he turned slightly and gave a sly wink to Ronna. "You'd better be careful what you say about her in front of me. You don't know it, because she can't tell you—you're holding the hand of my granddaughter. Her name is Olta, and she drives the young Yustega men crazy with her looks and charming ways. She gets those qualities from me you know. Ha! Ha!"

"Grandfather! Please, tell her what my name is . . . where we're from . . . what we're doing here!"

Olta hadn't released her grip on Panti's hand. As Ronna spoke, her hand tightened against Panti's each time his name left the old man's lips. P anti w as blushing, a nd f idgeting, a s he n ervously shifted h is weight from foot to foot. Each time she heard his name Olta would glance up, make flirtatious eye contact with him and smile brightly. Like Panti, she had a special flicker in her eye.

The grandfathers gave her a synopsis of their history as friends. She had heard part of the story before—at least one side of it. Olta commented how remarkable it was that after so many years, and the miles separating them, how the two men were so blessed by their personal totems. They were given a unique opportunity, to meet again before each made his journey to the spirit world. They knew her remarks were genuine and appreciated her encouragement. But it was obvious Olta was only interested in learning more about Panti.

"Grandfather, please tell Panti that I must leave and go home for a few minutes. Ask him to wait here until I come back. I won't be long."

Okeena repeated Olta's message. Panti looked at her and nodded affirmatively, to acknowledge he understood her grandfather's words. She squeezed Panti's hand tightly, released her grip as she turned, and ran out of the lodge.

The two men continued their marathon conversation until a group of noisy children was sent to interrupt them and let them know the feast Okeena had ordered was done. It was ready to be served. The Yustega village and their foreign visitors would have full bellies tonight. Roasted venison, turkey, fish, corn, and squash were the evening's menu. Later, they would dance and play sporting games to celebrate the grand reunion between their elderly leader and his friend from long ago.

After what seemed like forever to Panti, Olta reappeared. She had changed her clothes, combed her hair, and tied a fresh magnolia blossom to a long, delicately braided side lock. Panti looked closely at the set of incised turkey bone necklaces encircling her neck. Some artisan had rendered a herringbone design and had delicately carved it into each bead. He couldn't help stare at her as she continued to smile. Olta reached out, and again took his hand. She was stunning. He couldn't take his eyes off her.

Following the meal, the dancing, singing, and other festivities began. At dusk the women and children left the lodge to go about their customary activities in other parts of the camp. Olta was noticeably disturbed. She didn't want to leave although it was tribal custom that she must. Only grown men, both those of her people and the guests, would remain in the lodge. Women were socially excluded from partaking of either the black drink or tobacco. Both of the plants, which produced these products, were controlled and consumed only by the men.

Frustrated, Olta leaned toward her grandfather, and whispered, "Please, ask Panti's grandfather to tell him that when he has had enough of your secret ways to come and find me. I'll be walking along the river." Ronna translated the message to Panti and casually pointed toward the direction in which she would go. Panti nodded in acknowledgment and looked into her bright eyes. He felt his fingers being squeezed, and then her warm grip reluctantly turned his hand loose. Olta took several steps away, then turned back for a second before resuming her exit. She broke into a high-legged, happy skip, and disappeared into the twilight on her way to the river trail.

Panti soon tired of the dull conversation between his grandfather and the loud-voiced Yustega patriarch. Often the talk between the two was completely unintelligible to him. The languages shifted, depending on who was talking, as the old men practiced the other's language. Each was delighted he could speak another tongue. When a pause in the rambling discourse arrived, Panti took the opportunity and excused himself. He hastily walked away in the direction of the river trail, and his form quickly faded into the shadows.

Darkness had descended on the Yustega village. The brightest fire was in the lodge he had just left. Throughout the camp smaller fires gave residents some defense against the cool damp air that now pervaded the river bottom. The wood fires provided light as people hurried to finish their routine daytime chores. Wood smoke, carried aloft by the heated air, mixed with the heavy air and resettled to the earth. A ghostly, shifting haze was suspended just above head height. An immense golden moon hung low in the bright sky to the east. It was rising and was well above the cloud formation that partially obscured the horizon. Its size was still distorted and it would soon appear to become smaller and intensely brighter as its orbit caused it to climb higher into the sky. Rays of silver moonlight filtered through the moss-draped live oak trees lining the forested side of the trail Panti followed. Scattered shadow-shifting beams of brilliant light shone onto the ground and illuminated his way as he walked along the unfamiliar pathway.

Panti was surprised how far he had traveled on the path. He still had not caught up with Olta. He thought to himself. "She's toying with me. She's probably hiding somewhere along this trail. She'll probably jump out of the bushes any minute, trying to scare me." Not many girls that he knew would have ventured alone so far away from other people in the dark. She was not only attractive; she was brave, too!

The trail angled more directly toward the river and opened onto a sandy beach. As he walked into the clearing, Panti saw Olta sitting on the beach, basking in the soft moonglow. He whistled softly so not to alarm her. Hearing his signal, Olta turned, sprang to her feet, and dashed to meet him. She vocalized rapidly and uttered a series of words, nearly all of which he couldn't understand. "Panti! You've come to find me? I knew you would . . . I had a strange feeling that you'd come." She reached toward him with outstretched arms and threw them around his neck. She entwined the fingers of her two hands behind his head and locked them in place. Olta stood on her tiptoes, closed the distance between their faces, and without any kind of warning took Panti's lower lip between her lips. As Olta's lips contacted his, she pressed them together firmly. At the same time, she pushed her body closer and tighter against his. Taken completely off guard, but delighted at her advances, Panti hesitated. He wrapped his arms around her in a subconscious effort to pull her closer, and in an inexperienced urge he responded by locking his lips tightly against hers. An unfamiliar flood of warmth raced through his body. Briefly, he pulled his lips free from hers, looked down into her eyes, and saw her pleasure-filled smile. He quickly returned his burning lips to the warm, moist mouth of this beautiful Yustega maiden. The couple stood together in this embrace, each totally overcome by their feelings. Somewhere across the water, in the dense head of tall cypress trees that lined the opposite bank of the River of the Stone, came the resonating voice of a lone barred owl. The hidden bird announced to all that listened in the world of night that these young humans had found one another—and were in love.

Over the next few days, Panti and Olta became inseparable. The couple was together from sunup until late into the night. They worked hard at their language skills. They questioned either grandfather when necessary to help them translate key words in their race to know each other better. They did remarkably well, because Okeena had told Olta he thought it would be better if she mastered the Calosa tongue. He insisted they would be able to converse sooner if only one language was concentrated on. Okeena was wise.

After three days they could hold a simple conversation. Olta clearly understood the Calosa words she heard on the morning of the fifth day. She was shocked when Carta announced he and his men were leaving the next morning. Tearfully, she looked at Panti's solemn expression and saw the remorse in his eyes. She asked, "Must you leave me so soon? Can't you stay with me for just a few more days?"

Visibly shaken, Panti answered her in a sad tone of voice. "No, I must leave with the others. If I stayed here I doubt I'd ever walk through my homeland again. I'd fail the hopes of my family and my totem. If I stayed here, and tried to leave for home later, I'd not survive the dangerous trip alone through the lands of people hostile to the Calosa. I must prepare myself to leave you. You must understand."

In anguish, Olta screamed, "How can you do this to me? Take me with you!"

"You'd leave your home, your family, and your people to be with me?"

"Yes! I love you! I've loved you since you first stepped out of your canoe onto our village beach. That's why I took your hand in mine! I never want to be apart from you! I've prayed to my totem about us. I'm sure it's pleased I've found you, Panti the Calosan. Yes! Please, take me with you!"

Okeena, standing nearby, overheard their discussion and interrupted his crying granddaughter. "Panti our way is matriarchal, like yours. But, my totem has told me, that even though our customs are to the contrary, you children are destined to be together. Your bonding will commemorate the long friendship and the two lives that will end before much longer. Ronna and I must travel separately to the spirit world. We'll both rest better through forever knowing you two are mates. Right, Ronna?"

"Yes, but if Panti wants to take Olta as his wife, isn't it customary he stay here with you. He must live in the land of her people, not leave!"

"Yes, it's our tradition. My blessings alone won't allow her to leave. We must consult with Yult and get his approval, and then talk to our priests. Carta must agree with your plans, to be sure there's space in the canoes for an extra person, and there are sufficient supplies to accommodate that additional person."

Happy, but worried about the way negotiations were going, Olta stopped crying, and again interrupted her grandfather. "Come, Panti, let's find my father and mother so you can ask their approval to take me with you. If they don't agree, and the priests say no, I'll go anyway!"

"Are you sure you want me to ask? I'll ask only if I'm convinced you're serious. You realize, don't you, I can't promise that you'll ever see your family . . . none of your people again!"

Olta gestured, and excitedly said, "Yes! I want to be with you forever! I'll be your best friend and lover—your helper and companion through life. I'll make you happy as your wife, and bring you many children. Yes! Yes!"

Olta's parents were unhappy to hear the couple's request, but finally agreed and promised to urge their religious leader to support the couple's wishes. They consented because Panti, the strong Calosa warrior, had pledged to take care of their daughter. He assured them he would make her happy. Panti now had to convince Carta to agree Olta could come along.

Ronna and P anti explained t he situation t o t heir e xpedition's leader. They told him what had happened between the two young people and that Panti wanted to take Olta to become his wife. Carta was quiet. It was clear to them both he was weighing all aspects of this strange request. After a long, thoughtful silence, he said, "I'm amazed these people would allow one of their daughters to leave! I'm not blind to the ways of love. I've noticed that Panti and this Yustega girl were growing close. Ordinarily I would be happy for you, Panti. You are a good man and deserve to find happiness—here at some faraway spot, or in the land of our ancestors. Ronna, you know there's limited room in our boats. We can't safely carry another person. Although I respect both of you—I'm sorry but I must deny this request."

"Then I'll not go back with you! I'll stay here with Olta. I'll build a canoe and we'll travel home later!" Panti blurted out. He was irate because of what seemed an insensitive decision.

Ronna spoke up, in a calm but firm tone. "Don't talk foolishly. I can easily solve your dilemma." Placing his hand on the shoulder of his Yustega friend, he said, "Okeena, may I stay with you for my remaining days? M y son shall b ecome h ead of m y family and this union between his son and your granddaughter can only make each of our bloodlines proud and strong. Olta can have my seat in the canoe. I'll stay here with you!"

"Grandfather! I won't let you do that!"

Okeena raised his hand, and said, "Ronna, my brother, you can remain here, and live out your days among my people. Even if I should leave this life first!"

Ronna spun around and spoke to Carta. "See, I've solved the problem. Panti and Olta will make the trip with you . . . she in my place. I'll stay behind!"

Carta, taken off guard by the turn of events, cleared his throat, and with his voice of authority, he said, "You're a noble man, Ronna. I'll respect your decision. I'll take this girl in your place. She must understand before we leave, she'll work as a member of our group.

Modesty on her part, among so many men, while we're traveling, could result in some miserable memories of her first sea voyage. I'll see that everything possible is done to meet her private needs while we're away from land. If everyone is in agreement she should gather her belongings, load them aboard our canoes before dawn, and say her goodbyes. We'll leave just as soon as it's light enough to see."

Panti awoke before dawn, and nudged his grandfather to rouse him. The two walked to the canoes where the Calosas were busy loading their gear into the huge dugouts. A few of the Yustegas, who had befriended the foreigners, were waiting to see them off. Some brought gifts and food. They wanted to wish the visitors good luck for a safe voyage. Soon, Olta, her parents and siblings, and Okeena joined them. All was ready. The moment of separation was near.

Okeena stepped forward and spoke to the group. "Calosa friends! We've enjoyed having you among us. It saddens us to see you go, knowing our pathways may never cross again. But, as you leave us, you leave one of your own, my brother Ronna. He'll always remind us of this period of friendship. In return, you also take one of my people with you to share a new life with Panti. May your totems protect each of you on your journey home and through life!" Okeena walked over to Olta, embraced her, and whispered, "My child, you've been allowed to break our tradition, but you must never forget your own people. Always remember that you must be happy and forever free of any regrets because of this decision you've made. Smile often, think of us from time to time, and know that we are all pleased you've found Panti." He wiped his eyes and turned away. He walked to Panti and took his hand briefly before walking over to join and console his somber-faced son, sobbing daughter-in-law, and their bawling children.

Panti hugged Ronna and in a low voice he spoke with difficulty. "Thank you, Grandfather. Be forever happy with these people." He turned, took Olta by the hand, and started toward the canoe.

"What's wrong Panti? Why are you talking like that this morning?"

Wiggling his tongue as he delicately probed the inside of his cheek, Panti slurred, "I think I cracked a tooth last night trying to break open the shell of one of those nuts. It sure feels like I did, anyway." He continued turning as he and Olta started to walk away.

Ronna blurted, "*Wait*! Take this to remember me." He reached down and untied his sheathed knife from around his waist. "After all, someday it would have been yours anyway. Tell your father he can handle it now and then, and even talk to me from time to time in the spirit world about it, but it's yours to carry and use. The handle . . . your beautiful totem carving already speaks and identifies the knife as yours. Carry it proudly. Use it wisely and with skill."

"Thank you, Grandfather. I'll miss you!"

Visibly in tears, Panti turned and stepped into the bobbing canoe. He sat down next to Olta, picked up his paddle, and joined the laboring paddlers as the heavy canoe started moving with the river's current. Shouts of goodbyes echoed through the misty recess of the curving river bottom. As the flowing water carried the boats along and they entered the first bend downstream from the village, Panti and Olta turned around and waved in a gesture of finality to those they would never see again. The canoes rounded the wide-sweeping oxbow and the world of the Yustegas was no longer visible. It and its people had become memories.

CHAPTER 18

THE CANOEISTS MADE GOOD TIME DOWN RIVER. In less than two days they reached the Gulf of Mexico. Whenever practical they combined sails and paddles, but it was the strong, outflowing river current that carried them swiftly to open water. Olta had never seen the ocean before. She was in awe as the sparkling green salt water filled her visual senses. She could see all the way to the glistening, sun-drenched, offshore horizon.

Both she and Panti became noticeably moody once the trip started. He became quiet and aloof whenever he had time to think about Ronna. Olta was silently concerned. It had sunk in that it was unlikely she would ever see her family again. It hadn't taken long for both of them to slip into a state of mild depression.

The others understood their predicament, appreciated their sadness, and openly sympathized with Panti and Olta. They gave the couple the space necessary to regain their attitude and composure. Olta's feelings for Panti finally overcame her melancholy. She worked to cheer him up. She manipulated him into frequent simple conversations. Her speech rhythm, the broken Calosan language was offered intermittently, almost staccato, as she gathered her thoughts. Olta hesitated momentarily as she carefully mentally arranged her words before she spoke her newfound language. "Ever since I was a little girl I've heard my people talk about this Great Water. It's everything I was told it would be." She cupped her hand and reached down into the water, and dipped up a handful. Olta brought it to her lips, tasted it, spit out the remainder, and sputtered. "It tastes exactly as I was told it would—salty!"

Panti's attitude improved when he temporarily forgot his grandfather and his cracked tooth and yielded to the questioning words uttered by Olta. Their spirits lifted, the conversation continued, and they started to work with the men in the canoes.

Finally, on the open sea, the man in the stern steered and trimmed the simple buckskin sail and the boat turned south. Generally, he navigated close to land unless unfavorable wind directions forced him to occasionally tack away from the coast. Everyone else aboard was busy working. They continued to remove bark from the hickory staves. Panti carefully examined each of them and marked the pieces he liked. At home, after the wood had dried, he'd painstakingly work it with his specialized bone and stone tools. The bow would be shaped into a flattened, tapered, double-ended, spring with a handgrip at its center. At each end of the bow he would carve a groove for attachment of a bowstring made of twisted fiber or deer sinew.

Panti was a master bow maker. His long bows and arrow shafts were highly prized among Calosa hunters and warriors. Not only did Panti's bows propel arrows to greater distances, their increased power resulted in improved accuracy at those extreme ranges.

There was little leisure time during the trip home. Even the helmsman had extra duty and was sometimes kept busy pulling in large king mackerel or other kind of pelagic fish caught on the long trolling line they towed from the stern. Olta was given the responsibility of cleaning the fish the men caught. She confided to Panti that she had never eaten so much fish. He knew her diet would undergo major changes when she started life anew among the Calosa, but he kept that to himself.

During a tack offshore, the tops of the tallest coastal cabbage palms disappeared below the eastern horizon. Suddenly, Olta screamed out in surprise. An adult bottle-nosed dolphin, one of a pod merrily following behind the boat, had surfaced and exhaled directly into Olta's face. She had leaned overboard to wash fish filets in the clear water racing by the canoe's hull. *Whoosh*! The animal's blow-hole opened and a gush of the dolphin's smelly breath struck Olta's face. She had inhaled simultaneously with the animal's exhale.

Gagged by the odor, and startled by the sight of such a large toothy mouth so close to her face, she raised up away from the water and shouted. "*Ugh*! What was that thing? Its breath was foul! It smells worse than one of the mud flats close to the shallows where we gathered scallops yesterday. No, it smells like something worse. Like some dead fish that's full of maggots and has been melting and rotting forever!"

Panti calmed Olta by assuring her the animal wasn't trying to inflict any harm. "It's a dolphin! Haven't you seen one of them before?"

"No, I haven't!"

"They're not a fish. They breathe air like we do. I've never heard of one bothering people. Look, back there!" He pointed toward the stern and continued talking, "There's a whole group following us. *Wow*! Look out there!" Panti shouted and again pointed as one of the sleek, streamlined dolphins leaped completely free of the water in a high graceful arc. "They love to race our canoes."

The wind conditions were favorable so Carta decided they would sail the calmer inland waters back to their villages. The canoes and tired crews left the Gulf and went inside, into the Great Bay of Dolphins. They turned south, into the Sound that separated the barrier islands from others fringing tighter to the mainland, and sped toward home. They passed many Calosa settlements scattered among the islands, but none of the men lived so far north. Their villages were closer to the Great Seashell Island. They sailed through the night and reached familiar territory shortly after sunrise. Their destination was in view.

Exhausted, they paddled the last half-mile to reach the beach, inside Grassy Bottom. Panti saw that as soon as the canoes were spotted by the lookout, everyone in his village stopped whatever they were doing and headed in their direction. His father was leading the parade to meet them.

Barto stepped into the water and grabbed the bow of the lead canoe to help stop it. The excited, yelling, and waving passengers leaped into the water. They were overjoyed their long journey was nearly over.

Standing on the beach at the head of the crowd, an elated Pundon screeched, so all could hear. "Welcome home, everyone! You've been gone far too long. Our lodge will echo with tales of your adventures! Where's Panti . . . and Ronna?"

Waist deep in the water, already unloading cargo, Panti answered, "I'm here, Father."

"Where's your grandfather? Did something happen to him? Tell me, did he leave you? Has he gone to the spirit world, son?"

"No, Father, he's safe, but we did leave him behind."

"You left him *behind*? Why did you leave him? Who's that person passing you things?"

Nervously, and in hesitant phrases, Panti placed his hand on Olta's arm and answered his father. "This is Olta of the Yustegas. Grandfather told us many stories about her people. Remember, he told us of his adventures as a young man with a Yustega warrior named Okeena? Well, by chance the two of them met again on the River of the Stone. Grandfather decided to stay behind with his old friend so Olta could have his seat in the canoe and come home with me. I've chosen her to be my wife. She's accepted! She's Okeena's granddaughter. Grandfather was very happy when I left him and asked that I explain this all to you. He said you'd understand."

"Yes, I'll come to understand. Your grandfather's a good man. He talked often of this man called Okeena. It's good that they are once again together. We must be happy for him. So, this woman is to be your wife, *huh*?"

"Yes. We want to get married as soon as we can. In fact, after we've rested a few days Olta and I will go down to the great leader's village and find a priest to marry us. In the meantime, I'll begin to build a place for us to live here . . . with your permission."

Smiling, Pundon looked at Olta, then answered his son. "Of course. After all, this is your home."

Olta adapted quickly to her new environment and her new way of life. She shared a crowded sleeping space with other single women, and during the day she helped in routine women's work around the community. This consisted of gathering and preparing food, maintaining the water supply, and collecting firewood. Olta also learned all aspects of the netmaker's craft. She did these chores with Panti's mother, Corla, and his younger sisters.

With the help of his close friends, Barto and Kardah, Panti spent his days finding materials to build a small hut in which his new wife and he would reside. When the dwelling was finished to his satisfaction, Panti called Olta aside for her approval. "Shall we make the trip to the capital tomorrow? Are you ready to become my wife?"

"Yes, I'm ready!" She exclaimed with a blushing smile.

"Good. Let's get things we'll need loaded into my canoe this afternoon. We'll start out early in the morning. It'll take at least half a day to get there."

Panti couldn't sleep. For most of the night he wandered through the dark village. He talked softly to the dogs, or visited the lonely lookout at his observation post. Panti's rest came in spurts of dozing. Waves of anticipation aroused him to a state of personal emotion he had never experienced before. Tomorrow he would proclaim to a priest, his totem, his ancestors in the spirit world, and his peers that he was marrying this beautiful Yustegan woman. He knew his totem had selected Olta. It was destiny that had united her with him and his people.

Shortly before sunrise the canoe left the glassy surface of Grassy Bottom and entered the wide bay that separated Panti's village from the mouth of the Great River. As Panti paddled toward the rising sun, Olta admired the invigorating fresh air and the beginning of a beautiful sunrise. Birds, of every size and description, were leaving their night roosts on nearby mangrove islands. In long flight lines or tight flocks and as individuals they were dispersing in every direction. They were headed for their favorite daytime haunts to feed and do whatever it is that birds do to pass time and enjoy life. An enormous raft of tightly grouped diving ducks, after spending the night sleeping like bobbing corks on the open water, lazily parted to create an opening to allow the canoeists passage through their uncountable numbers. Hundreds loudly quacked in scolding disapproval of the human closeness that woke them and temporarily divided their ranks.

Panti steered toward the northern end of a long island four miles across open water from the easternmost point of the Great Seashell Island. When this far point was reached, they traveled behind it and entered a large red mangrove-lined bay. With an unobstructed view of this bay they sighted the silhouette of the capital city. This, the largest of all Calosa communities, was the primary political and religious center of the kingdom.

Olta mentioned it first. Puzzled, she pointed, and questioned, "Is that a large hill I see in the distance through the haze? I thought you told me the land of your people was flat!"

"It *is* flat! Well, except for our villages. The most ancient of these are really quite high. The mounds you're pointing at, which extend above the mist, are the highest that my people ever built . . . as far as I know! There are some taller hills a few days travel south of here on a large island we call 'Land of the High Hills.' When I was a boy I traveled there with my father and grandfather to trade with some of our distant relatives. They're really big!"

Panti and Olta walked hand in hand up the long, sloping, hard-packed shell path. It led them to a series of large, palm-thatched lodges, on top of the highest mound. Few people were about this late in the day. Those who were, stared or smiled when the happy couple walked by. Panti returned the occasional greeting with courtesy. Olta mostly blushed, turned her head aside to avoid eye contact, and tucked in her chin. She was convinced these strangers knew what she and Panti were doing—headed in the direction they were going.

A wrinkled old man, with a deeply furrowed, acne-scarred face, slowly rose from a low stool and stepped out of the shadows in front of a large building as they approached. He raised his hand in greeting, and said, "Aren't you Panti, the son of Pundon?"

Surprised, Panti extended his hand to reciprocate the elder's greeting. "Yes, I am. Do I know you?"

The bent-over, nearly toothless old man laughed, and continued talking. "I've seen you around from time to time at important functions. Ha! You may not recognize me because I'm not wearing my cape and mask. I'm Turlto. I'm the chief priest of the Calosa nation. I've known Pundon since his name-giving ceremony when your grandfather

212

brought him here from his village over at Grassy Bottom for me to conduct the ritual. Ronna and I are from the same generation."

"How do you know me?"

The old shaman smiled again, cackled loudly a time or two, and pointed toward the buckskin tote bag Panti had slung over his shoulder. "Your reputation as an artist and craftsman precedes you—and always will wherever you travel. It's said that no one among our people has ever been so gifted—as skilled as you. I guessed who you are because of the fine art work on your hunting bag. I'm sure no other Calosa artisan has ever created anything as beautiful. Your use of such vivid colors and detail amazes me! Now, tell me, what brings you two to the capital, and this place in particular?"

"This is Olta. She was born among the Yustega people. We met when I went there with a group, including my grandfather, Ronna." Panti interrupted Olta's introduction to tell the priest of his grandfather's sacrifice, how he had made it possible for he and Olta to be together, then concluded. "I asked her to become my wife and she agreed. We have the blessings of her family and her tribe's religious leaders. We're here to be married. I'm looking for a priest to marry us!"

"Will I do? It would be an honor to marry you two." Turlto said, interrupting Panti's train of thought.

"You . . . the head priest of my people would do this?"

The old man scowled and blurted out in an irritated tone, "I said it would be an honor!" Turlto pointed toward the stools in the shade. "Sit and rest while I gather my assistants and have them announce a wedding will take place." Within minutes, the *boom-boom* sound of signal drums and the *too-ta-toot* of conch horns announced to all within earshot that a wedding was going to take place.

It wasn't long before dozens of happy, smiling, and whispering people were seated on the bare, smooth, crushed shell-surfaced floor inside the temple lodge. They seemed eager to witness the marriage and be involved in their nation's most popular ceremony.

About two dozen teenage girls assembled in the front of the open-air hall and seated themselves in a formal prearranged semicircle behind the wooden altar. This structure was decorated with a variety of carved masks and totems. Panti leaned over and quietly told Olta that the displayed carvings represented the various family groups of the Calosa nation. Soon, the girls stood and began a non-musical chant, which erratically rose and fell in volume. This series of rhythmic utterances by the children was setting a serious tone and developing a mind set for the hushed audience.

The chanting intensified, reached an echoing crescendo, and then dropped in volume until it became a dull-sounding, barely audible drone. From either side of the altar two robed and masked figures marched into the building. In unison the four turned, bowed to the chorus of chanters, and spun around to face the audience. At that instant, a fifth figure joined them. Dressed in a long-trained cape, which completely covered his body, Turlto the high priest proudly strutted into the grand temple.

His cape was a beautiful pink hue. It was made from thousands of carefully positioned, overlapping, and skillfully attached roseate spoonbill feathers. In coloration the garment closely matched the priest's full headdress. This was made from the larger and stiffer wing feathers from the same species of bird. Turlto's face was completely hidden behind a wooden mask. The deep relief carving of his mask's three-dimensional features was highlighted by a series of vertical wide bands of color. These accentuated an over-sized nose and brows. Eye openings in the mask connected the high priest with his seated followers, the mystic realm of the Calosa religion, and the reality of the outside world.

Turlto had been called to the priesthood at an early age. He quickly advanced, passing through the demanding maze of different degrees of priestly levels. Like his predecessors he would remain high priest until the spirit of earthly death called him to the next world, and he took his position seriously.

In a booming monologue Turlto announced to the assembly they were gathered to witness a marriage ceremony—to bond Panti and Olta together as a family unit. The subdued chanting continued as his powerful voice rose above the background noise and he beckoned the couple to approach him.

Panti and Olta stood, then hand in hand timidly walked to the altar, and joined the old priest. Turlto pranced around the pair. With one hand he shook a large rattle made from the shell of a box turtle. In the other he held a long tassel of partly braided human hair. He waved this in rhythm to the rattle. It was rumored that this very thick tassel of hair could be used only by the high priest. It was said to contain locks from the heads of all the Calos' who had ruled the Calosa people since the beginning of time. Turlto began to circle the couple and broke into a singsong chant.

When it seemed the excited priest would collapse from exhaustion, he stopped his chant and dance, faced the crowd, and tried to catch his breath. After a short gasping pause, and many deep breaths, Turlto spread his arms and announced, "People of the Calosa—and the unseen living souls of our ancestors who have joined us—you are to be witnesses today of the sacred spiritual bonding of this young couple. Some of you may know Panti personally, others may have heard of his brave deeds as a warrior or perhaps his talent as a gifted artist. His chosen woman is Olta. She is a Yustegan who today wishes to become one of our people by marriage. Her people have approved this bonding. Together they will make our people stronger!"

"By the powers bestowed upon me by our great leader, mighty Calos, both he who still lives and rules and those who have departed, I publicly announce and affirm that Panti and Olta are united as husband and wife. The Calosa nation supports their union and all peoples shall honor and respect this marriage."

Panti reached into his bag and withdrew a folded piece of buckskin, and carefully unfolded it. Inside were two identical necklaces. Attached to each one was a giant tiger shark tooth. Holding one up by its macramé braided rawhide, he placed it around Olta's neck, and spoke to her. "My wife, I too shall wear one of these as an amulet. United as we are by marriage, we shall also be joined to ward off evil from this day forward, as we walk through life together."

Olta took the other amulet and reached up to encircle her husband's neck with the cord. As she did, Panti kissed her.

His work finished, the tired priest turned and left the temple. His four assistants followed him. They had not performed any visible function in the just concluded ceremony—other than adding their voices to the chants. Several people from the audience approached and surrounded the couple. Those who knew Panti extended their congratulations. Others introduced themselves. All wished them well. Panti had recognized a few of them earlier who were close to his own age as they came into the temple. Shyly, Olta leaned her head against her husband's shoulder and responded to their comments with smiles, soft sighs, and blushes.

CHAPTER 19

THE DENSE SEAGRASS PARTED WITHOUT RESISTANCE as the canoe moved across the mirror-like surface covering the shallow grass flat. The boat bumped the soft bottom a few times, before coming to a sudden stop next to an exposed sandbar which had been uncovered by a falling tide. In a few hours it would be submerged again and nearly invisible when the tide changed and the water returned. Panti lowered his pushpole. Repositioning his grip, he took the long slender staff in his right hand, and probed it into the bottom's ooze. Using it like a cane to maintain his balance, he stepped out of the stern into the knee-deep water. After breaking his feet free from the mud's strong suction, he walked forward and grabbed the boat's bow. With a forceful lift and tug he slid the canoe halfway out of the water onto the sandbar so the boat wouldn't float away while they left it unattended. With a firm handgrip on each gunwale, Olta cautiously rose to a squatting position. She was carefully balancing herself to avoid falling out of the topsy-turvy, round-bottom canoe. Still crouched, she gingerly side-stepped overboard, trying to avoid stepping onto a clump of razor-sharp oysters mostly hidden by floating pieces of grass and the cloudy water kicked up by Panti's efforts.

"This grass tickles my legs and feet!" Olta exclaimed as she bent over the boat and picked up two large baskets made from woven palm tree roots that were stacked inside the canoe. The soft mud and wide-bladed turtle grass didn't slow her passage and she soon caught up with her husband.

Together they wandered around the edge of the hard, water-packed sandbar searching for buried and barely submerged mollusks. The siphon holes produced by the former gave away their hiding places. Within m inutes the baskets were nearly full of large clams, whelks, and clusters of huge, fat oysters.

After lugging the heavy baskets to the canoe, Panti said, "Help me collect some of this grass. We'll cover the shells with it to keep them alive longer so we'll have a supply of fresh food for our trip."

They pulled handfuls of the wide-bladed turtle grass from the bottom, s wished i t t hrough the water t o remove l oose material, a nd placed several inches of the wet grass over their shells.

"Where are we going? Why are we taking so much food with us?" Olta asked, curious about their destination because they hadn't made any travel plans.

"We're going inland, away from the coast. Food won't be as plentiful there. It'll be harder for us to find."

"Why are we going there?"

"I want to take you to the 'Land of the Big Trees.' With any luck we'll be in time to see something special . . . something magical I've only heard about from our storytellers, but never seen." Panti told her. As he spoke, he gave himself away with his impish grin. She knew right away that he had some kind of a surprise planned.

His words did not quench his wife's curiosity and she kept the line of conversation going. "Land of the Big Trees? Something that's special? What are you talking about, my husband? Are you still under the influence of the black drink you shared yesterday with the men after our wedding? Why do you speak in such riddles? What's so funny about what you just said?"

Panti laughed aloud and answered his wife. "You'll see soon enough."

For the remainder of the day the couple leisurely paddled or poled through the confusing array of look-alike mangrove islands. Now, dark was swiftly overwhelming dusk, its envelope catching up with the travelers. Panti pressed ahead in the silver-gray dimness of twilight, carefully negotiating the rhythmic surface currents and power of a strong incoming tide. The flowing water raced from the Gulf of Mexico and entered the bay through a narrow pass. Later, its velocity would diminish, but not until it spread through every bay and bayou. The level of the flowing water would eventually lap on the edges of the dry uplands, then recede once again to repeat its perpetual cycle. An error in navigation or a misjudgment of balance here could result in sudden capsize, an unexpected swim, and the loss of food and equipment—or worse.

Because of Panti's seamanship skills the couple landed safely on the leeward side of a wide, wind-exposed open beach. Unless it completely died during the night, the stiff breeze would keep insects away and the newlyweds would rest comfortably through the night—when they finally slept. It was on this night, at this very private place, beneath the dark, star-filled sky that they consummated their marriage.

The predawn sunglow began its grand entrance on the world of the Calosa. It spread its brilliant preamble along the expanse of the eastern horizon. The newlyweds awoke and made love once more. Not long after the sun cleared the mangroves the couple resumed their journey. Panti paddled and poled east toward the rising sun. After crossing the southern end of the bay they meandered through a narrow, deep, and mangrove-lined tidal creek. Soon, the character of the landscape changed when Panti steered the canoe into a high-banked narrow channel. Olta, entranced and maturing because of their first night together, was nodding off into staggered periods of half-sleep and short naps. She noticed the difference. "What's this place you're taking me? This doesn't seem to be a natural waterway. It's not like any I've seen before. It's so straight."

"You're very observant, Olta! This channel was dug by my people. When I was younger I helped dig it, and since, I've worked on its maintenance. There are many canal networks in our land. This one leads into the interior of this part of our nation and connects with a small river at its other end."

"Which way are we headed?"

Panti pointed eastward. "We'll head for that horizon . . . there . . . where the sun rises into the sky. If the water that flows from the Land of the Big Trees is deep enough we'll be there in a day or two.

Now, just relax. Enjoy the sights and experiences of my homeland. I love my secret places that I'm taking you to. I'll carry you to these strange and beautiful lands, attend to your every need, and in every way rejoice that you're my wife and life's companion."

The protected passage through the Calosa canal was pleasant and peaceful. When they reached the far end and floated into the small stream, Panti turned the canoe sharply left, and slowly paddled against the creek's gentle, downstream flowing current. Stunted red mangroves and other saltmarsh plants lined its bank. They had entered the transition zone that mixed the divergent worlds of salt and fresh water. They hadn't gone far upstream when cabbage palms and tall slash pines began to increase in number and size. The river's dark acidic water snaked southwestward out of the interior, from the general direction of where Panti had said earlier they would travel.

By mid-afternoon the ecosystem had completely changed and Panti maneuvered the canoe through narrow but well-defined cathedral-like passageways crowded with tall moss-draped cypress trees. They were approaching the origins, the headwaters, of this beautiful subtropical stream.

Olta was suddenly startled to full consciousness by a strange sound which had originated somewhere ahead and was now loudly echoing through the flooded cypress. " What *was* that noise?" S he blurted out, breaking the stunning stillness that now prevailed, as the weird sound trailed off and was eventually muted by the thick stand of countless gray and green trees. Again, the mournful noise resounded through the trees. *Krrr-owww!*

"*Aha*! I love that sound. To hear it tells me we're entering another world. One dominated by freshwater and inhabited by different and interesting kinds of wild creatures. Many animals and birds that live here are not often found in the coastal lands of my people. I think that's why I love to come to these places. They're so much different! That sound is made by a marsh bird we call the 'crying bird.'

Let's be quiet to see if we can find it. Sometimes they're easy to spot. Other times not. They're loud but very secretive."

Putting his index finger to his lips, Panti whispered, "*Shh.* Keep a lookout on the sides of the wide pond ahead of us."

The cypress had become enormous. These were indeed the stoutest trees Olta ever saw. They weren't as tall as some kinds of trees in her homeland but they were the thickest trees she had ever seen. These were ancient pond cypress. Sometime in the past, passing winds stirred up by major hurricanes had topped the oldest trees. The younger trees in this strand would also someday be similarly damaged and none would ever attain their potential full height. Downed trees, and the fallen tops from those survivors which still stood, growing as testimony to their endurance, lay in disarray through the wetlands. Had their crowns not been broken off by powerful winds, the oldest trees would have been 300 feet tall.

The fallen trees were festooned with a variety of shade-tolerant plants. Dozens of different terrestrial and epiphytic ferns, bromeliads, and orchids were thriving on the living and dead cypress. Everywhere, long roots of strangler figs were reaching down for the water. They were connected to mostly stunted trunks growing high in the cypress. These trees originated from partly digested seeds randomly scattered in the fecal deposits of birds. The stoutest vine-like roots had already connected to the flooded ground.

The unique, partially submerged knees of the giant trees, which had evolved through time to provide a life support system for the stately cypress in their flooded environment, were everywhere, too. These protruded above the water's surface, like sentries, around their respective connected tree. These root extensions not only provided oxygen from the atmosphere to the tree, but they were also covered with—many nearly concealed by—a variety of plants. Minimal sunlight reached the understory of this shaded ecosystem in the summertime because of the dense canopy. The deciduous cypress would be bald—without needles—through the coldest part of the year.

Small flooded openings among the huge trees split off from the main pond. As they passed one of these, Panti stopped paddling and whispered, "Look off to your left at those gnarled trees growing by themselves in the center of that pool. Do you see the ones with all the dead-looking ferns growing on their limbs? The ferns will spring back to life right after it rains next time. Do you see the tiny lilac-colored flowers clumped along the outer branches . . . on the twigs . . . among the ferns? They're orchids."

Panti steered the canoe toward the island-like group of trees. When he and Olta were under the canopy of luxurious plants he reached up and in a few moments finished picking a handful of the dainty flowers.

"Here, these are for you. They don't have a very strong fragrance but I love their color. Don't you?"

"Oh, yes, thank you. They're so beautiful. I'll put some in my hair."

Olta selected several sprays of the orchid blossoms and inserted them above her left ear in the undecorated leather headband encircling her glossy, jet-black hair.

The hen limpkin was startled at the sight of the canoe. She dropped the apple snail clamped in her long beak, and crouched to conceal herself in the blue-flowered pickerelweed. The anxious bird peered through the lush emergent vegetation. She tried to figure out what this strange object was. She had never seen a human being before, much less a canoe with two of them in it. The bird glanced away for an instant and checked her three half-grown chicks, which were intently watching her every movement. A barely audible clucking sound from their nervous parent caused the young birds to hunker down. They froze, all motion stopped. Moments earlier, they had been moving around, busy exploring the limited world of their floating nest platform.

Before the interruption, their mother had been working diligently to remove the soft body of the snail. The invertebrate was securely housed, firmly attached to the convoluted inside of the round brown shell. Had the intruders not disturbed the limpkin, her long decurved beak would be dangling the delicious morsel in front of one of the hungry chicks. Their brave mother was now taking time out to respond to this unexpected threat.

She started her theatrics with ancient feigning tactics. These time-tried techniques were usually successful. They were developed eons ago by primitive birds. The ruse protects eggs or young when predators are drawn away from the faker's nest.

After making a series of plaintive sounds, the limpkin displayed herself to the intruders. She leaped into the air, did a somersault, and then collapsed in what looked like a death throe. She landed in a heap in the water at the outer edge of the dense pickerelweeds a few feet farther away from her nest and defenseless young. Still completely visible to the invaders, she extended her left wing. This was dragged behind her, and with a repertoire of convulsive leaps and agonized-appearing thrashing movements, she distanced herself further from her chicks. She was trying, at all costs, to convince the humans she was at death's doorstep so they would follow her.

"That crying bird must have a nest close by she's trying to protect!" Panti whispered, as he began to back paddle. When the heavy canoe's direction of motion reversed, he spoke again. "I don't want to frighten her too far away. Something bad could happen to her or her eggs if I did. We'll go on our way and let this bird do what she's supposed to do."

Olta had already noticed a special element of sensitivity in the way her husband interacted with wild things. He seemed to genuinely care about their survival, unless the animal or bird was considered one of the traditional food animals harvested by his people. She was delighted when he decided to withdraw from any closer contact with the frightened bird.

As the canoe left the pool, and reentered the main flooded run, Olta reached down to the surface of the black, mirror-like water and picked up a floating limpkin feather. She added the bronze-colored feather to her headband, next to the orchid sprays Panti had picked for her. As they meandered through the open waterways between the cypress, another distinctive *Krrr-owww* reverberated through the trees. When this farewell, "*I fooled you!*" wail trailed off into silence the cypress strand was once again stilled, except for the sound of rippling water passing the canoe's hull and dripping from the rhythmic lifting and stroking of Panti's paddle.

Panti found a place for them to spend the night. It was a traditional campsite located on a small pine island—an oasis-like dry upland retreat surrounded by the flooded cypress forest. While he busied himself knocking down the vegetation to form a clearing for them to camp, Olta unloaded their sleeping gear from the canoe. She noticed small piles of old, sun-bleached seashells.

223

"How did these shells get here? Aren't these usually found in the tidal waters? How could they have gotten so far inland . . . away from salty water?"

"Hunters and war parties have camped here. I've camped here a few times. We always brought a good supply of provisions, and empty shells mark our temporary campsites. We'll leave empty shells here, too. Speaking of food, shall we eat oysters tonight?"

"Yes, let's roast them. I'll get them ready to cook if you'll get a fire started." Olta was slowly becoming accustomed to seafood, the mainstay of the Calosa diet. In her former life, as a Yustegan, she had never tasted seafood. Food known to her that came from the water was limited to a variety freshwater fish, crayfish, frogs, and turtles of several species.

Panti smiled and nodded before walking into the head-high palmetto thicket to gather firewood. He carefully watched where he stepped and scanned both sides of his route several feet ahead of where he intended to go. He knew this was the prime habitat of the dangerous giant rattling snake. He must be very careful. To be struck and pierced by the long curved fangs of one of these large venomous snakes was certain agonized death. Fallen pieces of pine were scattered everywhere and Panti soon had an armful of the dry wood. He returned to the camp without confronting a rattlesnake.

In the meantime, Olta had collected a small pile of dry twigs and was breaking them up to be used as tinder to start the fire. Panti picked up his small bow and shaft fire-starter and fitted the parts together. Soon, its friction-generated heat produced small red coals at the base of the spinning shaft. He placed the tinder next to these, pursed his lips, and blew his breath. Panti directed steady puffs of air toward the coals to supply oxygen and help start the fire. The fire flared in the tinder and soon the flames of the rosin-filled pine limbs reduced the wood to a hot bed of glowing coals. Panti leveled these out and placed the enormous oysters Olta had separated and washed on top of them. To put them directly on the coals, he held the oysters with over-sized tongs he had made from a partially split green stem he had cut from a nearby cabbage palm. In a few minutes, they heard the sound of boiling fluid inside the shells and seconds later the faint explosive sound whenever an oyster popped open. They were done, ready to be gingerly retrieved from the heat with the tongs. When they cooled enough to be handled, the fully cooked, delicious animal inside the parted shell was removed and eaten.

After they finished their meal, Panti stoked the fire. With their appetites satisfied, they reclined on their tightly woven sleeping mats, watching the sky slowly darken as the sun slipped behind the western horizon. Night quickly descended on their bedroom. Far off in the cypress strand a barred owl announced it was active and hunting in the darkness, *Hooo, hooo, hooo-wah-hooowaah.*

As full dark quickly approached, Olta noticed small blinking lights around them. These started out low among the palmettos but after a few moments they dispersed and their tiny lights were everywhere she looked. She was familiar with these flying beetles. She remembered, when as a child, she had joined her Yustegan playmates and happily collected the strange blinking bugs. That is, once she was convinced that by touching them she wouldn't be burned. The insects mystified both youngsters and adults everywhere they occurred because of the light they generated. Other than fire, light in and of itself was an incomprehensible natural phenomenon confined to heavenly origins—created by gods and totems and sometimes demons.

Overwhelmed by the sight, Olta asked, "I've never seen so many of the light bugs before! Have you?"

"No! I haven't! This is the magical night I wanted us to see together for the first time. I knew the time of year lightning bugs develop, come out of the earth, and are able to fly was at hand. I told myself if we were in an area like this at the right time we might have a good chance of seeing it happening ourselves. *Oh*, just look at them all! I never imagined there would be so many! I've heard it said by storytellers that sometimes they're so numerous there seems to be more of them than there are stars in the sky. I believe it! My people call this 'The Night Stars Are Born.' Some of the priests have told me the tiny lights represent the souls of the dead who have returned from the other side to visit us. Very few people ever witness such a thing. We're so lucky! See, these shark tooth talismans we wear are already bringing us good . . . not evil."

What seemed to be tens of thousands of fireflies continued to emerge from the forest litter around the bases of the saw palmettos. They flew higher and higher into the darkness. Their blinking lights were everywhere. Silently watching the spectacular and rarely observed event, the couple snuggled closer together, and soon their heavy eyelids closed as each drifted off to sleep. They would dream of giant trees, strange-sounding limpkins and owls, and little flying insects with strange flashing lights in their soft bodies.

CHAPTER 20

PANTI AND OLTA SPENT TWO MORE NIGHTS IN THE land of the big trees, admiring and exploring the sights and sounds of the unique environment. On their third morning in the strand, the cypress trees were becoming noticeably smaller, almost dwarfed. The canoe floated out of the dense cypress dome and onto a vast flooded prairie. The tree line abruptly ended. This wetland system of coarse grasses stretched to the horizon, its plane only broken by scattered tree islands. These small islands—hammocks—of upland were dominated by clumps of cabbage palms. Unseen to the travelers, the shallow water on which Panti poled the canoe was moving with an indiscernible current toward their common destination. Hydrologically the vast freshwater wetlands of the prehistoric south central Florida peninsula formed a broad unified floodplain. The water contained within this system slowly flowed south with an imperceptible current until it eventually reached and mixed with seawater in the Florida Bay or the Ten Thousand Islands regions. Rainfall and overflowing lakes far to the north nurtured this globally unique ecosystem. Their canoe was being carried along at a snail's pace by the invisible flow, but the journey proceeded because of the steady pushing of Panti's long pole against the mushy bottom, steering them through the shallow marsh.

Panti and Olta were suddenly invigorated by the smell of fresh sea air. The distinctive aroma was being carried deep into the belt of mangrove islands by a brisk seabreeze. Their trip into the freshwater interior had ended two days before when they reached the periphery of intruding saltwater, where the clear outflow from the Land of the Big Trees began to mix with a much different quality of water. This mixing zone resulted in a very productive and rich estuary. It was at that point that the couple encountered stunted red mangrove trees. These were precariously rooted on the edge of an inhospitable cattail- and sawgrass-crowded freshwater marsh lining the tidal creek. The changing vegetative types—a transition zone—signaled to Panti they would soon reach the broad estuary of the Ten Thousand Islands—known to his people as the Waters of Many Islands.

Panti patiently maneuvered the canoe through a series of small bays. They were still far from open water, substantially distant from the outermost barrier keys, which fronted directly on the Gulf of Mexico. The small islands offered them protection from the wind and chop caused by the breeze's unobstructed sweep across open water.

"We'll begin to turn off to the right now. Our home is off in that direction." Olta turned as Panti yelled over the wind and pointed north. "Our route home will be mostly well-protected from rough water. We'll pass the Land of the High Hills. They'll be off to our left. If I can see them through the haze I'll point them out to you."

The l argest o f t he p eripheral islands h ad w hite s and b eaches exposed to the Gulf. They looked similar to some of the larger mangrove islands near the Great Seashell Island. The days were long and tiresome as Panti poled the canoe through countless shallow mangrove creeks and bayous.

On the afternoon of their second day in the mangroves, Olta suddenly lifted her left arm, pointed, and exclaimed, "Look, Panti! I see two or three canoes over there! Slightly behind us! Do you see them?"

Panti, who was standing up to best use the push pole, was a few feet higher than Olta and could see much further than his wife. He hesitated momentarily, then replying in an apprehensive tone, he said, "Yes. I've been watching them for quite a while! There are three canoes, and it looks to me like each is carrying five or six people.

228

Don't be afraid! I'm sure they're my . . . *ah* . . . our people. Others wouldn't dare to travel this deep into Calosa territory. They seem to be heading in the same direction as we are and I'd say they're in a big hurry. We'll try and catch up with them just beyond that mangrove island ahead, the one with the fish hawk nest on this end of it. I've got to find out why they're in such a hurry? I'm sure something important's happened! Can you help me paddle to make better speed?"

Olta dropped the slippery animal she had just cut free from the inside of an enormous quahog clam. It fell into a large wooden bowl with others of its kind and she tossed the still hinged-connected bivalve shell overboard. She picked up her paddle and dipped the blade deep into the water. Olta was determined to help her excited husband catch up with the other canoes. She recognized the sense of urgency in his strong and calming voice.

*   *   *

"Hello! Where're you men going in such a rush?" Panti yelled through cupped hands when he and Olta had nearly caught up with the lead canoe. Their vessel was now close enough that someone in one of the boats could hear him over the wind. Nearly exhausted, the couple had approached the strangers from an angle. The three canoes slowed when those in the lead canoe saw Panti waving at them. They saw he was straining, trying desperately to narrow the distance separating them, before they moved too far ahead.

A middle-aged man in the stern of the first canoe replied in a gruff, loud voice. "Who are you? Why do you interfere . . . try to stop us?"

Panti caught his breath, and said, "I'm Panti, of the Panther Clan! We're from the Great Seashell Island . . . far to the north. This is my wife, Olta. We're on our way home. When I first saw you I could tell you were in a rush. I thought something must be wrong because of the all-out effort you were making to get somewhere. And no one was chasing you! I know something important's going on. Who are you people? Why are you in such a hurry?"

"You're right! We *are* in a big hurry!" The man said, then turned and spoke to the others. "Everyone rest! Take a breather while I take a few minutes to answer this young man! He turned to face

229

Panti, and said, "I'm Runda of the Sacred Deer Clan. We're from the village on the island across the waterway from the Land of the High Hills." Runda was apparently leading the canoeists. He pointed toward the west and resumed talking loudly, but in a less belligerent tone. "We started out on a hunting trip to the 'Great Grass Prairie'. Before we reached the river that would take us inland, we encountered invaders in giant boats who had landed on one of the large outer islands. We attacked and skirmished with them. After a two day stalemate we were reinforced. We killed one of them and finally drove them back into the sea, but our force suffered many casualties. Had we been a war party with many arrows they wouldn't have escaped! Now, I must hurry to the capital and tell the great leader Calos about this invasion. I suggest you follow us, for your own safety in case those strange warriors return with a larger force."

Panti had to know more. "Who were these intruders? You say they were strange men . . . how so? Could you and your warriors not kill them?"

Runda answered him sarcastically. "Panti of the Panther Clan, you certainly are full of questions for someone so young. You speak like a man experienced in warfare. I'm sure we could've killed them all if you'd been with us to single-handedly overpower their strange and frightening thunder weapons."

This comment angered Panti and he responded defensively, irritated at what he considered to be this man's unjustified sarcasm. "I've been at war against my people's enemies a few times and taken lives. I have five locks of our enemy's hair, from the heads of those I killed in close battle, hanging from my war saber! I've made my enemies tremble and flee!"

With what seemed to be the core of the conversation ended, the stranger's canoes began to move again. Paddling hard to keep up with Runda's faster boat, Panti pressed the conversation, and asked,

"What was so strange about these men? How were their weapons different?"

"These men were not like us . . ."

". . . Not like us? What do you mean?"

"They were light-skinned. Their faces were sickly, almost white color, not unlike the feathers of long-necked wading birds! Some had their faces covered with black hair. Others had polished skin and were wearing strange headdress. Their skin was as bright as the sun! I'm sure their skin would have blinded us if we hadn't covered our eyes when they directed the brilliant flashes at us when we attacked! Their spoken tongue was unlike any we had heard before! Some of their warriors used weapons that smoked. They sounded like the loudest thunder during a summer storm! The men were short in stature but their boats were gigantic. They were larger than anything we ever saw before! We drove them off the beach and watched them sail away. Many large sails, the color of the clouds in the sky, carried them across the sea.

"If anyone knows who these people are, our great leader will. When I was sure we had driven the strangers away, I decided to go to the capital and report what's happened. I've dispatched another canoe with two men to alert all of our villages scattered through this region. They'll get the signal fires started. I have to hurry. We'll see you again at our destination. I'm sure a combination of your curiosity and responsibility will draw you there!"

With those words of finality Runda gestured and gave orders to the others in his company. Because their canoes had more paddlers they quickly pulled away from Panti and Olta.

Panti couldn't believe what they had just been told. He sat stone still except involuntarily shaking his head in disbelief. Returning to reality, he spoke to his wife. "We must hurry! I must get there as quickly as I can! It sounds to me as though sea demons have risen out of the depths of the Great Water! They've shown themselves and their evil intentions to harm my people. That was a grave mistake. One they'll regret!"

* * *

After two more days of dawn to dusk paddling, the fatigued couple was now in sight of the capital. Its tall silhouette was visible in the distance, jutting above the low mangrove islands. Panti told Olta he estimated it would take another half-day before they reached their goal.

All islands they passed on this part of their journey, which were inhabited by Calosas had fires burning on them. These fires were set on permanent dirt-covered platforms built expressly for this purpose and positioned for maximum visibility on each village's highest point of land. Signal fires were only lit as an early warning system to notify the widely scattered Calosa clans something important was happening and what action was required. In every direction Panti and Olta looked, there were canoes filled with warriors. All were bound for a common destination.

Panti pointed toward the Gulf of Mexico, now visible through a narrow pass between two barrier islands. A plume of smoke was suspended over one of the islands. Still pointing, Panti said, "According to that smoke signal, the great leader has summoned all the nation's warriors to his war council, except those who must remain at each village as a militia. Signal fires like that one off to the left are now lit at all our settlements. All the way from here to the Bay of Danger."

Olta replied to her excited husband. "I've never seen so many people on the water at the same time."

"There's more canoe activity than I can ever remember, and everyone's going in the same direction. *Oh*, I hope we're in time! I don't want to get the outcome of a warrior's council second hand. Only the great leader and those close to him will know what's going on, and I want to hear it from their lips!"

Olta reassured her husband. "It looks as though we'll get there in time. By the looks of things ours won't be the last canoe to arrive."

It was early in the afternoon, when they paddled into the wide canal leading into the protected basin. Panti's people had constructed this impressive entrance to the town centuries ago when the site was selected to become the political and religious center of the Calosa nation. Many of the canoes jamming the basin had been pulled out of the water onto the bank, beyond the reach of the tide. Later arrivals were tethered to these, some partially resting on the muddy bottom while others floated free. In the center of the crowded terminal, all tied together and firmly anchored, were a group of about a dozen large high-bowed and wide-stern war canoes. At maximum capacity these each would hold 20 armed warriors, and because of the manpower they were very fast.

Panti maneuvered their canoe to a spot he selected. Unable to beach it, he asked Olta to secure the bow to the canoe ahead of them.

Then he took his wife's hand and using nearby boats as bridges they walked across their hulls, carefully balancing themselves to avoid falling into the water. After they stepped ashore onto dry ground Panti led Olta to a small crowd of people, and made an unexpected request. "Please, stay with this group of women and children while I join the assembly. I'm sorry but it's for men only!" Before Olta could say anything, her husband had left her standing there as he dashed up the trail toward the large, over-crowded, and very noisy lodge.

As Panti sprinted toward the building he thought to himself. "There won't be any rumors now. Everything—each instruction and piece of information delivered by the leader and the war chiefs will be personally heard by each of us."

The sound and rhythm of the ceremonial drums announcing the arrival of the tribal leaders intensified. Panti's eyes scanned the assembly. He hoped to find a familiar face in the crowd. He saw his best friend, Barto, sitting near the front. He maneuvered in that direction and squeezed through the tightly closed ranks to join his pal.

Barto was surprised—no, astonished—to have Panti sit down beside him. After taking his hand in their customary shake of friendship, he slapped Panti on the shoulder, and asked, "How'd you get here on time? I thought you were still taking your time showing Olta the scenery—and other things! Ha! When we saw the signals at home and started our fire, everyone was sure you'd miss this landmark event."

Panti leaned close and his lips almost touched the ear of his nearly deaf friend. He gave Barto a concise rundown on how he and Olta had learned about this meeting and what actually caused it. Barto listened intently, nodding occasionally as Panti spoke close to his ear, telling him about their chance meeting with Runda and learning of the skirmish with the strange invaders. Before Panti explained the situation to him, Barto had no idea why this unusual council of warriors had been called. Neither of them could remember such a gathering happening before in their lifetimes, nor had either ever heard of such a historical event.

Almost through telling his tale, Panti paused, smiled, and went on to end his part of the conversation. "You of all people should have known that I'd be here. The power and destiny of my panther totem wanted me to be here!" He stopped talking when a man suddenly stood up in the center of the crowd.

The man raised his arm and clenched his fist to get the audience's attention. After introducing himself as Celti, one of Calos's key militiamen and the war chief, he announced the territory of the Calosa nation had been invaded by an unknown adversary. According to the long-established plan, now that this warrior council had assembled, all signal fires in the coastal network would be extinguished before sunset. The women, who had stayed at home, would have already collected a sufficient supply of wood should the relighting of signal fires become necessary. Militia sentinels were on standby, ready in case the invaders returned. He described their boat and its sails and said the instant they were sighted on the horizon, at any point along the coast; the signal fires would be relit.

"All rise in the presence of the great Calos!" A loud voice resonated from a domineering-voiced, pink-caped figure that had strutted to center stage. Panti recognized this speaker. It was Turlto. The high priest verbally guided the audience into an obligatory mood of united respect for their leader. Turlto was doing this with vocal tones and physical actions of a much more serious nature than when Panti had last talked with him.

The din of conch horns and portable drums announced the approach of Calos, and his imminent entrance into the building. A moment later, he entered the lodge, strutted down the aisle, and joined Turlto. He was followed by six stern-faced subchiefs who remained the required few steps behind him. The loud applause and spirited chanting from his assembled warriors gave him pleasure. Calos smiled despite the seriousness of the moment. He was a tall man and both handsome and muscular. His body was adorned with colorful body art and gold bands and bracelets circled the biceps and wrists of both arms. A heavy, twisted gold necklace with an attached pendant hung from around his neck and rested against his broad chest.

The origins of his metal jewelry were forgotten. Legend had it that these adornments were brought with the early Calosas from the land across the Great Water. Any gold the people now obtained through trade was dedicated to the ceremonial use of Calos. Therefore, it had no real value among the Calosa people. Chert was more valuable.

Calos was the paramount king-like leader of the Calosa nation. His name was a continuum of a traditional legacy of leadership, passed down a direct bloodline to the eldest male heir of a sitting king, to the next generation—an individual predetermined to ascend to the primary ruler position. He was now nearing middle age. Calos became the Calosa leader while in his late teens.

He was elevated to the position following his father's unfortunate and untimely death. The previous Calos, also a popular leader, had succumbed to a massive foot and leg infection. Irreversible blood poisoning and gangrene had ravaged him after his left Achilles' tendon had been severed. The sharp, poison-shrouded barb of a stingray he stepped on while swimming with his children impaled his foot. His son had done an exceptional job of leading the nation since his father's death. During the current Calos' reign, life had been good and mostly peaceful. His first major crisis was at hand—and it was far more serious than any ever faced by his predecessors. Mysterious invaders had dared enter the territory of his people and he must respond. He knew he had to deal with these issues with decisive power and tenacity.

Calos raised both arms and slowly circled to face each man in his audience. This was a personal effort to establish a one-on-one spiritual connection with his warriors. For the hundreds of men seated around him, it seemed he was making eye contact with them individually. He was personally asking each of them to give their best service in the nation's needs. They were expected to fearlessly and ferociously defend and protect their political and religious leaders, their people as a whole, their families, their way of life, and the lands claimed by the Calosa nation. To gain this resolve, each warrior would psychologically bond with the wholeness of the will of Calos. Lowering his arms, Calos began to speak. At first, he spoke slowly, testing the volume of his voice so that each man could hear what he had to say. "Brave warriors—defenders of my people! You represent the best of our nation . . . our enemies shall always retreat at your approach. We are proud to see so many of our gallant men assembled here today. Yes, if those who would dare invade our land could see as many brave men of the Calosa nation as I now see, they would cower in the dust and quickly flee from our territory. Your response to our call—the many signals asking you to gather at this meeting—was timely. Each of you being here is of the utmost importance to the successful planning for the defense of our people and their freedom.

"As I look out among you, I see many warriors that in the past my father or I publicly recognized for their brave contributions to our society in the face of battle and other adversarial times. Those of you I refer to have each been battle-tested. The youngest of you have not yet been offered a fight. You have not had an opportunity to take the life of one who is an enemy. Nor have you sent your first arrow or dart in anger at an enemy. Because of the problem facing us as a people, the one we will soon outline, your time to pick up your weapons and kill our enemies may be at hand. I want to thank you in advance should we be forced to make war. I hope that each of you remain safe through any battles that lie ahead.

"Romta, my advisor for territorial affairs will now speak to you. He will explain why we have been brought together at this special meeting." Calos again raised his arms and shouted, "Hail, my mighty warriors!"

In unison the audience leaped to their feet to acknowledge his final personal remark, as Calos stepped back a few feet and sat down in an elevated, throne-like chair. Their response to his words was a unified rallying cry. "Hail, great Calos, brave leader of the Calosa people!"

Romta was much older than his monarch. When the gray-haired, w ell-wrinkled elder walked t o t he speaker's circle h e d id s o slowly, almost hesitantly. Motion was difficult for him. He had a serious limp, and his posture was somewhat slumped. During his long distinguished career as a diplomat, Romta had served three leaders. Except for minor uprisings by non-Calosa people living within the region controlled by Calos, peace had prevailed in the nation for a decade. He had negotiated treaties with several of the smaller tribes whose borders connected with those of the Calosa. When a much younger man, Romta was selected to lead the first diplomatic mission to the large islands across the Great Water. He developed trade agreements with many different peoples and cultures. Later, his subordinates regularly traveled to those lands to keep the lines of commerce and communication open with those trade partners. His dealings were not secret, but he reported only to Calos. It was Calos who determined how far down the chain of command, or to which class level, details about his policy or negotiations tied to trade would reach. Without problems on the borders, which required combat, the average Calosa citizen would never learn of any trade negotiations or sanctions. All Calosans were at liberty to practice free trade with their neighbors, or any other people associated through treaty with the Calosa.

In a strong, steady voice, Romta said, "Defenders of our nation, I welcome you. Thank you for coming to this important meeting. I know it was difficult . . . a hardship . . . for many of you to be here. Great Calos has asked me to give you a report on some interesting news about foreign affairs."

He would not tell them that two, fast oceangoing sailing canoes were at this very moment underway at sea, speeding with the wind, and headed for the Big Southern Island. He had dispatched a skilled group of diplomats overseas. They were led by Romta's assistant, Ruad. He was sent on this secret mission to determine the accuracy of rumors, which had reached here from time to time, about strange people that had already invaded those foreign lands.

"Now, this is the situation as I know it to be—what we've learned about the recent landing of strange men in the Waters of Many Islands. Some of you may have heard stories and rumors about strange men that are said to have visited the islands that lie far across the dangerous Great Water." He paused, gathering his thoughts. "*Aha!* I see astonished expressions among you! Some of you may not have heard this news before.

"The unexpected contact, which Runda of the Sacred Deer Clan and his companions made with the unusual-looking men a few days ago, was our first meeting with these invaders. They are an unknown race of people from far across the Great Water—from where the sun sleeps. We have learned they first visited some of the faraway offshore islands some time ago. Probably within the lifetime of the youngest of you warriors who are here today. At first, they were friendly and simply traveled through the islands looking for a water passage to some unknown land they were searching for. A few years later, they returned with a larger force, made demands on the island people, and finally

237

open warfare raged for a time—and still does—between many of the island tribes and these foreigners.

"Their smoking weapons and small shoulder-held bows which shoot short arrows, as Runda has described, are superior to our weapons. Overall, their war campaigns were successful despite the large numbers of brave warriors who fiercely fought against them. Time, and time again, these interlopers were victorious, and over time, they subjugated and enslaved the people on many of the islands.

"We're reasonably sure the men Runda's hunting party encountered were an advance group sent here as scouts by their leaders. They continue a mad, unrelenting search for something they hold in high esteem. Runda was correct in repelling them. We must not offer our hands in greeting or friendship. They're troublemakers and their wrath is cast wherever they travel. We've learned through our diplomatic contacts that they are mortal men. They do die as we do. They are not gods or superhuman demons. Our warriors can kill them with common weapons. We suspect they will return, perhaps sooner than later. Each of us must remain in a state of readiness, be mentally prepared to meet them in battle, and defeat them soundly. They must never dare return to our homeland."

CHAPTER 21

A N UNCOMFORTABLE PASSIVE CALM PERVADED THE mood of the solemn-faced men who were sitting in the lodge. Their expressionless eyes gave away their soul-searching, depressed attitudes. Each individual's personal apprehension and disbelief fueled the mindset of those assembled in the lodge. Each warrior was absorbing the implications and seriousness of the old man's message. To a man, each contemplated what this meant to him personally. From the tone of Romta's message it was perfectly clear that a war was inevitable. Warfare could be a glorious element of life for a well-trained and experienced warrior. But it also brought death, pain, suffering, widows, and orphans.

Panti was shaken by the serious words uttered by Romta. Like the hundreds of other men in the lodge he was overwhelmed at the announcement. He closed his eyes and became completely lost in serious thoughts. "Invaders? We'll crush them like ants if they dare return! But, if they're as powerful as this elder has claimed many of us are going to die in battle. I've just taken a new step in my life. I've married Olta. Now, I'm threatened by the risks our warriors must face if we make war against this new enemy. But, no one ever promised me life would be fair or long . . . I wonder?"

Panti leaped to his feet, and yelled, "Wise Romta!" to get the old man's attention, and then excitedly said, "If a conflict with these strangers is inevitable why don't we become the aggressor and take the battle to them—alongside our weaker allies across the Great Water? Send a legion of our best warriors to fight side-by-side with our oppressed southern brothers. United, we could drive the invaders back to wherever it is they came from! I, for one, would join such an expedition." Throughout the audience, one-by-one men began to stand up, in support of Panti's suggestion that Calos launch a preemptive strike. They repeated his pledge to volunteer.

Romta, mentally quick on his feet, instantly responded. "Please! Please, be seated!" Once the crowd quieted, he said, "Our war council has talked about sending a large army of fighting men to help the island peoples. It has been ruled out as an option because of logistics." He turned slightly, looked down, and spoke to another man who was seated in the inner circle. He asked, "Bandon, do you have further comments on this man's suggestion?"

Bandon was a tall, powerful-looking man who wore an eagle feather headdress. He stood and saluted Calos, then slowly turned his colorfully painted body around. He rotated 360 degrees to face each serious expression glaring at him from the crowd. Bandon was one of the six men who had entered the lodge with Calos, and appeared to be about the same age as the Calosa leader. Panti had met Bandon, the Calosa nation's most decorated warrior, before. They had once fought side by side in a fierce skirmish with a party of Tequesta warriors from far across the Great Grass Prairie. It was during this heated hand-to-hand fight that Panti counted his first success in battle when he single-handedly killed a Tequestan adversary with his knife.

"*Aha*! Panti, of the Panther Clan! It's been a long time! My friend, your idea is noble and a good suggestion, but it simply isn't feasible. For one thing, we don't have enough seaworthy canoes to launch such an expedition with a sufficient force, but more simply put, it's just too far. We must wait for these men to come to us!"

Barto nudged Panti with his elbow and spoke to his friend in a hushed, questioning tone. "*He* knows *you*? Panti, you never cease to amaze me!"

Bandon was still talking. "We must be patient. If they dare return, we'll assemble and pounce on them like a mighty panther on a deer! Time will be our ally. We'll be prepared to defend our homeland.

"In the meantime, our people must maintain a constant vigil. When you return to your home village, each of you are to make, or have made, an additional war bow and 50 feathered arrows fitted with war points. It might be important for those of you who are skilled in the use of the atlatl to equip yourself with an additional spear-thrower and several extra darts as well. We're convinced these strangers will return. It's only a matter of time. We must be ready to assault them on both land and sea. We'll attack whenever and wherever the opportunity presents itself. Tell those who live in your villages they are not to live in fear, but you warriors must assemble quickly whenever you are called on to drive these evil men away. We must have such overwhelming power, in both terms of men and weapons, so none of them will ever dare meet the mighty Calosa in battle again!"

The meeting was over and men scattered throughout the island-city to visit with friends or relatives before leaving for home. For many it would be a long and grueling journey. Panti and Barto stood in the long angle of shade cast by a giant false mastic tree. Like others in the tree's shadow, they were escaping the afternoon inferno-like heat of the spring sun to privately discuss the leadership's announcements. A young man walked up to them, timidly introduced himself as Durna, a novice priest, and addressed Panti. "Turlto the chief priest would like to meet with you before you leave for home. Can I tell him to expect you soon?"

Apparently thinking about something else and annoyed by the impolite interruption, Panti scowled and replied in a hostile tone of voice to the question. "Yes. You can let him know I'll be there in just a few minutes . . . just as soon as I'm through talking with my friend." Still irritated, he then continued his conversation with Barto. A few moments later, when they were saying their goodbyes, Panti told Barto where he had left Olta near the canoe lagoon. He asked him to find his wife and tell her where he was going and that he'd join her soon. "Don't tell her too much about what went on at the meeting. I don't want her overly concerned. Remember, she isn't completely at ease

241

with the ways of our people yet!" With that, Panti turned and walked into the blazing sunlight in search of the old priest.

Small noisy throngs of adults were everywhere. Loud story-tellers were expounding the virtues of the Calosa; reaffirming to the citizens why they were known for their bravery, ever-victorious fighting ability, and feared by all men. All were true statements, for the Calosa had never tasted defeat or felt the heel of oppression since their ancestors had arrived in this land. These orators presented accurate oral histories about past wars and threatened great harm would befall any invaders. Panti had never before seen such unified public opinion build so quickly against any enemy. He, and everyone else, were certain the strange-looking men who had confronted Runda had brought down the wrath of all the gods and sacred totems worshiped by his people.

The Sacred Deer Clan was not known for quick aggression. At least, not as highly esteemed as the warriors of the Panther Clan. Panti had since learned Runda was a fighter of high reputation. He had repelled the demons and given the Calosa time to plan.

Turlto frowned as he collected his thoughts. Then in a serious tone, he said, "Panti, these are alarming times for our people. I've had many visions. I've grown to doubt the lives of the generation to follow yours will have the freedom you and I enjoy today. To safeguard the souls of my people I must do everything possible to please the Great Spirit who continues to protect our people. I must keep my mind, and spiritual being, connected to the other world. To do this I'm going to ask your help. You're the finest craftsman living. Every creation of yours is a thing of beauty. Each captures the essence of our nation's relationship to our gods and totems, which our people have always held in high esteem and worshiped. I've come to realize you have a special connection with the spirit world. Our people now need, more than ever, help in maintaining a favorable and intimate relationship with the powers living in the other world; the good spirits which give us prosperity and power. Those mysterious unseen icons on which our religious foundation rests must continue to favor us as a people."

Panti's anger seemed to have waned when he responded to the priest's words. "I understand what you're saying, Turlto. But . . . how can I do more than physically battle those who'd attack us? How can my talents and abilities do more than that . . . than my skills as a warrior? I'll serve our people in any capacity. You know that. You shouldn't have any doubt. I'd never decline any request to serve the gods who control the destiny of my people."

"It's often been whispered that you're different from everyone else. Some say that the totem of Panti is at the zenith of its power and equally balanced in each of your souls. Your clan's warriors insist the panther totem is a provider of some kind of a protective blanket to those who worship it. Men from other clans pray that its good will flow into their lives, too."

Turlto gestured with both hands as he spoke to Panti. The solemn gaze in the priest's eyes conveyed the conviction in his heart, as he continued. "I'd like you to consider an important request. You can give me your answer later, if you wish. I want you to make a series of miniature carvings of your totem. I envision them to be a little larger than the one you made for the handle of your knife. I'll see that one reaches every village in our land. With protection granted by your totem, every Calosa man, woman, and child will be spiritually shielded through any hard times they must endure because of the actions of the race of evil light-skinned men.

"Having one of your spiritual totems in each of our villages will bring strength and comfort to our people. Anxiety, because of worry about imminent war, will be diminished for the non-combatants. If I were to commission someone other than you to create these statuettes they would be crudely fashioned and likely scorned by the very god we hope to please."

Without hesitation, Panti said, "I'll do it! But it'll take time. I'll begin as soon as I can and when I have a sufficient number done I'll deliver them to you. After you've sanctified them as gifts to the good will of the mighty god which they represent, your priests can distribute them to the villages."

Turlto was pleased that Panti had agreed to his request. He grinned broadly, and his few, evenly grit-worn, and yellowed teeth showed, when he said, "Yes, they will be sanctified with pomp and circumstance. And, you, my son, will be rewarded in the afterlife and glorified by the storytellers when it's your time to make the journey there!"

Olta w asn't p leased s he h ad been a bandoned. H er h usband, Panti, had left her—just walked off and left her with complete strangers! Soon, she made an excuse and slipped away from the group of friendly but unknown people. She discovered and picked some wildflowers for her headband to impress her husband when he returned.

Although she offered no words of discontent, Panti could tell she was unhappy about the situation he had pushed her into. In silence, he untied the canoe, dipped his paddle into the clear water, and they began the last part of their honeymoon trip.

"You're awfully quiet. Are you upset with me?" Olta cautiously asked her husband, once they had cleared the entrance of the gateway canal, reached open water, and the bow of the canoe was pointed toward home.

Panti grimaced and replied quietly between clenched teeth. "No! This toothache of mine started again just before the council ended. It's really bothering me. It feels like the crack is getting wider. Each time the tooth begins to ache again it hurts worse than before! I couldn't even hold a simple conversation because of the pain. I was antagonistic to people I didn't even know, and for no good reason other than that my jaw hurts. I'm sorry, but I don't feel much like talking for a while. Please bear with me until the pain passes . . . if it does. By the way, the flowers in your hair are beautiful . . . you're beautiful and I love you!" Olta's smile returned.

Over the next few days, Panti alerted the people at his village of his need for special pieces of wood. He hoped they might find pieces during their routine activities. The material would have to be suitable for carving the stylized statuettes Turlto had commissioned.

Soon, with the help of his neighbors, he was beginning the process of collecting sufficient materials to start making the scores of totem figurines required for this project. Before Panti started to actually begin carving, he concentrated on his personal weapon making. He skillfully worked small chunks of the chert he brought from his wife's homeland. He produced the deep-penetrating and deadly bifaced arrowheads—the war points—that Bandon ordered all warriors to arm themselves with. With his well-trained artist's eye, and skilled use of the point-knapper's specialized tools, Panti began the tedious process of turning ordinary-looking flat rocks into deadly projectile points.

With a doubled-over scrap of deer hide protecting his left hand against t he s harp s tone, h e s elected a nd p icked up a small i rregular piece of chert. Inspecting it carefully to find a starting point, he placed the thicker portion in his leather-protected palm, and picked up a small hammer he had made from a piece of deer antler. After concentrating on the stone's features, and outlining the final product in his mind's eye, he began to systematically strike the flat piece of chert at the perfect angle and with experienced controlled force. Panti knapped points by skilled application of the percussion technique. Small flakes of stone broke away each time the hammer struck. Some flew aside, others bounced off his skin, and dropped onto his lap. Soon he was satisfied, and the roughed-out triangular piece was set aside. When others had been formed to the same stage of completion, all would receive more detailed shaping and sharpening.

* * *

Eight somber-faced, hunched-over men sat in a semicircle inside an open wing attached to Calos's residential lodge. Calos, the supreme leader of the Calosa, was seated on a high stool, facing them. Like his haggard advisors he appeared to be completely depressed. He spoke haltingly in a monotone, synonymous behavior with low morale and depression. "If what our emissary has reported to you is true Romta, is it still your opinion we can expect a force of the strange men to eventually attack us?"

Romta, Calos' diplomat, answered his monarch. "Yes, great Calos. It is! Ruad, our emissary to the islands, reports it's true these men landed o n t he s outhern i slands. They h aven't a rrived r ecently. They have done so on several trips over many years. Their giant boats brought them across the Great Water, from the land where the sun sleeps. They are a cruel race. Their leaders quickly overpowered and enslaved the island people. Their language is known as 'Castilian.' Some of the people Ruad talked with had escaped captivity and managed to return to their homes in outlying villages far away from the evil men. As slaves they learned to speak the stranger's tongue . . . had been forced to! Ruad invited a couple of former captives, a husband and wife, to return with him. They speak both the tongues of the Calosa and Castilians, should we ever need interpreters. The demons have enslaved the island people and Ruad is sure, and I agree, if they over-power us in a war we will suffer the same fate."

Calos stood up abruptly and interrupted Romta. He had heard enough! He bowed his head, and said, "Our original plan—to assem-ble our warriors and attack these men with an overwhelming force, should they return, will remain our course of action. From time to time, send others down to the Great Southern Island to learn more about their strength and habits. We can only wait and get ready for what seems to me will be an inevitable bloody conflict. I'm confident that my people will be victorious!"

* * *

Fifty of the panther clan totem carvings were to be produced by Panti and delivered to Turlto. The nation's high priest would accept them with a formal series of public religious incantations and mystic spiritual ceremonies. Turlto had announced, because of a recent godly vision, only he could receive word the panther clan's god had agreed to accept the idols. Only then would the statuettes be delivered to the Calosa settlements scattered through their territory.

Panti and his apprentices were making great progress with this project. He had carefully taught his students the proper use of measur-ing devices and different cutting tools to assure their work would pro-ceed satisfactorily. As each step of their training was completed, he would teach them something more, like how to deeply gouge those areas where a specific depth of wood had to be removed to form the head, neck, peculiar arms, the tail or curved symbolic kneeling legs of the half-man, half-cat creature.

The woodcarvers were diligently working on the totems when Panti looked up to see his friend Barto sprinting in their direction from the beach where the canoes were kept. When close enough, Barto shouted, "Panti!" Coming to a sliding stop, he continued talking in an excited tone, between deep breaths. "Your father and I, and a few oth-ers, were setting gill nets on the far side of Grassy Bottom and discov-ered some manatees. Pundon . . . your father . . . says they're mating.

246

We should be able to take one out of the group without interfering with the natural order of things. Ha! He says one less male will reduce the competition between the others. He's waiting . . . still fishing . . . and sent me back to get you and a harpoon and any other gear you think we'll need!"

Panti stood up and spoke to his helpers. "Keep working on the shapes. I'll be back just as soon as I can." Panti said, as he stood up, turned away, and dashed toward home to find Olta and get his harpoon. After quickly explaining to her why he was leaving so suddenly, he took down his prized spear and its connected coiled line from where they were stored out of the weather. He then kissed his wife tenderly, and then Panti and his best friend raced downhill to Barto's waiting canoe.

Marine mammals and their byproducts were very important to the Calosa. Dolphins, manatees, and sometimes small whales that beached themselves during those rare events, offered more diversity to the Calosa diet. The mammalian skin and fat was processed into oil and used for waterproofing, preserving leather and wood, and as a fuel for small clay bowls traditionally used as lamps.

Except for the narrow, undulating, band of rippling current flowing through the mouth of Grassy Bottom, the water was like glass. Deep paddle strokes moved the canoe quickly across the slick open water of the bay. Panti could clearly see his father, Pundon, and the others off in the distance. They were silhouetted against the thick red mangrove shoreline. A few yards to the left of their position he could make out frothing water where the manatees were gathered, and moving about in the shallows. As they drew closer, Barto exclaimed, "Did you see that, Panti? One of the manatees lunged completely out of the water. Look! There goes another one."

"Those are males leaving the water when they try to persuade a cow in the group their affections are serious and they should accept them as a mate." Panti broke into a chuckle. "Imagine having something that ugly making love to you? Much less, that heavy!"

The manatees were all adults. Calves were not mixed in because a cow's previous calf would be out on its own before its mother was ready to mate again. The mostly passive but receptive females acted as though they were trying to escape the amorous intentions of the males. Each female would mate with multiple males during the three week period they were sexually active. Some of the adults approached a ton in weight and were close to 12 feet in length. The frantic pushing, shoving, clamoring, even climbing, and tumbling males kept the water agitated. From a distance it was a scene of massive gray bodies creating rough water with geyser-like spurts—a pandemonium of whitewater. Panti and Barto could see at least ten of the giants at any one time. The manatees would soon be at the mercy of the hunters as the men closed the distance. Panti stopped paddling and started getting his gear ready.

"You boys made good time," Pundon yelled across the water to his son, Panti, and his friend Barto who were approaching in Barto's dugout. "I think one is all we need. Don't you have enough ribs left to work with from those that died from the cold last winter?"

"I have enough bone and if the village doesn't need much more oil we can take just one to eat. It'll be a lot less work! I'll get ready. Someone pick out a male that I can get close enough to without getting Barto's canoe swamped or broken up. I'm almost ready."

Panti reached down and picked up the coil of braided line. It was made from strands of fiber stripped from the thick, fleshy, and sharp-pointed crushed blades of the cactus-like century plant. Calosa women harvested and twisted the fibers into strong line from which they made gill nets, seines, and rope. He positioned the carefully coiled line on the small bow platform of the canoe. It would uncoil without snarling when Panti threw the harpoon at a manatee.

The harpoon's head was made from a forked deer antler, which Panti had carefully ground and sharpened. He had pierced the main shaft of the point and it was through this hole that he attached the line. The harpoon point was not overly tightened to the long white mangrove pole to which it was connected. Once the head of the harpoon was embedded deep in the flesh of a manatee the pole would disengage and fall away, to be retrieved. Because of the spear's length and weight it wouldn't be cast with an atlatl as a dart would be, but rather thrown javelin-style with the strong arm of the thrower producing all the force. Barto inched the canoe forward toward the mass of manatees. Panti stood poised, with his harpoon resting on his shoulder, and ready to aim and release it at the selected animal. Barto, who was now nearly completely deaf was talking very loud—so he could hear himself—as he described the individual he thought would be the best target. "Get ready! There's a male right in front of us that's moving up on that big female. Straight ahead!"

"I see him!" Panti said as he lifted the harpoon off his shoulder and bounced it in his hand to engage the best grip.

"Get ready . . . now!" Barto yelled as he worked his paddle to brake the canoe.

The canoe continued moving ahead as it began to slow, still a few yards away from the group of preoccupied giants. Panti heaved the heavy harpoon toward the manatee targeted by Barto. It left his hand with all the force his powerful body could muster. It was headed for a deadly entry of the manatee at a vital place, hopefully in the precise anatomical region he aimed for. Panti was not cruel. He always wanted a quick death for his prey.

Thud! The sharp point struck and deeply penetrated the body of the huge manatee. The animal was still moving ahead because of its momentum, but it was mortally wounded. Within minutes it quivered and died before the line inside its body cavity even had a chance to tighten. Panti's throw was so forceful, and his point so sharp, that the pole had not fallen away but had followed the harpoon's head deep into the manatee's flesh.

"That was a great shot! And, as usual, a clean kill," Barto said, congratulating his friend, as he began to back up the boat, pulling the floating carcass along with them and away from the other manatees that were still concentrating on their courtship. The group was completely unaware that one of their kind had just been killed and was now being taken by their species' only predator—a man.

"That was a good kill, son!" Pundon yelled to Panti as he and another older man brought their fish-filled canoe alongside.

"Between the manatee and your fish we'll eat well the next few days, won't we?" Panti replied as he looked down into the canoe.

"We sure will! Along with the usual small fish, we managed to catch many mullet that weren't smart enough to jump over our nets. We were lucky enough to net a small but fat green turtle too.

"How's your toothache today, son? Any better?"

249

"It was really bad last night—I didn't get much sleep! When I deliver some of the totem carvings to Turlto in a few days I'm going to ask him to look at my teeth and see if he or anyone else can do something to relieve the pain. Maybe they have some powerful medicine that will make the pain stop."

CHAPTER 22

SEVEN YEARS HAD PASSED SINCE PANTI AND OLTA became man and wife. During their happy years of marriage, nothing changed in the land of the Calosa. There were no wars, nor any large-scale invasion by the mysterious fair-skinned men. During this period, the strange-looking people did return to the same island their predecessors had. Calosa warriors living near the Land of the High Hills region assaulted the landing party and quickly drove them off.

Life and death remained ordinary. People grew older, children were born, and Calosans of all ages died. Panti's and Olta's family had doubled in size. A strong son, named Ronna, after Panti's grandfather, was born in the second year following their nuptials. Geno, a delightful daughter, followed him three years later.

Intermittently, Panti lived in excruciating pain because of his chronic toothache. Calosa doctors and medicine men had examined his troubled mouth from time to time over the years. Nothing could be done to repair the cracked tooth. They usually offered their traditional prayers for his good health and prescribed a few herbs and special concoctions for him to use as painkillers. But none of the remedies really worked and he continued to suffer.

Actually, what was going on inside his mouth was serious, and could become life threatening if the infection persisted. While eating mockernuts in Olta's village years before, Panti had made the mistake of trying to crack one of the rock-hard nuts between his teeth. Instead of breaking the shell of the nut he had vertically cracked the second molar on the right side of his lower jaw.. Over time, a severe chronic abscess formed around the roots of the damaged tooth and was causing this perpetual toothache.

"One of the medicine men wanted to take a stick and a hammer and knock the broken tooth out of my mouth!" Panti told his cousin Mando who was visiting him for a few days.

Mando confirmed what Panti had been told about the usual dental treatment for such a problem. "They do that to the old men in our village. Especially when their teeth loosen because of age. Why didn't you lct them remove it? Be done with it!"

Panti grimaced at the suggestion, then looked away nervously, before he replied. "Because I don't think it's loose enough yet!"

Although as adults they saw each other less frequently, Mando knew his cousin well. He knew Panti was a brave warrior, skilled at his various crafts, and now was a good father. He also knew his cousin was afraid of pain.

"As soon as I decide it's loose enough I'll let them take it out. Come on, let's go over to the prairie on the far side of Grassy Bottom and try to kill a deer." Panti purposely changed the subject as he shoved off from the beach toward deeper water, and then stepped into the canoe where Mando had already seated himself.

After completing the delicately carved totem statuettes that were now prominently displayed at the religious center of every permanent Calosa village, Panti had directed his talents to other art forms. When the challenging enterprise of doing the carvings to solicit the good will of the god of the Panther Clan was finished, Turlto, the high priest, persuaded Panti to carve a series of spiritual masks. These would be used at the capital city, but sometimes his itinerant priests would visit other population centers and take ceremonial masks along for religious functions. The wooden masks represented the many facets of the Calosa theological culture and religious experience. They were worn by the priesthood during specific ceremonies, and used to decorate the altar at the spiritual center of their religion, in the temple overseen by Turlto.

The head priest knew that features represented on the existing masks would be basically improved in Panti's versions. They would be superior replacements for the masks carved long ago by Panti's less talented predecessors. Turlto had watched Panti's skill blossom as he boldly developed a new proportional dimension to his carved creations. It was this deep-featured relief carving that set his work far above the rest.

Fifty beautifully carved, kneeling, half-cat, half-man figures had tested Panti's talents. His use of vivid, permanent, and new colors also brought fresh life into the series of ritual masks he was creating for Turlto.

"Panti, the magnificent masks you create are unlike any others I've ever seen. Mighty Calos himself often talks to me about your special abilities. He told me he's chosen one of your clan's totem figurines, which you carved, for his personal altar, and his family lineage isn't even remotely connected with your Panther Clan. You, of all the artisans alive in the world today, have most impressed our mighty leader—he who is the living heir of powerful forefathers. Great Calos is the rightful ruler of all lands and waters where the eagle soars and fishes."

"Wise Turlto, you embarrass me with your praise. I'll be pleased to start work on the masks as soon as I find time. I must finish this special pot first

*   *   *

The village was alive with activity because an approaching canoe had been sighted by the lookout. His signal horn sounded the alarm to announce that the arrival of friendly visitors was imminent. A canoe with four men aboard was coming toward the village from the south—from the direction of the city of Calos. Panti stopped what he was doing and joined a small group of noisy children and friends on the beach to watch the canoe as it sped closer. He noticed the serious look on the straining faces of the paddlers.

Pundon was the first to speak when the canoe landed, he asked, "What brings you men here in such a hurry?"

The man in the front of the boat stepped ashore, and replied, "We've been sent here by great Calos himself! Where's Panti? Is he here? I must speak to him at once!"

"Here I am," Panti said and stepped forward to weave his way through the group of villagers. He was in serious thought. "Why does our great leader send these men to seek me out?"

"I've been sent here to bring you sad news. I must tell you that great Turlto, our great priest, is dead! He died in his sleep two nights ago," the messenger exclaimed in a somber tone and with an anguished expression on his face. "Mighty Calos has appointed Feda to replace Turlto as head priest. Feda asks that you come to the capital as soon as you can. He wants to discuss work projects Turlto may have given you when you and he last talked."

Panti was completely shocked. He couldn't believe the messenger's words. He continued, in an uncontrollable stammer, "What . . . happened to Turlto? He was fine . . . it appeared . . . it seemed to me . . . he was in good . . . health when I . . . when I last was with him."

"I was told by another priest that he died peacefully as he slept. Feda has announced he'll call a council of priests soon. I'm told that will happen after he talks with you."

"Why me?"

"Great Calos and Feda want you to help plan the funeral. Turlto had no family or close relatives left. Feda said he needs your artistic abilities for planning Turlto's burial. When shall I tell our great leader you'll be in his presence?"

"I'll be there in two days!" Panti replied as he spun around, lowered his head, wiped the tears from beneath his eyes, and dejectedly walked away. Everyone knew he wanted to be alone.

The burial of Turlto would be a major tribute to a person of such prominence. Six months following his death, hundreds, if not more than a thousand people, assembled to honor the life of this famous man. Turlto had navigated the spiritual course of the Calosa people for more than 50 years. High priests from neighboring tribes had been invited and several were in attendance. Even rival chiefs unfriendly to the Calosas had sent representatives. Arriving at the crowded burial site, Panti and Olta were ushered to join the Calosa hierarchy.

The large, high, and flat-topped structure where the funeral was being held was primarily made of sand. It was the traditional burial mound used for the internment of Calosan royalty and other key persons who lived at the capital city. It was located on the edge of the mainland to the southeast of the capital. Much of this was spoil that had been excavated elsewhere during canal construction. The sand was hauled to the slowly enlarging burial site by the canoe load. A broad palm trunk stairway surmounted the steep-angled pyramid-like mound.

Exquisitely carved totems, masks, and brightly painted symbolic banners, all the work of Panti and his growing number of apprentices lined the open-air burial site. Finally, with all guests in their places, the ritualistic burial ceremony was ready to begin. The blare of horns and pounding drums signaled to the assembled mourners that Calos had arrived with the new high priest and their retinue. When Calos and his court of sub-chiefs had taken their places, Feda, who had succeeded Turlto as head priest, began the mystic incantations. These chants would soon send two of Turlto's three souls to the unseen land of the dead. There, the departed dwells for eternity in the tranquillity of the hereafter in the company of the Great Spirit. The first soul to leave the body was poised to begin its special one-time function before being reborn in another spiritual level. In life, this soul had reflected the image of the deceased onto the surface of still water—a mirrored human image. It would leave Turlto's body first, and journey to the spirit world on the other side of life. There it would prepare Turlto's place in his afterlife. Once completing this mission, the reflective soul would enter the body of another living creature at the beginning of its lifetime. The soul would continue metamorphosing into diminishing-sized creatures until it reached the tiniest form of life imaginable to the Calosas. Then it would disappear.

The second soul—Turlto's powerful and dominating shadow—would leave the physical world at the time the priest's carefully arranged skeleton was covered. This soul would assume the priest's exalted place on the other side in the land of the dead. Through eternity Turlto's shadow spirit would dwell alongside with and obediently serve the Great Spirit God. Through Turlto, and other priests in His domain in the land of the dead, His good graces would forever be bestowed on the Calosa people.

255

Turlto's bones had been removed from the charnel house, transported to the burial mound, and his complete skeletal system had been precisely positioned face-up in the grave. The morticians had properly oriented all bones as they had been in life. Turlto's social position required this anatomically extended repose. The bones of lower class individuals would be consolidated with those of others, bundled, and buried in a common pit in another section of the burial mound.

Since Turlto's birth, his third soul lived in the pupils of his eyes, and would reside in the grave with his mortal remains. This soul would protect Turlto's grave through eternity. The well-dried, ghostly white bones were surrounded by a variety of objects and implements that Feda thought Turlto might have use for in the afterlife. Among them were his personal religious totems, pottery, clothing, and weapons.

"Great leader and people of the Calosa nation!" Feda had finished his funeral chants and started to speak in a more coherent monotone, but still in the priestly-style. "We are gathered here to pay final tribute to a noble and wise man who has lived many years among us. He touched the lives of all Calosans during his long life of good deeds among his brave and faithful people. Although his work here was unfinished, the Great Spirit God has called him to the other side. He will soon be with the Divine Creator and will join His great council. From that other place he will continue to be a benefactor to our people and a protector of our way of life. Long live the souls of Turlto! Long live the great Calos!"

One by one, mourners left their places, joined a line of solemn-faced people, and walked to the precipitous edge of the priest's grave. Each person walked around the gaping hole, and with a foot pushed sand over the brink. As Panti took his turn and kicked sand into the pit, he noticed a scrimshaw-carved manatee rib he had once presented to his friend as a gift. It had been placed on the floor of the grave next to Turlto's right hand. Standing there, peering at another man's earthly finality, Panti hoped the Great Spirit God would be pleased when Turlto's soul picked up the rib and admired the artwork, as the living Turlto often did.

The cascading sand fell over the bones. They were soon covered. Sand continued to be shoved into the grave by the silent mourners until it was filled. Now free, Turlto's second soul left the world of the living and passed through the invisible curtain into the other side and everlasting life. He was forever at peace alongside the Great Spirit. Panti knew the gods who protected his nation were smiling in their secret places. That Turlto was among them was pleasing to them. All would soon be good again in the land of the brave and strong Calosa.

CHAPTER 23

JUAN PONCE DE LEÓN WAS A NATIVE OF SAN SERVOS,
León, in the region of Castile, on the Iberian Peninsula of Europe.
An adventurous young man, Juan Ponce was trained as a soldier during the conflicts that led to the final defeat of the Moors in his homeland. In 1493, his first opportunity to fulfill his youthful dreams came
when he sailed to the New World with Captain General Cristóbal
Colón[1] on his second voyage to the Indies. A time or two, Juan Ponce
had traveled back to Europe, but the financial opportunities in the
Western Hemisphere beckoned him to return. In 1502, he returned to
Hispaniola and founded the city of Salvaleón de Higüey. He married
and remained on Hispaniola with his wife Leonor. She bore him three
daughters and a son. In 1506, he temporarily left his family when
drawn to regional exploration by his restlessness, inquisitive spirit, and
quest for greater fortune. That year, he led a successful invasion and
conquered and settled the island of San Juan Bautista de Puerto Rico.
After his forces subjugated the native aboriginal inhabitants, and
enslaved them, he was appointed Captain General of San Juan. Juan
Ponce was given responsibility for both civil and criminal jurisdiction
on the island. His success in that position eventually led to his appoint-
ment as lieutenant governor. In 1509, King Ferdinand of Castile named
him governor of the island of San Juan.

---

[1] Christopher Columbus

In 1511, Diego Colón, son of the Grand Admiral, won a legal battle with the Castilian crown and regained all of his late father's rights and privileges. These included control over the political and financial affairs of the Indies. After becoming viceroy, Diego Colón removed Juan Ponce as governor and appointed a friend as his replacement.

Juan Ponce de León made a major career change. For the next two years he developed a large-scale farming operation on San Juan. He was again successful and made substantial amounts of money. This financial base provided sufficient funds and lines of credit for him to underwrite the full cost of another expedition. This time he would look for a rumored prize—an island the native peoples called Bimini.

Following his dismissal Juan Ponce often complained to family and close friends that he lost considerable amounts of money because of the interference of powerful people. He claimed they added undesired responsibilities to his duties, which despite his hushed objections created his strong civil and military career. His widely proclaimed, but insincere dedication to the crown masked his intense personal ambition. Accolades continued to be heaped upon him because of the military successes and his good work in the eyes of the far-removed royalty.

On March 3, 1513, he sailed north from San Germán, San Juan, with three ships in search of Bimini, and its fabled fountain of youth. The existence of this fountain was a legend among the native peoples of the northern Caribbean Sea. Although some Castilians accepted this lore as fact, the search for this mystical fountain was not a serious consideration in Juan Ponce's new venture of exploration. He discounted the reality of such a fountain, one that would rejuvenate people who bathed in or drank its water.

In early April 1513, he and his forces landed on a scrub and palmetto forested beach on the eastern shore of a large land mass. A friendly greeting soon turned into a confrontation with hostile Indian natives. He recalled his people to their two caravels and larger supply ship, known as a nao, and sailed back southward. Juan Ponce's chief pilot, António "Antón" de Alaminos, convinced him this was an island, just another of the uncharted Bahamas. The coast was lushly vegetated and because it was springtime a variety of coastal wild flowers were in full bloom. Coincidentally, it was also the period of Easter, so because of an obligatory religious sensitivity and visual sense of beauty, Juan Ponce de León named this new island the flowery Easter—the Florida.

It was here, during this same voyage, as his ships approached the coast, that he and his seamen discovered—but did not comprehend its importance at the time—the powerful surface current of the northward surging Gulf Stream. For a time, the ships had difficulty negotiating against the unrelenting flow of the Gulf Stream. Moving closer to shore, the two caravels sailed free of its influence and anchored. The nao, the *San Cristóval*, could not find bottom to anchor and was swept out of sight. The next day, the three ships reunited and continued sailing south. Day after day they skirted the shoreline. After seeing and naming the Florida Keys "The Martyrs" on May 15th, the ships were forced to make an extended westerly tack because of adverse winds. From some point, west of the southernmost Florida Keys, the three vessels again initiated a tack to the northeast. This was the direction in which Antón Alaminos calculated the island of Florida to be. When a lookout, high in his lofty perch, announced land was again in sight, the pilots of the vessels brought them cautiously closer to the land. Frequent heaving of lead lines to determine the water's depth was required since the clarity of the water was now reduced as they moved inshore. Before them stretched a strange panorama, a much different land. Countless mangrove islets appeared to be marching out, or making out toward the sea, to meet them. After reducing sail to slow their forward speed and turning more northerly, Juan Ponce, who was aboard the flagship *Santa Maria de la Consolacion*, decided to drop anchor inside a small bay with a deep water entrance. This anchorage was next to a narrow island with a white sand beach along most of its northern edge. The decision was made to land because as they continued to sail north a major cape of land was visible off to their northwest. The further north they sailed it became obvious this cape and the easterly shore were converging, and their passage would ultimately be blocked. Because of the lush vegetation it was the opinion of those aboard the ships this island might contain collectable surface water. The decision was made to make landfall. Their supply of drinkable water aboard the ships was dwindling, and the responsible leaders of the expedition thought it appropriate to try and top off all tanks.

The captain of the lead caravel was Juan Ponce's long-time friend Juan Bono de Quejo. Once he was satisfied the anchor was firmly set, he directed a landing party to go ashore and check the island for potable water. Juan Bono then joined Juan Ponce who was relaxing on the sterncastle of the caravel. The former governor was watching the activities as the boat full of men and water casks made the short row to the white beach. He guessed all of them were anxious to walk on firm ground. The captain asked, "Governor, what do you propose we do after we fill our casks, should the men find water?"

"Juan, if we don't find water here . . . do we have enough on board if we turn back today, until we can reach known sources on Cuba?"

"If it's properly rationed w e s hould h ave more than e nough, Governor. For us, and your two tough horses!"

"If the men find water, we'll go north for three or four more days—a few more leagues from this place. I'd like to try and circumnavigate this beautiful island. It's so green and lush. It's not dry and rocky like so many of the uninteresting smaller islands I've seen in this new part of the world."

After landing, the water-collecting party hiked across the beach. They struggled as they hauled barrels through dense, head-high sea oats. Once they reached the low ridge that appeared to be the highest point on the island, the men split up into three two-man teams. Each couple followed the narrow ridge where clumps of tall cabbage palms were growing. Each team selected a spot to dig, and with spades they dug a series of deep test pits. These were dug straight down until soaking wet sand was reached. Any surface water saturated in the sand- and shell-mixed soil would slowly seep into the hole. This water was taste-tested. If fresh, the hole was enlarged, and became a well. After any disturbed floating sediment settled out of the sand-filtered solution, the clear drinking water was ladled up and poured into their kegs. When filled, the barrels were still light enough to be rolled to the boats and carried back to the ship. The water was then poured into large water casks aboard the ships.

Using this method to locate water was a common way of finding drinking water by mariners. Within minutes, clear water was trickling into the holes. Soon, this was being dipped into the small casks.

Two ships remained at anchor, rafted together, for eight days while water was slowly collected from the wells. It was a period of relaxation for the expedition's leaders. The days passed while crews labored aboard their ships on routine maintenance projects, or details collected firewood on the island. The *San Cristóval* was careened in shallow water so minor repairs could be made to her rudder. Ballast stones in the bilges were shifted, depending on the side being worked on, and she was pulled over by the top of her mainmast by strong beach-anchored lines and heavy-duty block and tackle. While resting on her beam in the shallows, leaning far over on her side, the ship's bottom was scraped clean and recaulked. Later, she would be turned, careened again, and the opposite side similarly treated.

Juan Ponce, ship's captain Juan Bono, and chief pilot Antón Alaminos were poring over paperwork in the open air of the sterncastle deck. Suddenly, the captain shot upright from his leaning position over the chart table and exclaimed, "*Governor*! Did you see that?"

"See what?" Juan Ponce answered in a puzzled tone.

Pointing toward the northeast, the captain said, "I saw something move past that narrow opening in the trees . . . the far one between those islands at the head of this bay." He strode to the deck's forward railing and quickly glanced around his ship looking for someone. He leaned over the rail, and screamed, "*Espinosa*!"

"Yes, Captain!" A middle-aged but still dark-bearded man responded loudly as he ran across the main deck, stood beneath the captain, and looked up at him.

"Lieutenant, I saw something . . . perhaps a small boat . . . move across that opening . . . out there!" The captain pointed again, and continued, "Have your men arm themselves. Ready a small boat and move onto the cay to protect our seamen at the wells. It could be more of those damnable savages!

"Have Sergeant Alvarez go tell the other captains to send a squad of soldiers ashore with you! Eight of you from each vessel."

"Yes, sir! At once!"

In just minutes, Lieutenant Espinosa led a force of 23 helmeted, armor-clad soldiers ashore. Each man carried weapons and round shields onto the narrow beach. Sixteen of the men held crossbows and lances, the others, including the lieutenant, had heavy matchlock arquebuses over their shoulders. All wore both sword and dagger. The lances and the forked staffs, which would be used to support the weight of the primitive muskets when aimed and fired, had dual use. When the soldiers stepped over the side of their boats into the water, these were used as walking sticks. They helped support, even extricate the overweight armored squad when they sunk deep into the soft bottom.

Lieutenant Espinosa announced in a commanding voice, "After you light your matches from the fire pot, form a double-staggered skirmish line midway between the well-diggers and that wall of dense trees on the far end of the island. If some of those devil heathens are stalking us they'll likely come out of those trees rather than have a try at us from the water."

"Lieutenant! What's going on?" One of the seamen across the waving sea oats yelled as the military men began to fan out near their planned defensive positions.

"Continue collecting water, but be ready to retreat to the ships should you hear gunfire. Captain Bono thinks he saw something . . . he's afraid it's more of the damned natives. Be ready to move back toward the beach and your boat if hostilities break out. We have no idea how many of the devils may be watching us. We can't hold back a large force of the bastards for long if they're determined to attack!"

Runda, the leader of the Calosa hunting party, glimpsed the tall, bare masts of the ships, and the motion of their wind-ruffled, brightly-colored flags and pennants, sticking up above the red mangrove trees. The warriors in the five dugouts were astonished and at first some were very frightened. Never before had such a sight been seen by anyone in the Calosa nation. Initially, each man felt an urgency to flee, but Runda responded quickly and they hid themselves by moving closer to the trees. They would avoid detection should the lookouts Runda saw perched on the masts, in little fenced platforms high in the air, look their way. After a brief argument over immediate withdrawal, which was favored by some warriors, the majority of the hunting party decided it would be prudent to approach this specter with an air of bravery to determine just what it was they were confronting.

Runda tried to calm the fears of the group. Almost as if speaking to himself, he said, "Perhaps what we've just seen is a sea god who means no harm to us! It may have seen us and has come to reward us in some way."

One of his more apprehensive companions in another canoe spoke up in a nervous tone. "What if it's a sea demon sent here to kill us? We should withdraw and spread the alarm!"

Runda responded with firm authority. "No!" Next, he selected someone to serve as a messenger, and sternly issued further orders. "Tinya, take your canoe and the two men with you and return to our village. Tell our village leader, Hatchi, what we've seen and ask him to send messengers to all the nearby villages. Warriors from each neighboring village must be sent here quickly to help us. You must hurry! We'll work our way through these islands and confront this thing. If it's an enemy we'll kill it!"

Runda was certain that he and his warriors had not been seen as they carefully maneuvered through the small islets. They kept the screen of dense red mangrove trees between themselves and their destination. The Calosas had no idea of the size of the force that was prepared to meet them. Their concealment did not provide them with the opportunity to make strategic observations. They were completely unaware they didn't have the advantage of surprise.

Twenty-four Calosa warriors worked their way through the tangled mangroves. They moved toward the open beach area beyond the trees. Not a twig snapped, nor did a tree move, and no bird cried out in alarm to give their presence and position away. Each warrior moved forward until they reached the edge of the tree line. Perfectly concealed, they looked across the tall grass toward the beach, and then stared dumfounded, glancing at one another in total disbelief at what they saw. In view were three enormous tall-masted boats with strangely-dressed, white-skinned men swarming around on them, each occupied in doing some kind of work.

Still closer was a group of these men. They stood upright in a double line, sharing conversations, but all looking in the direction of the warrior's hiding place. Whenever a man moved the sun reflected on his polished armor, which covered their upper bodies and heads. The shiny metal was radiating strange flashes of light, like sunlight sparkling on the water. Runda issued a whispered message that was relayed among the ranks. "We must be careful. Stay low to avoid being struck by one of the magic light beams."

To himself, Runda assessed the situation. "They're men— armed and lined up in a defensive position to protect those already on this island and the others who remain on those enormous boats. That they've assumed a battle line tells me they're an aggressive people. I'll try and talk first. I'll tell them they're unwelcome here. I know in my heart that in the end we'll have to attack and fight them to drive them from our land!"

Runda told the men he was going to show himself, chance the light beams, and try to talk with these strange people. "If I'm killed or captured, attack them furiously and try to drive them away. Attack in a series of small groups so they can't tell how many of us are here. Cause them to believe you're a very powerful force of warriors." He stood up, stepped out into the open, and began walking toward the Castilian soldiers.

A front line musketeer shouted, "Lieutenant! Look, it's one of those damned savages!"

Lieutenant Espinosa bellowed orders. "Stand ready, men! He's stopped and has raised his hand. I believe he wants to speak with us. Rodriguez! Go to the *Santa Maria* and tell the governor what's going on here. Ask him to send that Indian we captured and brought with us from the last landing place back with you as an interpreter. Be quick!"

Runda stopped and waited. He glared at the shiny-skinned men, noticing that many had thick black hair on their faces. It was not unlike that of the black bear. He assumed the lone man had left to speak to someone in higher authority. He thought, "These men can't make decisions."

Soon, the soldier returned with another man. This new man was unlike the strangers. Like the Calosas he wore no clothing other than a loin cloth. From his skin color Runda judged this person was from another native tribe, one unknown to him. This man talked to Lieutenant Espinosa for a few moments, then bowed his head and hesitated. Suddenly, the lieutenant shoved him violently in the direction of the Calosa. Only then did he turn and leave the group. Haltingly, he approached Runda. Still a few yards away he paused, smiled, and raised his arm in greeting as he nervously started to speak. Runda understood a few words but could not make out the complete message being relayed to him.

Runda raised his arm and waved his forearm from side to side in an effort to signal the man to stop talking. Slowly and deliberately, carefully choosing his words, he said, "You, and these strange-looking people you travel with, are not welcome here! You've dared to invade the nation of the mighty Calosa people and you must leave right now, or you will die—here in my land and far from your own people!" The Taino interpreter cringed and dropped his arms in despair when he heard the word *Calosa*, and this man's serious warning of ultimate death. Visibly shaken, he rejoined the Castilian soldiers and relayed the parts of the sentences he understood to Lieutenant Espinosa.

Runda silently asked his totem, the sacred deer, to protect him. He swallowed hard, exhaled through clenched teeth, turned around, and began to retrace his steps to rejoin his hidden companions. He had taken a few strides toward the green refuge—the concealment among the dense mangroves waiting to hide him—safety was just a few more steps away. *Boom!* He heard the loud noise behind him and heard a whirring sound as an unseen ball of lead sped by his head, just inches from his right ear.

Startled at the sound, Runda threw himself to the ground. He sought protection in the deep sea oats. He heard the thunderous sound repeat itself. *Boom! Boom!* Frightened, he asked himself, "What's that sound? It's not thunder. What strange magic do these people have to use against us?" Runda started to crawl toward the safety of the tree line.

Twenty-three Calosa warriors stepped from the mangrove fringe and raised their powerful bows. Twenty-three war points sped on a lethal trajectory. Most fell short. The Castilian soldiers were on the outer boundary of the range of the Calosa arrows. The warriors stepped back into the foliage and disappeared from the Castilian's view.

Lieutenant Espinosa knew there was an advantage to distance, so he ordered his small force to move back a few more yards out of

266

arrow-shot. The well diggers, alerted by the gunfire, abandoned the wells and were busy loading the last of their casks into the small boats.

Lieutenant Espinosa shouted excitedly to his troops, "There must be 50 or 60 of the bastards hidden in those trees! Lancers! Go to the boats! Musketeers! On my signal—we'll fire a volley into the trees and then withdraw to the boats, too. Ready? Now!" *Boom! Baroom*! The matchlock muskets which had been casually aimed and resting on their yolk staffs, fired in near unison, and a cloud of thick smoke enveloped the shooters.

From their hiding place the trembling Calosa warriors cowered at the sound of the gunfire, and the sight of a ghostly pall of dense smoke drifting toward them. By now, a very frightened Runda had rejoined them and was again in command. No one had been struck by the fusillade of musket balls.

Someone yelled, "They're running! When they're in their boats we should attack—full force!"

Runda agreed. He shouted, "Follow me! Keep low! Don't move the grass and give us away!"

As the Castilians pulled away from the beach, Runda and his battle-ready warriors rushed up to the edge of the grass. Even though they lacked any real protection, they had the option to hide. The last of the small boats was still in range and 24 arrows were released in its direction. This time, six arrows struck human targets. Three of the soldiers screamed in pain, fell backwards, or slumped over to fall against the boat's bottom. One of them was mortally wounded. An arrow had fully penetrated his unprotected neck. A second was lodged in his shoulder. He died before the boat reached the caravel.

The seamen aboard the nearest ship responded. *Baroom*! Louder, roaring thunder again sounded and a geyser erupted from the water, which separated the adversaries. It was much closer to the Calosas and they were all soaked as the load of metal fragments fell short.

The warriors scrambled for dear life, running back toward the questionable safety of the tree line. The Castilian gunners, manning the rail-mounted, swiveling five-pound verso cannon readied to reload the gun and fire another round. Another clap of man-made thunder echoed through the mangrove islands, but the target had vanished. Flights of nervous birds veered away from the sound. Others, feeding or loafing, nearby on the beach panicked. They took spontaneous flight as the cannon-load of shrapnel struck the white sand of the beach. It was a direct hit on the spot where milliseconds before the taunting Calosa had stood in defiance.

For two more days the Castilian ships r ode anchor. Having repelled the Indians, Juan Ponce was convinced they had withdrawn and were no longer a threat. His captains agreed such was the case and concurred the repair projects should be completed. After all, another day and the work would be finished.

"Governor! Look," Lieutenant Espinosa screeched at the top of his lungs, "there's at least a score of fully loaded canoes coming through t hat c ut! Some of them a re double-hulled! There must be close to a hundred of the savages coming toward us!"

"Lieutenant, ready your men!" Juan Ponce said as he turned and picked up his arquebus from the rack near his cabin hatch. "Load scatter shot and bring all the swivel guns to bear on them. Fire when they're within range. If we can keep them at a distance we'll be safe from their weapons. Have a squad armed with muskets and crossbows take the larger of the small boats and try to intercept them. Tell your soldiers that they're to try and capture one or two of the red devils."

Boom! *Boom*! *Baroom*! Five pounds of large metal fragments left each of the six rail-mounted cannons. One of the lead canoes received a direct hit and four Calosa warriors tumbled over dead, killed instantly. Two fell into the canoe and another pair dropped over the side and disappeared. Two other warriors in the canoe were miraculously uninjured, but when they witnessed the sudden bloody fate of their canoe mates, they leaped overboard and started to swim ashore. As the other Calosas withdrew, after seeing so many casualties among their forces, the rowboat raced toward the swimmers. They were violently snatched out of the water to become prisoners of the Castilians. The captives were stripped of their waist weapons and breechcloths. The two naked men cowered as the small boat returned to the *Santa Maria*, its mission accomplished.

The remaining canoes kept their distance as the small cannons maintained sporadic fire. No more Castilians would die this day, but losses continued among the Calosas when the bravest ventured too close.

"Juan, we have an outgoing tide. Let's weigh anchor and leave this dangerous place to those infernal savages." Juan Ponce suggested to Captain Bono, and then added, "We'll sail south by east and make another search for this elusive place the Indians call Bimini. One day I'll return to this beautiful land with a force of arms sufficient to overpower such cowardly bastards! One day these sneaky heathens will pay dearly! Did our Indian interpreter ever tell you who these people are?"

"Yes, he did, Governor. That is, he muttered in fear and desperation when I asked. He called them . . . it sounded like, 'Calosas . . . are devils on earth . . . they are *cannibals*!'"

Juan Ponce de León looked toward the beach and then stared at the Indian canoes, raised his fist, and yelled. His loud voice was carried on the wind. It crossed the water, and filtered through the mangroves but was unintelligible to those to whom it was directed. "I'll return! You've not seen the last of me! I'll crush you, you godless heathen bastards!"

Captain Juan Bono was a veteran of many dangerous confrontations with the stubborn indigenous peoples of the Indies. Rightly so, he was afraid the warriors would be reinforced, then attack in overwhelming numbers. They might sacrifice themselves in a human swarm to board the vessels. The Castilian soldiers and sailors would be no match for a large force of these demons if they successfully boarded the ships and the battle raged in close hand-to-hand combat. He responded, "Yes, Governor . . . Menéndez!"

"Yes, Captain?"

"Notify the other ships to make ready to sail, and cast us loose from them. Put your deck crew on the anchor and get your men on the sheets! We have a favorable wind. Unfurl the sails and be quick about it before we lose the tide and wind and those infernal Calosa Indians catch us!"

The ships beat to windward to the south, and seven days later sighted a series of small sandy cays to their starboard. The clear water around these islands literally teemed with sea turtles. The expedition anchored for three days and the men of Juan Ponce's expedition caught, trussed, and stored 170 green and loggerhead turtles aboard their ships. They slaughtered countless numbers of seabirds and killed 14 West Indian monk seals. Their supply of fresh meat was ensured for the remainder of their voyage. The turtles would remain alive for extended periods if kept damp and shaded. Antón Alaminos appropriately named the islands "The Tortugas" because of the abundant sea turtles.

The expedition sailed on to Cuba and later traveled northeastward again through the Bahamas, searching for the elusive, legendary island of Bimini. Hurricanes forced long delays, but eventually Juan Ponce de León's mostly unsuccessful expedition returned safely to San Juan on October 15, 1513.

CHAPTER 24

J UAN PONCE DE LEÓN MADE HIS FINAL VOYAGE ACROSS
the Atlantic Ocean to his homeland in 1516. He made the trip to
validate a royal contract with the new king, Carlos I. Earlier, in 1514,
Juan Ponce was authorized by the king's late grandfather, Ferdinand, to
return and settle The Florida. He had been knighted[2] by King
Ferdinand in Valladolid, Castile. During this ceremony, the sovereign
presented Juan Ponce with a series of awards and documents to commemorate his service to the crown and thank him for his allegiance and
service to Castile. He was granted permission to conquer and colonize
the land he had named. In 1516, Carlos I ratified the agreement. That
same year the Iberian Peninsula kingdoms of Europe, excluding
Portugal, united and the Empire of Spain was created. This powerful,
far-reaching colonial power would soon encircle the globe and drain
her colonies of their riches.

Returning to his enterprises in the Indies in 1518, Don (Sir)
Juan Ponce began the long process of planning his return to the shore
of Florida. It took several years to build the financial base with which
he could adequately fund his second expedition. Finally, in 1520, he
realized he was financially secure, time was fleeting, and he must prepare for this important voyage of colonization immediately.

---

[2] Juan Ponce de León was the first of the Spanish
conquistadors to be knighted.

At this time, Juan Ponce's old friend, his former chief pilot, António de Alaminos, was employed in the service of Captain General Hernán Cortés in his campaign of conquest in "New Spain of the Ocean Sea." In early 1520, Ponce sent a communiqué to Antón in Mexico, and invited him to join him on another trip to Florida. By mid-year, Antón had replied and informed his mentor he would soon be sent on an assignment to Spain by Cortés. He agreed he would come directly to San Juan just as soon as he returned. In early 1521, Antón arrived in San Juan from Spain, just a few weeks prior to the expedition's scheduled departure date.

The two met at Juan Ponce's residence where the final plans for the project were being developed by the expedition's principals. When the military and civilian leaders of the expedition had departed, Antón spoke frankly to his benefactor. "Governor, I would be pleased to serve as your chief pilot on this voyage. I'll also agree to a short-term stay wherever it is that fate and the sea takes us. But, I must return to New Spain and rejoin Captain Cortés when you no longer have need of my services. I've pledged to return to his service."

Juan Ponce paced the veranda of his residence, carefully considering Antón's conditions for joining his team. He stopped, spun around, and said, "Antón, I accept your fair terms. Once we've established a settlement, and you've finished the work to be done within your field of expertise, you'll be returned here to Puerto Rico. Or, to Cuba if you prefer. I'll have to send a vessel back here for more supplies anyway. There you can make ship connections for New Spain to rejoin that gloriously lucky bastard Cortés. Ha! I'm sure you'll be back with his forces in six months time—agreed?"

Without any hesitation, Antón said, "Yes, Governor, I accept. It'll be a pleasure to be in your service again."

* * *

The caravels lurched, pitched, and almost broached, each time they surfed stem-first down a steep sea swell. The ships slammed and shook when they nosed into the next ridge of blue water they overtook with rhythmic frequency. A stiff following wind had been steadily pushing the heavy, overloaded, full-sailed vessels along on their dead reckoning course. They were coasting, paralleling the distant shore-

272

line. Land was only visible to the lookouts that were precariously perched high in the crow's nest on each ship. Those on watch in their teetering vantagepoints could only glimpse the distant terra firma briefly, whenever their boat reached the highest crest of a swell, before it pitched and slid down the roller coaster mountains of water. They held on for dear life and prayed that the standing rigging would hold against the fury of the sea and wind.

These 140-ton, triple-masted caravels were square-rigged for ocean-going travel. Commercial caravels used for inter-island or coastal trade and transportation were smaller 50- to 60-ton vessels and traditionally equipped with lateen sails. The caravel was the ship of choice because of its shallow draft, seaworthiness, carrying capacity, speed, and ability to sail to windward. The uncharted waters on which European ships sailed in the New World were often extremely shoal. Submerged coral heads, shallow reefs, and other hard bottoms were a threat to the wooden-hulled vessels. The excellent shallow water handling characteristics of these ships allowed the sailors to approach closer to the land, enter shallow bays, or even ascend rivers.

The two ships, among the largest in their class, left San Germán; a seaport on the island of San Juan, on February 26, 1521, bound for the incompletely charted land named the Florida. The expedition's leader, Juan Ponce de León, had named and claimed the lush green flowering island for the now consolidated Spanish crown during his first voyage there during Easter, 1513.

The sun had turned into a crimson fireball and was about to drop from the brilliant, purple-streaked, red-orange tinted, and iridescent glowing sky. All heads of those sailors above decks on the pitching caravels were turned left, facing the horizon. The men's stare was fixed. Their eyes drank in this rare beauty granted to those bound to the sea.

Alfonso Fernando, the captain of the flagship, the *Leonor,* was speaking to Juan Ponce as the two experienced sailing men flexed their legs and gripped the security of the rail much tighter. Just in time. The caravel pitched, slid down another breaking ridge of water, and rammed her bowsprit into the next. "The sunset is incredibly gorgeous this evening and these seas are mountainous! We're making good time, but I hope the wind shifts so we have to beat more northerly. These sea conditions are putting too much strain on the ship and the livestock. We've already had to destroy more horses than I had hoped, Governor."

"When the wind picked up I was afraid we'd take some losses in our herd, Captain. You and I know that broken legs are always a risk when rough seas must be crossed with horses aboard. I feel sorry for the poor beasts. The men are probably happy though! The cooks have fresh meat to cook. I'll admit, it's a welcome change from the salted fish and bacon and that damned cassava bread. Have many of the swine suffered the same fate?"

"None, sir. They seem to have more sense and stronger legs than the horses. The pigs lie down as soon as the sea gets rough. So, we don't usually need to suspend them in body slings like we do the horses. The horses can't seem to overcome their need to stand. So, if the motion of the deck suddenly changes angle or pitch, their weight shifts if they're not completely supported by their sling, a leg may flex in the wrong direction, and the long bones snap."

Juan Ponce wasn't happy about the high mortality among the small Iberian horses he had personally selected to accompany him. So, he opted to change the subject. "Have the midday position notations been made and the chart updated?"

"Yes, Governor. According to Antón's quadrant tables we're very close to the little island where you landed in 1513, but we're about six or seven leagues west of it. I asked him to superimpose both his dead reckoning traverse board notes and the quadrant readings on your chart. The two positions are remarkably in close proximity."

Juan Ponce interrupted the captain. He said, "Antón Alaminos is not only an excellent navigator, he's my friend. You know, don't you? He was with me in 1513, when we found the Florida. Did you know he returned to the Florida twice since then as pilot with other expeditions of exploration? Once, he even returned to the same spot we visited together in 1513—the place from which the natives drove us away. They drove his group away, too. He was badly wounded by the bastards that time! We're fortunate to have him along as a member of this expedition. He has a technical mind and in a crisis he has good surgical skills."

"Good, Governor. We'll continue on this course through the night. After sunup we'll begin to look for a feature on the coast where we can make landfall. If this weather persists and we don't land soon we'll certainly lose more horses. The crewmen are exhausted . . . as I am . . . these ships have taken a beating."

Juan Ponce was excited, and rambled on, "I'm determined to colonize this island . . . this place I've named the Florida. Eight years ago I raised my fist in defiance and swore I'd come back and conquer this land. I vowed to take it from the heathens who dared assault me for no justifiable reason. Here we are, my friend, with a strong force of over 200 men and women and livestock. Soon, with certainty, will come a day of reckoning with the savages if they choose to be aggressive. Our sick priestly passengers will have their work cut out for them as they go about trying to Christianize the ferocious bastards who drove me off that cay in 1513."

Ever efficient, the captain changed the subject. "There's still too much water beneath our keel to cause us to heave to tonight. So, during the night I'll have the helmsmen begin to inch more to the east—head closer to land. We'll look for a secure anchorage in the morning. If we're in sight of the coast."

First mate Pedro Alvarez interrupted their conversation. "Captain . . . and your Excellency!"

"What is it, Pedro?"

"We're taking on water. All this slamming of the hull has loosened some of the planking and it's beginning to open up on the port side. Carpenters are already working on it. The crew will man the pumps to bail if this becomes necessary. Once we arrive at an anchorage, we'll have to make permanent repairs . . . to both vessels, I'm sure. The *Santa Magdalena* must have similar damage. Those priests and friars are still forward by the rowboat too, Captain. They're all huddled together in their misery—vomiting and praying."

During the night the wind came around. It now blew more from the east. The caravels, bearing on a north by northeast compass heading, were now on a beam reach. Before dawn, the two sailors were beginning to have a difficult time holding the tiller true to the heading. They connected a small block and tackle between the long arm of the steering mechanism and the railing. This eased the load the rudder's pressure was exerting on them.

The helmsman was carefully watching the compass. He shouted to his companion, who was watching the redness of dawn peek above the eastern horizon. "Diego! Wake Alonso and let's get him aloft. It's light enough to see!"

A soundly sleeping, snoring seaman stirred in the mass of snoozing bodies scattered on the slippery deck. Still half asleep he kneeled on one knee and stretched. Yawning, he slowly rose to his feet. "See anything yet?" He sleepily asked Diego who had called him to muster and begin his long day aloft.

"No, not yet. Not from down here on the tiller deck. When Alfredo and I hoist you up to your crow's nest you'll see many leagues beyond the horizon we can see from down here. But I wouldn't trade places with you. *Ha*! Just look up and check out the way the top of that mast is lurching!"

Alonso stretched again, twisted his torso to loosen up, and said, "Let me take a leak, grab some bacon and a water jar, and I'll be ready. Looks like we're going to have some good weather today."

Alonso hadn't been cramped in the crow's nest long when he saw the faint darkness—a bouncing dark green line—far away and across the still-raging sea. His eyes were at a height of about 65 feet above sea level. The line in the distance broke the continuity of the red dawning. He shrieked, "Diego! I see land . . . 20 degrees off the starboard bow! Wait, I think I can see more land dead ahead of us too, but further away! Wake the captain and the pilot!"

Juan Ponce had already been awakened by all the loud voices and activity above his head. Unlike the other men aboard the *Leonor*, who always slept on the caravel's deck, he had a tiny stern cabin on the port side of the ship. This cramped cubicle was beneath the helm station and was reached by climbing down through a small hatch. It contained a bunk and a chart table, but the chamber didn't have enough headroom for him to stand fully erect. He quickly rolled out of his bunk, threw on a cloak, climbed to the deck above, greeted the helmsman, stepped to the lee rail, and relieved himself over the side. Juan Ponce then proceeded to the upper deck of the sterncastle and joined a happy pair of men, the ship's captain Alfonso Fernando and chief pilot António de Alaminos.

As he ran his fingers through his mostly white hair and beard, Juan Ponce yawned, and said, "Good morning, Captain . . . Antón. What's all the excitement about?"

"Good morning, Governor, we have land in sight. Our lookout judges we're about five leagues west of it, but there's also apparently some land further north of our present position. Shall we—with this favorable wind—bring her toward the shore and then coast north? The land will give us some protection since the breeze has gone around to the southeast and it will certainly be easier on the livestock and the hull."

"That's a good plan, Captain. We don't want to sail by and miss seeing some bay that will give us protection. Proceed! I'm going to have a bite of hardtack and bacon. Then I'd like to review the charts. Antón, are we well north of the place of our 1513 landing?"

"The old man's worried! He's hoping we're out of the territory of those Indians who attacked us in '13. Why does he dwell on that and get so apprehensive?" Antón thought to himself, then responded to his leader's question, "Yes, your Excellency. We're about ten leagues further north of where we landed eight years ago." Then to himself, while rubbing his throat that had been pierced by a Calosa arrow only two years earlier, he added, "I hope that's far enough!"

Over the course of the morning, Captain Fernando occasionally brought the *Leonor* into the wind. He was purposely slowing their headway so the slower *Santa Magdalena* could catch up with the flagship, and plans for coasting could be made. One on one discussion between captains was always best. The distance between the vessels had to be shortened to allow voice communication. Signal flags were inappropriate when a common navigation decision was to be made. The ships were brought nearly rail to rail and the captains talked for a few minutes. It was decided they would come to within a half-league of the coast and then turn and sail north until they found a harbor they could safely enter. The morning passed as they steadily approached land.

The chief pilot was receiving his customary routine half-hour reports from the hourglass handler for determining the caravel's speed, the lookouts that checked for threats, and the depth checkers who began to cast their lead lines when the inshore water became much cloudier. Pointing northward, he repeated the most recent of the crew's observations. "Governor, I'm told there's a wide opening between the easterly coast and that northerly point or island we can see over there— that flat island making out toward the sea. From the color of the water, it looks as though it's deep enough for us to pass into that broad bay. We'll hug this distance from the easterly white beach and hold our present heading."

Agreeing with Antón Alaminos, Juan Ponce faced the captain and said, "Go ahead, Captain."

A voice above their heads interrupted, "Captain Fernando!"

Alfonso Fernando looked up at the crow's nest, and yelled, "What is it, Alonso?"

"Captain, I see smoke! Actually it's like a chain of smoke dotting the coast from many separate fires. They keep showing up. They're being lit from south to north with our progress. They're signal fires of some kind—I guess!"

"*Aha*! I see the black smoke. A billow of it's rising up behind the trees that line the beach. Keep a sharp eye!"

"Governor . . . did you hear . . .?"

". . . Yes, I did. I just saw a plume of smoke rise above the beach directly opposite our starboard beam. Someone has seen us and is spreading the word. I hope they're friendly!"

* * *

"What is that? They must be sea spirits! No! It's them!" Choap the Calosa lookout said, then yelled loudly from atop his observation platform, "Light the signal fire! The evil strangers in the great sailing canoes have returned! We must alert our people!"

His backup, who was half asleep on the ground a few feet away, jumped to his feet, then up to the platform, looked out toward the windblown Great Water, and turned to face the busy village. He blew several loud blasts with his conch horn. The day the Calosa people feared was at hand. Viewed from high on the village mound, 25 feet above the water, the fully rigged caravels were a foreboding ghostly vision as they inched above the horizon in the early afternoon light. The ships bounced about in sea chop and swells and their distant forms radiated as distorted images through the heat waves. These magnified the distant and unearthly countenances. The most feared of all their fears bore down on the alarmed Calosas.

"Light the fire! We're to make black smoke . . . as black as we can! Blow your signal horn again and alert our warriors to gather their personal things and meet at the boats for a council. I'm sure we'll join a major war party soon!"

"Signal fires . . . the black smoke . . . the white-skinned people have returned! They've dared enter the borders of our nation—for the *third* time!" Panti said to himself, after noticing the dark smoke rising far to the east. He saw it when he happened to look up to take a break from concentrating on detailing his latest carving project. He was making a deer head with removable ears. Ever alert, this was his normal behavior. Since a boy, he always *had* to know exactly what was going on around him. He watched impatiently as men from his village dutifully started their fire. They were using the long established system of smoke codes to pass on the alarm. They were notifying Calosa settlements on the chain of islands north of them. Soon, fires would be burning as far as the southern shore of the Bay of Danger at the northernmost remote Calosa encampment on the frontier.

Panti joined his friends at the fire and casually questioned the village's lookout. "What does the smoke tell you?"

"It's the strange people! The same race our people battled two different times near the Land of the High Hills. They've returned in two giant boats, each with many white cloud-like sails. The smoke tells us that if they keep coming in the direction they are, very soon they'll enter the Bay of Calos! Can any of you believe this is happening? They dare enter the very heart of our land! You're our village war chief, what are we going to do?"

Panti lowered his head, closed his eyes, and concentrated for a few seconds. With a serious tone, he said, "First, we'll prepare ourselves spiritually. Then, each of us with wives and children will spend time with our families. We'll be patient until a messenger from our war chief Celti, or mighty Calos himself, arrives. The words in the smoke will tell us what we must do to fit into the great leader's plan. For myself, tomorrow, after I take care of the personal things I mentioned, I'll cross the mouth of Grassy Bottom and travel overland to the point on the Great Seashell Island where the sun rises. I'll reconnoiter and judge for myself what role we can best fill. Who among you will join me in this quest . . . to see these demons close-up . . . with our own eyes? And slay them!"

"I will!" Barto said, and walked toward his friend.

"And I shall!" Exclaimed Kardah as he stepped forward to join them.

Soon, a group of 18 battle-tested warriors, matured in the ways of war in border and tribute conflicts, assembled in a unit. Scores of similar groups of warriors were uniting throughout the Calosa nation. Each man at the Grassy Bottom village would retire with his family and personal spiritual totem. Tomorrow, those who were to go with Panti would take up their weapons and follow him to the ends of the earth, or to their burial place if that's where this dangerous journey led them.

Each village dispatched its best fighters, the primary defenders of the proud and fierce Calosa nation. This call to arms assembled the largest force of warriors ever brought together to challenge a common foe. All knew this would not be some quickly done and over with war. Usually, when some weaker tribe infringed on Calosa hunting territory, or failed to deliver agreed upon amounts of goods in tribute, they were immediately overpowered. Panti and every other Calosa male knew this would be the battle of all battles. For eight years, Calosa warriors had lived to become part of this great episode in the history of their proud people.

*   *   *

"Captain! The backside of that large, flat island off to our port appears to have deep water. From what I see from up here I'd judge at least for a half-league westerly of its eastern point." Alonso shouted down from the best vantagepoint around.

"Good. Keep an eye peeled!" Captain Fernando said, then turned, pointed, and casually commented to his first mate, "Pedro, we'll anchor and raft the vessels there, about 100 yards off the beach. We need to be out of arrow range in case our being here invites any hostilities from land. As soon as you're sure the anchor's set, send a small boat ashore with a squad of musketeers and a farmer to evaluate the land. He'll need to see if this island has enough pasture for the live-stock. Well diggers should be sent ashore, too, as soon as practical.

"At first light tomorrow, send a troop in the bark to that distant white leveled-out point we can see to the north of this anchorage. They can do a similar evaluation."

Again, glancing up at the crow's nest, he shouted, "Alonso!"

"Yes, Captain?"

"From up there, what's the lay of the land at the head of this bay?"

"I don't see any white islands in the distance, Captain. Those I can see seem to be overflow mangrove cays." Occasionally pointing in different directions, he continued talking, and said, "It appears there's a sound, which leaves this bay and runs off to the west and north. It seems to me there's outflow from a large river sweeping around that white point north of us. I think I'm right, because of the color of the water. About halfway between here and that flat white point I can see the color line where the dark river water is mixing with water coming in from the sea."

Over the next few days, task forces were dispatched between the ships and the two points of prominent land. A supply of good water was found and several large wells were dug on the large southern island. Work crews began building temporary housing near the wells for the colonists. Grasslands were found to be limited, but those settlers who were experts in animal husbandry assured Juan Ponce there was enough grass to support the hoofed animals. He was concerned because the livestock were still being kept aboard ship and none of the crowded animals had seen the sun for over three weeks.

During the first few days, some of the islands and nearby mainland were named and charted by Antón Alaminos. Two among the names he chose, with Juan Ponce's approval, were descriptively simple. These were South Level Port and North Level Point—respectively, the land closest to their anchorage, and the distant white beach of the northern point across the bay. He mapped the bay bottom from a steady flow of information being given to him by a team of bottom sounders. These men, using small boats, randomly checked a grid of line-of-sight water depths with lead lines between the two points of land. Although there existed a general mood of apprehension among the Spaniards, and the few Caribbean Taino Indians who had been forced to accompany them, it was the opinion of the military officers this would be a secure and defensible harbor. But then again, when Juan Ponce considered how many columns of black-smoke he still saw, he wasn't so sure.

During daylight hours, the two ships were moved closer to the beach to shorten the distance shipboard supplies and equipment had to be moved in the small boats. Pens and corrals were hastily constructed on the large South Level Port Island. These would contain the fowl, sheep, pigs, goats, and cattle. Once ashore, the horses would be tethered at night and hobbled during the daytime so they might forage for themselves, but not wander too far away. Plans made before the voyage started would eventually be implemented and they would soon begin to clear land and develop improved pastures. With the corral facilities completed it was time to begin unloading the livestock.

One by one, the animals were hoisted through hatches. Still wrapped in slings, each was lifted free from the foul-smelling air of their dirty, tight-quartered position in the holds. They were lowered onto the upper decks of the caravels.

"Alonso! Diego! Have you ever seen a chicken *swim*?" a deck-hand named Raul asked, broke into a hysterical laugh, and tossed a struggling rooster over the side. The noisy startled bird tried his best to fly but was only able to remain airborne for a few seconds. With a heavy splash, he crash-landed into the green water. Foundering and beating his wings, the soaking wet sinking bird could not manage to reach the beach on his own. Fortunately, a man in a returning empty boat rescued the cock before he completely sank and drowned.

"Raul! That's enough of that foolishness! Lower the coop into the next boat and take them ashore all together and make sure they stay dry!" Captain Fernando scolded.

The livestock were unloaded the same way as the rooster, but this time it was operationally acceptable. A section of railing was removed and the resisting, bucking, distraught, and refusing-to-move horses and other animals were shoved off the deck into the water by crewmen. They had no choice but to swim ashore and then be herded to their corrals.

Occasionally, as the days passed, Indian canoes were sighted and some even dared to come close to the connected ships for a better look. It seemed to the Europeans the natives were going about peaceful pursuits. Neither people made any attempt to make contact with the other. Juan Ponce noticed this. He commented that most of the canoes came into the harbor from behind North Level Point, or from the direction he had been told the sound was located. All were traveling to another point of land on the eastern shore, then disappearing behind it.

The living quarters made by the Tainos were crude but adequate. These were framed with poles and covered with folded green fronds cut from the many cabbage palms that dotted the island. Satisfied that work was on schedule, Juan Ponce called a meeting with the caravel captains and other officers to discuss the next step in the ambitious plans for the development of his colony. "Now that the animals and people are housed, we must begin building fortifications here and at North Level Point. If a party of hostile savages decide to pay us a visit we must be ready for them. Captains, now that the ships are empty, your men should start careening operations and quickly make any hull repairs necessary on your ships."

* * *

Panti and his band were concealed perfectly. They blended completely with the dense foliage and were far enough away from the Spanish perimeter they would not be easily detected. The Calosa warriors had established a temporary camp west and inland from where the Spaniards were busy building a more permanent base. The strange activities in the Spanish camp were being watched around the clock. Nothing went on there that wasn't known to the Calosas.

"Kardah," said Panti, "the pain is returning. My tooth has started hurting again. In fact, it's getting worse. My jaw's been swollen for several days and my gum had a large soft bubble, like a boil, around the cracked tooth. The bubble broke during the night and I suddenly woke with a mouthful of foul-tasting, bloody pus. After it broke, the pain was relieved but it's still draining. Look! *Psst.*" Panti spit a blood-stained stream of saliva, spit a second time, and then said, "I'll go to Mando's village after we kill these trespassers and have that medicine man he told me about knock this tooth out of my mouth and be done with it."

"Panti! Look, there on the beach! What are those four-legged animals?"

Peering through the green screen of sea grape leaves Panti forgot his discomfort. Staring in disbelief, he answered, "I have no idea! They look something like giant deer, but look at their hairy tails and the long hair growing on their necks. And their strange-shaped heads—they're huge! They're all different colors and none of them that I can see have antlers!

"Look! They're tame. Those men are leading them around and they don't resist. They just follow behind, obediently like a dog. What are they?"

Barto, Panti's closest friend, also whispering, said, "I don't believe it! Look there, I don't believe it, but I see a man riding one of the beasts! Listen to the strange sound the animal makes."

Panti was intensely interested in the interaction between these strange men and the stranger beasts they rode. He was completely fascinated by the horses. During his turns watching the Spaniards, he studied all visible actions and techniques between the men and weird beasts. He also noticed that at night these creatures were vulnerable, since they were not well guarded. Thirty-five Iberian horses, survivors of a group of 50 that left San Juan, were tethered to a zigzagging line stretched between several trees. It was obvious to Panti that all anyone had to do to take one was to slip up to them in the darkness, cut one free, and disappear with the animal into the brush. Panti made his plans, silently, and unshared. "I must have one of those animals! With one of those beasts I could move like the wind!"

* * *

The days dragged on without any contact between the Calosa and the Spanish. Periodically, the men in Panti's war party would rotate to return home and spend time with their families. During his first visit back home he learned that regular communications between the capital and the outlying villages had been established. Messengers were sent out periodically to tell the people that great Calos and his deputies would decide soon when the all-out war would start.

Panti's father, Pundon, made the short trip to Panti's camp to relay the message. "Son, I'm here to tell you that mighty Calos has decreed our combined force will attack the evil people the morning after the night of the full moon. That's less than a week away. Great

Calos has gathered over 600 warriors and as we speak they're preparing for this great battle. What are your plans? Shall I send word that you and the men from our village will join the main battle group?"

"No, you may tell the war chiefs that when the main force attacks by water, we'll engage the enemy here on the land. They are many and are well fortified. We'll press them and try to drive them from the land to their boats. Then we'll burn what they've built on our land."

"Be careful, my son. We pray your totem will be strong and you count many victories as you bring death to these evil people. Please, be very careful."

That night, before the bright moon rose to illuminate the landscape, Panti made his move. With all the talents of stealth he could apply, he moved alone, out from the protection of the dense cover, and toward the line of horses. Picket fires surrounded the Spanish encampment and shadowy sentries moved between them. The dark line of sleeping horses blocked the firelight and Panti slithered through the vegetation invisibly silent on the dark side.

"*Shh!*" Panti soothed the animal he had selected. Other than a large, peculiar white facial mark, and white socks on its front legs, the long-maned horse was mostly jet black. The animal did not remain quiet as he hoped, but neighed and snorted as the ghostly human figure approached from behind. Panti paused and stiffly waited. The horse quieted as Panti stroked his flank, exactly as he had watched the Spanish horsemen do. When the horse's sound brought no reaction from the sentries, he continued. With his right hand firmly around the carved totem handle, Panti lifted his knife from its sheath. At the same time he reached up and took the rope rein with his left. With one sweeping motion of the glistening black obsidian blade, the horse was free, and turning in the direction Panti was leading him. In a moment they were in the jungle of trees and headed directly across the Great Seashell Island. Panti was leading his prize captive toward the beach on the Great Water.

Panti led the horse into the low surf. When he was knee deep he turned right and they waded for a few hundred yards along the edge of the beach. At dawn, when the Spaniards discovered the horse was gone, Panti knew they would follow the animal's hoof prints. They would only be able to track him as far as the water's edge. When he was satisfied that they had moved far enough down the beach Panti and the animal left the water. After they crossed the open beach, Panti tied the horse in the trees, backtracked, and carefully and completely filled and brushed out the hoof marks and footprints that pocked the beach.

CHAPTER 25

G OVERNOR! GOVERNOR! YOU MUST WAKE UP AT
once! We're going to be attacked! Hurry!" Antón Alaminos
screamed and frantically shook Juan Ponce.

"Wha . . . what is it, Antón? Who's attacking?"

"It's the damnable heathens. There are hundreds of them in a
flotilla. They're forming their canoes in an enormous semicircle
around our ships. They've stopped just out of musket range. They
must've been gathering all night but the sentries didn't know they were
there until it was light enough to see!"

"I knew it! Those bastards were biding their time . . . building
their forces to a strength they thought capable of overpowering us.
We'll give them a fight they won't soon forget . . . I knew it!"

Captain Alfonso Fernando was pacing back and forth, waiting
for Antón to rouse Juan Ponce. His heavy footprints had started to
wear a depression in the shell-surfaced courtyard fronting the group of
palm-thatched huts occupied by Juan Ponce, his servants, and close
associates. The settlement was awakening because of the commotion.

The captain abruptly stopped his nervous march and issued an
order to his first mate, Pedro Alvarez. "Go to the *Leonor* and fire a
saker from the ship to signal those at North Level Point. The smaller

cannons, the falconets or versos won't be loud enough for them to hear. We must let them know what's going on!"

"Yes, Captain!" Pedro said as he spun around and walked to the small boat standing by, ready to take him to his anchored ship. As he seated himself in the rowboat, he thought, "Thank God we finished bottom repairs before the savages made their appearance. The ships are ready if we're forced to leave. There are so many of them. God help us!"

Within minutes, three noisy six-pound saker cannons, with their muzzles pointed toward the Calosa formation, were fired from the ship. Discharged in succession, one after the other, this was the prearranged signal between the Spanish camps to warn each group that a conflict with the Indians was imminent. The solid-shot balls fell among the crowded canoes. Geysers of water erupted high into the air.

As the Spaniards hurried to reload their guns, a dozen catamarans broke formation and left the Calosa armada. To form a catamaran, two canoes were sparred together. A lightweight woven platform of palm roots bridged the space between the hulls. The strung-out line of boats was rushing toward the caravels. Since the two ships were still rafted and connected together, some of their fixed cannons could not be turned and brought to bear on the Calosa canoes. Ten strong paddlers aboard each catamaran raced toward the ships, while another man remained crouched on the platform.

Despite the hurried efforts of the two-man gun crews, the small cannons were not ready to fire by the time the nearest canoe had bravely approached within 50 yards of the *Santa Magdalena*. The crouching man on the lead canoe stood up. In his right hand he held an atlatl. He bent over, picked up a five-foot long dart, and fitted its concave, feathered end to the spur on the rear of his spear-throwing stick. In an instant, the chert-headed dart was catapulted toward its target. The dart's speed and range were increased six-fold because of the combined force generated by the warrior's strong arm and his atlatl.

A Spanish crossbowman who had been watching the unfolding saga from the rail of the *Santa Magdalena* fell dead. His armor and flesh were deeply pierced by the speeding force and deadly accuracy of the stone-headed, white mangrove- and maidencane-shafted, dart. Before the canoe veered away, the warrior threw several more darts in rapid succession and another soldier at the caravel's rail died. The other catamarans continued the assault but the frightened and wary Spaniards had dropped to the deck and later volleys of darts found no targets.

The Calosa forces in the canoes continued this strategy, attacking each time the cannons were fired. Wave after wave of canoes continued the offensive. Casualties on both sides mounted until the early afternoon when the Calosa warriors suddenly withdrew.

In late afternoon Juan Ponce consulted with the expedition's military officers whom he had asked to gather in his hut. Pacing nervously, he stared at the bare-ground floor, and launched a tirade against the strong-willed adversaries who dared try to foil his dream for colonization of the Florida. He ranted, "We must protect the vessels at all costs, yet we must not leave our camp unprotected. If the heathen bastards take the ships we'll be completely at their mercy. I want the ground tackle and the ships protected day and night. If they cut us loose from our anchorage and the vessels ground we would be lost! We'd be unable to escape if their force grows larger. Most of the musketeers should be assigned to the *Leonor* and the *Santa Magdalena*. They'll keep the savages back further than crossbow bolts can. They mustn't be allowed to get close enough to use their damned bows and arrows!"

At breakfast a young Spanish lieutenant was sent to alert Juan Ponce. He burst into the mess hut, and exclaimed excitedly, "Your Excellency! I'm sorry to intrude, but I've been sent to tell you the Indians are back and are attacking our ships! They've tried to cut the anchors free but our musketeers have stopped them . . . so far!"

In a rage, Juan Ponce pounded his fist on the table, and yelled, "Captain!"

Alfonso Fernando stepped inside the hut. "Yes, Governor?"

"I think it's time we separated the ships. Some of the six-pounders are useless while they're rafted. If the screaming bastards are as smart as they seem to be, they'll soon think to surround the ships. If they do, all of our guns must be operational!"

"Yes, Governor. I'll see to it at once!"

Panti and his small force remained hidden in the tree line. The warriors under his command urged him to order the attack on the strange people. Now that the water assault was again underway they pressed him to attack immediately. He gestured in disapproval, and said, "We'll pounce on them very soon. Look, as we speak, many with the smoking sticks are leaving in their wide canoes. I'm sure they're being sent to defend the giant sailing boats. The time for us to act is getting close. Be patient!"

Panti glared at the Spaniards through the round sea grape leaves. He talked silently to himself. "That man with the white-haired face is their leader. I'm sure of that. He directs their every move with his loud voice and hand signals. He'll be my target. Without him they'll be much weaker."

"Get ready to follow me!" Panti exclaimed, then paused, and pointing toward the Spanish camp, he continued, "That man with the white hair on his face is my target. My totem has commanded that I'm not to allow any of you to interfere in his living or dying. Kill those near him, but he's mine! Is that understood?"

Each member of the war party looked at their leader and nodded in agreement. They already had fitted arrows to their bowstrings and were waiting for his signal to go ahead with their surprise attack.

Panti had not finished making his comments. He said, "This day is critical for our nation—the kingdom of the great Calos. I'm unafraid as I face injury or death again. Each of you must be in the same frame of mind if we're to succeed. Like each of you, I'm first a Calosan. I'm ready to engage in battle and, if necessary, die for my nation and people. Long live our great leader, Calos!"

As those words left his lips, Panti turned to face his enemies, and an arrow left the vibrating, humming string of his powerful war bow. One hundred twenty-five feet away a Spanish sentry died instantly. Panti's companions launched their arrows, and to a man each quickly sent a second shaft to follow the first, before dropping to the ground to hide again. Several Spaniards were killed and others gravely wounded even before the Calosa land-based attack was noticed. Hearing the screams of dying and wounded men the Spanish soldiers responded.

A frightened officer screamed, "Everyone withdraw into the breastworks! Musketeers! Come here and form a defensive line. Protect the people as they move into our fort."

Ten unprepared soldiers raced to the officer, lit their matches, formed a line, and fired their noisy weapons in the direction of the unseen Calosas. The lead balls found no flesh. Seconds later, six more of the musketeers lay dead and four others were seriously wounded, victims of the hidden warriors.

Juan Ponce had sought refuge inside the mess hut when Panti's force attacked. He protected himself by getting behind a heavy table, overturned by his bodyguards. The enemy was still unseen, so the men at Juan Ponce's side held their crossbows ready at their shoulder. They were trained to wait for adversaries to show themselves before releasing their deadly bolts.

Arrow followed arrow, but the small Calosa force remained hidden. Panti had planned to use this strategy to reduce losses and save the lives of his men, many of whom were his close friends. He had decided to continue the offensive from hiding until their supply of arrows was nearly exhausted, or an opening for close hand-to-hand combat presented itself. So far, there were no casualties among his warriors.

"Governor, we can better serve our company's defense if we withdraw to the breastworks."

"I agree," Juan Ponce responded, "but let's wait until we know what size force faces us in those woods, or at least until we can see and kill some of the devils!"

The officer hesitated, then nervously said, "Yes, sir!"

They didn't have long to wait. Panti signaled his comrades it was time to attack. One by one, the warriors dashed from their sea grape-shrouded cover. They agilely scattered to hiding places closer to the Spanish defenders. For a few seconds, some were exposed and easy targets for the trained marksmen guarding Juan Ponce. They died quickly, caught in a vicious crossfire of bolts and lead balls fired from inside the palm-thatched hut or the palm trunk fortifications.

Panti could see the white-bearded man through the cabin's doorway. He was gesturing and talking loudly as men near him fired their strange weapons. Panti's mind raced. "When we get closer they'll retreat to join the others behind the log wall. We must get closer and intercept them when they flee." Sensing the enemy would soon make that very move Panti yelled aloud, "Barto, and anyone else near me!

They're getting ready to run and join their main force. When they do, I'm charging with my saber. Those of you who have arrows left can cover me and whoever chooses to join me when I attack."

Six nervous Spaniards stepped out of the hut. Their weapons were at the ready, held tight against their shoulders. Each of the stern-faced men searched for a target. Juan Ponce, with drawn Toledo steel saber in hand, hesitantly stepped out behind them. Two more soldiers carrying pikes followed him. After leaving the building, the crossbow-men saw a few Calosa warriors running in their direction between points of cover. They all fired bolts, either at shadows in the sea grape thicket or directly at sprinting warriors coming toward them. The small force quickly began to sidestep toward the protection of the breast-works 100 feet away. Cranking their bows to the fully drawn position, each of the soldiers readied to place another bolt onto the track of his crossbow.

Seeing the Spaniards were abandoning their position, Panti quickly jumped to his feet. He had tossed his bow on the ground and now brandished his deadly war saber. Panti's "sword" was unlike the metal weapon carried by the Spanish leader. Panti had hewn and fashioned his from a piece of hard sea grape lumber. A handle grip was carved at one end, and leading away from that the thin blade curved gracefully. The leading edge of the saber was studded with a single line of eleven wicked-looking tiger shark teeth. A club-like projection on the edge opposite the teeth dominated the saber's tip. Five tassels of human hair and three eagle feathers were attached to it. It was a formidable weapon.

The group of cautious Spaniards had only managed to withdraw a few yards when two bodyguards were impaled by atlatl darts cast by the unseen warriors. Now that the Calosas were clear of large trees, their atlatls could be used to full advantage. The men struck by the high-speed darts would die a terrible death. In effect, these darts locked the armor of the victims to their flesh. Later, caregivers would be unable to remove the steel covering and the wounds could not be attended. Men severely wounded through their armor by an arrow or dart, and fortunate enough to be rescued and withdrawn, could not receive medical attention. First, they must bear excruciating agony as the wooden shaft was cut and shortened. The remaining stub and point was shoved, even hammered, through their body or extremity to remove the point.

Two more of the men protecting Juan Ponce fell victim to arrows. These lodged in their arms and legs, having purposely been aimed there by the Calosa bowmen to avoid striking the armor. Juan Ponce raised his saber to meet the oncoming warriors. The two crossbowmen still standing lifted their weapons to defend their leader. The first of these men to step forward was immediately downed by several arrows, fired by those warriors protecting the rushing Panti, Barto, and the others who had volunteered to join the close quarters attack.

The remaining crossbowman fired point-blank at Panti who was charging them at full speed and was closest, the greatest threat to Juan Ponce. Miraculously, as if all the stories of his greatness and powers were true, the speeding bolt struck inches short of its intended target. It imbedded in the moving blade of Panti's saber. It hit with such force that the weapon was nearly knocked loose from his grip. Panti stumbled. Regripping the saber with his left hand, Panti rose to his feet, and withdrew his knife from its sheath. With this firmly in his right hand he leaped forward to strike Juan Ponce. Panti felt an unexpected solid blow to the left side of his body. As he slammed to the ground he spun halfway around to see that one of the lancers had swung his pike—rather than jabbed with it—and connected with a bruising impact. Stunned, Panti hesitated briefly, then struggled to regain his footing. At the same time, he twisted and lunged forward to parry the swing of Juan Ponce's gleaming sword.

His primitive sword met one of the world's finest edged weapons when the sabers of the two determined men made violent contact. Panti was the stronger of the two and his second full-force swing knocked the saber from his adversary's sweating hand. Panti raised his weapon and screamed words unintelligible to his enemy, "Your people dared return to the land of the mighty Calosa! Despite our warnings! For this mistake, you and all those with you are going to die! I am Panti, of the Panther Clan! I am the Calosan who has come to kill you! My totem and mighty Calos have sent me to slay you and all your people."

Juan Ponce de León was no coward. He sneered and drew a stilleto from a scabbard on his belt. He spit in the face of the enraged

Indian who was yelling in his unrecognizable tongue. Legs apart, he braced himself for the attack and screamed defiantly, "Come on! You red-skinned, heathen bastard! Your gut will yet taste my cold steel!"

Panti didn't see the wounded lancer coming up behind him. He staggered as the pike point pierced his back and penetrated his shoulder. In a quick reaction, Panti spun around with outreached arm and his saber struck the Spaniard in the throat. The impact of the saber was so forceful, and the shark teeth so deeply imbedded in the soldier's neck, that the weapon was pulled out of Panti's hand by the weight of the soldier as he collapsed, dead in a growing puddle of his own blood.

Turning quickly after changing hands with his dagger, in desperation Panti lunged blindly toward Juan Ponce. The Spaniard stepped back, but not far enough. As Panti fell forward he drove the black blade of his knife deep into the right thigh of Juan Ponce with a downstroke stabbing thrust. He felt the resistance as the obsidian struck bone. Juan Ponce screamed, fell backwards, landed on his back, and kicked violently as Panti continued crawling on his hands and knees toward him. The Spaniard was trying to back up, yet at the same time kick away his attacker. Juan Ponce was trapped, and realizing the futility of escape he stopped fighting. Panti saw he had his adversary at a disadvantage when the man dropped his knife. He stepped forward, straddled his moaning enemy, and thought, "I'll cut his throat and be done with it. My wounds need attention."

Panti looked around when he heard the sound of his force's voices. They were screaming at him—warning him to withdraw at once. His fellow warriors were yelling and waving their arms to alert him that a group of soldiers were running in his direction from the fortifications. They were sent to rescue their fallen leader and were getting close. Panti looked down at the grimacing, frightened old man and waved his bloody knife. With words his fallen adversary could not comprehend, Panti shouted, "I've counted a great victory! I should kill you now, but you'll soon be a dead man anyway!"

Glaring with hatred, Panti reached down and tightly grabbed hold of a strange-looking shiny disk, which decorated the chest of his wounded enemy. Pulling his clenched hand away with a jerk, he tore the medal free, then spit at the screaming Spaniard. Panti took a few steps and bent down to retrieve his saber. He violently twisted and jerked the weapon free from the neck of the dead Spanish lancer, then turned, and dashed away. Panti stopped again, stooped to pick up his bow, and then sprinted into the veil of green sea grape leaves and disappeared into their diverse shadows.

The wounds on Panti's back were superficial. The Spaniard's lance had made a glancing blow. Its sharp, steel head had struck his shoulder blade, after it cleanly sliced through the tissue and muscle under his skin. Since it was not a puncture wound, he and his companions were in high spirits. Their brave leader was not seriously injured. Panti was more concerned about the condition of the prized knife his father's father had given him than his injury. After pulling it loose from Juan Ponce's upper leg he noticed that about an inch of the tip of the obsidian blade had snapped off. Panti thought part of his knife remained deep in the flesh of his enemy. "It's probably imbedded in the bone. I told him he was a dead man!"

Antón Alaminos was beckoned from the *Leonor* to assess the wound to Juan Ponce's thigh. He found his commander in pain and bleeding profusely from the jagged puncture wound in his upper leg. In a concerned tone, he asked, "Was it an arrow, Governor? The soldier that came to get me said he was told by someone that you had been wounded . . . by an arrow!"

"No, one of them got in close enough to stab me with a knife. He could've killed me if he wanted to, but I think my gold medal distracted him long enough that the men coming to my aid caused him to run. The thieving bastard pulled the medal off my blouse before running away! King Ferdinand himself . . . God rest his soul . . . presented me with that decoration the last time I went home to Spain. How bad is my leg?"

"I'll apply pressure to stop the bleeding, then clean the wound, and wrap your thigh with a bandage. You're lucky it didn't cut a major blood vessel. The wound looks clean but I'll have to watch it closely to be sure it remains that way."

Battles and skirmishes continued over the next few days. Despite heavy losses, the war chiefs leading the Calosa forces were determined to massacre the Spanish colonists and troops. Their arrows and darts were literally raining on the Spaniards who were bravely defending their positions. The Spanish were just as resolute to inflict casualties a nd k eep t he n atives a t b ay. They w ere b eing s uccessful because of the superior range of their arquebuses and cannon. Because of the blockade imposed by the Calosa canoes there were no connected lines of command between the Spanish forces. After hostilities started, communication existed only between the Spaniards fighting on the ships and those hunkered down in the fortifications at South Level Port. The smaller force of their embattled countrymen, who were stationed a league away, on North Level Point, were on their own. On the morning of the third day after the war started, a considerable amount of smoke rose over the northern outpost.

"Governor, how are you feeling this morning?"

"My leg is hurting—pounding slightly. I had a bout with mild chills during the night. Am I taking a fever, Antón?"

The makeshift doctor felt his leader's forehead, and said, "You do feel a little warm. Let me check and redress your wound first thing."

"What's the situation with the Indians? Do they continue the attack this morning?"

"There's smoke rising across the bay. Everyone seems to think that the savages have burned our other camp. It would seem our people over there may have been lost. We can't send a boat to check on their welfare until the fight with these naked painted devils is over."

Antón slowly removed the dressing from his commander's upper leg. The wound was closed but was continuing to ooze. It didn't look good, and this was evident when he said, "I think it prudent that we begin preparations to withdraw from this place. You need the care of a qualified physician."

"Is my leg infected?"

"It doesn't appear to be healing properly—if you're coming down with a fever. That's not a good sign."

"I came here to settle this land. I didn't travel back here to be vanquished by some unknown stubborn Indians. I'll not withdraw!"

Three days later, the swelling around his throbbing wound caused Juan Ponce de León to reassess his determination to remain in the Florida. Resentfully, he ordered that all fowl and livestock, with the exception of the horses, be slaughtered and cooked or smoked for use on a trip back to San Juan. Preparations were stepped up and all implements and property of value were taken back aboard the ships. The wounded were loaded aboard the *Leonor* and the horses aboard the *Santa Magdalena*.

An exhausted Juan Ponce issued instructions to his second in command, "Send out a party with one or two of the Indian interpreters and have them try to negotiate a cease fire with the bastards. Have them take some trading trinkets—the glass beads! We need to agree—to come to terms for a truce so we may send a group to the other camp to see if anyone survives. Tell the bastards they've won—again! We'll leave their land just as soon as we can bury our dead, load our ships, and give them gifts."

No one was found alive at North Level Point. To a man, the corpses had been stripped naked, disemboweled, and their eyeballs cut out of their heads. The Calosa believed that without eyes the souls of the dead would never find eternal rest. Lacking eyeballs, where one of the human souls resided, their enemies would be forced to perpetually move about the fringes of the spirit world. They would be unable to enter the other side and gain the blissful peace of death promised to the Calosa by their shamans.

The battle-experienced soldiers were appalled at the appearance of the victims. None of them had ever seen such severe mutilations by native peoples on other islands in the Indies they had helped conquer. Their opponents were certainly as savage as Juan Ponce de León had described them.

While hungry, carrion-eating birds soared overhead, drawn by the foul-smelling corpses, the bloated, maggot infested, and vulture-picked remains of the Spanish farmers and soldiers were summarily buried. This solemn and horrid duty finished, the small force withdrew from the site of the massacre. They returned to their ships across the bay under the watchful eye of gleaming, self-assured, and victorious Calosa warriors.

Two days later, the Spanish settlement at South Level Port was set ablaze by the last Spaniards to leave the beach. Their anchors pulled free from the bottom, the two caravels followed the swift ebbing tide flowing from the bay and racing toward the open sea. Antón

Alaminos had carefully marked his chart with the name he had chosen for the bay. "The Bay of the Calosa" described the body of water where they all had nearly died. Another notation in his script was written near the location of North Level Point. This bore the words, "The Place of Slaughter." These and related names identified the wide Bay of the Calosa for posterity, and the place where so many Spaniards were killed at the hands of a defiant and savage people—a proud people who stubbornly defended their homes and way of life.

CHAPTER 26

THREE DAYS OUT FROM THE BAY OF THE CALOSA, THE ships passed between the Tortugas and the Martyrs, and sailed into the yet unnamed Straits of Florida. After signal flags were hoisted high in the rigging of the flagship to signal the other ship, the caravels came together for the last time. They did so for a brief conference to discuss the future of the men and resources of Juan Ponce de León's failed Florida expedition.

The senior officer, Captain Alfonso Fernando, shouted to the captain of the *Santa Magdalena* as his caravel floated alongside. "You may take Chief Pilot Alaminos and a squad of soldiers, and whoever else wants to join you, aboard your vessel. Yesterday, the governor directed I change the course of the *Leonor*. Instead of sailing home, we're going to put in at Cuba. He's afraid he won't live long enough to reach San Juan. He seeks the aid of a doctor and a lawyer. He's already signed a document releasing you from your contract, and it also gives you permission to sail west to New Spain as you asked. You're authorized to sell the horses and equipment to Captain Cortés. The funds are to be later transferred to the governor's estate—to his heirs."

"Thank you, Captain. Are Antón, the soldiers, and the others agreeable to join me?"

"Yes, we discussed this in detail with the Governor—it was his idea. Antón's agreed to serve as your pilot. Cortés expects him to return to New Spain anyway."

"Good, you can tell them to come aboard my vessel when they're ready. In the meantime, I'll pay my respects . . . say my good-byes to his Excellency."

"Come aboard. Antón's below with the governor. I'll send word for him and the others to get their things together."

"How is the governor, and the rest of the wounded today?"

"He had a very bad time of it last night. He was feverish and hallucinating most of the night. The priests are alternating around the clock, and at least one of them is always with him should he want their spiritual care or need the last rites of our holy Roman Catholic Church. His thigh is now clearly diseased. The red line creeping up his swollen leg is much more visible and longer today than it was even yesterday. Antón told me his blood is poisoned, but he's strong for his age and will live until the poison weakens his heart. He could last but a few more days, or linger and suffer for weeks. There's no hope for him, and I'm afraid he knows it. It's so sad to watch such a great man die this way. I wish the red devil that did this to him had struck his heart direct-ly and had killed him outright! It would've saved the governor from this terrible suffering. We've calculated that 80 members of our expe-dition were killed or wounded in the battles with those bastards. We lost two more soldiers over the past two days, but all the others seem to be recovering."

Soon, the caravels parted company. One headed west, the other sailed east to find Cuba and hopefully some comfort for their fallen leader.

*   *   *

Panti recovered quickly. A doctor, who was told of Panti's band's casualties during their bold land attack on the Spanish camp, was sent to help them. He took charge of the injured warriors' medical care. He was assisted by a medicine man. To stop the bleeding on Panti's back, the wound was first cauterized with a thin, needle-shaped, fire-heated, chert blade. This sealed blood vessels to stop bleeding and prevent infection. As the doctor applied the various procedures of treatment, a different chanting song offered by the two caregivers accompanied each phase. Following cauterization, the wound was pinched together and covered with a thin layer of sticky white clay. The doctor worked delicately and slowly. While one of his hands held the separated skin together, the other applied thin strips of clay. The medicine man had worked this to the correct consistency. Panti's shoulder was bound with an uncomfortable tangle of thin cords to help hold the clay in place. Small amounts of blood leaked under the clay poultice. The doctor carefully lifted sections and withdrew blood from wherever it was seeping. To do this he used his mouth and a sucking tube. The tube was made from the thin-walled, hollow, wing bone of a pelican. Once the bleeding stopped, the clay was gently pressed back in place and all strips were smoothed into one unified bandage.

Three days later, the poultice was carefully removed and the wound inspected. It was cleaned with a liquid prepared from material in the medicine bag. Water and medicinal plants were placed inside a deep wooden mortar. Slowly, these were ground and mixed together with a hardwood pestle. A thick pad, made from several combined bolls of wild cotton, was saturated with the medicinal fluid and held in place with another network of cords. This treatment would be repeated every second day until the wound was completely healed. The scar would be large, not very pretty, and the story of its origins would be talked about many times in the future.

After the wound healed and the bandage was removed, Panti spent much of his recovery time with his horse. He had named the mare Mask, because of the white, elliptical-shaped blotch on her forehead. The irregular pattern extended beyond and around her eyes—like a mask. Just as soon as he was physically able he mounted the animal for the first time. He had carefully watched the Spanish horsemen ride the animals, so when he finally sat astride the mare's broad bare back his being there seemed natural. Slowly, the two became used to the other. The bond between them grew with the passage of time.

The small pasture and half-burned corral next to the destroyed Spanish camp offered Panti an ideal place to keep Mask. The eastern point of the Great Seashell Island was a favorite place for the Calosa to visit, and was often used for a variety of religious ceremonies. The site was not regularly inhabited because of the frequent rough, unsafe water on each side of the point of land. Since their everyday life centered on the mobility which boats provided, the Calosa preferred to live near much better protected waters.

Panti rode Mask along the bay beach to the spit of land on the shore of Grassy Bottom across from his home village. It was here that he kept his best canoe. After discussing the needs of the strange animal with Olta, they decided to change their place of residence. The Spanish wells were still functional. Since a quantity of water was essential for the horse, Panti decided the enemy's former settlement would make an excellent residence for him and his family.

* * *

Many days after separating from the *Santa Magdalena*, the *Leonor* reached the entrance of the fine harbor known as Havana Bay. Juan Ponce was in a state of delirium most of the time. With his body ravaged by the septicemic infection, he teetered on the brink of death. He was carefully taken from the ship to one of the area's finest homes. During a period of half-lucid reckoning, he drew his confidante Alfonso Fernando closer. In a weak monotone, he muttered, "Just as soon as we're berthed, locate a good lawyer for me. I must have my last will and testament drawn up immediately. My holdings in San Juan must be properly distributed to my heirs. You should send our horses west. Send them west . . . sell them to Cortés!"

In a soothing voice, Alfonso Fernando spoke to Juan Ponce. "Your Excellency, at this very moment the horses are sailing to Cortés."

The leading physician in Cuba was called to the aid of the fallen Spanish leader. "I'm sure the leg is diseased because some part—a fragment—of the weapon remains in the leg. Even if I could remove it, it would not save his life. It's too late!"

Juan Ponce continued to be cared for by the priests. He was given the last rites of his church. Soon after, he lost consciousness. He slipped away, and fell into a final, deep, and feverish coma. The conqueror of San Juan, and the discoverer of the Florida, died in Puerto Carenas and passed into history in July 1521. The exact date has been lost to posterity.

* * *

Life soon returned to a normal routine for Panti and Olta. They raised their children to become happy adults, and he continued his development as an artisan. The Calosa nation was at peace. Seldom were the strange light-skinned men mentioned anymore, other than at social events when the storytellers passed on accounts of the famous conflict and their people's victory.

Almost 20 years after the decisive Bay of Calos battle, citizens of the Calosa nation heard news that the Spaniards had returned. This time, the Europeans landed a large military force on the far shore of the Bay of Danger. From this beachhead the invaders marched northward and left a path of destruction, even beyond the River of the Stone. When they heard this news, Olta immediately feared for the welfare of her people. Panti's thoughts often drifted to memories of Ronna. How had his grandfather fared in his life among the people of his wife? During their quiet times alone, these fears and concerns were frequently discussed, but never shared with others. Private conversations were difficult in the open society of the Calosas. For the time being, the Spanish invaders purposely bypassed the lands ruled by Calos. Panti and Olta would not live to see the future collision of the two cultures— but their children would.

As they aged, Panti and Olta remained happy. Their union had been fortuitous and their lives enriched by the uncompromising love they shared for each other. This love, their common security, and the development of their children provided a special bond that controlled their marital relationship and passage through life. Not all was easy for this Calosa family when Panti's health started to decline.

When he reached his late forties, Panti's health started to seriously slip. It was now nearly 20 years since the battle with the Spaniards.

Olta assumed the family responsibilities that Panti was unable to fulfill. She was a strong and a caring wife and became the head of the family as her husband's health worsened. The episodic pain of his chronic toothache was often unbearable, yet despite the urging of friends, family, doctors, and medicine men, Panti continued to suffer. He resisted suggestions from anyone that he have the tooth removed. Panti learned that whenever the abscess and nearby subcutaneous cellulitis started to fester again he could treat it himself. He would lance the swollen gum with a stiff, sharp-pointed, leaf tip from a yucca plant. Puncturing the swollen gum reduced the painful pressure that periodically flared up, but the drainage provided no lasting cure.

After many successful, but unsterilized abscess punctures, it took only one such treatment with a germ-tainted, needle-tipped yucca leaf for Panti to self-infuse a lethal bacterium into his bloodstream. Over time, a subtle, slow-moving, massive infection, generated in the tissue around his split tooth, weakened him. It brought him a great illness he would be unable to conquer. Like the leader of the invading Spanish, Juan Ponce de León, Panti was slowly succumbing to a deadly septicemic infection.

When his physical appearance revealed the seriousness of his illness, those around him knew he would die soon. People with such severe mouth infections *always* died. In private conversations with priests, Panti asked that his mortal remains be given a special dispensation following his death. He and Olta were told they could be buried wherever they wished, including a site near their home on the eastern point of the Great Seashell Island.

Enlisting the help of benevolent friends high in the priesthood, Panti began to orchestrate the preparation of his final resting-place. He and Olta selected the spot, and Panti oversaw development of the place their earthly remains were to be buried.

Panti wanted his burial mound to be special. It would be made from the gray-colored, fine sand gathered from soil deposits far up the Great River. This dark sand had a special significance in the religious rituals of the Calosa. Being buried beneath it would elevate his status among his people even further after he had gone to the other side. He also let it be known he wanted to be buried in this particular spot so the sun would greet his mortal remains each morning through eternity. All who later visited his death shrine would learn of his work as a master craftsman, artist, and his brave deeds as a famous heroic warrior. They would learn, too, that here was buried the man among their people who rode the horse. No one in the Calosa nation was held in a higher level of awe—except Calos. The priests who tended his spirituality assured Panti that the storytellers would sing verse and tell tales of his great deeds until the end of time.

His last weeks were spent in the village on the shore of Grassy Bottom where he grew up. In those final days those who loved and admired him surrounded him. Olta was his constant caregiver. She held Panti to her breast while his will to survive, and his life, slowly drained from his mortal entity. The infection had won. Panti's souls passed into eternity.

Panti's remains were taken to the village's charnel house. They would decompose there while work on his burial mound continued. Laboring paddlers in double-hulled canoes strained to carry maximum loads of the gray sand from the mine on the banks of the Great River. Slowly, the mound took shape. As Panti had directed, this mound would be diamond-shaped and large enough to accommodate him, later Olta, and the few possessions they would need in the afterlife.

Months later, the mound was finished. It was announced throughout the Calosa nation when Panti's funeral would take place. Hundreds of people traveled to attend his burial—to pay their final respects to the legendary artist and warrior. He had touched all of their lives at one time or another.

Panti had arranged with religious leaders to be interred at the time of the first summer solstice following his death. The time approached. His wishes were to be carried out at noon on the longest day of the year—the day with the greatest amount of sunlight.

Feda, still the Calosa chief priest, assumed supervision over the ceremony. At his direction the morticians carefully laid out Panti's skeletal remains in their proper anatomical position while a choir of girls sang ritualistic melodies. His extended skeleton was positioned at the western end of the grave, the feet pointed east. The grave was partially back-filled, until just the top of the skull was visible. Three enormous manatee ribs were then passed to the priest who stood in the grave. He was waiting to receive and arrange the objects as they were passed to him. The priest placed the largest bone on the sand above where Panti's chest would be and aligned it with the position of the sun at the eastern horizon. It was pointed at the precise place the sun had risen that morning. The other two bones crossed the first rib at a point directed by the Calosa's head shaman, Feda. The outer end of each of the upper two bones were lined up toward the north- and south-facing points of the mound. Another layer of sand was placed over Panti's remains and the manatee ribs.

Olta walked to the edge of the grave. She was holding a beautiful, ornately decorated clay pot her late husband had made. It was the ultimate expression of Panti's creativity. She passed the ceramic vessel to Feda who opened the container and held it while Olta placed several objects inside it. The first item to go in was the polished golden disk that her husband had pulled from the chest of the fallen Spanish leader 20 years ago. The last object to be placed inside the pot was the black-bladed dagger with the splendidly carved Panther Clan totem handle. The tip was noticeably missing—it was somewhere on the Big Southern Island. Feda sealed the lid to the pot and solemnly passed it down to his assistant who was standing in Panti's grave. The priest loudly chanted a song as he placed the ceramic pot on the sand directly above the manatee ribs. He then stood up, walked to the eastern end of the grave pit, and waited. Another priest placed a bulky, rosin-coated ark made from manatee hide in a hole that was left for it between Panti's knees.

Wearing a stunning cape and headdress fashioned from the darkest pink roseate spoonbill feathers, Feda stepped to the edge of the grave. His emotions were concealed by a grim ceremonial death mask covering his face. He kneeled for a moment, then rose, and said, "We're gathered here to elevate the deceased—great Panti—to his place in the eternal life awaiting him on the other side of death, in the company of the Great Spirit God. Our traditions are strong. Our respect for the dead is great. As we send the two souls of Panti forward to the secret eternal life with our songs, his third soul—that which has lived in his eye since birth—will linger in, and protect this grave. It will guard the remains of Panti and the tributes to his life, which we entomb here today.

"At the same time, we have deemed it wise to sacrifice the strange beast that belonged to Panti. Its burial with him will please the totem of the Panther Clan. Its spirit will join with his on his journey to the other side and they will be together through eternity."

Another priest walked through the crowd, and the priests who had formed into a circular line closest to the open grave parted to give him entry. He was leading Panti's old horse, Mask, into the shallow pit.

He stopped to one side of Panti's remains. All were chanting a common message underneath the grim wooden masks that they wore. After loudly reciting another chant, the head priest stepped forward toward Mask. As he touched the nervous, blindfolded animal with a carved Panther Clan totem he clutched in his left hand, he raised his other arm. With a sweeping motion the arm fell and a shark tooth-bladed knife he gripped in his hand sliced the animal's throat. After this mighty swing, Mask collapsed instantly, following a torrent of her blood to the red-soaked ground. Without a sound she died in a heap. In the minds of those gathered around the grave, the horse's spirit had now passed through the invisible curtain to join Panti on the other side of life. Soon, the singing stopped, the grave was back-filled, the surface of the mound leveled, and the crowd dispersed and gathered in small groups. Storytellers started telling all who would listen about the honorable life and deeds of mighty Panti—the Calosan.

PART THREE

THE SURVIVORS

"Our men from Oklahoma and Texas are rough and ride well Leonard, but have you seen the rangy Florida cowboys who've joined us handle a horse yet? Look at those two!"

— *Lieutenant Colonel Theodore Roosevelt*
Tampa, Florida, 1898

CHAPTER 27

ASSISTANT LIGHT KEEPER IVORY CLARK SLOWLY climbed the tight-turning spiral stairway inside the tube-like wrought iron walls. It was downright cool this evening and the winter sun hadn't settled below the western horizon yet. A cold front was racing top speed across the Gulf of Mexico and blasting Sanibel Island with powerful wind and frigid air. Ivy thought, "This weather front'll sho 'nuff ruin Alice's t'maters if it brings frost 'long in b'hind it. The kids'll likely git sick 'gain, too." He shook his head as his thoughts wandered. "These oil cans 're beginnin' to git heavy. I cain't hardly believe I've been totin' 'em up this tower fer nearly 14 yars."

The wind howled through the tower's well-braced skeletal framework. Less experienced men would refuse to make the climb because of the deafening and frightening roar, but Ivy Clark was a veteran light keeper.

To avoid fatigue, Ivy occasionally switched the two-gallon can of kerosene between hands as he climbed. The supply of fuel it contained would be enough to top-off and later refill the special oversized oil lamp's reservoir. The lamp, high above his head, must burn and its light-magnifying lens continue to turn through the night. After all, this was a light that must *never* fail.

311

Ivy placed his water bottle and snack bag on the small wooden table inside the round, windowless watchroom, just beneath the glass-walled lantern room. He wouldn't dare open the double door and venture outside on the narrow gallery tonight, because of the unrelenting, screaming wind. He picked up the fuel can again and climbed the spiral, almost ladder-like flight of stairs to reach the lantern room and the lens.

Ivy set the can down, reached up and one-by-one removed and neatly folded the ten khaki-colored curtains. These covered the inside of the plate-glass storm panes. These drapes hung in place during daylight to prevent the sun's rays from reaching the bank of circular panels that formed the lens. The lens was centrally located in the room. If overheated by the sun, the expensive glass optics might crack. Next, Ivy carefully removed the soft dust cover, which completely shrouded the five and a half-foot tall third-order Fresnel lens. It was this precious French-made lens, when coupled to a turning mechanism in the watchroom, which gave the Sanibel Lighthouse its characteristic; a regionally unique identification—its personal flash pattern.

"This lens ne'er fails to amaze me each time I look at it," Ivy thought as he continued working. "How'n the hell did that smart ol' Frenchman have the wits to fig're out these optics? How'd he learn to 'range 'em so they'd bend 'n' consolidate the light into a beam? That the light projects so fer offshore is downright magical!"

Carefully opening a door-like panel of the lens, Ivy reached into the interior and withdrew the oil lamp. He picked up a small funnel, unscrewed the brass cap on the lamp's base, inserted the funnel, and topped off the oil reservoir. After replacing the lamp in position, Ivy raised the glass chimney and lit the wicks. The flame slowly spread along their charred edges and in an instant the three concentric wicks were burning evenly. He replaced the chimney and closely observed the flame. He'd adjust the wick height if necessary to avoid unwanted smoke. Black smoke created soot and this affected the clarity of the lamp chimney or the lens. Satisfied the light was burning properly Ivy closed the lens' access panel and went below to the watchroom.

Near the center of the watchroom was a large, brass framed, glass enclosed cabinet. Inside this were giant clockworks. Ivy took a crank handle from its storage place. He opened a small door in the clockwork case, and inserted the base of the handle into the appropriate turning socket. Slowly, he cranked the handle until he felt tension. This pressure told Ivy he had taken up the slack and was about to lift the heavy counterweight off its temporary daytime rest. He continued cranking the weight through the hollow central post of the tower until it reached the upper position at which the apparatus was ready to be engaged. Once meshed, the mechanism would continue working through the night. Holding pressure on the crank handle, Ivy released a nearby lever. The myriad assortment of gears started to turn and the lens began to slowly rotate around the lamp.

Ivy withdrew his timepiece from his trousers after climbing halfway up the stairs to the lantern room again. He faced the slow spinning series of glass rings, and waited for one of the bull's-eye prisms to reach his line of sight. When it did, the ground glass magnified the light and a sudden concentrated flash temporarily blinded him. Ivy managed to observe the time and make a mental note. He would remain in this position and, if the clockworks were synchronized, two minutes later another bull's-eye prism would turn into his field of view, and again blind him momentarily. "Perfect, the characteristic's right on the money. Lis'en to that damned wind!" Ivy said, to himself.

Every two hours, Ivy cranked the counterweight and time tested the characteristic of his light, while continuing to talk to himself. "If someone's out in this blow 'n' they see this light they'll have a chaince to reach safe harbor."

Not far from where Ivy was working, this exceptional black, moonless, and stormy night, an invisible electric impulse raced along the bottom of the Gulf of Mexico. It had originated far away—about 300 miles away—in Havana, Cuba. A manually keyed series of dots and dashes, known as International Morse Code, sped through the twisted copper strands of the submerged cable. The signals passed through the pair of cable huts west of the lighthouse. Then the speeding coded words went underwater again, to be intercepted in the telegraph terminal at Punta Rassa. From there, the electronic words continued their northern journey toward the U. S. Navy Department in Washington, DC. Ultimately, this message would reach the Government's network of politicians and military leaders.

Deciphered, the dots and dashes said:

> ". . . MAINE BLOWN UP IN HAVANA HARBOR
> AT NINE FORTY TONIGHT AND DESTROYED . . .
> MANY WOUNDED AND DOUBTLESS MORE KILLED OR
> DROWNED . . . PUBLIC OPINION SHOULD BE SUS-
> PENDED UNTIL FURTHER REPORT . . . MANY SPAN-
> ISH OFFICERS INCLUDING REPRESENTATIVES OF
> GENERAL BLANCO NOW WITH ME TO EXPRESS SYM-
> PATHY . . . "

Three weeks earlier, the second-class armored battleship, the USS *Maine*, had been sent to Havana, Cuba. She was dispatched as a show of force and American support for the insurgent Cuban nationalists. The *Maine* entered Havana Harbor on January 25th with a crew of 309 officers and enlisted men. After the explosion, on February 15, 1898, 250 men were dead and 59 wounded. Eight of these casualties would later die because of the seriousness of their injuries. A Spanish mine was suspected and within days the United States was on a war footing. Americans were unified—nationally incensed because of Spain's suspected treachery, and her responsibility for the loss of the USS *Maine* and its sailors.

The news of the disaster was slow to circulate in the vicinity of Punta Rassa. The agent-in-charge of the port's telegraph terminal was discreet. He didn't want to be criticized later by his superiors for leaking the contents of an official Navy Department dispatch. Over the next several days, more news of the ship's sinking trickled in.

Aware of this maritime tragedy, Ivy stopped at Punta Rassa a week after the telegraphed message became common knowledge. He had finished routine weekly servicing of the two harbor range lights that were located next to Fisherman Key. Ivy was on his way back to Sanibel Island, but whenever he was detailed to pull maintenance on these lights he also took the opportunity to pay his parents a visit.

Things had changed at Punta Rassa since he took the job offered by the Lighthouse Board. Most faces he saw these days were strangers. His old pals, Logan Grace and Jehu Rivers, were still chasing cows through the Florida wilds and moving them to Punta Rassa, but he saw his friends less and less as the years sped by. The tough and generous cattle baron, Jacob Summerlin, became infirm and left Punta

Rassa a few years after Ivy had moved to Sanibel Island. The crusty old cowman had now been dead nearly five years. After Jake Summerlin died, his faithful black man, the former slave Thomas Jefferson Bowton left Punta Rassa. He died happy, with his own people, in the Fort Myers colored quarters a few years later. Captain Gus Wendt took sick suddenly and passed away two years ago. No longer did his speedy sloop, the *Punta Rassa Pilot*, ply the waters of San Carlos Bay and the adjacent Gulf of Mexico. These days a sleek motor launch, bearing the same name boldly lettered in white on each side of its black hull, carried an aging Charlie Clark to and from the vessels he piloted. The harbor pilot was beginning to consider retirement.

Delighted to see his son, Charlie hugged Ivy's neck, and said, "It's sho good to have yuh stop by, son. How's ever'thin' ov'r on the island these days? Yer mama wants yuh to bring Alice 'n' the kids ov'r fer a visit as soon as yuh can. It's been a while."

"We will, Daddy. It seems to me that Alice ain't as lonely as she was in our early years on Sanib'l. It's hard to believe, but it's been ten yars since the Gove'ment released most o' the land ov'r yonder 'n' the homesteaders moved onto Sanib'l. She stays busy most o' the time wit' schoolin' our kids 'n' sewin' 'n' cannin'. Now that we've our own island church she spends a good deal o' 'er time teachin' book learnin' to the farmers' children 'n' helpin' out there. I'll try 'n' git us all rounded up 'n' come ov'r to see yuh 'n' Mama real soon."

The conversation between father and son drifted to the topic of the sinking of the *Maine*, as Ivy said, "I cain't believe those Spaniards were stupid 'nuff to do somethin' like that. The crew 'board a tender which come up from Key West late last week to deliver lamp oil filled us in 'bout what was goin' on. All the farmers I've tol't on Sanib'l 're ready to head fer Cuba 'n' drive the damned Spaniards back 'cross't the Atlantic. Reckon we'll be at war ov'r this, Daddy?"

"I believe it'll come to that. Sooner 'r later! Everyone I talk wit' is o' the same state o' mind. They're mad as hell 'n' wanna git ev'n. I believe war'll sho 'nuff foller. Those people cain't be allowed to git by wit' sinkin' our battleships—'n' killin' our sailors!"

The weeks passed and the *Maine* continued to be discussed wherever people gathered. It got closer to home for Ivy in early May.

His daughter, Esther, came running along the wide shell-surfaced walkway, which leads from inside the lighthouse compound to the boathouse on the edge of the bay. Ivy was working on the boat. Still yards away from him, panting, and almost out of breath, she blurted, "Daddy! Mommy says fer yuh to come to the house right away. There's two people on horses comin' this a-way! They're ridin' down the beach purty fast. Mama says they'll be here in a few minutes 'n' yuh should come home! Right now!"

"Okay, honey. Run to the house 'n' tell Mama I'll be there directly. Jus' as soon's I git the grease offa my hands."

Drying his hands with a rag while on a dead run, Ivy quickly covered the 100-yard distance between the boathouse and home. At the same time he reached the foot of his stairs, two lathered horses almost collided with him. Spurred on, they had vaulted over the low fence railing and continued galloping toward him after rounding the building. Just before running him down, the horses whirled to a sudden stop between him and the stairway of his stilted home. A shower of dusty, pulverized shell, kicked up by the animals, settled over him. To protect his eyes from the cloud of dirt he closed them and turned away.

Blinking, then squinting, Ivy turned around and looked up at the riders. He saw a grinning Logan Grace looking down at him. Logan shouted, "Ha, howdy, Mr. Lightman! Reckon yuh're su'prised to see the likes o' us! Ain't yuh? Jay, I believe the boy's done got fatter! Must be 'em Gove'ment-issued pork 'n' beans!"

"Naw, he jus' looks old'r to me. He's tired out from makin' all 'em babies. Ha!"

Surprised at their arrival, Ivy asked, "What'n the hell're yuh two doin' here? Why're ya'll in such a big hurry? An' the horses—who do these skinny ponies belong to? They ain't no cow chasers. Looks to me like yuh boys done kinda backslid in the cow pony department."

Jehu continued, and quizzed his old friend. "Hell, ain't yuh glad to see us, ev'n a lil' bit?"

"Why, yuh know I am!" Ivy said as he pointed toward the cistern. "Draw offa couple o' buckets o' water from that cistern fer 'em thirsty nags, after yuh hitch 'em to the braces on the lighthouse. Then come on upstairs. I'll go up 'n' warn Alice ya'll're here!" Ivy said, as he finished brushing off the sand and shell clinging to his shirt and trousers. Done, he clapped his gritty hands, turned, and started up the stairs.

As he climbed, Ivy cupped his hands over his mouth and shouted—purposely loud enough for his guests to hear his words. "Alice! Honey, we've got comp'ny! Yuh'll ne'er believe who the riders were! Guess who's jus' showed up? Hide yer good silver! An' my whiskey!"

As the three stood on the porch looking out toward the glistening Gulf of Mexico, Ivy grinned and asked, "So what brings yuh boys to my doorstep? Ya'll ov'r here deer huntin'? There ain't no loose women on Sanib'l. Not yet anyway!"

Logan smiled, winked at Jehu, and replied, "We was headed up to Tampa, but the damned steamer broke down. We had to be towed into the Wulfert dock to git it fixed. The boat's engineer had to send a small boat back to Punta Rassa to git some parts. Why, I told yer daddy this very mornin', jus' 'fore we got on the boat to leave Punta Rassa, what we were doin'. I told 'im to tell yuh we was leavin'. Neither 'un o' us thought that we'd git a chance to see yuh in person, Ivy. Ma always told me, 'the Lord works in mysterious ways.' We borrowed the sorry horses from a 'mater farmer to come see yuh. We cain't stay too long though. Maybe 'n hour, 'r two, tops."

"What the hell're yuh two goin' up to Tampa fer? Or, should I guess?"

"No! Ne'er yuh mind yer dirty-minded guessin'. We're goin' up yonder to 'list! To volunteer! An' then we're goin' down to Cuba 'n' help whip the sorry asses off 'em goddammed Spaniards!"

"Enlist? 'List in what?"

Jehu butted in, "That's right. We're joinin' the damned Army. We heard there's a calv'ry outfit that's been formin' in Texas 'n' is comin' down to Tampa by train from some place out yonder called San Antonio. They've been named some fancy name. I believe they're called 'Roosevelt's Ruff Riders.' Logan 'n' me 're fixin' to join up wit' 'em. Mister Jake's boy, Sam, up in Bartow done already 'ranged it. We'll show 'em candy-ass westerners what ruff ridin' is."

Following their visit, Logan and Jehu said their thank-yous and goodbyes to Ivy and Alice, grabbed their hats, and started out the door. Ivy was bringing up the rear as the three brother-like friends filed down the steps, one behind the other. At the bottom, Ivy hugged them both, and said, "Yuh boys be careful will yuh? Don't take any foolish chainces. Give my regards to ol' Cuba fer me. An' kick some Spanish ass fer me, too!"

As Logan turned, preparing to unhitch his borrowed horse, Ivy stepped forward with his right hand extended. His hand was met and tightly gripped by his friend's. Ivy fought back the tears, which were beginning to blur his vision, and continued talking in a serious tone. "Logan, take this 'long wit' yuh. It'll bring yuh good luck. It certainly has fer me since't I found it." Ivy pressed his hand even firmer into Logan's and passed his gold good luck charm to his friend.

Ivy turned slightly, faced the eroding spit of land where bay met Gulf, pointed in the direction of the barely visible mound, and said, "I reckon the spirit o' that dead Indian buried yonder'll see me through while 'is medal is in yer care."

* * *

The sprawled-out Army encampment was nine miles inland from the Port of Tampa. At the peak of the muster, 30,000 troops would crowd the area. After disembarking from the steamship at the commercial docks, Logan and Jehu managed to catch a ride to the military base on a rickety freight wagon. Like dozens of other freight haulers, this wagon was carrying supplies to the troops on a slow circuitous route.

The train carrying the Rough Riders hadn't arrived yet. After a systematic search through the maze of rowed white tents, and making countless inquiries, the Punta Rassans managed to locate the officer whom they had been told would be their contact. The company commander said that while they waited for their regiment to arrive he would temporarily attach them to his calvary unit. They were training in the pine flatwoods east of the city of tents.

Logan and Jehu trained hard. They knew the troops on their way from Texas had a headstart in becoming part of a well-tuned military entity. The Punta Rassa cowboys were determined to become outstanding soldiers.

The troop train carrying the horse soldiers of the 1st Volunteer Calvary arrived in Tampa on June 3rd. The unmistakable mournful sound of the train's whistle echoing through the pines and palmettos signaled its arrival. Logan and Jehu were released from their temporary assignment and reported straightaway to the makeshift headquarters of their regiment. The next day training maneuvers continued in the Florida heat. The self-assurance of Logan and Jehu swelled when they realized they had each already become every bit as good a soldier as anyone among the Rough Riders.

During a break from training, Logan asked, "Sergeant, who're those two officers?"

"The large man on the big bay horse is Colonel Leonard Wood. He's our regimental commander. The other gent on the small horse is Lieutenant Colonel Theodore Roosevelt, the Rough Riders' second in command. Like us, they're both volunteers. Look sharp while they're watching us! Make me proud!"

To catch his attention, Logan waved, then motioned to Jehu, who leisurely trotted over to where Logan was resting. Logan laughed, then whispered, "Let's show 'em two spit 'n' polish Yankees how good two o' ol' man Summerlin's boys can sit on a Army horse. C'mon!"

Frequently, during the rest of the afternoon Logan glanced at the two officers. He swore that the two men and their aides were watching, sometimes pointing at him and Jehu, as they demonstrated their riding skills.

Days passed. Finally, the rumor swept through the ranks that the unit had been selected to participate in the impending invasion of Cuba. Other regiments eager for the fight would be left behind. The Rough Riders moved toward the rail siding. A train would carry them to the port where they would board waiting transport ships. It seemed things were beginning to get serious—until it was announced they were not taking their horses on the voyage!

"Damn!" Jehu complained to Logan and a fellow volunteer from Oklahoma, "We done joined up to ride 'gainst the Spaniards. Now, we gotta walk! I believe—hell, I know—I ain't walked ten mile in the past five years. If my horse cain't carry me, I don't go! Whose idea was it to join this damn Army anyway?"

"Dammit, I don't recollect, but if Bob here 'n' the rest o' these western'rs ain't bitchin' 'bout this turn o' events, why're yuh? *Hush*! We've done come too fer now to piss'n moan 'bout it!"

319

Finally, a locomotive pushing coal-hauling cars was commandeered. The battle-eager men of the regiment climbed into the open coal gondolas with their gear. The train slowly gathered steam, and traveled the nine miles to the docks and the waiting fleet of transport ships. Soon, all men and their equipment were packed into the foul dark air, deep in the guts of the sweltering, overcrowded, steel-hulled vessels. Despite the deplorable conditions, no one complained. All were keyed up and anxious to get on with the war. But the fight wouldn't come for many days.

CHAPTER 28

DAYLONG TRAINING SESSIONS HAD BEEN CAREFULLY developed to help keep the morale high of both officers and enlisted men. But boredom soon began to invade the ranks. It gnawed at the war-eager spirit of the horseless troopers packed aboard the *Yucatan*. The transport swung about on her anchor at the whim of water and wind. Her position over the bottom was at the mercy of the currents which swirled in a constant change from tide to tide. Moored deeply and firmly into the muddy bottom of Tampa Bay, it was nearly a week before the anchors were winched aboard and coal-hungry boilers fully stoked. Free from the bottom, the fleet started to move toward some destination in Latin America known only to a few aboard the flagship.

After clearing the mouth of Tampa Bay, the armada turned south. Its boats and ships left the white-painted, brick tower of the Egmont Key Light Station and the adjacent six-inch gun batteries and fortifications of Fort Dade to port as they entered the Gulf of Mexico. The task force was subdivided into three groups after they cleared the barrier islands and reached the open Gulf. The invasion fleet had swelled into a mix of 56 vessels. It consisted of slow transports, arms-bristling warships, speedy patrol boats, and graceful schooners. All had one purpose: to carry men and supplies to the Spanish-held islands and to support those men as they defeated the enemy.

As the fleet moved offshore, the coast disappeared over the eastern horizon. The energies of the soldiers, once subdued because of inactivity, were restored and their goal-oriented morale had returned. First in small groups, then as a united army, the troops jammed the decks, and shrieked, "Remember the *Maine*; to hell with Spain!"

Day after day the fleet plowed through the blue-green Gulf water on their southerly heading. On the second day out, the long line of vessels passed Sanibel Island. They were far away from its black and brown light tower, beyond the range of its beam of light, and out of sight of Ivy Clark.

"What's the latest word, Sarge?" Jehu asked his sergeant, a regular Army veteran. "Are we landin' at 'Santiago' like the boys're whisperin' 'r 're we goin' down to Puerto Rico? I ain't no sailor but I can tell we've been headin' east fer the best part o' two days."

"Rivers, you know as much about where we're going as I do. Someone claims there's freight aboard that's marked 'Santiago de Cuba.' Some wise-ass civilian 'anchor clanker' told me this morning that we're nearing the eastern end of Cuba. He claims . . . at least he told me, that later today we'll turn and begin to move west, once we're clear of this end of Cuba. If the Spanish Navy's torpedo boats don't find us first, it's my guess we'll be getting our taste of this over-glorified war pretty close to Santiago."

On June 22, the Rough Riders had to use the *Yucatan*'s lifeboats to land at a dilapidated wharf at the tiny port of "Daiquiri," or on the beach next to it. This village was located 15 miles east of Santiago Bay. Like those brought to Cuba by earlier invaders, the few horses—and many mules—which had made the voyage were pushed over the side of their transports and forced to swim ashore. Horses, mules, and men drowned in the haphazard landing. The American forces moved inland and bivouacked about a quarter of a mile from the landing beach. By the next afternoon the *Yucatan*, other troop transports, and support boats and ships were still not completely unloaded. Unfortunately, small boats and barges necessary to move supplies ashore were not available, and much food was to remain on shipboard and unavailable during the campaign. Finally, despite the confusion and unclear objectives, orders to move out toward Santiago came down the chain of command. The exact location of the enemy was unknown and the 1st Volunteer Calvary joined the troopers of the regular Army—the 1st and 10th Calvary—to march along the narrow winding trails through the jungle-like wilds toward Santiago.

The next morning, with the opposing forces within 900 yards of one another, the first skirmish started at a place called "Las Guasimas." The Spanish were using the new German-designed Mauser rifle. This modern firearm used cartridges packed with smokeless powder and had great range and accuracy. The American regulars were still being issued old Springfield rifles. These used black powder, an antiquated carbon explosive of low energy, and a tremendous smoke producer when exploded. As a calvary unit, the Rough Riders had been issued Krag-Jorgenson .30-40 caliber carbines and Colt .45 caliber revolvers. Like the enemy Mausers, their weapons fired smokeless powder cartridges. Because of the undetectable origins of their gunfire, Spanish guerrillas operating outside of fortified positions remained hidden. The gunsmoke from the American regular Army rifles gave away their positions and exposed soldiers to Spanish sharpshooters.

"Jay, do yuh believe this! Here we was—jus' 'bout to he'p lick those goddammed Spaniards hidden in the woods yonder! An' they make us ride shotgun guard on a goddammed wagon train pull't by these sorry ol' mules."

The Punta Rassans had been detailed to a regimental mule train moving ammunition and medical supplies closer to Santiago. They were enroute to a place called "Juragua." Logan raved, "It ain't fair! Why'n the hell did this doctor have to pick us? Wit' all the niggers 'n the 10th why'n hell did he pick us fer this detail? Damned if I can figure it out. Let's git wit' it! If we can git these contrary mules movin'. Git mule! If we git goin' we'll soon be outta range o' the Spanish artillery. After we he'p move these wagons we'll git into the fight."

Logan and Jehu raced back from Juraqua along a rutted trail marked "El Camino Real" and rejoined the Rough Riders and L Troop near "Savilla." Until they fell off into totally exhausted sleep on the wet bare ground, they heard and reheard the successes the men of the regiment had experienced in the battle at Las Guasimas. They yearned for the brief firefight they had missed. Both were visibly shaken when they learned their troop had been the point unit when the Rough Riders were ambushed. Three of their comrades were killed and seven wounded when the hostilities started. Rumors persisted that tomorrow the troopers would assault the Spanish-defended San Juan Heights, a group of high hills overlooking and protecting Santiago de Cuba.

The Rough Riders were awakened from an uncomfortable night's rest on July 1st. Reveille was not sounded because the bugler was ordered to be silent. A bugle would have given away their position to any nearby Spaniards. Waves of hushed conversation swept among the sleepy troops when 0400 wake-up was ordered. While they slept, soaking dew had settled and completely wetted the exposed, shivering troops. During the exhausting forced march from the beachhead under the tropical sun and through humid air, most men had discarded every-thing heavy they carried the day before. The Rough Riders had fought fatigue the simplest way. They lessened their load. They turned loose of everything except their carbines, revolvers, and canteens. Most had neither bedrolls nor tent halves to protect themselves from the soaking-wet earth or the moisture sagging down in the air. The breakfast meal was simple. Uncooked bacon and hardtack w as washed down with weak coffee or tepid, untreated water from their own canteens. Many of the Rough Riders had dipped the water from the muddy San Juan River during the hurried crossing the previous day. Canteens were filled there contrary to direct orders that the water was unfit, but alas there was no other potable water available. Supplies of safe drinking water were still aboard ship.

Recently promoted and now a full colonel, Theodore Roosevelt, assembled the officers of the 1st Volunteer Calvary Regiment while the troops ate their morning meal. His voice boomed, "If we don't move against the high ground, they'll pin us down and cut us to pieces! I assure you, when their artillery finds the range after sunup it'll be no picnic!"

The Rough Riders would follow their charismatic leader into hell, a nd he k new i t. As t he h ighest-ranking officer i n t he v icinity, Roosevelt convinced himself the decision to go on the offensive was his alone to make. He turned to his orderly, and said, "Sergeant, have them saddle and bring up my horse, Little Texas!" Looking straight at an admiring second lieutenant, without pausing, he continued, "Lieutenant Day, I want a skirmish line from L Troop ready to move off the road into the thicket."

"Yes, sir!" The young lieutenant responded. He had inherited command of L Troop after the unit's captain had been killed and their first lieutenant wounded at Las Guasimas.

Leading his excited horse, Roosevelt melted into the jungle with the line of men of L Troop. These were tough and brave men, mostly from the Indian Territories. Logan Grace and Jehu Rivers were not far from the colonel when hundreds of racing Mauser bullets screamed through the air space above their heads. Like green snowflakes, bullet-torn particles of foliage began to fall around them as ricocheting slugs sliced through the trees at every conceivable angle and altitude. Logan yelled to Jehu, who was next to him. "Keep yer head down! Bend ov'r more! Git lower! I guess they're firin' at the half-breed Indian boys up at point. I swear they're aimin' way too high, 'r they flat don't see us!"

Trying to duck down even lower, Jehu replied, "Ha! Well, I'd say that's good fer us wouldn't yuh? The woods 're thinnin' out. I believe I can see open ground 'head o' us."

Shortly after the advance started, Colonel Roosevelt mounted Texas, and commanded, "Hold your skirmish interval at six feet, boys. Run if you can! Crawl if you have to!" He rode back and forth among the troops and bullets. His presence inspired the brave men around him and they continued their advance. Every step of the way Theodore Roosevelt encouraged his troops forward. "We're nearly clear of this jungle, men. I can see high ground! It's a hill! It's rising up out ahead of us!" Simultaneously, as their excited commander shouted his words, the Rough Riders dashed out of the dense jungle into a broad grassland and straight into another hailstorm of Spanish bullets. Logan yelled, "Look ov'r yonder, boys, on the top o' that hill! I believe those're big ol' cook pots I see." Someone nearby, concealed in the thick grass responded to his comment. "I believe they're sugar kettles. The Cubans cook sugar cane in 'em." Jehu, about two yards away on Logan's right, quipped, "Maybe they're fulla Spanish beans! I'm so hungry I could eat the ass end outta a rag doll!"

Logan laughed at his friend's witty remark, and yelled, "Those Spanish reg'lars 're shootin' at us from 'Kettle Hill,' boys!" The fight for Kettle Hill was about to start in earnest.

The Spanish Army was well entrenched in the earth atop Kettle Hill and the other nearby hills beyond it known collectively as the San Juan Heights. Their hidden snipers were everywhere. They were in the grass ahead or still shooting from trees in the forest through which the skirmish lines of Rough Riders had just passed. Most of the Spaniards on Kettle Hill were firing their high-powered weapons in volleys from trenches or breastworks located over the hill's crest. Not only were they too far back from the crest to lay down a deadly field of fire, their nervous commanders were hurrying the volley shooters. Because they were not given enough time to aim properly, their shooting was grossly inaccurate. The Americans were fortunate because their adversaries on the high ground were mostly shooting over their heads.

Soon, 500 Rough Riders had managed to reach the front. They found their colonel in a heated argument with a captain from the 1st Calvary Brigade. The troopers overheard Roosevelt as he screamed, "Stand aside! As the ranking officer here I'll order a charge. My God man, these men will be cut to pieces! Let my men through!" It was clear to all, Kettle Hill would be assaulted and Roosevelt's Rough Riders were about to lead the charge.

Trotting back and forth through the rallying troopers, Colonel Roosevelt announced the battle plan. "We'll advance in a series of rushes. Dash forward a few yards after they fire a volley, then drop into the grass. Don't fire until we get closer! You must have a clear target. Dash, then dash ahead again, and again!" The colonel spun his horse around to again face the rising slope of Kettle Hill, and yelled, "Come on, Rough Riders, follow me!" The regiment hesitated. Their commander had not issued the correct military order, nor did he utter his instructions loud enough. Bewildered when he noticed the troopers were not following his lead, he turned Texas around to face the men of his command, and showered them with blistering words. He dared ask, "Are you cowards? I said, *charge*!"

This time the Rough Riders surged forward on either side of their mounted colonel. He continued to urge his skirmishers on as he rode among them. Once satisfied his regiment was moving in the right direction, and at the pace he wanted, Colonel Roosevelt spurred Texas to join his troopers who had surged ahead and were leading the assault. Volley after volley of Spanish rounds coming down the hill brutally found targets.

Medical corpsmen were mixed among the advancing troopers. They tagged casualties who would later be treated by other medically trained soldiers. The dead were ignored. Later, their corpses would be gathered, identified if possible and buried by specially assigned details of survivors after the battle concluded. Many troopers with limited mobility, because of minor wounds, who were unable to continue fighting, were pinned with white tags. Those with more serious injuries wore blue and white tags. The most seriously wounded, men requiring immediate medical attention because of life-threatening wounds, were marked with conspicuous red markers. Those red-tagged would be the first to be evacuated once hostilities in the immediate vicinity had ended and the battleground was secure. The walking wounded withdrew for immediate medical attention. After their wounds were attended, and contrary to demands made by the field surgeons, these brave men raced back to the front to rejoin the regiment.

The Rough Riders did not try to conceal themselves as they moved against the Spanish. Soon, they overtook the forward-most squadron of the 10th Calvary, who were on their left. The Rough Riders were now at a position beyond which Roosevelt was authorized to lead them, but they pressed on. The black troopers of the 9th Regular Calvary, the famed "Buffalo Soldiers" of the earlier Mexican, Civil, and Indian Wars, were under heavy Spanish fire and were ahead of the 10th. Their white officers had been killed or otherwise knocked out of the action. Following their brave leader, the Rough Riders forced their way through the bewildered ranks of the Buffalo Soldiers. Seeing Roosevelt's leadership, the black calvary-men joined their white countrymen on the slow, deadly journey up Kettle Hill.

Logan Grace could see Jehu Rivers off to his right. As if connected by an invisible tether, in unison the Punta Rassans would rise, run forward, and fall back into the grass. They had managed to stay on the front line near their boisterous colonel who continued to verbally prod his troopers forward. How Roosevelt survived without receiving a serious wound was miraculous. Dynamite-filled shells were exploding overhead raining deadly shrapnel down on the advancing troopers. The shrapnel and whining bullets were inflicting increasing numbers of casualties. Every American knew the volley-shooting rifles and the field artillery on Kettle Hill and the heights beyond must be stilled. This must be done as quickly and efficiently as possible. Periodically, since the Krag carbines were now in perfect range, the Rough Riders shouldered them. Each was a marksman and Spanish casualties began to mount. Another volley of Mauser-fired bullets had just been sent toward the American line. The men of L Company, screaming saucy epithets as they rose again, sprinted forward.

"*Lo . . . Logan*! I got it that time!" Jehu shouted, stumbled, and fell into the deep grass. Logan, seeing his friend drop, dove to the ground toward the location where Jehu had fallen. He disappeared into the waving grass. Crawling on his elbows and knees, Logan hurried to reach Jehu's side. Reaching him, Logan carefully raised and cradled his friend's upper torso in his arms. He thought, "*Good God*! His mouth! Why, Lord? This is a good ol' boy. Why 'im . . . why now?"

"I got it in the neck! Buddy, can yuh believe this?" Jehu said with slurred words that were mixed with torrents of his blood as he clutched his throat. "I reckon I'm supposed to die in this damned ol' Cuba after all! Ain't I? I'd rather've been gored in the guts by a bull back home. I hate this goddammed place!"

Logan lied when he said, "Naw! Shit, yuh were shot a helluva lot worse't the last time we were down here." He knew! He could see from the amount of blood and the gaping hole that his friend was mortally wounded and was dying in his arms. Despite the gushing blood, Logan saw that part of Jehu's lower jaw, and much of his throat, had been blown away when the speeding Spanish bullet struck bone and tore flesh as it passed through his best pal's throat. Jehu clumsily tried to rise, but fell back, hard against the Cuban soil and Logan's blood-soaked chest. His words, mixed with blood, came slow as his body jerked involuntarily. He forced out a mutter only Logan could hear, "Logan! I see Jesus! Look yonder. He's wit' Mama 'n' Daddy! They're all wavin' fer me to come on into that light wit' 'em." Then Jehu Rivers sighed deeply, exhaling as he died. His lifeless frame settled firmly against his friend and the foreign earth that was soon to cover his mortal remains.

Logan stared down at his dead friend, wiped away the flood of tears, and promised, "I'll come back fer yuh, Jay! After I kill the Spanish bastard that did this to yuh!" Logan issued a blood-curdling wail, rose to his feet, and charged toward the crest of Kettle Hill.

The Spanish infantry had started to withdraw toward neighboring San Juan Hill and the heights beyond it. They would escape the full wrath of Logan Grace and "Teddy" Roosevelt and his Rough Riders. After t he h ill w as t aken, t he r egiment regrouped a nd rested. When additional units reinforced the American troops they attacked, but the Rough Riders did not lead the charge up San Juan Hill. Wounded and dead Spanish soldiers were treated or buried nearby. Most of the dead Spaniards had bullet holes in the front of their heads. Deadly accurate slugs from Krag carbines of the American forces had struck them when they exposed themselves to participate in a volley firing.

Like many of his brave comrades, Logan's luck would also run out this day. San Juan Hill was much steeper than Kettle Hill. Its grade of incline did not offer the concealment advantage the deep grass that fronted Kettle Hill had. The Spanish had a better field of fire for their artillery, which was positioned on the upper heights, and the riflemen dug in at the top of San Juan Hill. Soon after the assault started, an arching Spanish shell exploded high above L Company. It released a metallic shower of shrapnel. One piece found Logan, who at this wrong instant was flat on his stomach. The falling piece of speeding iron smashed through his left knee, just missing a major artery. After what seemed an eternity, Logan was wearing a red tag on his chest and was being gently placed in a mule-drawn wagon by medical corpsmen. He was bound for the field hospital at Siboney for treatment. Logan was unable to keep his promise. He would never see Jehu Rivers or the battlefields of Cuba again.

CHAPTER 29

LOGAN GRACE HAD BEGGED A RIDE ACROSS SAN
Carlos Bay from Beau Duke, the operator of the Punta Rassa pilot
boat. Beau was headed in that direction anyway. He was carrying the
Punta Rassa pilot out to the sea buoy to board a waiting inbound cattle
steamer. They had chugged away from the dock just as soon as the
engine on Beau's boat had built up a sufficient head of steam.

As the vessel bumped against the structure Logan thanked the
men and tossed his valise and cane onto the weathered planking. With
Beau's help he carefully climbed off the boat onto the Lighthouse
Service pier.

Logan had written Ivy from his bed at the Key West Naval
Hospital. After he was given medical attention in the field at Siboney,
he was transported aboard a hospital ship to Key West. Logan recuper-
ated in the military hospital there, until well enough to be furloughed.
In his letter, Logan wrote he would be coming for a visit, but didn't
specify when. He purposely did not tell his friend anything else. He
wanted to wait and tell him the whole sad story in person.

It so happened that this morning Ivy was up in the brown and
black light tower on duty. He was inside the lantern room, going
through the usual morning routine. He had already extinguished the oil
lamp and covered the lens with its soft protective shroud. Now, one at

a time, he was unfolding the khaki-colored curtains. He hung them from the oversize cup hooks at the upper corners of each of the ten glass storm panes. Ivy noticed the pilot boat approaching the dock and hurried his work, as he thought, "I wonder what brings Beau to our pier this mornin'? In a few minutes he was done and cautiously backed down the ladder-like stairway to reach the watchroom.

Dim but slowly brightening sunlight flooded the watchroom through the stairway opening and the eight skylights in the ceiling above him. Ivy took the binoculars from their place inside the storage cabinet and unlatched the top and bottom door bolts. These secured the heavy double set of doors that led outside. He shoved open the doors to the gallery and stepped out into the brisk air. He turned right. After a few short steps he reached the north side of the tower's observation platform.

With the eyepieces of the heavy glasses firmly over his eyes, Ivy panned the bay and quickly found the pilot boat. He focused and watched as a tall figure was helped onto the pier. The person waved to the men in the boat then turned and looked directly at the tall dark tower looming ahead of him. He stooped and picked up a piece of luggage and a walking stick. Turning and looking back for a last peek and final wave to the boat, the figure then started walking slowly toward the lighthouse compound. Despite the poor light Ivy could tell the visitor was a man and he was hobbling.

"I'll finish up here 'n' git down to the walkway 'n' meet 'im. Looks to me like he could use some help wit' 'is suitcase." Ivy looked again but couldn't make out whom it was coming to visit the light station.

This trip along the wide concrete walk was going to take longer than it used to. "Dammit, my knee hurts like hell! Now I know how bad ol' Cap'n Gus's leg must've hurt when 'is wounded knee acted up. I shoulda been more careful when I climbed outta the boat." Logan said to himself in a barely audible voice. "I shoulda listened to the doctor 'n' stayed off it 'til it was all healed up. But I've gotta see Ivy! It cain't wait no longer!" He still wore his Rough Rider-issued broad brimmed hat. It was the only souvenir of his third—and last—ill-fated trip to Cuba.

By now the light from the cloud-hidden sun had fully cleared the horizon of the mainland. Ivy reached the ground and walked toward the unrecognizable early morning visitor.

"Good mornin', sir, can I give yuh a hand wit' that valise?"

"Damn it to hell! Cut the crap! I ain't no sir! Don't yuh reco'nize yer poor crippled buddy?"

"Hot damn! *Logan*! It's yuh. I had no idea!" Ivy yelled and ran the few feet still separating them. They embraced like two long-lost brothers. Then Ivy stepped back, gave his friend of 25 years the once-over, and said, "Logan, yuh look like holy hell! How much weight've yuh lost? Yuh're as skinny as a cane stalk. That red beard sho changes yer looks. I declare! It's mostly gray! Why're yuh limpin' 'n' usin' a cane? Where's Jehu'?"

"Damn, slow down, Ivy! Please, one question at a time. I've got lots 'o t'ings to tell yuh 'bout, but all in good time. Right now let's git my weary tail to a soft chair 'n' maybe yer ol' lady can brew us a fresh pot o' coffee. That good lookin' Alice ain't left yuh yet, has she?"

As the pair slowly made their way along the path, Logan explained that he had been seriously wounded in Cuba and was sent to Key West for hospitalization. He grimaced and talked haltingly as he described his injury. "My damn knee was so mangled I feared they were gonna cut off my whole lower leg. My luck held out though. A navy surgeon tucked ev'r't'in' back'n place 'n' sewed it up. I'll show yuh the scar later if yuh wanna see it. It ain't very purty! Part o' my leg's missin'. The doctor told't me that I'd be stiff-legged fer the rest o'my life, but he said that wit' exercise it'd begin to bend some later on. Hell, I'm gonna straddle a horse'n chase cows 'til I croak anyhow so what's a lil' stiffness in a leg? Sho as hell beats the alternative! Anyway, I done 'nuff walkin' in the Ruff Riders to last me a lifetime."

Logan told Ivy he couldn't stay too long. He had to report to someone up in Tampa to be discharged from the volunteer Army. Then he wanted to visit family in Wauchula and upstate. He told Ivy he planned to come back to Punta Rassa as soon as he could. With a little help with his balance, Logan made it up the stairs to Ivy's quarters.

Alice Clark was never happy to see Logan Grace show up at their doorstep. But, when asked by her husband, she dutifully left her darning and made the coffee and served it in a friendly manner. She also brought food to the table—fresh-baked clabber biscuits and some of the sea grape jelly she and Esther had put up at the end of last summer. She knew Ivy and his best friend wanted to be alone. She could tell this was a serious visit—unlike their usual get togethers when they drank too much whiskey and spoke way too loud. They were always much quieter when Jehu wasn't around. The three were always inseparable. Suddenly, it came to her and she thought, "Where *is* Jehu?" Just as immediate, Alice sensed something was wrong. "Something's happened to Jehu! Logan's come here to tell Ivy some bad news! I can just feel it!" She also knew that there were important manly things they wanted to talk about—crude things she didn't want her children to overhear. She would act to prevent her youngsters from hearing the profanity she knew was inevitable. "Esther, go find and gather up your brothers and the four of us will go down to the pier and catch supper."

Esther, the oldest of Ivy and Alice's children, was 12 years old. Like her mother, she wore her long blonde hair twisted into a tight crowning bun. She was a delightful miniature Alice, a carbon copy. Esther rose, politely curtsied to their guest, and left the living room to find her two younger brothers. Once out of the room, she shrieked, "Logan! Bobby! Where're yuh boys hidin' at? Come here! Right now! Mama wants yuh both in the front room."

It wasn't long before two barefooted, towheaded boys shyly shuffled into the living room. Both were shirtless and wore faded bib overalls. The youngest was holding one of the family cats in his arms and the other held a glistening, blue-black, eight foot-long indigo snake draped around his neck.

Logan, surprised to see the snake, spoke directly to his namesake. "Logan, yuh 'n' yer lil' brother've sho 'nuff done growed since't I was here last. Where'd yuh git that big gopher snake, son? Now, I mean to tell yuh he's a real beauty. Yer ma's mighty tolerant lettin' yuh bring a snake inside the house. An', one that big! My ma would ne'er have allowed it! If I'd ev'r brung a snake into the house . . . why, she'd've whipped my ass! *Oops, sorry, Alice!* I meant to say *my butt*. She'd've worked it ov'r big time wit Pappy's wide ol' Army belt!"

The shy boy blushed, tucked his head, to hide a grin and said, "I catched . . . caught 'im in the field by the beach the other day. Bobbie 'n' I was lookin' fer gophers fer Mama to cook wit' a pot o' rice when a big ol' gopher snake—this very one—tried to slip down a gopher's hole. But, I catched 'im by the tail 'n' pull't 'im out. I'm fixin' to turn 'im a-loose tomorrow. Daddy says he's much too purty to keep in a croker sack, plus when he's free 'gain he'll he'p the cats eat the rats we have 'round here."

"He sho 'nuff will! He's a dandy, fer sho! Yuh boys be careful 'round 'em gopher holes. Big ol' diamondback rattlers live in 'em too, yuh know?"

"Yes, sir! Daddy's already warned us 'bout that."

Ivy stood, walked over to his son, and said, "Logan, yuh can take my grains wit' yuh in case there's somethin' swimmin' 'round the pier bigger'n a mullet. But, be sho yuh've got the free end o' the line tied to somethin'. I don't want some big ol' snook pullin' my gig 'n' pole 'n' yuh clear ov'r to Punta Rassa. Sister 'n' Robert can catch a bucketful o' mullet wit' their snatch hooks. Ya'll can easily git at least a couple o' dozen fish. They've been schoolin'—buildin' a big pod und'r that pier fer the last few days. What we've left ov'r aft'r we share wit' Keeper Shanahan's family next door, 'n' what we don't fry ourselves this evenin', we'll put in the smokehouse early tomorrow mornin'. Ya'll mind yer mama 'n' be real careful not to fall offa the pier! The tide'll really be rippin' by there now."

The two were alone at last. Logan's tone of voice changed and his words became serious as he looked Ivy straight in the eyes, and said, "Yuh sit right where yuh're at, so I can tell yuh somethin' we gotta git behind us."

Ivy was astonished, and thought, "Those 're *tears*! He's cryin'. This must be serious!" Tears were filling Logan's eyes and flowing down his cheeks.

"Goddammit, w hy're yuh c ryin'? What's g oin' o n? What's happened?"

"I left Jehu down yonder in Cuba!"

"What do yuh m ean—*left 'im*? He d idn't git mixed up w it' 'nother Cuban whore 'n' fall in love 'gain, did he?"

"I wish that were it! He's done gone, Ivy! Jehu's dead!"

"*Dead*! What do yuh mean *dead* . . . how . . . what happened?"

"He got kill't by a Spanish bullet 'n' died in my arms!"

334

"Lord have mercy!"

"I couldn't stay wit' 'im! We was ordered to leave anyone that was kill't 'n' keep on advancin'. It was the hardest t'ing I ev'r had to do in my whole life! I got hit in my leg a few minutes later 'n' they toted me off in a wagon. I couldn't git back to 'im like I promised I would. I ne'er was able to learn anythin' 'bout what happened to his body. But I know that he's buried somewheres on the slope o' San Juan Hill. He's prob'ly buried in a' unmarked grave wit' some other brave Ruff Riders who died on that damned battlefield that same day. Right at the end he told me he saw Jesus 'n' 'is mama "n' daddy. Jehu died peacefully."

Logan stood, reached into his pocket, withdrew his hand, and said, "Here, this's yers." He flipped Ivy's good luck charm to him and between sobs, he said, "It worked fer me, I guess. I reckon I'm livin' proof it worked . . . it jus' don't . . . Ivy, it didn't have 'nuff power to protect both o' us."

Ivy caught the gold disk in his hand. He clutched it tightly as each man broke into tears again. They cried uncontrollably over the loss of Jehu Rivers.

For the next hour they talked about their deceased friend and the many ways that knowing him had enriched their lives and made them far better men. They were still sobbing when Alice and the children returned from their successful fishing trip. They found Ivy and Logan sitting on the north porch. Each held a half-full glass in his hands. A half-empty bottle sat on the table between them.

Logan wiped his face with a wet, tear-soaked handkerchief and tried to smile. He finally managed a grin and beckoned Alice and the children to join them. "Ya'll come sit wit' us. He'p me cheer up ya'll's daddy. I done brought 'im some sad news 'n' I reckon he'll tell ya'll hisself later. In the meantime, did yer daddy ever tell yuh kids 'bout the time he drown't a full-growed deer?" Logan asked, with that unique mischievous twinkle that still persisted, even now fully into his middle age.

"No, sir!" Esther blurted out. "Tell us 'bout it, Uncle Logan! Please?"

Logan smiled, turned in his chair, pointed toward the beach, then glanced at his old friend across the table, and said, "Why, I sho 'nuff will. It was right out yonder. Weren't it, Ivy?"

Ivy glared at his old friend, then broke into a wide smile. He nodded in affirmation to his daughter as he continued to flip, like one would a coin, the gold medal once torn from the blouse worn by Juan Ponce de León by a brave Calusan. This was indeed a special disk— a good-luck piece—of great power. It had brought his best friend back to him.

Logan, ever the consummate storyteller, laughed and continued his tale.

EPILOGUE

IN 1888, A SIGNIFICANT REDUCTION WAS MADE IN the size of the Sanibel Island Lighthouse Reservation. The Lighthouse Board determined most of the reservation's acreage to be surplus to their needs. They released the land under the land give-away program of the Homestead Act. Just after the end of the 19th Century it was again downsized to its present boundaries. Only after homesteaders occupied Sanibel Island did this wild barrier island begin to change. Since then, dramatic alterations to its biological and human character have never really slowed. At first, farming was the core of the island's economy. After 1888, growing high quality produce proved to be a successful enterprise for some hard-working individuals for nearly four decades.

When rail lines left Tampa and began to snake down the state and one-by-one connected the sleepy communities of Florida, waterborne transportation along the Gulf Coast started to wane. The Atlantic Coastline Railroad crossed the Caloosahatchee and reached Fort Myers in 1904. In 1912, the Florida East Coast Railroad was completed to Key West.

After years of searching, Charlie Clark finally managed to find his replacement. He retired as harbor pilot for Port Punta Rassa in 1903. He and his wife, Naomi, left Punta Rassa and comfortably and quietly lived out their lives upstream from the port on the riverfront of the Caloosahatchee near Iona. By 1910, both had died and were buried upriver at a private cemetery in Fort Myers.

Ivy and Alice Clark watched their three children grow to become fine contributing citizens in a growing and modernizing Florida. Ivy retired from the Lighthouse Service in 1914 and he and Alice spent the rest of their days at the place they had inherited from her parents on Fisherman Key. The couple had been blessed with a good solid marriage, and their lives together were never difficult. Alice remained a down-to-earth gentleperson, a loving wife, and a concerned mother until the end. As the years passed, Ivy lost contact with Logan, but occasionally a letter or Christmas card sent by his old friend from somewhere in Florida reached him. These communications would bring on a flood of memories—some warm, some not so warm, and even some downright dangerous recollections of their shared lives as young men. Ivy always wrote back, inviting Logan to visit, but his friend never returned to Sanibel Island. Ivy and Alice made a grand trip before settling into retirement. They traveled to Fort Myers by motor vessel, boarded a train, and visited family in Tampa and Savannah. Ivy got to see his birthplace in the pinewoods of Georgia one more time. He passed away in 1928. Alice survived him by eight years. As both wished, they were buried side by side in the small homesteader's graveyard on Sanibel Island. Their gravesites have been long unmarked.

Logan Grace's life ended in Taylor County, Florida, during the great influenza epidemic of 1918. He was a long way from Punta Rassa when the flu knocked him down. He passed away at his younger sister's home where he was visiting at the time. He was interred near Perry at his brother-in-law's family burial ground—the Carlton Cemetery—on the southern outskirts of the lumber town. Until the time of his final illness, Logan was still a hard-living, tough-talking, and witty Florida cowman. Unlike most of his peers, he didn't die broke though. Logan had remained a bachelor throughout his lifetime, and managed to put together a modest estate. His surviving siblings were surprised after his death to discover their oldest brother had a substantial amount of money nestled in a well-guarded secret account at the Wauchula State Bank. But, they were really shocked when they learned Logan had willed the bulk of his assets to the second child of Ivy and Alice Clark. To someone named Logan Grace Clark.

In 1926, another severe hurricane struck the shoreline of south-west Florida. Like its terrible predecessor of 1873, it destroyed most of the improvements at Punta Rassa. By '26 the Florida cattle-shipping industry was already dying and Port Punta Rassa was never rebuilt. The storm surge produced by the hurricane inundated not only Punta Rassa but also Sanibel Island. The flooding salt water ruined Sanibel Island's productive soil for the short-term. The agricultural economic base of the island completely died and never recovered.

The 1926 storm also altered the island's shape. Point Ybel flooded and was overwashed by strong currents and breaking seas. This resulted in severe erosion at the point. The diamond-shaped mound of gray sand and the mortal remains of Panti the Calusan and his Yustegan wife, Olta, and the bones of the horse he stole from Juan Ponce de León were swept away by the powerful forces of nature.

Little evidence of the existence of the once powerful Calusa society remains above the surface of the earth to immortalize their passage and interaction with primitive Florida. For posterity, they left us scattered heaps of piled-up shell. Since the Calusa's extinction, these mounds have formed small islands of dry uplands in the vast mangrove forests. A few obscure waterways they engineered and excavated continue to survive. No other structures or improvements mark their presence or passage through time.

In the capital city of the United States of America, far away from the shores of the former Calusa kingdom stands a cluster of buildings of diverse architectural design. These are collectively known as the Smithsonian Institution. This is an edifice of human and natural history and their scientific documentation. Some of the collections housed here bear testimony to man's so-called progress in the Western Hemisphere. The Smithsonian's scientists and collections record and preserve many of the earliest Native American cultures. Since European contact in this hemisphere, many of these civilizations—and some of them were acutely advanced—were totally destroyed because of the actions and demands pushed on the indigenous peoples by the greed, and the political and religious attitudes of the European conquerors. These attitudes immediately violated, and eventually destroyed, the social integrity and lifestyles of the unique and independent aboriginal peoples.

In one seldom visited section of this museum stands an almost forgotten dusty, tall, and glass-fronted cabinet. Engraved words on a brass plate screwed to the frame of this cabinet read:

"Dr. Francis Corning Expedition—Sanibel Island,
Monroe County, Florida—1883."

Inside the cabinet, for serious archeological students to examine, are a series of neatly tagged and labeled artifacts. On the lower shelf are two wooden, well-detailed, carved ceremonial masks, a splendidly carved atlatl, stone-headed dart foreshafts, and a magnificently formed primitive saber studded on its business edge with eleven gigantic tiger shark teeth. These teeth are indubitably the largest teeth of this species in the Smithsonian's collections. On the middle shelf are three exquisitely etched manatee ribs along with black and white photographs of these large bones still partially buried in dark sand.

At eye level, on the uppermost shelf, sits a very beautiful glazed clay pot. The surface of the clay around the outer circumference of the pot is covered with a wonderful series of pictographs. These detailed etchings seem to be rendered in chronological order. These are a progressive outline of a place of being and a proud tribute to a lifetime of personal achievement. Next to this pot is another engraved brass plate resting on a tiny easel. The plaque reads:

"This decorated ceramic pot and the variety of artifacts within it were discovered in a Calusa Indian burial site on East Point, Sanibel Island, Monroe County, Florida, in April 1883. This collection is on loan to the Smithsonian Institution by Ivory and Alice Clark, residents of Port Punta Rassa, Florida."

There is no mention of Juan Ponce's de Leon's medal on the plaque to indicate it is anywhere in the cabinet. This gold disk is not among the artifacts, originally stored for eternity inside the clay vessel by its creator—Panti of the Panther Clan—the Calusan.

THE FINE PRINT . . .

I HAVE LIVED AND WORKED ON THE COAST OF Southwest Florida for over 50 years. In 1953, as an impressionable teenager, I watched helplessly as earth-digging machinery legally ravaged an enormous Calusa Indian mound. This Native American burial place was nestled in a dense red mangrove forest on the eastern shore of Estero Bay, south of the community still known as Coconut. The heaped mixture of long-dead seashells and sand from the desecrated mound, and everything else buried in it, was being systematically excavated. It was to be used as base material with which land developers were building roads in Lee County, in a poorly regulated Florida. Among the artifacts collected at the doomed site that Saturday were: a complete human skull and associated remains, a beautiful chert atlatl dart point, glass Spanish trade beads, numerous whelk shell hammers that had once been hafted to wooden handles, tiger shark teeth, and a variety of pottery shards. Had they not been rescued, these human remains and artifacts would have been pulverized and overcoated with asphalt like those from many other prehistoric sites in the region.

This awesome event resulted in my lifetime fascination with Calusa Indians. A few weeks after my experience near Coconut, the subject inspired me to create a composition for a writing assignment in my 11th grade English class at Fort Myers High School. My short story brought to light the fictional life of a Calusa Indian named Panti. Panti was a brave, fierce-fighting, Calusa warrior who was present when his people had a second engagement with the Spanish explorer Juan Ponce de León, who is credited with "discovering" Florida. Through the years, I never forgot Panti. As time passed, my interests diversified but I continued to develop the life story of my character in my mind. I often shared elaborate tales of the Calusan's adventures with my close friends and family. Like his creator, Panti matured over time.

Charles LeBuff

In 1960, I received a federal law enforcement commission after I began a long career with the U. S. Fish and Wildlife Service and moved to Sanibel Island, Florida. During my 32-year tenure with this agency I protected primitive Calusa and other historical sites on federal lands along the Florida Gulf Coast between northern Tampa Bay and the Ten Thousand Islands. This included the mound I describe in *The Calusan* as the location of Panti's home village on the outer shore of Grassy Bottom—modern Sanibel Island's Tarpon Bay.

I am convinced that in the 21st Century the residential and burial sites of the Calusa will receive substantially better protection than they did in the 19th and 20th. However, vandalism will continue at the well-concealed, more remote sites. Little of any real value, other than important archeological resources, has ever been unearthed by those grave robbers who continue to pilfer these sites. Vandals are drawn to their clandestine operations by persistent rumors and tales of buried gold. Although scant, the historically documented evidence from the 17th Century tells us that the Calusa had insignificant amounts of this metal, yet their burial sites continue to be violated. Anyone who observes unauthorized activities at Native American sites *anywhere* should immediately report the crime to the closest law enforcement agency.

In *The Calusan* I deviate from the written accounts pertaining to the death of Juan Ponce de León. The historical account tells us he was wounded in a thigh by a Calusa arrow, not during hand to hand combat with a savage Calusa warrior who was wielding a knife.

My story includes the subsistence harvest and artistic use of the West Indian manatee by the Calusa. To me this seems a logical use of an existing sustainable natural resource, however; there is no scientific evidence that the Calusa utilized manatee parts. Only pre-Calusa fossil manatee bones have been uncovered in the lower, more archaic levels, of Florida middens and mounds investigated by professional archaeologists.

There is no ethnohistoric evidence that the Calusa sailed their watercraft. I've convinced myself that in a specialized marine- and water-based society such as theirs, they would have developed the rather simple technology of sailing.

I created the full-size reproduction of the famous "Key Marco Cat," which has been incorporated into my cover layout, and in the text of my book as the major religious totem of Panti's Panther Clan. The genuine Key Marco Cat is a Calusa artifact. It was uncovered during a bona fide archeological dig on Marco Island, Florida in 1896. I carved the figurine from a piece of native Sanibel Island buttonwood. I then hafted this carving to a blade of lace obsidian. I commissioned an obsidian knapper in Oregon to make the blade. The original half-cat, half-human kneeling figure is in the collection of the Smithsonian Institution. It does not have,

342

nor did it ever have, a blade attached to it. My interpretation of this unique carving is a major theme in *The Calusan*.

Any logs, charts, or navigational documents kept by either Juan Ponce de León or António de Alaminos to record their Florida visit(s) together have been lost. One chart, known as "The Pineda Chart," was printed in 1520. It was probably drawn by Alaminos, or under his direct supervision, and was based on his navigational data. He was chief pilot for Alonso Álvarez de Pineda during a voyage of discovery along the Gulf Coast in 1519. Historically, it is undocumented if Antón Alaminos actually traveled to Florida with Juan Ponce in 1521. In my opinion, the two adventurers were close friends, so I took the liberty of putting them together one last time.

In 1601, 80 years after Juan Ponce de León's death, the official Spanish Grand Historiographer, António de Herrera y Tordesillas, included a summary of Ponce's Florida visits in his famous work, *General History of the Deeds of the Castilians on the Islands and Mainland of the Ocean Sea*. In *The Calusan*, these events are historically balanced and based on the writing of Herrera.

The Calusan is a work of historical fiction but my interpretation and presentation of Ponce's landings in Southwest Florida are historically accurate and described with little influence from "literary license." Sometime in the future, if written substantiating documents are ever discovered from this period, someone may come forward and irrevocably prove that Ponce's 1513 landing place in Southwest Florida was not Panther Key in the upper Ten Thousand Islands as I have described in *The Calusan*. Readers who are familiar with this region of Florida may have guessed this island to be the location of Ponce's 1513 Gulf Coast landing site described in my book. Some modern historians argue that Ponce's party landed somewhere in Charlotte Harbor (not too far north of Sanibel Island) both times. But based on Herrera's text—and that's all we have to go on—Charlotte Harbor does not fall into the description of either of the landing sites.

Herrera tells us that in 1513, while Ponce was approaching the Florida west coast from offshore, he observed "islands that make out to sea." The Spanish historian continues, and tells us that after coasting, Ponce's party found an opening through which the three vessels could safely negotiate. The passage of his ships through most narrow Gulf Coast passes (inlets) situated north of Sanibel Island would have been difficult because treacherous sand bars and shallows blocked their entrances. During this period of exploration in unknown waters, Spanish sailors were acutely aware of the relatively recent loss of Columbus' flagship the *Santa Maria*. She ran aground in shallows off Haiti, and sank in 1492.

Clear passage over the bottom to reach today's Panther Key or San Carlos Bay would have little risk when either was approached by a cautious pilot coasting from the south. From a 16th Century mariner's viewpoint, only the Ten Thousand Islands *or* the string of barrier islands which run north from Sanibel Island, can be accurately described, at least north of the Florida Keys, as *islands that make out to sea.* Factually, Panther Key and Sanibel Island meet this description, so I selected them to be the fictional landing sites—the former in 1513, and the latter in 1521.

Will we ever comprehend the human elements of what really happened to the ill-fated second expedition of Juan Ponce de León to Florida in 1521, when he gravely erred and entered the Bay of Calos? I hope *The Calusan* has tendered an answer, and an adventure or two getting to it.

—*Charles LeBuff*